LAST LINE OF DEFENSE

CHEVALIER PROTECTION SPECIALISTS - BOOK 5

LISA PHILLIPS

TWO DOGS PUBLISHING, LLC

Paperback ISBN: 979-8-88552-001-0

eBook ISBN: 979-8-88552-000-3

Published by: Two Dogs Publishing, LLC. Idaho, USA

Cover by: Ryan Schwarz

Edited by: Christy Callahan, Professional Publishing Services

1
———

Her sneakers whispered on the waxed hallway floor. The murmur of voices neared, around the next corner.

Soraya Adams eased open the closest door and ducked into the room. It was as dark as the rest of the classrooms this time of night. The college campus was all but deserted, only inhabited by early risers or those who had pulled an all-nighter.

Two people passed in front of the door and headed down the hallway. Neither of them would know she was inside the room. Waiting.

Not only could she not afford for them to know she was here, but she couldn't even allow them to see her face. Anyone with a basic awareness of what was going on in the media would know who she was. So far she had barely managed to skate under the radar. She'd done that only thanks to aid from a concerned third party. Despite helping, that woman scared her more than the corporation who wanted her silenced. Travers Industries was using all the resources at its disposal to accomplish that.

Soraya was on the run.

The voices drifted away, and she emerged from the room.

The door clicked shut behind her, and the sound echoed down the hallway. Soraya stood utterly still for a second, waiting just in case someone else was around. At least, someone other than the contact she was here to meet.

Her gaze drifted over a poster on the far side of the wall. The campus newspaper, front-page article. It was like looking into the past—her past. But that was a long time ago now. In the last couple of weeks, her face had been plastered all over the media. Every accolade she'd received for her work in journalism had been stripped.

Now she was being hunted as a criminal.

Soraya had zero credibility. But when she had the evidence in hand, the world would have no choice but to listen to her.

Pressing on, she headed through the science and technology building toward a lab at the end. Coming here was a risk. It was also her last chance to get the information she needed. Soraya would expose those who saw only the power they could have in the world and not who they hurt to get it.

If she succeeded, she would get her life back. The only option she was willing to accept. Nothing less than to put everything to rights and end this running and hiding where she couldn't contact her family for fear of putting them in danger.

Soraya would clear her name.

She knocked lightly on the lab door and let herself in. His instructions had been clear, and she was determined not to do anything that would mean he didn't cooperate. She'd had disgruntled sources before. People who changed their mind about being interviewed or came up with a different story all of a sudden. For whatever reason.

Then there was the last man she had interviewed.

Greg Benton, a man whose brother worked for the same company she was trying to expose, had been killed in prison just hours after talking to her. Now she was on the run, being chased—probably by the same people who had orchestrated his death.

"Daniel?" She crept into the room, which was dimly lit by a couple of undercabinet lights. The rows of lab desks and stools were clear and tidy, left that way by cleaning staff. Computers had been stacked on the shelves of one wall, behind locked glass cabinet doors. "Are you here, Daniel?"

She shuffled through the room to his office in the corner. Halfway across, he emerged. Dark hair stuck in every direction, as though he had slept on his desk. He even had a deep crease in the skin of his cheek.

"You're here." He shook his head as though clearing the cobwebs of sleep and looked at his watch. "You were supposed to be here two hours ago."

"I'm sorry." She closed the distance between them. "It was harder than I thought to get here from Colorado Springs." She shifted the backpack off her shoulders and swung it around to retrieve the chip she'd brought.

Soraya pulled out the lunch pail and handed it over.

Daniel stared. "That's it?"

"Inside."

He turned to his office with a frown on his forehead. "Let's take a look, I guess."

He sat at his desk, and she hovered by the doorway, unable to sit down with all the energy and lingering adrenaline coursing through her. She also wondered if she would fall asleep as he'd done if she sat for any length of time. Instead, Soraya shifted her weight from side to side as she waited for him to connect the chip to his computer.

"It's so tiny." She shook her head, not liking inane conversation at the best of times.

She dealt with facts and preferred to get to the point as quickly as possible. That meant any peripheral information had to be discarded fast. It was either relevant, or it wasn't. The size of the chip didn't mean anything other than that it had been easier to carry as she traversed the country in search of this man.

Only the fact that the chip itself wasn't equipped with a GPS locator meant she was still one step ahead of everyone chasing her.

Weeks before, Daniel had reached out to her online, offering a white flag. Lending a hand so she could mine this thing for information using an air-gapped computer—a laptop with no access to the internet. No way for anyone to track them or hack the chip.

"I appreciate you bringing it all the way here." He clicked his mouse and frowned at the screen of his computer. "The chance to look at this thing?" He blew out a breath.

"Do you think you can get into the source code?" She paced behind him.

"Let me see what I can do."

Soraya figured that meant he needed space to work.

She wandered to the window and peered out between the slats in the blinds. No one moved outside as far as she could see, but that didn't mean she was safe.

Venturing out at all was a risk, let alone meeting with someone even if Daniel might be able to provide knowledgeable assistance.

She could hear Lana's voice in her head.

Ditch your phone. Toss it in the trash, and don't look back. Keep moving. Use only cash, and switch out these fake IDs every couple of days.

She should have written it all down. Not that she needed to do that to remember it, but a hard copy left a record of what had happened. It could be the only chance she ever had to tell her story.

Maybe she would put it all down later—after life got back to normal and she could find her way to writing a book about her experiences. Soraya needed to tell the world the truth about what had happened.

She was getting ahead of herself, though—and assumed that when this was over, she would be either not dead or not in jail. Neither of which was a guarantee at this point.

"Huh."

She turned from the window. "Did you find something?"

"It's definitely outfitted with the ability to track anyone when it's up and running."

"I know it works with wireless networks," Soraya had to be careful to parse out information. She could put Daniel at risk if she told him everything. "It can be outfitted to a lot of different things to provide pinpoint accuracy in targeting."

"And from what I'm seeing, it would appear that any admin can alter every single record."

Soraya hadn't known that. "Like rewriting the information?"

Daniel nodded. "Any record can be altered. Admins have full ability to make global changes. They can change the program. They can modify everything it spits out, and any command given can be adjusted in any way at any point. Total control."

Her stomach churned. "Anything else?"

"The way it changes the inherent program? The person who put in the original command wouldn't know it had been changed. It preserves that and then makes adjustments under the surface."

"So an admin can not only change whatever they want, but they can do it without anyone knowing?"

"Yes," Daniel said. "It's very specific about that."

Soraya lifted both hands and ran them through her hair, grasping handfuls of the long dark locks at the back of her head. The sting in her scalp meant she was pulling too hard. But it was the only thing that could keep her from freaking out.

The implications meant…

Her gaze drifted over framed degrees and awards on the wall. The one at the end said, "Travers Industries."

She spun to Daniel, pieces falling into place in her mind. "Travers Industries is a sponsor of your department?"

"Don't worry." He sat back in the chair. "A representative of theirs will be here soon."

She took a step back. "What do you get in exchange for handing the chip back to them?"

"You think they need that?"

Soraya snatched it off the desk before he could grab it. "You might not, but I do."

The chip was her ticket out of this. If she didn't have evidence, she didn't have anything.

Before he could detain her, Soraya raced out of the office and through the lab. She saw flashing lights in the hallway and used a secondary door. It led to a smaller computer lab.

She ran to the window, flipped the latch, and pushed it up.

Two thick arms banded around her from behind and lifted her feet from the floor. Soraya kicked her legs, banging against his shins.

He grunted and lowered her, his grip loosening.

Soraya twisted and elbowed him in the nose.

A gunshot exploded across the room.

Daniel's body jerked straight, then started to fall.

She turned and scrambled out the window. Glass shattered after another shot, inaudible over the ringing in her ears. Every part of her stung, and a tear wet her cheek.

But there was no time to think.

Move.

Soraya raced across the grass, not even thinking about where she was going. She simply had to get out of there.

Lights flashed against her back. A horn honked, and she realized multiple vehicles had pulled up behind her.

She spun around, anticipating the shot that would drop her any second—the one to end her life.

"Get in!" Lana leaned out of the driver's door and slammed her hand against the side of the vehicle. "Now!"

Soraya dove for the back door.

They drove for thirty minutes, the car full of people all sitting in complete silence. Soraya's mind raced through what'd happened. "I can't—"

"Don't say anything." Lana pulled over in a deserted area, miles from anywhere.

Is she going to leave me here?

Everyone in the car got out, except Soraya and Lana.

The older woman turned from the front seat. "Sorry I didn't get here on time." She shifted and handed an envelope back to Soraya.

An envelope filled with money.

Lana handed over something else. Soraya recoiled. "I don't want a gun."

"You need to go. Don't trust anyone." Lana's voice was stern. "You'll never escape these people otherwise."

"If I disappear, it leaves Travers free to do whatever they want." It just wasn't in her make up to allow corruption to stand. Even if standing up for what was right put her family in danger and left her with no life, just destruction.

"Then you wait, and I'll tell you when it's time to come back." Lana handed over a manila envelope. "This is your life now."

2

Virginia

Judah gripped the phone, praying his boss would pick up.

He had to get Badger and then get them both out of here. But if the team didn't know where he and Badger had been taken, that would be pointless.

"O'Connell."

When Zander answered, Judah could barely talk. Finally, he managed to choke out, "Z…"

"Judah?" Zander's presence filled the line. And his order. "Talk to me."

Judah blew out a breath. "Trace the call. Z—"

A heavy weight slammed into him. Judah dropped the phone and spun around. He nailed the guy with a punch to the stomach before he even looked to see who it was. Didn't matter. Not when the team was all that counted right now.

He followed up with a punch to the jaw. Every muscle in his arm screamed, but this wasn't the worst that'd ever happened to him.

Judah needed to be out of here, though.

He shoved the man away and kept coming until the guy's head hit the wall. His eyes rolled back. Judah let him drop to the floor, already headed for the exit.

He doubled back and searched the guy for a gun. Just a phone, no pistol.

Judah bit back a curse he shouldn't say and checked the hall. He couldn't get to Badger with the number of people hanging around. Not just Peter Benton, but others who worked for Travers Industries.

Whether he liked it or not, they had discovered something in his history.

Zander was on his way. Judah knew that for a fact, even though their call had been cut off.

The way he knew the rest of the team wouldn't rest until they found Judah and Badger. All he needed to do was find somewhere to sit tight.

Wait for them to show.

Judah heard voices approaching. He ducked back into the room where he'd left the unconscious man. And the phone with its angry tone that he could hear through the handset even from across the room. He stayed out of sight while two men turned the corner and headed down the hallway. He peered through a crack in the door.

One of the men…

Judah couldn't believe who it was. He swallowed a choke and tightened his grip on the door, making sure he didn't reveal his presence there as former president Holland Raleigh strode down the hallway with an associate. The guy with Raleigh didn't look anything like a Secret Service agent. They were assigned to protect him for the rest of his life.

Somehow the guy had ditched that detail, and he was here?

Maybe it was because he was at work, operating in his position at Travers Industries. But being here and participating in interrogating Badger and Judah? The whole thing barely made sense.

His brain spun at the implications of it all.

They disappeared at the end of the hallway. Judah ducked out and decided to follow them, just in case he was mistaken. But how could that be? President Raleigh had been out of politics but stayed in the business world and recently took a position at Travers Industries. Both he and that company had been in the middle of everything Chevalier Protection Specialists had been involved with for the past few months. From Nora's father, Stephen Gladstone, and the night an airplane had exploded, killing Raleigh's wife…all the way to this abduction.

Travers Industries was up to something, and they didn't want anyone figuring out what that was.

As far as Judah was concerned, Raleigh was in the middle of all of it.

But if he couldn't get out and let the team know it, what good was that information?

Judah peered around the next corner. The former president and the man he was with stopped to talk to two other men. Before he could figure out where to hide, another couple of men approached from behind. He heard their voices first.

Judah was surrounded. He rushed across the hallway, uncaring that he would be seen. There was no time to lose. He prayed and twisted the handle of the door across the hall. It gave way in his grip, and he barreled into the room.

It was a lobby, but they weren't on the ground floor.

Judah heard shouts and the pounding of boots behind him. He could successfully lead these men away from Badger. It wouldn't get him out of danger, but it might distract all of them long enough for Zander to show up.

He bypassed the elevator and headed straight for the stairs.

Every muscle in his body screaming, Judah punched his

way through the fire door into the stairwell and raced down. He then grabbed the rail on the landing between floors and propelled himself around to the next set of stairs.

And down.

His head spun as he fought to retain his equilibrium long enough to reach an exit door and slam into the alarmed bar. Nothing sounded, but he disconnected a kind of clip that meant the door swung open and hit the wall outside.

Judah raced off down the deserted street before the door bounced back.

A black SUV pulled up at the end of the street, stopping at the mouth between the two buildings.

Judah stumbled, nearly falling at the relief of knowing Zander was there.

Until the window rolled down.

The first thing he saw was the gun pointed at him. Then the face behind it, the one holding the weapon.

Before he could duck to the side, out of the line of fire, the man called out to him. "Get in, Lance Corporal Havig."

Before he could decide what instinct to follow, a commotion erupted behind him. The door hit the wall again, and multiple guys spilled out. Armed and ready to use their weapons on him.

The back door of the SUV opened.

Whatever lay in front of him, Judah knew what was behind him was worse. So he climbed into the back of the vehicle.

It sped away before he even got the door shut. Bullets pinged off the side of the SUV, and he ducked, flinching at the impact. Nothing shattered.

He frowned. "Bulletproof?"

There were three men in the vehicle. The driver, the front passenger, and the one beside him. The two not holding onto the steering wheel and hurtling them down streets both aimed guns at him.

None of them said anything.

"My friend is back there," Judah said. Worry for Badger sat like a bad curry in the pit of his stomach. "We need to circle around and help him."

"You'd be wise to worry about yourself right now," the man beside him said.

"As opposed to worrying about the fact you guys are with MI-6?" He could read secret intelligence service in everything they did. Even the way they were sitting.

It didn't take a highly trained genius to figure it out. Which was good because he was only one of those two things.

"Care to share what that was back there?" The guy beside him was the chatty one.

Too bad Judah wasn't about to "play ball," as his American friends would say. "No, I don't think I will."

Information was traded as currency. He might never have been a spy, but that didn't mean he was unaware of exactly how that world worked.

If he gave up what he knew, he would be left with no leverage.

Perhaps he was a valuable asset. More likely they needed him to do something because he was expendable, or he had information they needed. Either way the power was with him, considering he could withhold anything.

No matter how forcefully they asked.

"Why are you guys picking me up?" He figured it wasn't so they could save his life, although he didn't actually know.

"For our own amusement, I'm sure."

Judah quit talking. Except for one thing. "As long as there's tea, wherever we're going."

"Depends on whether you cooperate."

Judah sat back, exhausted. He put on his seatbelt and stared out the window. Which turned into praying for Badger and the rest of his friends. What else was there to do? These guys weren't going to say anything to him on the road. He could fight for his life, but it would only end up with him getting hurt or killed. No way they'd have left the doors unlocked.

Not the first time he had been out of options.

The aches and pains of being tied to a chair and beaten while questioned swelled in him as the sensations all stretched and came awake. Probably he'd ignored the state of his body too long, and now his mind couldn't continue doing that any longer.

He felt his eyelids lower and then the sharp jab of a red-hot sting in his upper arm.

Judah pushed out a breath. He'd never liked getting shots, least of all when he didn't know what was in the plunger just pushed down.

He tried to form words, but everything softened into a blur until he felt as though he were floating.

He awoke to the sound of an airplane engine. That low drone rumbled under his cheek, pressed against the wall beside the oval window. But this was no passenger airliner. It was a private plane, bigger than Zander's.

He kept his eyes closed, thinking through everything involving the team, and then Hannah and Badger. For once in his life Judah actually liked where he was. The people he worked with had become family, and he got to live close to his sister and her husband.

What wasn't to like? His work meant he could feel clean. He made a difference in the world. He was in a good place, except that the past had finally caught up.

All the hope he'd had that the British government would leave him alone?

Nah.

He pushed a long breath between his lips.

"You're awake, then."

Judah fluttered his eyes open. "And you've got the kettle on?" He glanced around, as though expecting to see a kitchenette on a plane—one that came with a plugged in electric kettle. Lit up and rocking with the rolling boil going on inside. "I'm thirsty."

"How many sugars?"

None. "Two."

The man got up, returning moments later with a steaming mug. Suit trousers and a white shirt, no tie. No ring. Analog watch. No identifying marks or tattoos. Hair cut recently. Forties, and fit, even though he worked in an office. Civil service. Her Majesty's Government. He'd probably killed more people than Judah would over the course of his entire life.

"Thanks." Judah accepted it. *Probably poisoned.* "I'll be sure to enjoy the last tea I'll likely ever drink."

His only regret was not saying goodbye to his friends and family. He would never know if Badger had been rescued. Or what Travers Industries wanted with Chevalier. If his sister would have kids, or how his cousin was doing.

What would have become of his own life.

The guy settled into the seat opposite him. "You think we'd waste the expense of grabbing you just to end your life? I'd have sent Her Majesty's finest to put a bullet in your head, and no one would ever know it was us."

"Maybe you should've." Judah drank the tea anyway. "What do you want?"

The civil servant studied him with green eyes that had seen—and done—plenty, and he hid it well. But Judah had lived the first few years of his life under the thumb of his African home nation's worst leader. His uncle.

He knew how to see the truth people hid.

This man would kill him, wipe his hands, and walk away. Thereafter he would never think of Judah again, or what his life might've meant to anyone who cared about him.

This guy had no soul, something Judah knew well. He'd

nearly lost his own years ago, and part of him had been gone since. He didn't know how to get that missing piece back.

The bit that would make him whole again.

"You cost us an asset in Jalalabad," the man said. "That means you owe us. And we are here to collect."

3

Four Weeks Later
Abuja, Nigeria

Preteen boys and girls filed out of the classroom at the end of the school day.

Soraya gathered up papers. "Don't forget worksheet four. It's due on Thursday."

"Yes, Ms. Albert." The girl slung a backpack strap over her shoulder and smiled at Soraya.

Maybe sixth-grade teachers weren't supposed to have favorites, but Soraya's credentials meant she'd done a lot of internet searches to figure out what to do here. She figured it didn't matter if she liked some better than others.

Teaching English was enjoyable, except that she had no love for poetry. But that was fine because she was having them read a young adult fiction novel—and in three weeks, they were going to watch the movie after school.

Two female students picked up their notebooks and followed the girl out, glancing at each other as they went to the door.

Soraya stared at their backs as they strode out after her

friend, whose name was Mayeni. As far as she knew, the girl had an older brother who took care of her in between transactions for his illegal businesses. Thankfully the girl had a solid head on her shoulders, which meant Mayeni steered clear of what she didn't need to be involved in and always got her homework done on time.

Still, the vibes weren't good. Something had been brewing between the girls for the weeks since Soraya got here.

She grabbed her own folder and followed the girls out.

The hallway teemed with chattering kids. The sound of footsteps and laughter rose as they filed to the doors and moved outside.

Soraya nodded to the "maths" teacher—she'd learned that was the British term when she arrived. Thankfully, she taught English, so it didn't weird her out saying that as she referred to her subject every time. Still, the poetry unit was coming up. She hoped things resolved themselves before then and she wound up not actually having to teach it.

How Lana had managed to put this entire identity—a whole life—together so fast was something she'd thought about over the weeks alone in her tiny apartment.

Soraya headed for the main doors and stepped to the side to observe the playground outside. The middle school shared it with the neighboring elementary, but those kids hadn't been released for the day.

Mayeni walked beside the curbing that ran around the swings area, where the ground was covered in a kind of springy bonded rubber.

The two girls who'd followed her out of Soraya's classroom closed the gap. One of them hip checked Mayeni off the curb, onto the rubber. The girl cried out as she fell, her papers dispersing across the ground. The other two stepped off the curb and stood over her, laughing.

Soraya raced down the concrete steps, set her things on the curb, and crouched beside her. "Mayeni, you okay?"

At first her American accent had been a curiosity, but that seemed to have worn off. The fact she was settling in here wasn't something she was entirely comfortable with. She would be leaving soon, and this wasn't home. But right now wasn't the time to contemplate her life.

The girl blinked. "I'm okay."

Soraya lifted her to standing.

Mayeni winced, as if her hip hurt.

Soraya said, "Girls…" in her teacher's voice, then pointed at the loose papers on the ground before Mayeni could retrieve them. "Pick those up. And apologize for that disrespect."

The apology was a mumble at best. The girls shoved the papers at Mayeni, who limped away toward home.

Soraya pointed at the door. "Inside, both of you." They turned to the door together, and a glance passed between them which Soraya imagined involved rolled eyes.

The principal, who they all called the "headmistress," stood at the door. As Soraya approached, she crossed her arms. "I'll sort this, Ms. Albert."

"I'd like to check on Mayeni."

Her boss nodded, not missing an opportunity to look disapproving. It was one of her best skills. "Ask my secretary for her address."

Soraya figured the house was within walking distance, but that probably meant it was more than a mile or two away in this part of the world.

After a ten-minute drive, Soraya arrived at Mayeni's house and parked across the street.

The teen stood on the doorstep.

Soraya slid the thin strap of her purse across her body and rested it on her left shoulder. Glasses would complete the look, but it was far too hot to have plastic sliding down her nose. The slacks, buttoned blouse, and flat shoes completed what she thought of as her "teacher" ensemble.

Given Mayeni's brother and his friends were milling around the front door, she wanted to look as harmless as possible.

Soraya crossed the street, avoiding the potholes full of muddy water. "Mayeni?" She smiled as though they'd run into each other at the bakery. "Can I talk to you for a second?"

"Go inside." The brother flicked two fingers at Mayeni, and the girl scurried inside, head down. Still limping. But since none of the men out here looked at her, they didn't notice it.

"Everything okay?" The brother had an expansive chest, thicker than his waist. His legs were two sturdy pillars covered with ratty jeans. Two gold rings and a chain. Interest flared in his eyes.

Beside him were two others, one with a scar on his neck and the other with far too much stubble on his face. He almost had a beard.

"I'd like to speak with Mayeni about the short story she wrote for English class." They would figure out soon enough that she was the American teacher the neighborhood all seemed to have found out about.

"Let's go inside." The brother nodded. "Have some tea."

The two men with him shifted, angling toward her as if their intention was to assist her if she didn't want to go. Like the two girls who had shoved Mayeni off the curb, it reminded her of times she was bullied at school. All those old inadequacies surged in her. Until she had to push them back and wonder why she still felt like that little girl even though she was a grown woman.

"That won't be necessary." She could have taken a step back, but that would look far too much like a retreat. The woman she was now didn't plan to back down. "I'll just catch her at school tomorrow."

The brother motioned to his two guys. Both moved to stand behind her, blocking her route to the car—unless she circled them. Would one grab her?

"Like I said"—Soraya lifted her chin—"I'll talk to her tomorrow. I really think her story could be published. I know a couple of publications accepting short stories. I'll give her the information, and she can use the school computer if she wants to submit."

As if that was why she was here.

Soraya turned. "Excuse me, gentlemen."

Beard guy's lips twitched.

The brother grabbed her arm. Soraya pressed her lips together.

Beard guy said, "We don't need her." His voice had a crisp British accent. *Very nice.* His eyes differed from the others', but he played the part well. Who was he?

No one you need to worry about.

The voice of reason in her head sounded a whole lot like Lana, even though she'd only met the woman a couple of times. It was still advice that would keep her alive.

"Mmm," the brother's voice rumbled.

She glanced over her shoulder and saw the look in his eyes.

"We might not need her, but I *want* her now."

"And when I report you to the police?" She lifted her chin. "What then?"

He chuckled. "The police?" He laughed louder.

Soraya used her free hand to slide the zipper on her purse. With two fingers, she eased out the pepper spray.

A meaty hand snatched it from her. She whirled back, but it was the scarred man.

"We have too much to do tonight." That British accent.

She refused to be distracted by him when he was likely an awful person not deserving of her time or attention. "I'm sure we can take this up at another time…if you have somewhere to be."

Soraya kept all her attention on the brother. He was the real threat here, not either of his guys. Although, all three together wouldn't be something she could fight against—even with the pepper spray, which had been tossed on the dirt.

She didn't plan to be around when the worst happened, but she would for sure report Mayeni's situation to the authorities. And pray they actually did something to help the teen. Situations like this were hit and miss, even in countries with established child welfare systems. Nowhere was perfect.

"I should go." She side-stepped, despite his grip on her arm. All she'd wanted to do was make sure Mayeni was all right after that incident at the school. Soraya needed to lay low, not get tangled up in something messy.

He chuckled and started walking toward the house.

"Ouch. You're hurting me."

The other two crowded behind her.

"Let go."

Soraya was dragged inside, and the door shut.

———

THIS WAS the last thing Judah needed. He was here to get the job done, and this woman—whoever she was—shouldn't factor. But he still didn't plan to allow her to get hurt by these guys.

Judah went to the kitchen and pulled a soda from the ancient rattling fridge. He popped the top and listened to the hiss.

"You gonna get anyone else one of those?" Banjoko lifted his chin, that vicious scar of his flashing in a strip of the sun from the side window.

"Get your own." Judah took another long pull from the can.

Mobo, the ringleader of this operation and older brother to that teen girl, started to tug the woman toward the hall.

"We have things to do. Can't we leave that until later?"

Mobo glanced at Judah, his expression full of displeasure.

"I thought this thing was time-sensitive." Judah shrugged like it was no big deal to him. "She can wait, can't she?"

The woman looked at him like he was her savior.

"He probably wants first go," Banjoko said.

The woman whimpered.

"He's right. There's not time for this." Mobo shoved her to the couch.

She stumbled and slumped onto the dirty cushions.

Judah had been trying to get in with these guys for two weeks. Now he'd finally done it, he didn't like potentially messing that up by trying to save this woman whatever indignity Mobo had planned. When he got info on the older man MI-6 wanted them to lead Judah to, he would get the teen somewhere safe and out of here.

Mayeni reminded him entirely too much of Aria, the daughter of his teammate Eas—who he had now reconnected with. Which made him think of his friends. His family.

Judah just needed to get this job done, and he could get back to them. Probably. Hopefully. Anything would be better than pretending to be some tourist who'd outstayed his welcome and wanted to get into the kind of warfare where there were no rules.

"Put her in the back," Mobo ordered. "I'll talk to Mayeni, and then we go."

Judah swept past Banjoko, not willing to allow the guy to take that task—and get out of it whatever he felt like taking in five minutes before Mobo ordered them to head out.

"Let's go." He hauled her toward the bedrooms.

The end of the hall had a closet with a lock on the outside. Inside was empty except for a bucket. Mobo hadn't put his sister in there since Judah had been here, but Banjoko told him all about his friend's favorite method of disciplining his sibling when he felt as though she got out of line.

"Let me go, please," the woman whispered. "I'll take her

and get out of here. He'll never see either of us again. We'll escape while you're gone."

Judah wanted to reassure her, but it didn't get him to his goal of completing this job so he could return to his life. And yet, when he did get back—knowing he'd left her here—would he be able to live with himself?

He stopped at the closet door, wondering who she really was. The woman wasn't Nigerian, not with that American accent. But then, neither was he.

The last thing he needed right now was to find himself attached to her.

"Please." She turned to face him. "I can make it worth your while." She shifted closer, but the look in her eyes spoke loudly in opposition to what her body was doing.

Still, his own took notice. Attraction sparked in him, but he realized she thought he was the kind of man who would help her if he were going to get something out of it. She thought using her body was a way to escape this scary situation.

"That's the kind of teacher you are?" He looked her over, shoving an expression of disgust onto his face.

The last thing he needed was to get tangled up with this woman. She was nothing but a complication he didn't have time for.

He'd have made a joke about it if the guys were around. They'd never have doubted what he would choose to do. The boys knew him, and he was part of Chevalier because he belonged.

This place? Judah didn't want to be here any more than this woman did.

She huffed, fear still in her eyes. "Do what you want then. I guess you don't care about anyone but yourself."

She was gorgeous. He'd give her that. Even just a few weeks ago, he'd have been interested. Truth be told, he'd have fallen for her in five minutes. His heart just did that—jumped off a cliff every time he was attracted to someone.

But this woman couldn't deter him. "You don't even know me."

"I know exactly who and what you are." She leaned in. "And it's something I wouldn't bother scraping off my shoe."

You have no idea. Judah pulled open the closet door.

"Please don't put me in there."

He could probably give her, or the teen, the key. Together they could get out. But when Mobo found out that Judah had orchestrated the escape, his "in" with these guys would disappear.

He was walking a fine line here. And an even finer one with MI-6. The last thing he wanted was for something to go wrong that meant he couldn't go back to his life.

She was intriguing, and he wanted to do the right thing, but tonight was his shot at finding the guy MI-6 needed him to locate. Mobo and his buddy were going to get Judah to the place where the guy was rumored to live.

Once he had that guy secured, he'd get out of this mission and back to his life.

If the rest of Chevalier hadn't written him off already.

Judah didn't know if they'd accept him back or if the team wasn't willing to allow him into their lives again. But his sister would—and her fiancé.

It didn't matter what it took. Judah wanted out of this mess and back in the life he'd had.

The one he actually wanted.

Judah felt a shove from behind.

"Gimme a sec." Banjoko pulled the string on the bare bulb that hung in the closet and muscled her inside.

"Hey." Judah grabbed his arm and yanked back. "Didn't you hear? We've not got time for you to be doing that."

"No?" Banjoko held the woman against the back wall.

She whimpered.

"Maybe you should watch," he said. "You'll learn something about your place here."

Judah glared. "Want me to tell Mobo you're wasting time sampling his merchandise?"

The woman shivered. Judah didn't look at her face or he'd see if a tear rolled down her cheek or not. He didn't need to know either way.

She couldn't be someone he fell for. Not now.

"Get out of there." Judah shifted, about to crouch for the weapon holstered at his ankle.

Banjoko slashed out, and Judah saw the flash a second before the hot sting erupted across his shoulder. From his collar bone, all the way to the outside of his arm.

He gritted his teeth together, grabbed the wrist holding the knife, and punched Banjoko in the jaw.

The big man didn't move.

Judah squeezed the bones in his wrist. It was like he didn't even notice the crushing grip. The other man had nearly fifty pounds on him and was wearing flip-flops, sweatpants, and a T-shirt over which he wore a leather vest like it wasn't ninety degrees outside.

This was going to hurt.

Judah punched him twice. Diaphragm and jaw again.

Banjoko grabbed Judah's wrist before he could punch a third time. Judah saw what was coming and ducked to the side as Banjoko slammed his head down to headbutt Judah.

His forehead glanced off the blood on the shoulder of Judah's T-shirt.

The woman grabbed the bucket and slammed it down on Banjoko's head. The big guy crumpled to the floor, out cold.

Judah took a step back and held his hands up. "Hold on."

She held the bucket above her head, breathing hard.

"I'm not with them." He glanced over his shoulder. "You don't need to knock me out."

"I don't believe you."

There was no time to explain who he was or why he was here. He needed to go out with Mobo tonight and find out where the target lived. That had to be the priority.

Judah tried to shrug. Pain stung his shoulder, and he hissed. He glanced down at the blood soaking his shoulder and pulled back the collar of his shirt to take a look. "Ouch."

Movement out the corner of his eye gave him a split-second warning. But it was already too late.

She swung the bucket down on his head, and everything went black.

4

Last Chance County

The weight of his pack hung from his shoulders heavier than usual, forcing Zander to acknowledge it as he pushed strength into his arms and legs. All the way to the top of the hill.

He slowed enough to glance over his shoulder and saw the other members of Chevalier Protection Specialists right behind him. Closer than he'd thought they would be.

Zander grinned and crested the hill. There was no more stopping. Not until he was at the base of the hill on the other side, right behind the huge house where they lived. It had been built by the man who'd owned this entire valley for a hundred years before a group of Vietnam veterans—most of whom turned out to be terrible humans—started the town.

Good for the team because this community was secluded enough to run an international operation from here. Also, because the house had been built with so many rooms. The place was currently the home of ten people and a dog. That should've been an odd number of humans, but for the fact that Judah's room was currently empty.

Zander slowed his pace behind the house, hung his head, and set his hands on his thighs. He breathed hard, feeling the burn of exertion that meant he'd pushed himself. Something he strove to do every single day. As the team leader, he had to be the first one in, the last one out, and the one who made sure everyone else operated to the best of their ability.

Andre clapped him on the shoulder. "Why does it feel like that was about four miles longer than it needed to be?"

"Speak for yourself." Lucia eased off the straps of her pack and handed it to her husband. The two of them headed inside.

Next to approach was Eas, whose wife Karina might have once been an operator, but she now taught fitness classes in town. She'd opted to stay behind and make lunch. Zander had a sneaking suspicion it might be because their daughter Aria was having a rough week at her job and needed her mom close when she got home.

Badger and Hannah were the last to pass him, holding hands despite the fact that both were breathing hard and sweating from the exercise. Zander figured it didn't matter what he put them through. The two of them would just smile at each other and carry on.

Zander followed them into the house, heading toward his room first. Nora had been napping when he left, and he hadn't wanted to disturb her. The note he'd left folded on her bedside table lay flat now. She was up, but he didn't see her in the room. Then he heard the distinctive sound of retching coming from the bathroom.

He filled a glass with water at the bathroom sink and handed it to her as she sat back from the toilet. He crouched. "Doing okay?"

Her face was pale, her lips lighter than they should be. She rolled her eyes, evidently amused even if there was little spark to it. "They really shouldn't call it morning sickness." She sipped some water. "But all-day sickness doesn't quite have the same ring to it."

He touched her cheeks and kissed her forehead.

Her next prenatal appointment was in a week, and they would get to see the baby on the ultrasound. Sometimes he couldn't believe this was his life. After years of operating with a team of guys, he'd met and married her within just a few weeks, after they'd realized neither of them had reason to wait around.

Zander had been married before. Not for long, as it had mainly been a disaster. But considering his ex-wife lived in town and was happily married to a police lieutenant, he was always sure to give her a hug when he saw her at church.

Both of them were in a much better place now than they'd been when they tied the knot.

Zander had married the woman of his dreams, and she was pregnant with his child. Something he wanted for everyone in his life now. Simply because he knew how wonderful it felt to be loved and accepted this way.

But with two members of his team no longer working with them, Zander wasn't likely to get his wish. Isaac was in prison after returning a stolen nuclear warhead to the government. Judah was MIA.

She made a face. "Did Ted give you the update yet?"

Zander shook his head.

Nora held out her hand. "Let's go."

They found the rest of the team in the living area, milling around and chatting with water bottles in one hand. He looked at each one, registering how much they had drunk so far. Badger's was barely touched.

Zander motioned to it with his finger. Badger lifted it in salute and drank. The guy had been shot just a few weeks ago and was released back to regular duty again. Out of all of them, he was the one everyone kept an eye on. The guy might resent that at times. Zander just figured it meant they cared about him. The way they all cared about each other.

Karina said, "Dinner is in the crockpot. But I think I'm going to take Aria to see a movie later." She looked at Eas. "Want to come?"

Eas kept his features neutral. "Is it going to be another romantic comedy?"

"Does that mean no?"

Both of them smiled.

Eas leaned in and kissed her. "I'll meet you at the diner for dinner after the movie."

"Sounds good." Karina got herself sparkling water from the fridge.

Zander pulled out his phone and squeezed the power and volume buttons, holding the device to his mouth like a walkie-talkie. "Team meeting, Ted."

The reply took a few seconds—longer than he'd have expected. "I'm on the phone. You'll have to come down."

The team had renovated the downstairs in the house and converted it into a sort of command center, complete with a massive office for their technical specialist. Beside it was a conference room big enough that when they all packed in there, it didn't seem small. A couple of offices.

A room at the end was a storage closet, but the back was connected by a tunnel to the bunker under the warehouse next door. Something deemed necessary after everything that had happened the last few months.

It had given the guys something physical to do while they waited to hear word about where Judah might be. When days had stretched into weeks, and weeks had stretched into a month with no sign of their British teammate, the tunnel had been finished ahead of schedule.

Zander went downstairs to find Ted. Lucia and Andre went with him.

Ted wore a wireless headset, the mic covered with foam in

front of his mouth. He paced back and forth across the room. Pretty soon, they would have to fill in the worn channel he was making on the floor. The kid wore skinny jeans and a comic strip design on his T-shirt. His dark hair needed cutting, but Zander had told him to wait until right before his wedding to do that. The guy was supposed to get married on New Year's Eve to a local police detective. Something they had all assumed Judah would be able to attend.

Now it was looking like that might not happen.

The pit in the bottom of his stomach deepened to an ache. As much as he wanted his friend back, Zander also wanted to know he was all right. In the last few weeks, anything could have happened to him. He'd been injured after Travers Industries kidnapped Judah and Badger. Since rescuing Badger, they'd seen no sign of Judah.

"Yes, sir." Ted nodded. "I understand. It's just that—"

Lucia shifted next to Andre, both frowning.

"I can do that, sir. Absolutely." Ted paced some more, then stopped. "No problem at all." He pulled the headset off and blew out a breath. "The director of the FBI."

"Everything okay?" Zander said.

Ted shrugged. "He's not overly happy, but he's going to talk to the director of the Department of Clandestine Service about us doing a job for her. We're not exactly their favorite freelance team, but the information I just gave them helped the CIA keep all their South American operatives from having their identities leaked."

Zander walked over and squeezed the back of the guy's neck. "Good job."

"You guys were the ones who got that information. I just forwarded it on." Ted blew out a breath, bracing. "I asked, but they didn't have anything about Judah. Nothing concrete, at least."

"So what did they have that isn't concrete?" Andre asked.

Ted slumped into his chair. "A couple of German agents

mentioned something on a job in Paris about a former Royal Marine who'd been co-opted by British intelligence into doing some off books jobs for MI-6."

"So it's hearsay at best." Lucia folded her arms. "But it's actionable, at least. We can find the Germans and talk to them. Figure out where they got the information from."

Zander figured that wasn't a bad idea. He just needed to get a few things straightened out first. "What did the director want you to do?"

Ted glanced at him, and Zander knew he realized he wasn't getting away with it.

"Just tell me."

Ted frowned. "He advised me to stay away from Travers Industries."

"So they're under his protection?" Zander asked.

"Or he knows what's going on over there, and he has people dealing with it." Ted rolled his eyes. "It sounded more like he thought it was risky, and he's worried about us. Or he thinks we care about further damaging our reputation."

Andre snorted. "Probably doesn't want to risk losing you as an off-book asset."

Zander had always figured that they could still get work even with a bad reputation—for bringing the previous director of DCS to justice. Thank you very much.

They could pick and choose what jobs they did regardless. If it didn't work out, the group would probably get hired as wilderness firefighters. There were plenty of things to do in the world that involved facing down an enemy—human or not.

There were wars to be fought in so many ways. He just disliked the ones where only words were exchanged, and the outcome was achieved by manipulation. Zander had no desire to become what his father had been. He would much rather be able to look at himself in the mirror and respect what he saw.

"I'll put out some feelers," Zander said. "See if the bureau has anyone working on Travers Industries and this big project they're about to announce."

"I'd rather find Judah," Andre said. "I'm struggling to care about a company that should know better."

"They're the reason he's gone." Lucia turned to face her husband. "If not for Travers, half the stuff that's happened to this team wouldn't have."

"We take the good with the bad," Andre said. "I have you back. Zander has Nora. Eas reconnected with Karina and found out about Aria. Badger met Hannah. Nora, Hannah, and Isaac found out they are all siblings." He paused, worry creasing his brow. "If we don't find Judah, how can we make sure he's all right?"

Lucia nodded. Andre tugged her toward him, and they hung onto each other.

Zander figured they weren't the only ones working on this Travers Industries thing. He turned to Ted. "Anything on Lana lately?"

Ted shook his head. "She's gone completely dark. But we all know that doesn't mean she's unaware of what's happening here."

"We need a plan." Zander rolled his shoulders. "A way to get inside Travers Industries and find out what's going on there."

"A reporter was trying to out them a few weeks ago." Ted turned to his computer and started typing faster than Zander's eyes could track. "They essentially buried her. No one knows where she's gone, and all the articles she'd written disappeared along with her research. The rumor about her trying to expose them is exactly that. A rumor."

"A whistleblower?" Zander scratched his jaw. "At least she knows more than us. If she isn't dead, we need to find her."

5

___

Soraya lowered the bucket and stared at the men on the floor, breathing hard. The realization of exactly what she'd done hit her. The massive guy had gone down like a tree, out cold. The British guy had tried to tell her he wasn't one of them—which was a bald-faced lie if ever she'd heard one. He'd only been trying to get out of a situation where he could face the same thing.

As if she would spare him when the two of them were as bad as each other—and Mayeni's brother was worse than both of them combined.

She needed to get out of there.

Soraya left the tiny closet before she realized she was still holding the bucket. But maybe it would come in handy. She needed to get Mayeni and go before the brother could stop either of them.

As she came down the hallway, Mobo exited the bedroom.

Soraya swung the bucket up and ran toward him. If she could do this fast, it would be before he could rally. She knew squat about fighting but figured surprise was better than nothing. And it had worked with the other two.

Mobo lifted his arm, and the bucket slammed into his elbow.

Soraya swung it up again. Before she could bring it down, a gunshot exploded in the hallway as loud as a firework. She hissed a breath and realized she was watching Mobo fall to the ground. Blood on his chest.

She gasped and spun around, the bucket clutched in front of her like a shield.

Banjoko stood at the closet door, over the unconscious British man. Holding a gun out. He swung it toward her. But before he could squeeze the trigger, the unconscious man erupted off the floor and punched Banjoko in the back of the thigh.

The gun went off again. Soraya screamed and clapped her hands over her ears. She couldn't stay out here in the hallway, or she would probably be killed. She jumped over Mobo, who was struggling to breathe and staring up at the ceiling. He grabbed for her, but she twisted the handle—dropping the bucket—and rushed into Mayeni's room.

The girl sat on her bed, books on her lap and white, wired earbuds in. Tears streamed down her face. She blinked. "Teacher?"

Soraya slammed the door shut. The girl had a dresser to one side of it, so she rounded the thing and muscled it in front of the door with a whole lot of grunting and straining. Out in the hallway she could hear the muffled thuds and thumping of a fight going on. But thankfully, no more gunshots.

She spun to the girl. "Is there somewhere you can go, someone you can stay with?"

Mayeni yanked the earbuds from her ears by the cord and shifted to the edge of the bed. "My aunt and uncle live close. Mobo never lets me go over there."

"You like them? Do you think they would take care of you?"

The girl nodded.

"Pack as much as you can as fast as possible. But you can probably come back for the rest of it later." After the blood had been cleaned off the floor in the hallway, and the police had arrived to take the rest of them into custody. "Give me your phone and gather your things."

Mayeni handed over her cell, unlocked.

Soraya dialed 1-9-9—that had taken some getting used to—and set the phone on the bed. She didn't want to talk to anyone, least of all the emergency dispatcher that answered or whichever cops showed up. She also couldn't afford for her voice to be recorded on anything that might be connected to the Cloud. It was too risky.

She pulled in a long breath and blew it out slowly, then went to the window and forced it up past the creaking and straining. "If we can get to my car, we can get out of here."

"I'm ready." The girl had a backpack with her school things and another sack over her shoulder, rounded with belongings stuffed inside.

"Let's go." Soraya climbed out the window first, then assisted the girl with her things. They crept around the side of the house.

Crossing to her car on the street meant exposing themselves, but she prayed for the first time in a long time. They needed some kind of cover. A way to stay hidden. Wasn't that in the Bible somewhere?

"Come on." She put the girl in front of her, so any shot from inside the house would hit Soraya first, and maybe the girl could just run through the night to her relative's house. The world was a dangerous place, but some good people were in it.

They raced to her car, and Soraya glanced back over her shoulder.

The British guy stood in the doorway. If she weren't scared she would be killed at any moment, she might consider that he was extremely good-looking. Plus, that accent of his didn't hurt.

Maybe if she'd met him in a coffee shop. Or on a college campus years ago when she'd been a student. But out here there was no way she would ever trust someone like him.

Mayeni got in the passenger side. Soraya scrambled in, turned the engine on, and hit the gas. The girl directed her to a house not so dissimilar from the one they had just left, but without the dangerous men and the blood. Soraya's hands shook as she rounded the car and opened the passenger door for Mayeni.

The front door of the house opened before they even reached it. A hulking man stood there. But as he spotted the teen approach, his face softened. "Come in."

The girl accepted the man's hug.

He said, "Auntie is in the kitchen."

Soraya stopped at the bottom of the steps with Mayeni looking back at her. "Go ahead."

"I'll see you at school?"

Soraya wasn't sure she would even be able to go back. Not now that she'd been involved in something like this. She settled for saying, "Be safe. Okay?"

The girl nodded and disappeared inside with her things. The uncle waited until she was out of earshot before saying, "Is he dead?"

"He was still alive when we left. But it didn't look good, so who knows?"

"I'm tempted to go finish him myself."

Soraya nodded. "I know what you mean."

Despite the fact she could never imagine herself taking a life, the sentiment remained. A man like Mobo shouldn't be able to guard a precious life like Mayeni's. And yet, he had been given guardianship over her.

"Thank you."

Soraya nodded, turned away, and headed back for her car. Over her career she had reported on stories of family neglect and abuse—situations where one parent cared nothing for the children they had created and did nothing to help them. All she could do was write the best article she could so that as many people as possible were aware of those kinds of circumstances.

The one she remembered most was the time a young boy who claimed abuse from his father had returned to his childhood home and burned it down with the father, the stepmother, and half-sister inside.

Such a tragedy, the selfishness that had cost so many lives. Trauma victims lived their lives like the walking dead sometimes, whether the scars were visible or not. Overcoming something like that in a person's formative years was so much more challenging than any other time in life. It took a whole lot of courage and a robust support system—if one was even available.

Like with Mayeni and her aunt and uncle.

Soraya kept a strong hold on the steering wheel all the way home. Once she had gathered her own things, she could decide where she would go next. There was no way she could stay here when something like this had happened. The last thing she needed was to get involved in a hot situation—even if it had nothing to do with her own problems.

Or would it all blow over?

Maybe the worst was that the headmistress would look at her with that disapproving stare, and then afterward, things would go back to normal.

Or as normal as they could be when a person was on the run from their own government and hiding out in another country under an assumed identity.

She should call Lana and ask for advice. But that number was only for the worst of emergencies, and Soraya wasn't sure this qualified. Still, maybe it was time to pack a bag just in case. So she would be ready to go if it was necessary.

She parked in her regular spot, collected her mail, then headed up the stairs to her tiny third-floor flat.

With a little digging, she'd figured out that it was a place Lana seemed to have kept in this country. Though, Soraya wouldn't exactly call it a home. Maybe it was some kind of safe house, because it certainly wasn't a random place they'd chosen to stash her. It seemed more established than that.

Soraya let herself in and closed the door behind her, musing that rote tasks didn't do much to settle her.

Especially not when the lamp across the room flicked on and that good-looking British guy sat on her couch, holding a smartphone.

A light flashed in front of him, blinding her for an instant.

JUDAH LIFTED his gun and held it at the woman. "Take out any weapons you have and put them on the table." Her eyes widened, her face losing some of its color in a way he didn't like, and he realized something about her just from her reaction.

She gasped and dropped everything in her hands. "I don't have any weapons. What are you talking about?" The contents of her purse lay on the floor of her entryway, along with her phone and all her mail. A water bottle rolled under the entryway table.

He kept his gun trained on her. "So tell me who you are, then."

"I'm a teacher." She swallowed hard, her hands raised as though trying to ward off something. "At Mayeni's school."

It might be partly true, but he could see on her face that it wasn't entirely accurate. There was more to her.

"I'm supposed to believe that?"

He used his free hand to upload the photo he had just taken of her to a search app that would try to find her face on the internet. He figured that was the only way he would get the truth of who she was.

Unless this woman was like him.

But given her reaction, he concluded she was not.

Who goes around in a place like this unarmed?

Ted, the computer tech Chevalier Protection Specialists employed—and not just because he lived in their house and had for years—would have given him a full workup on her. But considering Judah was currently on the run and supposedly working for MI-6, that wasn't an option. Like going home to Last Chance County and his friends and family, resuming his old life wasn't an option.

As long as MI-6 thought they had a hold over him, it wouldn't ever be possible to go back.

"I don't have anything to do with Mobo or any of his businesses"—her chest rose and fell with each gasping inhale—"if that's what you're asking."

"Maybe not." He tried to rein in his frustration. "But you certainly managed to get yourself in the middle of it."

He was supposed to be with Mobo and Banjoko right now, meeting their contact who supposedly had information about where Judah's target lived. The fact it happened to be in this part of the world where all his childhood triggers seemed to lurk around every corner didn't exactly sit right. But he figured he at least blended in here. It wasn't like they could send an agent that wasn't black and have them go unnoticed. Then again, his British accent made him more memorable than he'd like.

He'd never been able to do any other accents with skill. Probably why they hadn't recruited him straight out of the Royal Marines to work as a spy.

Then again, given what had happened on his last mission, he wasn't exactly MI-6's favorite person. Which was why they thought he owed them. Judah was now under their thumb, whether he liked it or not.

Judah's friend Isaac had been a CIA agent. Maybe the US clandestine organization was different, but MI-6 could be ruthless when they wanted to. Which seemed to be all the time.

"I'm not in the middle of anything!"

Judah just stared at her. Most people filled the silence, and wound up saying more than they intended.

"I didn't know that would happen!" She gasped again. If she kept that up, she'd pass out. "I just came over to check on Mayeni because she got picked on at school. And she fell."

"And…?"

"You think I'm going to tell you where she is?"

Judah gritted his teeth. She thought he wanted to find the girl? For what? "I'm assuming wherever she is, it's somewhere safe."

"Of course." She huffed. "What kind of teacher do you think I am?"

"Mmm."

"What is that supposed to mean?"

She was gathering her strength, probably born of frustration but he would take it. That surge of energy would fuel her to face whatever was going to happen next. The woman was beautiful, and at any other time he'd have let himself be swept away, but there was no way he could do that with what was happening right now. She would only get caught up with MI-6 as well—used as leverage to further coerce him into operating for them.

Judah wasn't naïve enough to believe that if he found this one guy, who was the head of an international guild of assassins, for goodness sakes, that it would be over, and the British government would let him walk. But doing this job would give him leverage for the next job.

No way could he fall for this woman in the meantime, with everything the way it was.

He looked down at the screen of his phone and the search results that had come up. *Journalist disgraced.* "Soraya Adams."

She gasped.

A second later, she turned for the door.

Judah shot across the room after her.

She scrambled with the handle and got the door open two inches before he slammed his palm on the wood, and it shut.

He crowded her against the door. "So you're a journalist. But you lied about a story, and now you're a teacher in Nigeria for some reason."

Her body sagged. "Why don't you just shoot me? I don't want to talk about this." She sucked in a shuddering breath.

Judah pressed his forearm against her shoulder blades and held her against the door while he looked at his phone. He scrolled with his thumb and got an overview of what happened. Two words stuck out to him. "Travers Industries?"

"I guess I learned the hard way not to mess with a company that has so much influence."

"What did you find out?" He was getting an idea of what happened, and whatever she said would be one side of the story, but it wasn't anything good if Travers was involved. She might even need the help of Chevalier Protection Specialists. Something he couldn't give her.

But he knew where to send her.

"I was given a chip…anonymously," she said. "It arrived on my desk one day. A little package that I had no idea would cause all this. Otherwise, I never would have opened it."

The only chip he knew of was the one Karina, Aria's mother, had been asked to steal from Travers Industries—by Lana, the head of an organization who seemed to operate in a gray area between good and evil.

Was it the same chip his team had fought so hard to keep?

She continued, "I took it to an…expert. And was told by…this person…that embedded in the chip's code was something that shouldn't have been there. They're about to roll out this proprietary federal phone system, and it gave me serious pause. Whoever sent me the chip was trying to expose the fact Travers Industries wants full control of all the information that will be transmitted on it."

"Can't most electronics companies see everything on their network?" He wasn't sure why that meant Travers was so dangerous.

"Sure, but this one will be used by government, federal law enforcement, and the military. Travers Industries will be able to control *all* of the information. They can look at everything, but they can also change whatever they want. And manipulate any of it. Without anyone knowing."

"And they caught on to the fact you knew, so they had you disgraced."

She twisted around and looked at him. "They killed someone who was supposed to be helping me, but he was one of them, and they nearly killed me."

Now she was here.

Judah stared at the woman who had essentially walked into his life. But how was it possible no one had orchestrated it considering the enormous coincidence that made? "Who sent you here to hide?"

Whoever it was couldn't possibly have known he would also be here.

"A contact I made."

Judah scratched at the growth of beard on his jaw. It angered British intelligence that he'd insisted on it, but the beard reminded him of Zander and his teammates. So he kept it, and he wasn't going to shave anytime soon.

"One of us is being manipulated," he said. Actually, he realized it might be more than that. "Maybe both of us because I know I definitely am."

"I'm not manipulating you."

"You met me, didn't you? So it was either because I know exactly who can help you fix this situation you're in. Or you're here because my job is bigger than what I've been told so far."

He didn't doubt that MI-6 had lied. They might well have dragged him right back into his old life, on the opposite side of his team.

Judah didn't like the sound of that at all.

She sputtered again. The woman didn't get any words out before a pop, and the sound of glass shattering, brought him around in time to see windows explode.

Pop. Pop. Pop.

The entire row of windows shattered, and glass sprayed across the room.

He grabbed the woman. "Get down."

6

Judah tugged Soraya all the way to the floor. "Careful on the glass."

The shots had stopped, but he didn't figure that meant they were out of danger.

"Get to the bathroom," he said. "You have a tub in there?"

"Yes." She looked at him, confusion in the crinkles of her brow.

"Get inside. Keep your head down until I come back. And don't let anyone in unless it's me."

Judah waited until she was halfway across the room before he grabbed his gun and headed outside. He used the stairwell, ignoring the smell as he raced down the concrete steps to the ground floor and pushed out the exit door. A rush of humid night air hit him.

In the distance, an animal howled.

Judah headed for the side of the building with visibility of the windows that were shot out. Whoever fired could be on a neighboring building. Or in a vehicle, and they'd simply aimed up. No, the shots had been almost straight. They all hit the wall above the TV and not the ceiling, which meant the person couldn't have been on the ground, firing up.

He figured if someone who wanted the reporter, Soraya Adams, taken out, firing warning shots was one thing. But now, she would be scrambling. They would have to move as fast as possible to find her and kill her.

Which meant they would be headed for her apartment now.

He'd gone through all of this with Badger and Hannah a few weeks ago, when Hannah's handler had been killed. The shooter pretended to be an assassin. Or he *was* an assassin, and he'd blamed it on his brother. Judah had never been able to get that all straight. But what they did know was that the shooter's brother worked for Travers Industries.

The same company she was running from.

As he told her, there was no way this could be a coincidence. That meant someone had manipulated them into meeting each other. He wasn't willing to accept anything else. Not when believing in coincidence meant he was naïve and wouldn't realize the truth of what was happening around him. Or to him.

Judah found a spot to sit and waited.

He crouched in the dark, holding his gun in front of him, and listened to the rush of every breath in his ears.

Seconds later a man emerged from the building beside Soraya's.

The name suited her. It was mysterious and interesting —like her.

But he couldn't allow her to distract him. For the first time in his life, he needed to not fall in instalove with a woman the first time he saw her. After all, it had never actually helped him before. In fact, it was probably more of a hindrance. Often it tended to get him in trouble. And that was the last thing either of them needed right now.

The man crossed in front of Judah headed to her building. He was bathed in light from the street lamp by the front door.

Judah recognized him immediately.

But that was impossible. He was dead.

Casper Cunningham had been killed in Afghanistan four years ago. He was the MI-6 asset Judah had been blamed for the loss of, which was why they were targeting him now. For the favor they thought he owed them since they believed him responsible for Casper's death.

Judah had believed it as well.

The guy got the door open before Judah managed to move.

Judah's options were limited. He settled on lifting his gun, squeezing off a shot, and embedding it in the brick in front of Casper's face.

The guy spun around, let go of the door, and raised his own weapon.

Judah fired another shot and shattered the front door glass to the apartment building.

Casper backed up, reflexively retreating from the threat of death.

It was definitely him.

This guy planned to kill Soraya? There was no way Judah would allow that to happen.

He'd never liked the guy, anyway.

Judah fired another shot closer to him.

Casper backed up again, turned, and ran. Choosing to live to fight another day, no doubt. Or, he was simply a coward at heart. Someone who snuck up on a defenseless woman and took her out because a powerful company wanted her dead.

Or he'd been ordered to do it by British intelligence, though that was a harder sell.

Maybe there was another reason entirely. But Judah didn't have time to figure it out.

He ran across the street, watching for Casper, just in case the guy planned on doubling back to see who had shot at him. Then he pounded upstairs as fast as he could and shoved his way into the apartment, where he wedged the door shut with a chair. The bathroom was the only closed door down the hall.

He knocked. "It's Judah. Open up!"

"You never told me your name. How am I supposed to know it's you?"

"If it's not me, you can hit me over the head with a bucket again."

The door opened.

"You've got backbone," Judah said. "I'll give you that."

Soraya lifted her chin. "I've got a whole lot more than that."

Judah opened his mouth to reply with a quip, and he would have. He'd have taken that bait and run with it any other time than right now. But instead of falling back on those old habits, he said, "We need to pack up and leave before the person who came here to kill you comes back."

She blinked. "What's wrong? What happened outside?"

"Nothing. Let's go."

"So I'm done here? Like life-ending stuff?"

He nodded.

She pushed out a long breath. "And nothing happened outside?"

"You being here, hiding out, has been compromised."

"I was supposed to stay until she called me. I guess I can let her know I'm leaving on the way."

Whoever she was talking about, Judah figured they could help her.

"Get packed up." He headed back to the hallway and the living room.

He needed to walk off this unnerved feeling, or he would jump all over her demanding answers to every single question he had. First they had to leave, then he could pin her down and get her to talk.

If MI-6 didn't find him before they got away.

Once she was safe, he would get back in touch with them. Get back to the mission that had been thoroughly ruined tonight. He was supposed to be with Mobo and Banjoko right now, meeting with a contact of theirs who had information about where he could find the head of this assassin's Guild. Instead, he'd been dragged back into Chevalier's business.

But he couldn't get involved with Soraya. If his two worlds collided and MI-6 got wind of the team he worked with now, he would never be able to escape them.

All Judah needed to do was get her safe. Which probably meant sending her to Zander and the rest of the guys. They could help her do what she needed to do. Keep her alive and take down Travers at the same time. In the meantime, he'd be off fulfilling his obligation to MI-6.

Only, now that he knew Casper was alive, that changed things.

It made Judah wonder if the guy worked for the man Judah was looking for, as a paid assassin. There had been entirely too many of those consequences lately. And all roads seemed to be leading back to Travers. He could draw conclusions and make connections all he wanted. But without evidence, it was only guessing.

The idea that MI-6 was a hop, skip, and a jump away from Travers Industries was a scary thought. But once he got Soraya far from here and under protection, he could separate the two things again.

Judah would work the problem, even while he did what MI-6 expected. Like a double agent. The way Isaac had worked for his mother, Lana, deceiving everyone in Chevalier before he left them high and dry only to land in prison.

Judah shook off the frustration, caused by lingering adrenaline and his mind needing an outlet for his feelings. He would have found something to laugh about, only this situation was far from funny. He felt like a completely different person than the man who had worked with the team at Chevalier.

When they found him again? They might not even recognize him.

That was the worst of this. He liked who he'd been and the life he had in Last Chance County. It was nothing but a pipe dream now.

If he could find Casper, he'd be able to convince MI-6 he wasn't responsible for the man's death.

Before he could reason it all out, Soraya emerged from the hall with a duffel over one shoulder.

"Good." He grabbed her hand. "Let's go."

HE DROVE the car far faster than she was comfortable with, saying nothing as he navigated the roads in the pitch black outside the city. Until Soraya had to brace one hand on the dash so she could fish her phone out. It glowed in the dark. She turned the brightness down and dialed the number she was only supposed to call in a dire emergency.

She figured some gunman shooting out all the windows in her apartment qualified.

It rang long enough she wasn't sure the other woman was going to pick up.

"Hello?"

It took Soraya a second to realize the call had connected. "Yeah. It's me." She blew out a breath. "Someone tried to kill me. They shot out the apartment windows."

"Are you somewhere safe?"

Soraya wasn't entirely sure about this British guy's driving skills, but still. "I don't know where we're going. I'll let you know."

"We?"

She winced. "I have help."

She had a feeling he was going to drop her off as soon as they were somewhere he could get rid of her and drive away knowing she was taken care of. This wasn't the kind of guy who stuck around for the long term. He wasn't even telling her everything.

At least she knew his name. *Judah.*

Then on top of all of it something had happened outside her apartment. But Judah hadn't answered her question about that. Instead, he brushed her off and got them moving.

Which told her he at least understood the threat level.

"Whoever it is, put them on the phone."

Her tone didn't invite any argument, but Soraya wasn't in this mess because she willingly laid down in the face of things she was invested in.

"Maybe in a minute." Soraya needed to figure out what to do next. "Listen, Lana—"

His head whipped around. "What did you just say?"

"Is that him?" Lana asked. "Hand the phone over."

Soraya wasn't just going to let the two of them railroad her. "I'm the one calling the shots here." As if that were true. She glanced at him, then turned her attention back to Lana. "I need to know what I'm supposed to do next. Because my life just fell apart all over again, and I get the feeling I'm not going to be safe. No matter how far I go…or how deeply I try to hide."

"I'd say that's true." Lana paused. "Tell me who this guy is?"

Soraya wasn't sure she even had an answer for that. She shifted in her seat and asked him, "What is your full legal name?" She didn't want him ducking out of this.

He gripped the wheel, not answering. Finally, he said, "My name is Judah Havig." Then, "Put it on speaker."

"J-Ju…," Lana sputtered.

Soraya put the call on speaker. "One of you can fill me in

on what's happening here. Considering I'm in the middle of it."

Judah—she had to admit the name suited him—turned his head slightly toward the phone, but kept his attention on the road. "Lana?"

"I can't believe this."

"So you're saying you didn't know?" He shook his head. "As if I'm supposed to believe you didn't send Ms. Soraya Adams here specifically, knowing I was here as well?"

"I stashed her in a place that was safe, that I control," Lana said. "Now she's saying a shooter tried to carry out a hit? What brought you to her doorstep?"

Soraya blinked.

"She's the one who walked in on *my* operation," he said.

"I already know you're working for the British. So don't bother trying to sell me some other story." Lana huffed. "Who tried to kill her?"

"That's classified." His answer came entirely too quickly.

Lana laughed.

"Is it actually classified?" Soraya asked. The company that was looking to silence her had plenty of government contracts. That was what this whole business was about. Maybe the government was backing Travers Industries in the hunt for her. She had no idea. Except for one thing. "Because need-to-know would be bad for all of us."

"It's classified in the sense that I am a British citizen, and the people I work for also are. Our top-secret files contain information you won't find buried under red tape in the US."

"So the accent isn't fake?" Soraya asked.

Judah shook his head. The car slowed, and he glanced at her for a long second.

She wasn't sure what she was supposed to do with the expression on his face. If it weren't for the fact he clearly had a job going on and was likely some kind of spy, she might like to spend time getting to know him. But that wasn't going to happen. And for whatever reason she didn't want to think about, it made her sad.

"This is not a situation where I need you to go all James Bond." Lana's "no arguments" tone was back.

"Why," Judah said, "is this another one of your kids who doesn't know they have a bunch of siblings?"

"She isn't my child. However, I have taken responsibility for Soraya Adams and her situation."

"Why does that not fill me with confidence?" Judah's question seemed rhetorical, and neither of them answered.

"Where am I supposed to go now?" Soraya swallowed against the lump in her throat. She had barely any belongings on her and only the knowledge in her head to leverage with. Everything else was gone. The chip. All her gathered research.

She knew she'd done the right thing, but the fact she couldn't see her family caused a sharp pain in her chest she didn't like at all. Nobility might be nice; it just didn't keep a person warm at night.

Things had to be better than this.

They needed to be, or Soraya wasn't sure she would survive.

"We'll figure it out." Judah reached over and squeezed her knee.

She wanted to grasp his hand and not let go.

"You know Travers is hunting Soraya," Lana said. "Right?"

"If you're after help, you came to the wrong place." Judah shifted in the seat, his expression shadowed. "Why don't you call Zander and ask him."

"You've never heard that expression, the enemy of my enemy is my friend?" Lana said.

Soraya didn't like the sound of that. It was almost like they were on different sides of a war, trying to find common ground. Judah didn't seem interested in a truce. What did he know about Lana that meant he didn't trust the woman?

As soon as they got off the phone, she would ask him what he knew of her. That way Soraya would be able to tell if she could trust Lana. So far she had, and she'd believed the woman was trustworthy enough she put her life in Lana's hands. But Soraya didn't want to be naïve. If there was another side to this.

Am I nothing but a means to an end?

She had to find out.

"That doesn't work with me," Judah said. "Where do you want Soraya? I'll take her there. After that, it's up to you to keep her safe from the person hunting her."

"Who is it?"

He stiffened. "It doesn't matter who they are. It only matters that they're stopped."

He was hiding something. Soraya could tell, and she knew it had to do with the identity of the person who'd shot out her windows. Something else she needed to ask him. Again. If he wasn't going to share with her, then why should she trust him at all?

Maybe she had no allies in this. But she was stuck between these two people anyway, forced to rely on them for her life. If it wasn't for Lana, she would be dead already. And now she could say the same about Judah.

"What about Chevalier Protection Specialists?" Lana said. "Where do they fit into this?"

"They don't." Judah pushed out a short breath. "I'm not going back there."

"Because the Brits have you up against a wall?"

"It's more complicated than I realized," he said. "Who knows when the situation will be resolved."

"And it doesn't even occur to you to ask me for help?" Lana said. "After everything you know I've done, and what you can imagine I'm capable of?"

Judah shook his head. "There isn't time to get into everything you've done and why that would be a colossally bad idea."

"Lana gave me a clean identity and a place to stay." Soraya wasn't sure why she felt the need to defend the woman. But at least he would have a better picture of everything Lana had done. That had to count for something, didn't it? "She helped me stay alive. Kind of like the way you just did in my apartment."

"How well do you really know this woman?" He glanced at her.

"Better than I know you," she pointed out. "But for some reason, I still think we should stay together."

He shook his head. "That's not possible."

She shifted in her seat and tried not to think about what it meant that he was ditching her. Soraya didn't need to have hurt feelings over a guy she had only just met.

A blinding white light flashed beside her.

She frowned as it grew brighter for a split second. She realized what was happening and gasped. Then the impact came, a noise louder than anything she'd ever heard. Glass shattered. Judah roared.

Soraya's whole body jerked. Contorted.

Everything went black.

It took a second for Judah to realize he was moving. None of his limbs worked, his head swam, and everything felt as though he had slammed into a concrete wall.

His feet hit the ground. Someone had a grip on his armpits.

He was being dragged.

A second after that realization moved through him, everything went black again.

When he woke next, his cheek was pressed up against carpet. Not good carpet. The scratchy kind, like cheap office flooring. Or the trunk of a car. He did a head-to-toe inventory, moving each joint and the larger muscles of his body to see what was working and what wasn't.

His top lip was damp, and his nose—which had been broken too many times already—seemed to have been moved out of place again. *Ouch.*

He lifted his hands and realized they were secured together. In the pitch black, he fought to hold his focus on being conscious. Nothing else could be dealt with until he got this initial problem sorted out.

And it was going to hurt.

Judah laid his fingers alongside his nose, thankful his hands had been tied in front and not behind him. Yep, it was definitely broken. He clenched his jaw and pressed on the cartilage, shoving it quickly back into place. He covered the moan that escaped his lips with a few short breaths, like a woman in labor. Why did breathing always seem satisfying? At least it helped him focus through the pain. Then it had passed enough he could figure out what he was going to do next.

Before he made a plan, he needed to work out where they were.

Given the rumble under where his body lay, he would go with a moving vehicle. He felt around the trunk and found clothing covering a warm body. In the dark, he could only feel his way. He tried to be respectful in the process as he figured out it was a woman, and everything rushed back.

"Soraya."

She'd been in the car with him, shifting in her seat because of his comment about leaving her. Not that she cared enough to have hurt feelings, but he still didn't like it. They didn't know each other well enough for her to have been hurt, and it wasn't like he owed her anything. But she'd stiffened anyway.

Then the car was slammed into by another vehicle.

Lana.

They'd been on the phone with her at the time of the crash. Surely she would track the phone and figure out where they were. Someone would come and rescue them. Fully armed people who were trained in tactical rescue.

That ever-present ache in him to see the members of his team surged inside him. Like a small fire that suddenly whooshed into an inferno. It hit him all over again.

He missed them.

The boys of Chevalier were his family, as much as his sister Toni and her fiancé, Jeff. If he couldn't get back to them? Judah didn't even want to think about that.

He found Soraya's elbow, then her shoulder. He patted her

cheek and turned his hand so the back of his fingers were in front of her nostrils. He felt the exhale of breath. She was alive.

"Wake up." He patted her cheek a couple more times.

The two of them working together was going to be a whole lot more effective than just him on his own. Especially when she wasn't more than deadweight being unconscious. He needed her awake and fired up to get out of here.

"Soraya." He didn't like how his voice sounded, but that didn't matter. He needed to work the problem and not let his feelings get in the way as he always did. Falling too hard and too fast for a woman.

Even if she was entirely worthy of it, Judah couldn't afford to fall back in those old behaviors this time. It was better that he keep separate. That he didn't let his feelings get involved in this. Whoever took them, they couldn't know he felt responsible for her. That he cared.

The car slowed. Judah heard the squeak of brakes, and they came to a stop, though the engine kept running. A door slammed. Was someone getting out?

He braced. As soon as the boot opened, he was going to launch out and fight for both their lives.

Instead, the boot never opened, and a chemical smell tickled his nose. Judah sniffed. The last chemical he'd gone up against seriously injured Badger, and he'd been exposed too. Even if he hadn't suffered the same effects, he remembered it well. But there had been no smell.

What was this?

The smell filled the back of the car. Until it was all he could taste. The odor swallowed him up, and everything went black again.

When Judah woke next, the scene was entirely different. Instead of being in the pitch black of a car with Soraya beside him, the lights were too bright. But he recognized the scene well.

They were on an airplane.

Much like before, when MI-6 had grabbed him on the street, the handler who co-opted him into working sat facing him. Saying nothing.

Judah sat up from his slump in the chair and decided to break the silence. "This was all you?"

The guy just stared at him. "It's really too bad you didn't figure out the identity of the leader of that assassin's guild. But it turns out you gave us something better."

Judah wasn't going to argue why he hadn't completed the mission. Soraya had given him something far more critical to do.

He looked around to try and find her but didn't see where she sat. Or lay. Was she even on this plane?

Judah was about to ask a question when the guy's phone rang. Whatever conversation he had might provide intel into what on earth was going on here.

"Yeah?" The MI-6 officer paused. "That's the plan. We should be landing shortly. After that, it's up to you. I get what I want, and the merchandise is turned over to you."

So it was going to be an exchange? At least, Judah figured when the guy said "merchandise" that he was referring to Judah and probably Soraya as well. If she was here.

That realization settled in the pit of his stomach.

The officer said, "I want everything at the time of the exchange." Then he hung up.

Judah stared at him, trying to figure out if this was an action the British government was taking or if this guy was working independently. If he exposed a rat to the SIS, Judah could earn himself back some credibility. How did he even know this whole thing really was sanctioned? It could be he'd been strung along this entire time.

Duped into working for a traitor.

Alternatively, this could be exactly what Her Majesty's government wanted. Now that there was no way Judah could find out the identity of the head of that group of assassins he was supposed to locate, they were using him in an entirely different manner. Determined to make him worth something to them in one way or another.

And yet, they had no idea exactly how valuable he could be. Judah stared the guy down. "Casper is alive." He waited for that to settle in. "I saw him in Nigeria."

There was no way this guy didn't know. After all, he figured that shooting was why British intelligence found him and Soraya trying to run. Or they had some kind of tracker on him and discovered he was outside the boundaries of where they expected him to be. Judah didn't know.

"That's rubbish." The guy shook his head. "You just want us to keep you around, so you're making up anything to try and get me to hang onto you."

Judah wanted to ask about Soraya but couldn't do that. "I would have fought for my country if they gave me something to fight for. Instead, all you did was try to manipulate me."

"I should've appealed to your honor?"

Judah shrugged. That was exactly what Zander would've done. A thought that made him miss his friend. If he played this right, Judah could get himself exposed. Leave a breadcrumb for either Lana and her organization, or his friends, to find. Give himself a shot at going home.

That hope was better than believing he had none. Because denial was better than going insane.

The plane landed. Judah leaned over and pushed up the window.

All he saw were mountains and one building. They were in the middle of nowhere. Which meant it was unlikely there were surveillance cameras to catch what was about to happen.

"Let's go. Travers is waiting." The guy stood.

Judah assimilated the information as fast as possible. They were going to exchange him and turn him over to Travers Industries? "I'll feed you information. I'll be an asset."

He would figure out a way to contact Chevalier.

The MI-6 operative laughed. Then he pulled a black cloth bag over Judah's head.

———

THE WAFT of cold air that surrounded her let Soraya know she was outside. But she couldn't succumb to her body's need to shiver. Otherwise, the person currently carrying her down what she figured was the steps of an airplane would know that she was only pretending to be unconscious.

"Where do you want this one?" A deep voice rumbled under her cheek.

Where was Judah? Of course, not that she cared, considering he would have dumped her off somewhere. Although, if she were willing to admit it to herself, she did actually care about where he was and if he was all right.

Maybe they killed him.

Whoever had taken them, she figured this had to do with the tech company that wanted her silenced before she could tell the world what she knew about Travers' new phone system they were about to release. Who else could it be?

"Over there." The man spoke with a British accent.

Like Judah, a guy Lana knew—something that spoke in his favor.

Much like her identity being exposed and being forced to run, this was all happening too early. Too fast. Too much.

She couldn't assimilate what was happening quickly enough.

Panic swelled, but she beat the sensation back. Only having a cool head would help her figure a way out of this.

Lana was supposed to be working on things at her end. She'd told Soraya to hang on. Wait until it was the right time to come back and tell everyone what she knew. Soraya had no idea how Lana planned on accomplishing that, but she figured a woman with those types of resources knew what she was doing.

Lana had shown Soraya details of several operations she'd been involved in and how things had turned out. Soraya believed what she'd seen.

The fact she was in over her head now wasn't something that had escaped her. She had no idea what to do in a world of gunmen and kidnappings. The crash had left her achy all over, and she thought that maybe she had one black eye. It certainly felt puffy and swollen. Her cheekbone currently smashed against the man's jacket hurt a lot.

The man stopped walking and tossed her inside a vehicle. Soraya cracked her good eye enough to see the interior of the SUV. And then Judah was thrown beside her. Soraya shut her eyes again to make sure no one realized she was awake.

"They're here." The first voice spoke again.

The second was clearly in charge. "If they do anything you don't like, shoot them. We'll figure this all out after."

"You really think they have the identity of the guy who is coordinating all these assassins?"

The boss replied, "That's what they say. And they think it's worth enough we're going to give Travers Industries both of them in exchange for just that…and nothing else."

She imagined he motioned to Judah and Soraya. But considering she didn't look she had no idea if he did or not.

Her head still swam from something. A drug they'd given her, and maybe Judah as well if he was passed out too. He wasn't fighting to get them out of this, so she figured he was unconscious as she had been since the car accident.

However long that had been.

The boss continued, "Just as long as they think they're getting the better end of the deal."

"You think he was telling the truth about Casper being alive?" the underling asked.

"Who knows?" the boss said. "Seems like exactly the kind of thing I'd have said in his position, just to throw us off."

Both spoke quickly as they continued their conversation. Given their thick British accents, Soraya had difficulty processing their words, but she got the gist of what they were saying. Judah had told them something, and they weren't sure if they believed it.

He was tangled up in this, probably as much as she was. For some reason, Travers Industries wanted both her and Judah. The company was willing to exchange something the Brits wanted for the two of them.

The last place Soraya wanted to be was in Travers Industries' hands. Would they kill her or use her for something else?

An engine roared, and she heard the heavy whoosh of pneumatic brakes as the vehicle came to a stop. The back doors of the vehicle they were in slammed shut. Soraya shuddered, and she heard Judah let out a breath.

She whispered, "Are you awake?"

"Stay quiet for a bit longer." He kept his voice as low as hers, but there was a tone of authority in it. He was taking charge of the situation.

Considering how in over her head she felt, Soraya didn't exactly mind.

She'd thought he might support her when they were driving away from her destroyed apartment. Then he'd told her that he would drop her off somewhere and go back to his life. Now look where they were. Everything she'd tried to do was going to be erased. Travers Industries would make sure of that.

Like the rest of her life, she'd thought things were looking up. Only now it turned out they weren't. Soraya didn't know why it always surprised her. Nothing ever turned out differently.

Even though she and Judah were in this together, she needed to keep her focus on what she was trying to do.

Travers Industries couldn't be allowed to release their new technology. The phone system's overreach meant too many people would be exposed. Travers would have full control over all electronic information. Allowing it put people in far too much danger. Who knew how they would abuse that power? It couldn't happen.

Especially if no one knew the truth.

She had to protect herself. Keep her empathy from going overboard, no matter what happened to Judah. Travers might use threats against him to coerce her into doing whatever they wanted. She couldn't allow that to happen either.

There was a clang of metal, then a whir, and they started to move. The vehicle they were in was hauled up a ramp into a shipping container. Soraya peered out the windows as darkness surrounded them. She shifted to look out the back and saw only mountains and one building. Where were they?

The US, or maybe Canada. The Brits might have chosen neutral ground. A place they could get into and out of easily.

But that meant Travers would have to get them back across the US–Canadian border.

If that was the case, she and Judah could use it to get them out of this.

The back doors of the shipping container swung shut and the entire vehicle was swallowed in darkness. Even inside the car she heard the heavier clang of a lock being secured. Maybe even a chain, leaving them with no way to get out of the shipping container in order to escape.

A whimper fled her lips.

The truck under them began to rumble and they started to move.

Judah shifted. In the dark she couldn't make out anything, but she heard the rustle of his clothing, followed by a grunt and a mutter. "Ouch." Then his hand touched her knee. "Are your hands secured by plastic tie in front of you?"

"Yes." She didn't want to sit up for fear of headbutting him in the dark.

"Is there space between your wrists?"

"A little. Why?" The truck under them turned the corner, and she rolled onto him. "Sorry."

"We're going to get out of here." Before she could counter and ask how he figured they would do that, he said, "Bend your knee. Bring your hands down fast, over your kneecap. Force it between your wrists and you'll snap the plastic ties. But fair warning, it's going to hurt."

"I know." She bit her lip. "I've done it before."

"Earlier? Or some other time?"

"It doesn't matter." She didn't want to talk about any situation she'd been in. Not when it would bring back all that fear and add it to what she felt right now. Then she'd have a double dose of terror to try and get a handle on so she didn't flip out and become completely useless. Inconsolable, and unable to think straight. She needed to push back the fear and figure a way to get herself out of this that didn't involve him.

"We need to trust each other." His fingers brushed her shin, and he squeezed her ankle. "Work together."

She sat up, bracing her arms out so that she pushed him away as she moved. "Actually, what you need to do is stay out of my way."

8

———

Judah blinked. Had she seriously just told him to stay out of her way?

He backed up and found the side door, then cracked the handle and pushed it open so the dome light overhead turned on.

The interior of the car washed in yellow light.

Soraya lifted her hands and brought them down over her bent knee. She hissed a breath and shook out her wrists.

"You good?" As far as he was concerned, he was going to ignore that comment about him needing to stay out of her way. She would see soon enough that wasn't a good way to operate. If they were going to get out of this, it should be together. They were that much stronger and more effective as a team.

She nodded but didn't move.

If she wasn't convinced that was the case, Judah was happy to teach. He'd worked on squads in the Royal Marines, small teams that made up the battalion. And over the last few years, in the team that was Chevalier Protection Specialists. In fact, the last few weeks had been the first time in a long time Judah had worked solo.

He'd rather have backup and the support of people he trusted.

If Soraya didn't trust him, maybe he could convince her he was trustworthy now.

So long as they were working on getting out of there in the meantime.

"If you're not busy," he said. "Could you climb into the front and search the glove compartment? See if there's anything we can use to help us get out of here."

"The glove box?"

He nodded, realizing too late he should have used that expression for it. Even though they both spoke the same language, sometimes the differences between American and British English made things confusing. He'd learned to compensate with the boys, although occasionally he refused and left them to figure out what he was saying.

Now that MI-6 had traded him like a commodity they no longer needed—because they could get a higher price for him from someone else—he wanted to get back to his team. The Brits might show up again one day, but he certainly didn't owe them anything. And they were no longer in pursuit of him, trying to force him to work for them. They were going to complete the mission by making a deal with Travers.

They were giving him up.

The whole reason they'd co-opted him in the first place was all down to the fact that Casper had been killed in Afghanistan and they held him responsible. Now that he knew the MI-6 agent was alive, they had no leverage to hold over him.

But why hadn't Casper come back in the years since he was declared dead? A guy like that could ask for whatever he wanted from the people he worked for. He'd been an amazing spy. Now he was reduced to being a sniper? The fact there was an organization of assassins targeted in all this made him wonder if there wasn't a connection between

Casper and that group. Maybe he'd been tasked by them with killing Soraya.

It wasn't a stretch. But it wasn't something Judah needed to worry about right now.

He and Soraya needed to focus on getting out of this shipping container.

She climbed over the center console into the front passenger seat and opened the glove box. "What am I looking for?"

"Just tell me if you find anything other than papers." Although, Judah could cause a decent amount of damage with paper. If he had something to ignite it.

The middle row of seats had been folded flat for cargo mode—them being the cargo.

Judah crawled to the storage compartment in the back and flipped the latch. He discarded the lid to one side, and looked into the one-by-two-foot space. With only six inches of depth to fill there wasn't much inside. But it was enough for a box of latex gloves, a first-aid kit that might come in handy, and a tire iron. The spare tire was probably under the car, but he didn't think he needed that.

Likely he could cause a decent amount of damage with the tire iron. And if either of them got hurt, the first-aid kit might come in handy.

"There's a lighter under the papers."

Judah lifted his head. "Any juice in it?" He heard the snick, and a flame popped up.

"Looks like it works." She let go.

"Okay, hand it over…along with the papers." He crawled to the center console and reached out.

"What are you going to do with it?" she asked.

"Cause a kerfuffle." If she were interested in teaming up with him, then he would happily explain the plan. However, she had told him she didn't want to work together with him. "Unless you have an idea you'd like to try? I'm happy to go along with your plan." *Seeing as you have so much experience escaping kidnappers.*

That's what he wanted to say. But he held his tongue on that. She would probably think she was getting to him if he threw out attitude. Breaking him down so he might fall into line with what she wanted to do. Instead, he was interested in them meeting in the middle. Not in one of them being in charge, while the other one sat around with no clue what was happening or how to help.

She said nothing.

Judah took the papers and lighter from her, then climbed out the side where he laid everything by the back door, and the opening to the shipping container. They were moving, a breeze coming through a gap in the bottom of the door. Hopefully it didn't put the fire out. Because he needed this thing to create a ton of smoke.

Could he burn the latex gloves?

The last thing he needed was to fill the container with a load of noxious gas, so he held off on that one.

Judah pulled off his shirt and stuffed it along the seam at the bottom of the door to block the breeze. The icy-cold air prickled his skin, but he ignored it, laid out the papers in a stack, and flipped on the lighter. As each piece of paper began to burn, Judah added to it with the next one.

"I found a tissue box."

He glanced at her and accepted what she'd brought. "Thanks. That should help."

"Aren't you just going to suffocate us?"

"I'm hoping there will be enough smoke the truck has to stop. We're no good to them dead, otherwise they would have killed us already. MI-6 would have sent them pictures of our bodies to prove it, and then walked away with what they wanted."

Unless the Brits didn't want to get their hands dirty. Were Travers Industries only transporting them somewhere they could be killed? Judah didn't like that idea at all. He pulled out tissues and bundled them up, setting them on fire.

Right now, all he had to do was figure out how to get whoever was driving to stop and open the door.

After that, he would figure out what they wanted with him and Soraya.

The pile burned quickly.

"Move to the front of the car and crouch at the bottom corner of the container," Judah said. "You need to be low. The smoke will fill from the top down."

"Are you a firefighter?"

"My squad helped out fighting a few blazes in Afghanistan. But no, I'm not a firefighter. I work for a team who protects people."

"Is that how you know Lana?"

"Yes." But not in the way she was thinking. "And it's how we got on the radar of Travers Industries."

"Okay." That sounded an awful lot like she was acquiescing. But before he could ask her about it, Soraya moved to the front end of the car.

Judah needed more fuel for his fire. He went to the car and detached both headrests from the front row. Then he grabbed the lid for the rear storage compartment. The top was covered in a layer of carpet. It might burn.

He set it up, leaning the lid on the two headrests so that it hovered over the fire and the flames licked at it.

Then he went back for the gloves.

When there was enough of a blaze, Judah grabbed his shirt and stood at the rear of the car. He wafted smoke toward the gap at the bottom of the door. Hoping and praying with all the faith his grandmother had instilled in him that this would work.

That someone would see, and his efforts would be a beacon for his rescuers to come and find him.

Assuming his teammates hadn't given up on him entirely.

Judah fanned and prayed, fanned and prayed.

The container filled with smoke.

The driver hit the brakes. Judah slammed against the back of the car, and the truck began to slow.

SORAYA PEERED under the open rear door of the car, huddled on the floor trying to escape the smoke. With a great creak, the doors of the container eased open. Cold air rushed in. The kind of winter air found in northern states.

She had spent her college years living and working in Toronto, but Canada wasn't for her. She'd moved back to the US and been in search of year-round warmth ever since. Her parents lived in Georgia, which was warm enough. But who wanted to live their adult life in the same place they'd grown up?

After weeks hiding out, living in Nigeria, she may as well be in the Arctic right now. She certainly wasn't dressed for December in a wintry climate. Nor was she used to it.

She shivered against the floor of the container and watched as black smoke wafted out and wrapped around a man who stood there. He had a mean face, and a dark jacket. He didn't seem particularly surprised to find people in the container.

She spotted a flash of movement.

Judah launched himself out of the container with a tire iron. He tackled the man to the ground and Soraya heard the clang of the tire iron on asphalt. Then the dull crack as it hit bone beneath flesh.

She squeezed her eyes shut, but she couldn't stay here forever. She was exposed even in the corner where she now lay.

Her fingers had gone numb. Even the warmth of the fire didn't help to combat the cold from outside.

It was possible the driver only thought there was a problem and had come to check it out. Now he was being pummeled on by a former soldier. She doubted either British intelligence or a scary technology company would leave something like this to people who were oblivious. But what did she know? Soraya believed the truth was to be spoken, and people should do what was noble.

No company had the right to control the lives of those they were supposed to serve. Least of all people who were meant to be on the side of justice, like federal law enforcement. If Travers got their way, no one would be safe. Due process would go out the window. Convictions would be a joke. Evidence would disappear, or fabricated evidence could show up.

But if she couldn't get out of this container, what good was knowing all of that?

At least Judah was trying to fix the situation. She had an idea of who he had been before he showed up as some kind of covert operative. That should be reassuring, knowing he was someone who served his country with honor. But she just couldn't wrap her head around any of this.

She crawled forward to where she could get a better look under the door. Her muscles screamed, and the joints of her fingers were almost completely seized from the cold.

Someone could see her at any second, but she had to know how Judah was doing. The guy might not want anything to do with her, or her way of doing things, and maybe she'd insinuated she would leave him behind.

Either way, she didn't want him to die. She tried to convince herself she didn't care if he'd gone ahead with it and dumped her off somewhere safe. But she felt as though she needed to help him now, so she wasn't going to leave him in the lurch.

After all, what if he was right?

What if the only way to take down Travers was to do it

together?

Just because she'd been alone for a long time didn't mean she wanted her life to be like that forever, refusing to see any other way.

"Get a bag over his head!" a man yelled. "Now."

She frowned. That wasn't the man Judah had fought talking. There must be more of them than just the driver, and they were worried about someone seeing him. Which meant people were around, or he could be on a kind of security system that recorded video.

A man approached him, gun up.

Someone else shoved him away. "Don't kill him."

"Get his legs."

They were trying to take down Judah.

Soraya crawled on her elbows, now wedged partially under the door with her head turned to the side.

Judah jumped up, spread his arms to the sides still holding the tire iron, and turned in a circle. Putting himself in full view of anyone who could possibly see him. Exposing himself so hopefully someone saw him?

If Lana was looking for them, she'd find evidence they'd been here—wherever *here* was.

Lana had been on the phone with them when the initial accident occurred. Now Soraya knew it definitely hadn't been an accident—it had been British intelligence. Judah was working for them, and they'd turned him over to someone else. She couldn't believe he would've chosen to work for people like that.

"Come and get me!" Judah yelled—his back was tense, those broad shoulders with no shirt—seemingly not cognizant of the fact it was freezing out there and he had no protective clothing.

The other men wore coats and woolen hats.

"Maybe I could just hurt him a little," one of the men said. "They don't mind if he's beat up, right?"

Soraya wanted to hide and get away from everything that was happening. But she also had to do something. She scrambled to the driver's side and used the cover of the rear door to keep her from being seen as she eased it open and climbed in.

There was so much noise happening outside that she slammed the rear door shut, and then the driver's door. Inside it was much more tolerable. Plus, a crime article she'd written two years ago had put her in the path of a car thief gave her an idea.

She knew exactly how to hotwire this vehicle.

Soraya gripped the steering wheel but had to take a breath. She couldn't simply put the thing in reverse, hit the gas, and peel out of here. She would likely kill Judah if he was in the way. Or destroy the car as it hit the concrete. Still, the idea of running and escaping was like an intoxicating drug.

All she knew was that she had to get them away.

A man cried out. Judah, or the other guys? Did the driver even know who—or what—he was transporting when he set out? Or these other men, did they work for Travers?

Movement in the side mirror caught her attention. Judah's body jerked, and he went down. Falling below the edge of the truck so that she couldn't see him.

She gasped.

A gunshot rang out. The back window of the car shattered.

Soraya screamed and ducked down, realizing the seat had no headrest. She could be shot so easily. The way Judah had been overcome through no fault of his own, or a lack of skill.

With her head down by her knees, she could see the underside of the steering wheel.

Without overthinking what she was doing, Soraya pulled off the plastic cover and exposed the wires she would use to start the ignition.

"Get out of the car!"

She shook her head, even though whoever it was couldn't

see her. She needed to do this quickly or she would lose the element of surprise. *God, please don't let Judah be in the way.* Because she already knew what she was going to do. If this went wrong, she would kill a good man who shouldn't have been in this situation with her.

Soraya touched two exposed wires together and heard the engine roar to life. She checked for an emergency brake, released it, and put the car in reverse.

She hit the gas.

The car backed up. Soraya held the steering wheel straight and twisted to look out the shattered back window as the engine roared and the car picked up speed.

The car shot off the back lip of the container into the air. A gunman dove out of the way.

Soraya winced, then realized that meant she couldn't see anything, so she opened her eyes. Her hands still on the steering wheel.

The car slammed onto the ground, rocking the entire vehicle. Her face hit the steering wheel and she cried out.

It kept going, backward.

The tires bumped over a body, but she didn't stop.

One of the men lifted a gun and fired. The front windshield shattered with a hole punched out of the bottom right corner.

She screamed again, and the car turned. She straightened it out, her foot moved to the brake, and she jolted to a stop. Her window faced the gunman.

Judah lay on the ground by the container, completely still.

Another of the gunmen lay in her path—the one she'd run over. One stood to the right of the container truck, the other on the left. The guy on the left ran to his buddy.

Two standing together made a bigger target than one alone.

Soraya put the car in drive and hit the gas, headed straight for them.

9

———————

By the time Andre pulled the SUV through the security gate, he realized why they hadn't been given clearance to land at St. John's International Airport. "Whoa."

The airport was inaccessible by plane due to the incident that had happened on the tarmac. The team of Chevalier Protection Specialists had been forced to land at a private airport and drive through Newfoundland to the airport that hit Ted's radar.

They had no evidence at all it was Judah someone had reported seeing yelling and acting crazy before he was taken down. In addition to that, seconds later a car had run roughshod over several people.

The entire runway was covered with emergency vehicles, mostly fire trucks and police cars. Even hours later a helicopter was parked on standby. Though maybe it resided here and had nothing to do with the commotion of first responders.

Uniformed officers were peppered around the wreckage of a car, wedged under a container truck right on the edge of the runway.

It looked like the scene of a disaster.

Andre parked far enough away that they weren't going to be seen as intruding. But when the group of them piled out of two SUVs and all walked over to the scene of the accident, a uniformed officer broke off conversation with someone and headed toward them. The guy looked far too young. That didn't mean he was malleable and they would be able to walk all over him. The team had no intention of doing that in a foreign country. It could start all kinds of sticky international situations.

The name of the game these days was keeping their heads low, even while they tried to figure out what was going on with Travers Industries.

There was a chance they would never earn back their reputation as a team and get a spot with the Department of Clandestine Services again. They'd run missions for the director up until a few months ago. Zander was hard at work trying to repair those bridges, and they had a plan for how to do that. So far there hadn't been a whole lot of time, and on top of all that Ted was about to get married. But soon enough they'd figure it out.

Andre didn't care either way if they got those contracts back. They seemed to be busy enough as it was.

The Canadian cop scanned their group. "Can I help you folks?"

Andre glanced over his shoulder. His wife stood close to him. Beyond them were the duet of Badger—his army buddy before Chevalier—and Hannah, who'd been a Rochester police detective. Beyond the two of them stood Eas, a man on the FBI's Ten Most Wanted list up until a couple of short months ago. All in all, they were an intimidating group.

Andre lifted his chin. "One of the men possibly involved in this incident is a friend of ours, a member of our team." He pulled out his wallet and flashed identification so the guy would know he was prepared to be checked out and verified. And that he was an American. "We work in private security. We believe he was taken against his will several weeks ago and we've been looking for him since."

"That's right." Lucia took Andre's hand and laid her head on the outside of his arm, coming across as uncharacteristically upset. The woman was fire and steel. He knew this because of how much they had been through together. But right now, she played the part excellently. "We are very worried about our friend."

Taking the road of relative of a victim put them in a lower position, which meant the cop would feel it was within his rights to tell them to leave and he would get in contact with them later. He might feel sympathetic toward them and allow them to wait—hopefully in Bluetooth distance of the only building Andre could see out here.

The cop nodded, and his expression softened. "That's understandable. Truth be told, it's kind of crazy what happened here. I hope your friend isn't the one involved."

If the security cameras he could see didn't lead back to that building, he didn't know where they would find any footage of Judah that might be here. Ted hadn't been able to hack their system, which was why they'd made the trip all this way.

It had taken hours to get here, not even knowing if the incident that'd happened had anything to do with their friend. Maybe it didn't, and this was just another dead end in the search for Judah.

But none of them were giving up.

"Were there any casualties?" Hannah took a step forward.

The cop's eyes flared with interest. "There was no one here when we arrived. That's what has everyone so baffled. There are bullet holes and blood, but no injured or casualties."

"And you've searched the whole area?" Hannah said.

"Thoroughly." The cop nodded. "Now we're processing the scene and collecting evidence. When we run DNA, we'll be able to find the identity of the persons who were involved."

"But they're gone?" Lucia folded her arms.

It was the only concession she gave to how upset she was they had no leads on finding Judah. Everyone in the team loved him, and they were a tightknit group both before and after the addition of Nora, Lucia, Karina and Aria, and Hannah.

No one believed Judah left of his own accord and chose not to return. His sister was worried sick about him, stuck at home because her future mother-in-law was in the hospital with salmonella poisoning. If they found indication Judah had been here, Toni would be on the first plane out. Probably along with her husband to be, something no one on the team would object to.

They knew a number of highly skilled people.

And then there was Ted, the team's technical expert.

Even with all that, they hadn't found one single whiff of where Judah might be. For weeks now. It was beyond frustrating.

The cop nodded. "I am afraid everyone involved in this managed to leave before we were alerted there was a situation and we could arrive on scene. It's the nature of being this far out on the peninsula, I'm afraid. Not many close neighbors."

"Who alerted you in the first place?" Hannah was starting to sound like a cop and shifted her stance. Probably to shake off the sensation. She was no longer an officer of the law, but like him and the years he had spent as a soldier, those ingrained traits and mannerisms were hard to shake.

"We have a security guard here," the cop replied. "He saw the semi roll in with the container behind it, and what happened after."

Andre wanted to ask about physical evidence, but the cop might clam up and refuse to tell him. "What did he see?"

"Why don't you describe your friend to me," the cop said. "I'll let you know if that matches what we've been told."

Andre nodded. "He's of African descent, but he has an accent he uses sometimes when he doesn't know people really well. So he might've sounded British if he spoke."

How else did he describe a guy born in Africa who emigrated to the UK? He wasn't American. Andre figured what he'd said was better than the long-winded explanation of who Judah might pretend to be if this guy ever came across him.

"About five eleven. Two hundred pounds." Andre patted his shirt. "Big chested."

The guy could be a tank when he tackled you. It really was a shame he flat out refused to play football. Or "American football," as he insisted on calling it.

The cop said, "Anyone else with him?"

Andre thought of the briefing Ted and Zander had given them all on the plane, over video chat. "There might've been a woman, also a person of color. Slender with long dark hair. I think she's about five foot nine."

"Anything else you can tell me?" The cop gave nothing away.

Andre scratched his first assessment of the guy and realized he was more skilled than that. "Maybe their kidnappers? Like I said, we believe they were taken against their will."

The guy nodded. "I need to speak with my superior, and I'll be back shortly." He spun on his shiny shoes and strode back to the crowd.

Eas pointed. "I can get into that building by pretending I have to make emergency use of the bathroom. Then try to find out where the control room for their security system is located."

"Good idea," Andre said. "Keep us all posted if you can

get Ted access. We need to know if there was any recorded footage of what happened."

Eas nodded and took off.

A biting wind whipped across the runway and ruffled Andre's hair beneath the edges of his knit cap. He stuffed his hands in his pockets.

Lucia slid her arms between his elbows and his body. "We *are* going to find him."

Andre lowered his head and laid his cheek against hers. "Blood…and bullet holes?"

"You know he can take care of himself." She gave him a squeeze. "And I know you wish you were there to protect him. But we will find him."

Andre kissed her. He loved having his wife back in his life. He wanted to talk to her about having kids. But with the work they did, and both of them being full-fledged team members, having a family meant one or both of them staying home from missions and maybe even finding a different role.

Still, it remained a dream.

He was going to wait until Nora had her baby and see if it turned out Lucia couldn't resist the idea of having one of their own.

"I should call Zander."

She nodded, then wandered off to speak with Hannah and Badger.

Andre pulled out his phone. When Zander answered, Andre ran down everything they'd just learned.

"So it might've been him." Zander sounded as though he was determined to believe it.

Andre didn't blame him. "If it was, he's long gone. Possibly injured. Definitely in trouble."

"We're closer than we've been so far."

Andre ran a hand down his face. "We need to get him back."

Zander was quiet for several moments. When Andre was

about to speak again, his team leader and best friend said, "Eas got Ted into the airport's security system…and now our boy is muttering and shaking his head." Zander pushed out a tense chuckle, like releasing the valve on a pressure cooker for a moment. "Ted has the security footage. He's backtracking it now. We'll figure this out."

Andre took a few steps, just to try and work out the frustration. "Anything on this reporter woman?"

"Travers buried her," Zander said. "Which means she knows something about what they're up to."

"Tell Ted we need a lead on both of them. The woman… and Judah."

"Then it's a good thing I'm looking at what I'm looking at," Zander said. "Because she was here, and so was Judah. He fought them, but they hit him with a stun gun, and he went down hard. The woman backed a car out of the container."

"You mean, the car currently wedged under the back of the semi like a horrible traffic accident?" Andre winced.

"The two of them were dragged away to an airplane that took off shortly after."

"The cop never mentioned that." Andre shook his head. "The security guard who was a witness should've said."

"Could be they're in on it."

"I'll go talk to them and find out," Andre gripped the phone far too tightly.

"I'll get Ted on pulling the plane's serial number so we can find out everything there is to know about…" Zander's voice trailed off. "Then zoom in or something." He paused. "I don't care how, just get me a lead."

"We *are* going to find him."

Zander sighed into the phone. "Do it."

The call ended.

Andre stowed his phone. It stood to reason his boss was

feeling the same frustrations. They'd all welcome Judah into their group—and their lives.

We need to get him back.

He shut his eyes for a moment and prayed.

Then he got to work.

Whoever had been holding Judah up shoved him away and let go. With no strength in his legs, his body slammed on the floor. His hip. His elbow. His cheek.

Judah flexed his fingers on the cold concrete. But that was all he could manage.

Soraya was tossed similarly beside him. She slammed both hands down and managed to keep her head from bouncing off the floor. But that put all the weight on her wrists. She cried out and collapsed.

Judah rolled over in time to see the door slam and hear the lock turn. He slumped back and looked at the ceiling. "I guess it didn't work."

His body still hummed from the voltage that had coursed through him when they'd zapped him with that stun gun. All he'd been trying to do was draw enough attention to them in hopes somebody would see them. Maybe no one had.

Even with the car accident Soraya had orchestrated, no one had come to their rescue.

For hours.

Now it was clear no one knew where they were.

It would be par for the course with Travers Industries that

Judah and Soraya had been transported through a location where no one could possibly have seen them. Otherwise they'd have been hooded. Though, given the fact he'd set that fire and they'd essentially escaped, maybe the plan had originally been to cover their faces. Or bring them here via the shipping container.

Wherever here was.

Either way, they'd been dragged to a waiting airplane and loaded on board like cargo.

Soraya hissed out a breath. "I'm sorry. That was a dumb move, and I never should've tried it."

Judah shifted to look at her.

She shook her head and stared at the ceiling. "I could have killed you. I can't believe I did that."

He frowned. "You might have saved my life."

She huffed out a breath.

"Are you injured?" He couldn't believe he hadn't asked that first. *What a jerk,* as his American friends would say. "Did they hurt you?"

She squeezed the bridge of her nose, then smoothed her hair back. "My head aches…and my hip. But I don't think they did any damage."

"That's good." He'd wiped the blood from his broken nose off his face as best he could, but figured he looked a mess.

She looked around. "How are we going to get out of here? Assuming we're both ambulatory." She glanced at him, those dark eyes of hers full of concern. Almost hopeful.

"I'm fine." Probably about the same as her in terms of injuries.

He sat up and looked around. They weren't getting out of here anytime soon, considering the bare walls and the heavy lock on the door. He didn't like to use the word *impossible,* but some situations were worse than bleak. And this might just be one of them.

"I don't know how we're going to get out of here." Judah

didn't like the tone of his own voice. But it wasn't like he had the energy to change it. Maybe Soraya wanted to be here with the man he would be when he was stripped of his tendency to cover everything with humor. Or maybe all she wanted was to be distracted, even if it meant denial. "But if they brought me a cup of tea, I figure we could stick around for a while and be okay enough."

She stared at him.

Judah tried to chuckle, falling back on laughing it off. The way he did with everything. Except that was with the guys, who understood why he was doing it. Soraya was an unknown. And for some reason he felt as though her opinion of him was important.

Given her expression, she didn't believe him. "Like, British tea?"

"Milky tea. No sugar." As far as he was concerned, adding sugar defeated the entire point of drinking it.

"I had this roommate in college, and she would drink PG Tips."

Judah summoned a wide smile. "She and I would be friends."

Soraya winced. "She was killed by a guy on campus who was stalking her."

His smile dropped, and he reached over to place his hand on hers. "I'm sorry for your loss."

"It was a long time ago." She didn't shrug, though she could have. Sometimes it just wasn't right to brush things off. "She's the reason I became a reporter. No one wanted to talk about it, so I wrote an article for the campus newspaper and told everyone the whole story. All the evidence I'd gathered. The police took it up, arrested him. And he wound up being convicted."

"Wow. You did a great thing for your friend." He squeezed her hand and let go.

"I'm not going to let Travers push me around." She

squeezed her hands together. "I know I walked into something way bigger than just me. But if people's freedoms are on the line and I can do something about it, there's no way I'll lay down and let them walk all over me."

"I understand." He blew out a breath, wondering whether he should tell her. "Let's just say, I know what it's like to be under the thumb of somebody more powerful than you. And what it feels like when you're finally free."

And yet, in that journey of emigrating by boat from Morocco to the UK, they had lost Judah and Toni's younger sister. An experience that would be ingrained in his mind for the rest of his life.

Joining the military right out of school, there had been far too many similarities in the officers over him. Shades of the same things he had seen in his uncle, the general over the country where he had been born.

Working for Zander was the first time in his life he understood what true leadership looked like.

His friends had to be looking for him. There was no way they'd just let him go. Not if they thought he'd been captured.

Had British intelligence made it look like he simply walked away? After Isaac's betrayal that would certainly sting. But would they really trust what it looked like on the surface?

"I can't believe I did that with the car." She winced. "I really could have killed you."

"But you didn't."

"If I had, I don't know how I would ever have forgiven myself."

"Let's talk about what we're going to do." That was a better idea. "Talk me through what we know."

She nodded. "We only *think* it's Travers who took us. That's just a guess, right?"

"All we know for sure is that whoever's doing this, they have resources enough to bring us halfway across the world. Possibly through several countries in the process." That took a whole lot of cutting through red tape, or greasing palms. Something Travers Industries could definitely accomplish. "And it was British intelligence who handed us over."

"Like MI-5?"

"They are more like Homeland Security. They only work domestic cases. MI-6 is the CIA equivalent."

"And you work for them?" Her eyes widened.

"They think I should. Because they think I owe them for the death of one of their guys. But I saw him outside your apartment." Casper was the one who had shot up her place. "Now I have no idea what's going on. But the team I work for in private security, Chevalier Protection Specialists, they should be looking for me."

"Isn't that team run by Zander O'Connell?" She frowned. "He went up against Stephen Gladstone and exposed the guy as being a criminal."

Judah nodded. "Gladstone was the director of the Department of Clandestine Service. We did a lot of jobs for them, until he was arrested."

"In my research about Travers Industries, I found a connection to Stephen Gladstone. When I realized he was in prison, I went to visit him. But he wouldn't talk to me, so the lead went nowhere."

He felt his eyes widen. Gladstone had been trying to kill Raleigh, or at least he hadn't tried to stop it. "They were connected?"

She shrugged. "I don't know how. And it wouldn't make a difference at this point, considering he was killed." Her body stilled.

"What is it?" Judah said.

"I also spoke with Greg Benton recently, and he was killed in prison as well."

Judah hadn't heard about that. Greg had shot at Hannah, Badger's girl. His brother worked for Travers so far as Judah knew. "I doubt it's correlated to your actions, considering you met with one and didn't meet with the other."

The team had been fairly certain Stephen Gladstone had been killed for a reason. The top theory was that it happened because he'd spoken to Nora about the identity of her mother.

Maybe it was deeper than that.

"What I do know," he said, "is that it's definitely connected to Lana." He had to get her to see the truth he knew. "I don't think she's on your side, even if that's what she told you."

"So I was naïve?" She lifted her chin. "Even though she rescued me and gave me a safe place to be. Until you showed up."

He started to argue. "That doesn't—"

The lock clicked and the door swung open. Three men with guns walked in. The fourth wore a suit and was unarmed. "Judah, come with me." He glanced at his men. "He makes one move you don't like? Shoot him."

———

Soraya reached for Judah, but it was too late. "Where are you taking him?"

One of the men shifted and pointed a gun at her face. Soraya froze. Anything she might've said next got stuck in her throat.

The suited man was the one who spoke. "Someone will be here for you in a second." He shut the door.

Soraya scrambled to her feet, not even steady before the door flung open again. Literally a second and then someone else came in. She didn't much care about the identity of the man who stood there as she raced at him, fists flying, and pounded his chest. A suit. A tie. Could she use that? Thoughts of strangling him entered her mind. Before she could do any damage, two men grabbed her arms and pulled her back from the guy.

Soraya fought with them. She kicked one in the shin so that he let go of her arm and she could punch the other.

But he rallied all too quickly.

His friend grabbed both her hands and pulled them behind her back. The one she'd kicked glanced at the door while Soraya fought blindly.

"Sir?" he said.

Asking for permission for something. Probably to kill her. Soraya screamed, just in case anyone was interested that she needed to be rescued.

"Just don't leave any visible bruises." She knew that voice. But couldn't think enough right now to figure out who it might be.

The man in front of her pulled back a fist and slammed it into Soraya's diaphragm. She coughed out a breath, then tried to suck in more air that got caught in her throat.

He punched her again in the stomach.

She cried out.

Again.

Soraya sucked in gasping breaths and realized she was on her hands and knees on the floor. She looked up, shook her head to move the hair from in front of her face, and lifted her chin.

She gaped and nearly collapsed. "President Raleigh?"

He looked just as he had when he'd left office. She didn't much care for the new guy, but honestly wasn't all that interested in politics. She'd rather let someone else worry about that circus and cover stories that affected people in real, local ways, even as a journalist. Until she'd stumbled across Travers Industries and the threat they represented to the country, she'd left national stories alone.

Soraya glanced at the two men who stood beside her, but they didn't look like Secret Service. She was pretty sure he would still be assigned agents to keep him safe—probably for the rest of his life. These guys were more like the kind who'd blindfolded her and shoved her in a trunk.

Since they weren't holding onto her anymore, Soraya climbed to her feet. She held back the wince. She didn't want them to know how much that hurt.

He didn't want the bruises to show.

She knew now Raleigh was the one who had said that, but what did it mean? It reminded her of domestic violence cases she had reported on where the assailant managed to hide the wounds he had inflicted on his victim.

"I'd heard you were working for Travers Industries." She figured it was more of a figurehead type of role, but what if he was the mastermind behind the phone system they were about to roll out? "I'm guessing that's what this is about."

She needed him to tell her, so her suspicion could be confirmed or denied. Her entire job depended on information, and this was no different. Even if she was the victim and him the assailant.

"We can't have you telling everyone your half-baked theories." He stared at her. "Can we?"

And yet, she'd gotten verified confirmation it was true. In fact, until she dug into the chip and found out exactly what it was, she hadn't even been looking at Travers Industries.

Now they were firmly on her radar.

"So you're not even going to deny you're a liar," Raleigh said. "Because you know what I say is the truth. I'm sure there's a reason why you want to destroy Travers. But it's not going to happen. I won't allow it."

"Maybe you're used to everyone around you doing what you say." She shifted her feet, unable then to hide the wince at the stab of pain that sliced through her middle. "But I'm not exactly going to lie down on this one. Not with the power you'll have if that phone system rolls out."

The former president smiled. "You know, your earnestness

is very convincing. In fact, that's why you're here. You're going to be our new spokesperson."

She just stared at him. "Where is Judah?"

"We all have our roles to play here," Raleigh said. "Even me."

"And you think I'm going to work for Travers?"

"We're not going to pay you." His lips twitched.

Soraya wasn't going to back down, regardless of whether he thought she was less than nothing. So far beneath him, he didn't even have to entertain her as a nuisance. Not now that he had his hands on her. He thought she would just fall into line. Instead, she said, "Someone will be looking for me. Maybe you know her? Her name is Lana."

As his eyes widened, she realized she'd given up what she probably should've held back. Maybe she'd just given away everything, and now they were going to kill her. Then Lana and all *her* people. Was that what they were doing with Judah right now?

She didn't hear anything from down the hall, like screams as he was murdered.

Soraya's breath caught in her throat. She swallowed and tried to rally her courage, taking solace in the fact that Raleigh seemed genuinely surprised. "Oh, so you know Lana?"

She didn't know how their worlds could possibly have collided, but evidently, they had. Maybe during his term serving as president, he'd met Lana or learned of her.

At least he hadn't immediately murdered Soraya now. There was something to be said for that. And if that was the case, then maybe they actually needed her alive.

To do something for them?

"My advice?" Raleigh lifted his chin. "Worry about what your job is here and not about…*that woman.*" He practically spat those last two words.

No love was lost between them, apparently.

And now, she had set Raleigh on Lana's path. Thankfully,

that woman had far more resources to defend both herself and Soraya. Plus the skills necessary.

"So what is my job here?" If it was an actual job, and they gave her a computer or a phone then maybe she could figure out how to send a message to the outside.

Judah had told her the name of the company he worked for. Chevalier were famous now. Surely she'd be able to find a phone number online. All Soraya needed was an internet connection, and she could get a message out. His people could come to find him. She prayed he wouldn't be a dead body when they arrived.

That was the last thing she wanted. All because she had poked the bear—figuratively. Travers responded in full force. She was disgraced, her life nearly ended.

Now Judah would pay, too, because he'd been betrayed.

"You will be assigned a series of tasks," Raleigh said. "I've been assured they were made easy so there could be no confusion over what you are to do. I want no trouble with this."

"And if I refuse?"

After all, he had to know that she wouldn't simply obey blindly. No matter that it wasn't in her nature, who would in a situation like this? It would be un-American.

Which made her think about her British friend. She wanted him back. Even though they didn't know each other well, Judah had become part of this for her. It would be nice to look at his handsome face some more. Those dark eyes. His broad, strong shoulders.

The man was positively distracting.

Raleigh lifted a cell phone from the inside of his suit jacket. He unlocked it with his thumbprint and tapped the screen.

When he turned it toward her, she saw what appeared to be a video. But in the corner, it said LIVE.

A living room, with the kitchen far away at the top of the screen. Someone moved around the counter and walked to the couch with a mug, then sat. She lifted a book from the coffee table and opened it.

Soraya had sat on that couch many times. She had grown up in that house, the one that belonged to her parents. The one where her mother now sat reading in the living room.

"You will do exactly as asked or the price will be paid, but not by you." He shifted the phone in his hand. "Their blood will be spilled."

11

———————

"You don't do what we say? They die." The man spoke with a thick Boston accent, sitting across from Judah on the plane. Wherever they were going, he figured he wouldn't like it when they got there.

He didn't move from his seat. Judah just clutched the photo they had given him. A picture of his sister Toni and her fiancé. Both of them were on the street in Last Chance County, where they lived. Where Judah also lived. A place he hadn't been to for weeks now.

These people knew all about it.

They likely knew everything about him, and all the buttons they should press that would trigger his natural urges. Those deeply ingrained instincts that tried every day to keep him from living, trapping him instead in guilt over another person's death again.

Judah had few good things left in his life. He didn't want to lose what he did have. But it was something he rarely contemplated. He preferred to brush things off with the blasé attitude that Badger usually joined in with. But his friend wasn't here, and neither was the rest of the team. He'd been bounced around from MI-6 to Travers Industries. Taken from Soraya so he had no idea if she was okay or if he'd live the rest of his life with the guilt of knowing she had died because he hadn't been able to get them free.

Travers had won this battle. Judah couldn't let them win the war.

"So what am I supposed to do?" If he knew a little more about what Travers was interested in, maybe he could find some evidence to take with him when he got free.

He looked up at the man, the way he had with that MI-6 agent. The one who hadn't even bothered to give Judah his name. This man didn't either. Neither cared about him as a person, even with the homework they'd done on his life.

"This mission is time-sensitive, but I've been assured you're someone thoroughly capable of undertaking it." The man's eyes narrowed. "I trust you won't let us down. And if you do well, then there very well could be a future with Travers Industries division of international relations waiting for you when you're done."

"Really."

The man shrugged.

Judah set the picture of Toni and Jeff aside, laying it on the seat beside him. It would be the last day he ever rode in a private airplane—one day. But apparently, that wasn't going to happen anytime soon. It seemed like everyone in his life had one. But the plane he most preferred was Zander's.

Not that it surprised him. What he was missing were his friends, not the plane his mind seemed to want to dwell on.

He glanced around, trying not to think about what this guy was saying. "This thing is kind of old. Does it even have Wi-Fi?"

"Not that you'll be able to enjoy."

Unless Judah killed them all and stole someone's phone. Considering there were four guys onboard, plus this one talking to him, and each of the four was armed, Judah didn't figure that was especially likely. Not without getting himself injured. Or killed.

With everything that happened, he lost more and more of a grip on the dream. The idea he would get back the good he'd had for a while with Chevalier. Even if things with Soraya had been nice. Given the situation things weren't stress-free, but she'd turned out to be an amazing woman. Someone he'd like to see more of.

The man in front of him pulled out an envelope and handed it over. "Identification and the keys to a car. You'll find the weapon in the glove box."

He wanted to correct the guy and say, "glove compartment." But Judah didn't figure that would be met with warm reception. The guy probably didn't even know that British people had different terms for things. At least he didn't say the car's boot was a trunk. That was just wrong.

He waved the envelope in front of Judah's face. "You're going to have to concentrate. Because if I think you can't do this, the plane door gets opened, and you're taking a long fall with no parachute. Got me?"

Judah cleared his throat. "Yeah, mate."

Hopefully the guy wouldn't demand Judah call him sir. He would gladly dive out the door of his own accord if that was thrown on the table.

"A picture of the target is inside."

Judah found it, along with local ID—his photo—for an African country he'd never been to. Apparently, he was now a licensed driver in that country. And his name was Alexander Underwood.

The photo was the size of the envelope, and he slid it out.

Thankfully it wasn't anyone he'd ever met in person. And also, thankfully, he managed to contain his reactions, as if he had never seen the man's photo before. "Who is this guy?"

"His name is Yuri Amrakov. At least, that was his name at one time in his life. And along with a new name, I've been told other things have changed as well. Although I wasn't given specifics."

Whatever that meant.

The guy leveled a steady gaze on Judah. "But you knew that already, didn't you? As I am reliably informed, this man"—he tapped his index finger on the top of the photo—"is the father of your friend, the federal prisoner Isaac Amrakov."

"And you want me to kill him?"

"Why MI-6 wanted to know his name and where to find him, I suppose we will never know. Unless one of us asks them." He gave a small smile as though thoroughly amused with himself. "Which, of course, you will be too busy to do."

"This man is the head of an international group of assassins?" It was the guy British intelligence wanted to find. But Travers had a photo of him, and they knew exactly who he was.

"Do not be fooled by his age. This man is highly trained, and if you wish to return alive, you'll not underestimate him," the man said. "I'd hate for that to happen, considering I'll lose a bet. Plus, the company will be out a considerable investment."

Judah stared at the photo.

The Travers employee said, "I'm aware MI-6 requested you discover this man's identity and locate him. However, considering we can't have them speaking with him or even finding his base of operations, we have little time to accomplish this mission. Before long, they will begin to suspect they were given falsified information."

"So MI-6 traded that reporter and me"—he didn't need them to know he'd formed a bond with her—"to you guys, in exchange for information about this guy?"

The man nodded.

"I was led to believe Isaac's father was dead," Judah said. "Killed a long time ago."

"A man who governs a group of deadly assassins? You think he can't fake his own death?"

"Did Peter Benton work for them?" Judah asked.

The guy had been a Travers employee. Someone whose brother claimed he was an assassin, something that never sat right with Judah as far as explanations went. Whether Greg was the killer or his brother, both had been tied to this. It was a long shot thinking this guy even knew all the way what he was talking about, but it was worth the chance to possibly discover the truth.

The guy laughed. "Greg was nothing but a wannabe. Peter got himself killed. Now both of them are dead, and no one has to worry about telling Greg we were never going to put in a good word with the assassins and get him a place there."

So now he knew. If this man could be trusted.

Judah had always thought Greg's story never made sense. Peter had seemed to be a loyal Travers employee. Everything Chevalier found out had sounded only like a smokescreen behind which the truth remained buried.

"So you want me to kill this guy?" Judah pressed. "But won't that just mean one of his assassins takes his place as the leader?"

"Your job is not to worry about the vacuum and inevitable power struggle."

"Right."

This was good. Judah figured the minute he was out of range, in whatever vehicle they had left for him headed out to kill this guy, he would be able to make a stop and find a phone. Get word to the rest of the team that he needed help.

"All you need to do is kill this guy," the man said. "Which is why we will not allow distractions."

This didn't sound good.

"We will have eyes on you at all times. Any attempt you make to contact anyone by any means or even signal for help will be met with a swift end to your life and that of your family. Do not test me."

The intercom overhead buzzed, and the pilot announced the plane would be landing momentarily.

"Buckle up." He stood and pushed his glasses up his nose. "You wouldn't want to get injured. And I don't like damaged merchandise."

———

"Time's up." The heavy knock sounded against the door.

Soraya started out of her thoughts. She laid a hand on her chest and tried to breathe slowly. *You can do this. Whatever it is.*

She'd been shoved into a tiny office with no furniture and handed a dry-cleaning bag. Inside hung a blouse and blazer, which she'd been instructed to put on over her jeans.

She was also given a makeup bag and told to fix her hair. How, she had no idea. So Soraya simply pulled it back with a hair tie. If they weren't going to let her take a shower, something she didn't want to do in a situation where she was this vulnerable, there was only so much sprucing up she could do.

She had washed her face in the tiny industrial sink in the corner. The makeup had an entirely wrong skin tone, of course. She tossed the pale blush back in the bag and rummaged around, finding eye makeup and lipstick. The bare minimum was about as much effort as she was prepared to put into this when Travers Industries seemed to have no intention of explaining the situation.

Now the door shoved open. "Ready or not."

She spun to him and stood still under his assessment, some nameless blond grunt she didn't care about. His stare made her cheeks heat even while anger boiled low in her stomach.

He'd better not touch her.

"I will drag you out."

Soraya eased past him into the hallway and thought about

making a run for it. Two men turned the corner at the far end of the hall and her legs locked. Neither looked like the kind of man she wanted to run toward. The other direction? Nothing but more rooms on either side and a wall at the end.

There was literally no way out.

She turned to the grunt. "What am I going to be doing?"

Maybe he didn't know. Perhaps he only did as he was told, something she was unaccustomed to. Except of course when it came in the form of instructions from people she actually respected—which didn't include him, unsurprisingly. As if he'd have her best interests at heart.

"This way." He motioned with his gun down the hall.

Soraya would have to pass the two men coming this way. She kept her chin up, determined not to let any of them know she had a million journalist questions about who they were and what they were doing here. Then all the other questions about what they wanted with her.

Clearly she was useful to them, or they would've simply killed her. People disappeared all the time. She'd done enough articles on missing children to know that.

But that image he'd shown her of her parents' house told a story of its own.

If she was to go missing, they wouldn't stop looking for her. She hadn't seen the website asking for information as to her whereabouts. But Lana had told her all about it. And the regular vigils her parents had been having. How they went on the local news and pleaded for her return.

A single tear rolled down her cheek.

One of the men reached out to grab her as she passed. Soraya shrieked and jumped out of the way, unable to hold back that humiliating reaction.

She was out of her normal reserves with nothing else to pull from, making her think of her mother's insistence on relying on a heavenly being who had nothing to do with her as far as she'd ever been able to tell. Right now she was willing to concede the point she might have been wrong, especially if it got her out of here.

Soraya offered up a prayer because she had no one else to go to for help. She was all alone.

"In here." The man opened a door on the right-hand side of the hallway.

Raleigh sat behind a desk. Opposite it was a similar desk, two computers back to back forming a workstation for two people. Partners, or colleagues. As if she was ever going to have that kind of relationship with the former president.

"Take a seat, Ms. Adams." Raleigh waved to the seat at the desk opposite him.

The metal folding chair was cold under her jeans.

"No, that won't do." He got up, took a thick directory from a shelf of books, and asked her to lift up. He slid the book under her and put pressure on her shoulder until her legs gave out and she was sitting again. Her entire body was numb.

Soraya managed to glance over her shoulder and saw the gunman still by the door. Even if she wanted to elbow Raleigh in the face at that moment, an armed man stood there. She had no defense against him.

"Much better." Raleigh sat at his own desk in a tall-backed leather chair. "Put on the headphones, please."

She could hardly see Raleigh around the computer monitor that displayed a YouTube video. But it wasn't on the browser. The video was paused, opened in a media player app.

She frowned.

"The headphones, Ms. Adams." His voice was cold. "I'm sure I don't need to remind you what will happen if you don't cooperate. My friend behind you has certain…appetites. Ones I'm sure he can satiate with you."

Soraya didn't look at the man as she reached for the

earbuds in front of her and inserted one in her ear. She needed to be aware of her surroundings.

The frown on her face didn't lift. Playing through the earbud was a familiar Christmas song. "What is—"

"No talking." Raleigh gave the order.

Then the mouse on her screen swirled and clicked to play the video.

"No frowning."

Something inside her obeyed the order. She wasn't sure how she felt about that, but now wasn't the time to debate or foolishly fight a battle she had no way to win.

On the screen, two puppies frolicked on a couch. One slipped over the edge, and the other still had a mouthful of the other's fur so that both puppies tumbled onto the floor.

Any other day, any other time or place, she might have laughed. They were adorable.

"Good," Raleigh said. "Let's continue."

He played two more videos while she listened to Christmas music through the headphones. All the while trying to figure out what on earth was going on here.

"Nod, please."

At that order, something in her mind assimilated what was happening. She was being videoed, recording her reaction for some reason. She peered around the screen at Raleigh. "Explain what this is."

As though she had any authority at all.

"Don't do that again," he warned. "But we can edit that part out."

She was right.

"Why do you need a recording of me looking like I'm spending a day at the office?" Never mind that she'd never worn anything like this in her life. Not even for staff meetings, or that week the guy from corporate came to the newspaper.

"If you'd refer back to the screen…" It wasn't a question.

It was another order, given in that commander-in-chief voice he'd managed to retain.

She looked at the monitor. He dragged a window showing the video of her parents' living room into view, leaving it on one side of the widescreen display. On the other side, he opened a PDF document.

"You have three minutes to read this on your own, and then I expect you to read it aloud for the recording."

Her eyes widened as she read the first few lines. A statement, supposedly written by her hand. The first part sounded like a response to someone's question. But what was the question?

"This is ridiculous."

"The fact remains," Raleigh said, "you will read this statement in its entirety, or the men stationed outside your parents' house will enter their residence and shoot them."

Tears gathered in her eyes.

She wanted to be anywhere in the world but here. With anyone but these people. No, that wasn't true. She only wanted Judah back with her. She felt a thousand times more safe and secure when he was around, something she probably shouldn't dwell on overly much.

Soraya had to submit to being used by these people. They were trying to get ahead in the world, and gain more power.

If she didn't? She would never see her family again. All that would be left for her was to bury them.

It was better that she suffer than that her parents ever felt even the sting of one wound, just because she'd done her job and made herself a target of these people.

Soraya swallowed. "I need water."

A bottle was placed in front of her.

She unscrewed the cap and took a long drink.

"All that will be edited out, but throwing a fit will only waste both our time." Raleigh frowned. "Now read."

12

The earth radiated warmth Judah could feel against his skin despite the early hour. It was like being in a sauna. The orange sky stretched for what seemed like hundreds of miles, bathing the world in the glow of sunrise.

Judah parked a couple miles from the house, leaving the rusty beater off the edge of the dirt track as far as possible. That way if he had to use the thing to leave again—which was the plan—he wouldn't have to get it out of the mud first.

Africa might be in his blood, literally considering he'd been born here and lived here until they left after his mother was killed. But that didn't mean he had to like it. Too many bad memories.

Every time the weather was even remotely like this, he could taste that life on his tongue.

England was so different that it had been a shock to his system being constantly under that gray sky. The drizzle. But those years with his grandmother were the most peaceful of his life. He'd joined the Royal Marines when the restlessness couldn't be contained. Traveled all over. Wasted those years fighting wars that weren't his, all the while ignoring the conflict in his chest.

The target would see him coming. If Travers wanted Judah to sneak up on the guy in a way that would be effective, they should've let him parachute in.

Instead, he had to walk up to the front door.

If he didn't get shot before he reached it.

All they'd given him was a Glock and a pair of boots to wear instead of his trainers. How long had he been wearing these jeans and this T-shirt? He didn't even want to know how badly he smelled. He'd be a beacon to an adventurous animal out for breakfast.

Judah crossed between two baked trees, their trunks scratched by claws. The dirt puffed up under his boots as he headed for the boundary of the property.

Thinking about nothing but what he could see was better than thinking about his sister and her fiancé.

Toni and Jeff could take care of themselves, that was for sure. Even if Travers came after them—and Judah didn't manage to warn them—it didn't mean they'd get hurt. Or killed. Instead, whoever was sent to them, the way Judah had been sent to kill this guy, was going to be in for a surprise.

Judah glanced at the house, a rundown structure probably built as a farmhouse years ago. His gaze drifted to the ground, and he came to an abrupt stop, nearly tripping over his feet. He let out a long breath and crouched, four inches from a dark thread that shifted with the unseen air currents. Strung between two scrub bushes.

A spider stared at him from inside a hole in the ground, but that wasn't his biggest concern right now. Still, he willed the thing to remain where it was and not bother him.

"You're not the predator out here," Judah said to the spider. "Are you, mate?"

Judah looked around, found a palm-sized rock, and tested its weight in his hand.

He scanned the ground between him and the house, straightened, and tossed the rock about twenty feet away.

The second it hit the ground, a land mine exploded. Dirt spewed, displacing the air with a concussive force and the orange flash of the ordinance superheating. There was no way to disguise it as smoke filled the air.

This place was booby-trapped.

Judah took a step back from the tripwire directly in front of him. The one that would undoubtedly kill him when it detonated.

The homeowner had to have seen that blast. It was his security system, so Judah was about to have company looking to protect his life and property—unless he wasn't here.

Considering he knew the guy was a former Soviet agent who had faked his death to turn around and create an organization of hired assassins, Judah figured he'd be using the Glock in due time to defend his own life.

As long as the guy let him speak first, he had a shot that this might not be his last day on earth.

Cold steel pressed against the back of Judah's neck.

He froze. Started to lift both hands, fingers splayed out.

"Easy." The voice was gruff and heavily accented.

Judah didn't speak Russian, so they'd have to make it work. "Gun at the back of my belt." He kept his hands where they were.

As the Glock was tugged from under his T-shirt, the gun barrel never even moved against the back of his neck, not even a twitch. This guy had control.

"Any other weapons on you?"

Judah shook his head. "I'm clear."

If the guy shot him right here, Judah's death would set off a second ordinance—the one right in front of him. He figured this guy didn't want to draw unwanted attention, so he maybe had a few seconds.

"Your name is Yuri Amrakov." Judah took a breath. "Your son is Isaac, and his mother is Lana—but maybe that wasn't her name when you knew her. He likes watching Christmas comedy movies and hates marshmallows…if you're interested. He prefers swimming over running, and isn't a fan of bacon, which is just bonkers if you ask me."

"This is what you came here for?"

"Travers Industries gave me that gun so I could kill you. And if I don't? They'll hurt my family." Maybe this guy would care, but he doubted it. "But I want to talk about Isaac."

"My son."

Judah couldn't gauge the tone of his statement. His voice sounded muffled. He needed to see the guy's face to get a good read but wasn't about to turn around and risk a bullet between the eyes—before he was dismembered by an explosion.

"Yeah, he's your son," Judah said. "Everyone thinks you're dead."

"As it should be."

And yet, Lana didn't know. She'd killed people to get revenge for Yuri's death. It was the reason she did what she did, or so they'd thought.

"I need your help." Judah couldn't guarantee Travers wasn't watching this entire exchange. Maybe they even had a way of listening in. "We probably only have minutes before they realize I haven't killed you, and I've got no intention of doing it."

Travers probably had a way to ensure this man's death, like a UAV or something. They'd hear a whistle and know it was too late. Maybe Judah had only been sent here to draw the guy into the open.

"I'll kill you right now." The man didn't move or shift. Not even a twitch or a sound from behind that mask.

Judah flinched. "I know. But please don't."

"What do you want?" Amrakov let out a breathy exhale.

Judah tried to look over his shoulder. "Can I turn around? I just wanna talk, I promise." And now that he'd been stripped of the gun they gave him, he had limited options for killing this guy.

"Because I didn't make a move to kill you already?"

"Please."

"Very well."

Judah moved slowly, twisted around, and got a look at the guy. Bigger than him. Threadbare cargos with Judah's gun in his belt. A denim shirt with pit stains. A wide-brimmed hat under which he wore a plastic mask so that his features were disguised. Judah didn't even know if this was the guy, considering Travers had shown him a photo of Yuri.

Had they simply sent Judah here so this guy could kill *him*?

If Judah was wired up without his knowledge, they could use voice recognition to confirm the Russian's identity. Judah had to assume they were staring at him from somewhere. Or had a way to independently verify the kill, aside from taking Judah's word for it.

"I think we're both going to die in a matter of seconds," Judah admitted. "Unless you've got a way out of here."

The guy had snuck up on Judah. Maybe there were tunnels…or a vehicle nearby.

"You're the reason they're coming," Amrakov said. "You think I'm gonna help you?" Did he want to see Isaac? Maybe that didn't hold enough weight to be leveraged. "I'm not gonna offer you a position, that's for sure."

"I have to go through the motions here, or my family's lives are in danger," Judah said.

"So I kill you. You fail, Travers fails, and Uzhas loses nothing."

That was the name of the assassin's group? "Except you've lost your anonymity. The Brits are hunting you, and Travers clearly thinks you're a liability or they wouldn't have sent me here to kill you. Your life is in danger."

The man huffed. "As though I cannot make adjustments."

"They'll never stop looking for you. Travers…and British

intelligence." Both organizations would hunt him, or Uzhas—the group of assassins—until it was over.

"Yet, my point stands." The man removed his mask and hat. "Who will they be looking for?"

Judah sucked in a breath through his nose and bit back a word his granny wouldn't have approved of. *Plastic surgery.* No wonder this man hadn't been found yet.

He looked like…

SORAYA STARED AT THE SCREEN. On one side, her childhood home, where her parents were eating sandwiches for lunch at the dining table. The other half of the screen was a steadily scrolling stream of text she read.

It told her when to pause. When to smile.

Soraya swallowed. "Thank you for your question, Madam Secretary. I am nervous, understandably. But this is a great opportunity for me to put my skills to good use."

Smile.

"I'm unused to public speaking."

Pause.

"I've been working the last few days on being fully immersed in the tech that Travers will be offering the federal government. A lot of it is over my head, I'm afraid."

Chuckle. She didn't think she managed that exactly, but they were coercing her into recording her having this fake one-sided conversation. They'd have to live with what they got.

Soraya watched her dad take both her parents' plates to the sink and continued, "But I've seen it in action, and the system will save lives with the tracking accuracy and the fact there will be no dead zones in coverage. Each law enforcement officer who uses one of these phones will be that much safer as a result. Thanks to Travers' satellite network and their technology."

Her stomach churned, and her mouth watered as the sick feeling rose to her throat.

Longer pause.

As she obeyed that order, her gaze drifted to the corner of the screen. The computer wasn't connected to the internet, according to the icon there. So how was she seeing her parents live? Was that a recording?

Considering how Raleigh seemed to be remotely controlling the PC, she still doubted she'd have been able to send an email or some other mayday message without him knowing.

She had to get out of here. But how?

Soraya had nothing to bargain with. Could she escape? There were no windows. She had no idea where she was or how to get out, let alone whether she would survive. This place could be a prison for all she knew. Or some kind of facility, buried deep underground.

She shivered.

"Continue reading," Raleigh ordered.

The bile hit her tongue. Her throat seized, and she felt it coming.

She tried not to overthink what she did next. That kind of disassociation wasn't easy to achieve. She let her eyes lose focus on everything and encouraged the hitch in her esophagus until it spasmed hard enough she vomited on the computer keyboard. Some of it hit the monitor.

She retched until there was nothing left in her stomach, and all that came out were dry heaves.

Raleigh started to roar, but she couldn't make out the words over the rush in her ears. The gunman who'd been behind her kicked the chair.

The wheels rolled to the left.

His next kick was to her leg, just above her knee. The heel

of his boot got the chair. She sailed across the room, and the chair hit the wall six feet away.

Soraya slammed her hand on the paint to steady herself and get a handle. Calm down a bit.

She didn't get the chance before Raleigh grabbed her arm and yanked her out of the chair so hard her shoulder almost dislocated.

She slammed into him.

He bit out a vulgar expression and dragged her to the door, calling back over his shoulder, "Get this cleaned up!"

For a moment, she thought he meant her then glanced back and spotted the gunman's disgusted expression. The computer was toast, but she didn't look too much at the spread pattern. Thankfully there had been enough in her stomach to do some damage. But the raw acid at the back of her throat would make her voice hoarse for days, no doubt. She was a mess.

As if that were the worst of her problems.

"I need water," she croaked.

"You think you have the right to ask for anything?" He opened the door to the room she and Judah had been dumped in and shoved her in.

Soraya stumbled to the far side and slid down the wall.

Raleigh stood by the door, staring at her. "If this continues, life will become extremely difficult for you."

"Where's Judah?" The question escaped her lips before she even thought about holding it back. She wanted to know where he was—her only lifeline in this situation.

No one else even knew she was a captive.

"I would suggest you worry about your own situation, and not someone you can't save any more than you can save yourself."

Debatable. Even if it was a pipe dream, she still had to believe it. The moment she let go of the hope, it was over. She would be as good as dead. But that was better than costing her family their lives.

Would Lana be able to rescue her before then? Maybe she couldn't get inside this facility. Or whatever building they were being held in.

Assuming Judah was even still here.

Maybe he was dead.

Tears welled in her eyes. Soraya sniffed and tried to push away the emotion that wanted to overwhelm her. She had no intention of giving in. Through sheer stubbornness, she would hold onto her emotions and keep a handle on herself.

There was no other option open to her. Not if she wanted to get through this without losing herself in the process.

"What was that?" Soraya gasped. "Why were you recording me?"

Raleigh folded his arms across his chest. "Congratulations. You are Travers Industries' newest media spokesperson." He gave her a second to absorb that. As if it was sufficient. "After you came to us with your suspicions, we decided to team up and get the word out to everyone that this phone system is not only in the federal government's best interest, it will also be the best decision they ever make."

"Giving you the power to control all the information that goes across it?"

"I managed to change your mind. You came around and saw good sense, so you're going to be telling everyone who will listen that you've seen the light. As it were."

She saw a glint of his smile and looked away. "No one is going to believe it."

"Except for the fact that people believe what I want them to believe."

She knew he'd been into some shady things before he became the president, but most people believed he'd simply had a bad reputation all those years. That everything he'd done as the commander-in-chief said more about who he was than what everyone who'd ever worked for him wanted people to see.

After all, President Raleigh did what he needed to do to get people to back him. Evidently, that included coercing reporters into toeing the line.

Then there was what the media said about him. She highly doubted it was entirely objective and selfless of them to report the current narrative.

The grassroots groups either loved him or hated him.

Losing his wife meant Raleigh had reappeared on the national stage, whether because people were sympathetic to his grief or expressed the fact they were glad for his wife and the fact she'd managed to be free of him.

Soraya had no idea what the truth was. And instead of going all in, or all out, for a man she would never know personally, she'd decided instead she would be objective as much as possible. Do her job as a reporter and let politics take care of itself.

She lifted her chin, trying to ignore the taste in her mouth. "So it's all just a lie?"

"Whether it is or not," he said, "there's nothing you can do about it."

"And if I refuse?"

He couldn't possibly believe she would simply do as asked. She intended to fight back until the last second in her own way. Soraya didn't want to jeopardize her family. Now that she had a complete grasp of what was going on, she knew it was more important Travers was stopped than it was to save the lives of two people. Three, if they took out her sister as well.

More bile rose in her throat. But there was nothing in her stomach to accommodate the sensation.

No. She couldn't let them kill her family. But she also couldn't let them roll out this phone system.

"When is the launch?" She had to know how much time the country had.

His expression shifted. A slight twitch of displeasure. "Soon enough."

"What's the problem?"

"Nothing I need you to worry about." He grasped the door handle. "As I said, you just focus on doing what I asked."

It was a good thing he didn't need her to confirm she would obey that. Soraya had every intention of figuring out exactly what was going on. It was all information she would need, for when she inevitably brought the whole company crashing down.

And Raleigh along with it.

A light in the hallway flashed. Seconds later, an alarm sounded.

The door slammed shut.

What was going on?

13

____

The alarm sounded far too quickly. Eas pulled up short, stepped to the side and hugged the wall. "That isn't good."

Adrenaline flooded his body as though someone had come at him with lethal intent. It was just a security alarm. Thankfully, they'd gotten all the way inside before it sounded.

His team leader, Zander, spoke through their comms. "No turning back now."

In front of him, Hannah glanced over her shoulder. She shot him a look with a nod of her head that indicated she knew Zander was right.

Together, they continued down the hallway through this facility located in southern Utah. Hidden from the freeway that ran past it on the far side of the westerly mountains. The six of them—Eas and Zander, with Badger, Hannah, Andre, and Lucia—had traversed the land in the middle of the night, with Andre complaining about how cold it was the entire time.

It was all hands on deck in the hunt for Judah.

But no one was being careless. Zander had employed a team of Last Chance County friends to watch out for Nora and Ted back at home. No one was willing to risk anyone's safety. But they all wanted Judah back.

As soon as Ted had found the facility's location where Judah had been taken, they'd formulated a plan for how to enter. In the end, they'd found an employee with a prosthetic eyeball who gave him access to this place along with his key card.

Hannah had gone in undercover at a bar, got the guy drunk, and waited for him to pass out before the rest of them duplicated the card and sent Ted enough information about the eye he could 3D-print one for them to use.

Apparently, it wasn't a completely foolproof plan. But they had gained access to the facility, so what did it matter that they'd been discovered?

"Find him," Zander said.

Each of them responded, "Copy that," in turn.

They'd been divided into three teams. Eas was paired with Hannah, a former police detective who'd recently quit her day job. She'd managed to contain her curiosity about his entire situation so far. He figured the clock was about to run out on that.

The two of them made their way down an empty hallway.

The other team members spoke to each other, audible through their comms.

"Is there even anyone over here?" Hannah asked.

From the rear, Eas glanced over his shoulder. "No one behind us. Maybe this part of the facility is empty."

"The whole thing looked abandoned." She blew out a breath. "But if this is where Ted said he was brought, I'm going to trust that."

"As am I," Eas said.

"Has he ever been wrong before?" she asked.

Someone snorted. Probably in reaction to her question. But Eas didn't know who. "Everyone is wrong sometimes."

They paused at the end of the hallway. She glanced

around the corner. "I don't see anyone." She looked back at Eas. "I was glad when Zander gave the assignments. I wanted to get to know you."

He nodded, not sure what to say. Especially at a time like this, and considering Judah's future brother-in-law had said something similar to him. What was it about him that made people curious?

"I don't know about the dog, but your family is lovely." She grinned.

"Thanks." Eas turned the corner with a smile on his face. "Finally."

The hallway was filled with doors. Various rooms, each of which they would need to check. The two of them had to clear them one by one for their friend or any information about what Travers Industries was doing here.

He didn't like leaving his family behind to go on a mission. Even if this was his job, that had nothing to do with the fact he'd rather be home. Karina had been out of his life for years, and he'd believed she was dead. Now that he had her back—and he'd met the child they had together—she'd continued her peaceful life. Karina had opted to remain out of the career path he'd taken, the one she'd been in years ago working for Lana.

The last thing he wanted was for anything to happen to him with her thousands of miles away and put their future in jeopardy.

He opened the first door. "Clear."

Hannah did the same on the other side. It was empty.

Three doors down, he heard rhythmic beeping before he saw the occupant of the room. Laid up in a hospital bed, hooked up to all kinds of machines that checked his vital signs.

Zander's voice came over comms. "Did anyone find Judah yet?"

Eas studied the face of the man on the bed. He almost didn't look alive.

Badger responded for their pair, him and Lucia. "We just—"

A gunshot crackled across their communications.

"—resistance."

"You need backup?" Zander asked.

"All good," Badger said.

Zander came back on. "Andre and I took down a couple of guys. Found the network closet and got Ted hooked into the system."

Given what happened every other time they tried to hack Travers Industries, Eas hadn't thought that was an especially good idea. Ted had been forced to wipe his entire system once already, but he also knew what he was doing.

Eas stared at the man on the bed. "I just found Jerry Travers."

Another gunshot crackled across the line.

Lucia called, "All clear. Continuing on."

Hannah stepped around him into the room, where she noticed a clipboard beside the bed. She lifted it, flipped over the first page, and scanned the words there. "Looks like he had a stroke, and now he's in a coma."

Eas recalled his uncle's recent demise. A man he'd never met that he could remember but who seemed to hate Eas anyway just for his existence. "That sounds familiar."

Hannah turned. "So who is walking around with this guy's face, pretending to be him?"

Badger's voice came on. "Maybe Jerry has an evil twin." He paused. "Too soon?"

More than one person said, "Yes."

Eas didn't have to bother responding. Which was good. He didn't think he could talk about that right now, and maybe not ever.

Hannah studied his face, evidently realizing how he felt about Badger's words.

Eas shook his head. She didn't need to worry.

"Do I need to get into the mechanics of plastic surgery right now?" Zander said. "Because I was thinking we could just find Judah and get out of here."

"Or we could call the cops," Hannah suggested. "Surely they'll find evidence of criminal activity in a place where a billionaire is being held, and Judah was taken after he was abducted."

"Hmm," Badger responded. "I see your point there."

"Thank you," Hannah said.

"You're welcome, babe."

Someone groaned.

Eas was pretty sure it was either Andre or Lucia. Either way, Judah could need help quickly. That wouldn't happen if they were busy bantering. "I'm going to check the rest of the doors in this hallway."

"We're almost done with the second floor," Zander said. "Then we'll head back to you. I want to get a look at Jerry."

"Copy that," Eas said.

Hannah set the clipboard aside and followed him out since they weren't supposed to let each other out of their sight—something none of them was upset about, considering the stakes on this one and the fact their enemy had remained a mystery for months. The team had only recently begun piecing things together, and they still didn't have everything figured out.

The next door was empty. The one on Hannah's side caused her to pause.

She nodded to her teammate, then eased into the room.

He stood at the doorway, content to hang back if that was necessary. Watch her back. The way he'd promised Badger he would.

"It's okay." Hannah crouched, not talking to him.

Eas saw who was in there. He cleared the room apart from the woman, who Hannah was dealing with. After he'd confirmed there was no one else inside, he ducked out. But only far enough to say, "We found the reporter."

"Any sign of Judah?" Zander asked.

"We'll find out," Eas replied. "Maybe she knows where he is." He rounded the door jamb back inside.

"I can give you an assist if you like." Hannah held out one hand.

Soraya was in a sorry state, but that all seemed fixable with a shower and a change of clothes. She didn't have any visible bruises, though in his experience those were usually the easiest to heal from.

Hannah lifted Soraya to her feet, holding onto her elbow. The reporter who had gone missing from the public eye weeks ago. Around the same time as Judah. Had she been a captive of Travers Industries this entire time?

"Do you know where Judah is?"

Soraya pulled up short, her eyes widened, and took half a step back.

Before Hannah could speak, Eas continued, "We aren't here to hurt you. We're here to help."

"I know who you are."

Hannah said, "Whatever you think you know, I can assure you this is a good man."

Warmth birthed in him. Diminished slightly by the fact Hannah didn't know him well. But she knew his family, those he had chosen to be part of his life. They were her family too —some by blood. Still, she didn't know a lot about him because the important things couldn't be read in a police file or a newspaper.

Both of these women had no reason to trust him.

All Eas wanted was to go home to his family. He didn't owe either one anything, and Zander would understand if this was his last mission. But how could he tell the rest of the team?

Karina had given up this life, and he could as well. It was all he'd known for years. But maybe it was time for a change.

"Let's go." Getting them both out of here safely would go a long way to building that.

"Hold on." That was Hannah.

Eas checked the hallway again. When he knew it was clear, he glanced back.

Hannah's attention was on the reporter, Soraya. "We do need to know if you've seen a man here. His name is Judah, and he'd be a prisoner like you."

"Do you know who that is?" Eas asked. Maybe she had no idea.

The reporter nodded at his question. "He was here, with me. They took him away." Her face fell. Tears welled in her eyes, and one traced its way down her cheek. "I don't know where he is."

Eas relayed the information to Zander. His boss's reply came quickly. "I'll have Ted get into the surveillance. Find out where he was taken."

"We have another problem," Badger said.

Hannah stopped at the doorway and turned her attention to the open comms channel. "What is it?"

"Everyone we faced retreated. They didn't seem that interested in fighting back."

Eas said, "They fired on you, right?"

"Yes," Badger said, "but only to delay us going after them. We did anyway, and we came up against a steel door. We can't get through to the other side."

Zander came on. "Ted, can you get us through that door?" He was quiet for a second. "Copy that. Guys, on the other side of that door is a garage. Two vehicles just headed out a tunnel."

"They ran?" Andre said.

"If they did that, they left Jerry Travers here." Eas shook his head. "They cut their losses and decided he wasn't worth keeping. Which means even if we do all we can, it's unlikely we'll find anything here to help."

"Or there's another explanation," Lucia said over comms. "One we haven't thought of yet."

"Like what?" Badger asked.

"If I knew that, I'd have thought of it," was her reply.

Hannah sucked in a breath. Her gaze lifted to Eas's at the same time his mind came up with one word.

Bo—

"Bomb!" Lucia and Andre spoke simultaneously.

"We need to get out of here," he said. "*Now.*"

He stepped out into the hallway, the two women right behind him just as the building exploded around them, the world swallowed up into heat and darkness.

Eas was falling, and then everything went black.

14

Judah stared at the man, hardly able to believe who he was looking at. Not the guy he had come here to find, Yuri Amrakov. And yet, for some reason, he got the feeling this was exactly who he was looking for.

He pulled his thoughts from their spiral and gathered them back in. "You're the one who runs Uzhas?" The word meant "terror" in Russian.

He'd thought they were only a myth. Killers who show up under cover of darkness, and no one is left alive. Although, it had always bothered him how anyone could tell the story when no one witnessed it and the only person involved was the dead target.

Yuri nodded.

But it wasn't Yuri, was it? Or maybe it was.

The man he was looking at looked nothing like the aging Soviet agent Judah had been sent here to find. "I was approached about fifteen years ago. At the time, things weren't going well in my home country. Too many wanted me dead."

"Approached by who?" He wanted to ask about the man's family. Judah was pretty sure Isaac knew nothing about his father, but considering the fact the former Chevalier member had lied to them about a lot of things, the truth was, he had no idea.

Judah had tried to get Yuri to admit to an emotional attachment to Isaac. Telling him personal details about the man. Yuri hadn't even blinked. But given the mask that had been disguising his face, maybe Judah just hadn't been able to see it.

Now he had a good view of the man's entire face. It was the eyes that told the truth. Whether a person tried to disguise it, or not.

"Travers Industries offered me a way out of my…predicament." Yuri blew out a breath. "I made a deal with the devil, and I lost everything."

Judah nodded. "That seems to be a familiar tale when people come up against Travers. I just didn't know they'd been operating that long."

"The CEO has been around maybe the last thirty or forty years. I certainly heard of them back in the day at the beginning of my career."

"I know you were a Soviet agent."

Yuri's eyes widened. "You do, do you?"

He didn't betray even the slightest notion of an accent with that. After the muffled voice that had sounded like English wasn't his first language, all of a sudden now he sounded like a red-blooded American, as far as Judah could tell. It fit with the face, certainly.

Judah couldn't wrap his head around it. "How long have you been playing the part of Jerry Travers?"

His other question surrounded why Travers would want the guy dead now, at this point in things. If they were getting ready to release a new technology, surely they would like their spokesperson in the middle of it all.

There had to be a reason for the timing of why Judah had been sent here right now.

Maybe it was a setup in some way.

"I've been Travers in the public eye almost ever since then." Yuri shrugged. "Years now. Every few weeks they parade me around, then they dump me back here so I can train them."

"The assassins?"

He nodded.

Judah had to wonder. Travers had an active Twitter following, and he was in the public eye more than just every few weeks. And yet, all that could be fabricated easily enough. With all the resources at Travers' disposal, they could make a lot of things seem real that weren't.

Including giving a Russian agent a new face.

But had Yuri simply dropped into their laps, or had they approached him specifically?

That might be a question he never got an answer to.

Yuri said, "Uzhas works for Travers Industries, and they take independent contracts as well."

"How many assassins?"

"Seven."

"Is one of them Casper Cunningham?"

Yuri's eyes widened again. "I'm thinking you know more than you were aware of."

"And you're just happy to fill in the blanks out of the goodness of your heart?" Judah figured that wasn't the case but needed Yuri to confirm it.

The older man chuckled. "If you haven't figured that out yet, maybe you're not as smart as you think."

Judah frowned. Then he scanned one way until he looked behind him to the left. He rotated all the way around and looked behind him to the right. Then he looked back at Yuri. "How many are there?"

"At your ten o'clock, behind me and to the right, there is a grate in the dirt." Yuri spoke as though they were continuing a casual conversation. "When the time is right, you will make a run for it. Climb down—watch out because the grate is heavy —and take the tunnel to the end."

"How will I know when the time is right?"

"Oh," Yuri said, "you'll know."

"I'm going to need you to give me my gun back."

Yuri opened his mouth. His brows reached for each other. Before he could say anything, his body jerked and blood blossomed in the center of his chest.

They dropped at the same time. Judah grasped for the gun Yuri had, and the older man gave it up. "Tell him I thought of him."

Isaac.

There was no time to respond. Judah had to go.

He ran for the grate just as another bullet pinged off the ground beside him, spraying dust and dirt. He skidded to the hatch, lifting it as he moved behind the thick metal. A bullet pinged off the grate. Judah felt a hot sting on the back of his shoulder.

He didn't think about what that meant. He simply shimmied his legs in and dropped into the dark.

The floor slammed into him. He relaxed his body, folding his knees into his chest as he rolled to displace the force of his drop.

The grate was open above him, but there was no time to close it.

He scrambled up and tried to run down the hallway. His hands hit the floor. Judah pushed off with his feet, crawling for a couple of steps before he managed to get upright. The tunnel turned a corner.

Judah managed to slow his pace enough to look around before he went.

Clear.

The sound of people approaching the open hatch spurred him on. He raced to the end, unlatched the door, and found the lock on the other side. He engaged it. A dusty garage with a roll-up door at one end was on the far side. It looked flimsy enough.

If there was only…

The first vehicle was a rusty Jeep up on blocks, looking like it hadn't run in thirty years. Judah raced around it and found a Mercedes from the nineties—in fact, it was a model he'd been handed down from his granny just after he got his driving license, right before his eighteenth birthday. Toni had been so jealous.

He felt his lips curl into a smile. That was a good memory. One he was going to remind his sister of when he got back to Last Chance County. Which he *would*. There was no other option here, not now that he had so much intel to give the guys. Whether they let him back on the team or not, they needed to know.

A heavy thud banged against the door.

That lock wasn't going to hold forever.

Judah slid into the driver's seat. Several prayers rolled through his mind—for keys and enough petrol to get out of here. Also, not dying on the way would be good.

Yuri was dead.

Pain sliced through Judah's chest as though that bullet had hit him. *Isaac.*

He flipped down the sun visor and keys dropped into his lap. Judah turned over the engine and winced at the gas gauge. He wasn't going to get far.

Also, the garage door was down.

Risk it?

He hadn't gotten this far in his life by playing it safe.

Judah put the car in drive and hit the gas. It sped from the space and hit the garage door seconds later. The crash had him ducking down to take cover behind the wheel. Such as it was.

The door splintered on impact, and he burst through the other side in a shower of pieces. Shards. Dust. Judah coughed, even though the debris was outside. Light blinded him until he adjusted that visor, and got a look at the outside world. Miles of dirt. Probably more land mines.

Two parallel lines curved in the dirt. A path or the familiar route Yuri took to get out of here. Often enough, he'd left a visible trail.

"Thank you, Yuri."

Judah followed as fast as he could, taking corners like a rally car driver on those tight mountain switchbacks. The terrain was mostly flat, with trees and scrub. The house behind him…

He blinked and looked again at the rearview mirror. Then the wing mirrors.

Two Humvees were in pursuit.

Judah pressed the accelerator to the floor.

I need a phone.

Soraya came awake on a gasp. Everywhere around her was dark, and the air was laced with dust. She coughed, and pain spasmed through her chest until she cried out.

Someone moaned.

Or maybe that was the building around her. The whole facility.

She realized the place had exploded like a giant trap to murder them all. Another gasp, cough. She found she could move her hands, her arms. Her shoulder didn't feel great. She felt around her, in front of her face, and tried to move her legs.

Trapped.

She cried out, pushing against whatever was in front of her face. Soraya couldn't even think.

All she could do was let the tears fall.

She was going to die down here. Her parents—she would

never see them again. Her sister, too. Judah. Lana. Anyone, everyone she'd ever met. None of them would visit with her.

She even cried for the enemies she never wanted in her life, the ones who had wronged her so long ago she shouldn't even remember. Or care.

Soraya had no space to move, even if she could.

Another moan sounded.

"Help!" Her voice was barely above a whisper. She swallowed and tried again, louder. "Help! Is somebody there?"

That woman had been with her when the building exploded. And a man, scarred on his face. She knew him, but her mind couldn't piece the fragments together. All she could see in her mind was Judah. Had he been here? Her rescuers, did they know him?

Her thoughts dissipated, floating away from her. Too far to catch them back.

The debris above her groaned.

If it shifted, was she going to be crushed? Maybe she was about to find out.

"Help!" she yelled as loudly as she could, hoping someone heard her. "Help!"

"Hey." Someone coughed. The voice was hoarse. "Hey, I'm here."

Soraya turned her head to the sound. "Who's there?"

That groan moved through the building.

"Lord, don't let there be a secondary explosion." The voice belonged to a woman. The one who'd tried to rescue her?

Soraya tried to move again. "Someone help us!"

But who was even out there?

The debris moved. There was a great groan as a section above her slid away, and a shaft of light flooded the space where she lay. Barely bigger than the crawl space under a porch. Soraya whimpered.

"There are people down here!" The steady voice of a man

broke the buzzing in her head, that relentless pounding of her heartbeat in her ears.

"Help!"

Debris rained down, coating her until she had to close her eyes or be blinded. A whimper puffed out her lips. Scuffling and more groans filled her ears. Then shouted orders back and forth. The ear-splitting buzz of an electric saw.

"No, help her first." The woman, the one beside her.

"No can do, lady."

Soraya opened her eyes and saw a flashlight bob. The woman's face flashed in the beam, blood down one side. But her eyes were clear. It was the woman who'd found her, the one who tried to rescue her. And in retaliation, Travers Industries wanted to kill them all.

"Hey." A man's face drifted into view. "Let's get you out of here."

"My legs."

He looked down, then back at her. "Like I said. Let's get you out of here."

That told her nothing about the state of her lower limbs. Part of Soraya didn't even want to know what they looked like. There would be plenty of time to face that after they were out of here.

Debris was cleared from above them. More people than her mind could count right now moved around, most of them blurry despite her trying to focus. But she realized one thing. None of them had uniforms on. These weren't first responders, at least not ones who were on duty.

The man who moved around her, checking her limbs. He seemed competent. But he wore no helmet. In a situation like this?

He glanced at someone else. "Let's get that off her."

"Copy that."

Soraya wasn't exactly going to complain if they were less than professional rescuers.

She was lifted by her underarms. The man clasped his own wrists in front of her. She heard a signal given, then the weight lifted from her legs. Whoever had her in his grasp tugged, and she was pulled out from under it.

Finally she was out in the open, where the sun beat down, but the temperature remained close to freezing. Sweat chilled on her skin. She brushed at her face but felt only gravel. On her hand or her cheek?

She managed to get her legs under her, though pain flashed from her ankles up to her knees.

"I've got you." Strong arms lifted her from her rescuer's grip so that she was held against his chest.

She looked at his face. "Thanks."

He was as dirty as she was. With a scrape on his cheek and bright blue eyes. But there was a lethality to him. "I'm Zander. The rest of these people, I'm not sure you need to know who they are. Unless they're my team."

She frowned.

"Z!" A man raced over to them, a slight limp in his stride. "Have you seen Hannah anywhere?"

The man holding her up shook his head. "Not yet."

"Is she the woman who found me?" Soraya didn't know how to describe her. "With the other guy. Asian, I think. With a scar on his face. Is that who you're talking about?"

He laid her down. If he was with those people, Zander probably also wanted to know where Judah was.

"Where's Judah?" she asked.

They glanced at each other, then back at her. "Let's get you some medical attention."

Soraya started to object, then realized that probably wasn't the best idea. She doubted she could even walk right now. The idea she would be useless and have to rely on other people until she was healed didn't sit right. But give her a computer, and a phone, and there was plenty of damage she could do to Travers Industries in retaliation for this.

"I need a phone." She lifted her head. "They threatened my family, and I need to call them and check they are all right."

The second man, whose name she didn't know, glanced up. "There she is." He raced away, scrambling over debris.

Soraya looked at the scene around her. The wreckage of the building looked like some post-apocalyptic movie scene, where everyone in the world was displaced and left to fend for themselves.

All she could do was shudder.

Then she looked down at her blood-coated pants. She rotated her feet left and right, then pointed her toes and pulled them toward herself.

She wanted to throw up some more or pass out. Too bad she'd done both of those far too many times already today.

The man who'd said his name was Zander looked away from her. The expression on his face was as she would imagine someone about to commit murder.

As much as she didn't want to ask, Soraya's reporter instincts overrode her good sense. "What is it?"

"Lana." The way he bit out her name didn't change that expression at all.

Soraya twisted around. "She's here?" That was great. Lana would know what to do next, and they could make a plan to take down Travers Industries. After this? There was nothing she wouldn't do to fight.

Travers was going to pay.

"Maybe she's not exactly who you think she is." He spoke with measured words. "But we can figure that out after you're admitted to the hospital."

A tall man with Hispanic heritage ambled over, blood on his temple. Under one arm was a woman. Soraya couldn't tell who was holding up who. The woman held her elbow with her other hand, the arm tucked against her body.

Soraya said, "I hate hospitals."

The woman rolled her eyes. "Pretty sure we all do. That's why we have a team doctor."

"He's busy." Zander frowned. "But we'll get him to meet us."

"Do you know Judah?"

He turned that frown to her. "Do *you?*"

"He was here." She looked behind her, and saw another man pulled from the rubble. The second man she'd met sat with a blonde—the woman who'd rescued her. *She* was looking at Lana. Staring. In fact, both of them were. And it didn't look good.

"When?" The guy with the bloody forehead crouched. "I'm Andre, by the way. This is Lucia." He motioned to the woman, who smiled.

What did they have against Lana?

"When did you see Judah?"

Soraya frowned. "Why didn't you help him?"

"We've been looking for him for weeks," Zander said. "Does he need help now?"

"He's not here." And Soraya wasn't going to be either. Whoever these people were, she didn't trust them. She trusted Lana, who was coming over to her now with that determined stride. "I need to get out of here."

Lana nodded once. "I can make that happen."

"Hang on—" It figured Zander objected.

Soraya glanced at him. "Thank you for saving me, but I have to go now."

She had a lot of work to do if she was going to bring down Raleigh before more people got hurt.

15

———

J udah bumped along a dirt road toward a town that was still thirteen miles away. It didn't really matter what country this was. It wasn't as though he'd been trained for specific places, not when generic climates and terrain were easier to instruct. The team had done missions all over the world. In the military, things had been the same no matter where they were deployed.

Location wasn't a factor at all.

What he needed was a phone. And the town up ahead was the only place he would be able to get one.

The people who had killed Yuri were still behind him. But there was something to be said for Judah's ability to drive in a place like this. He'd been living in Nigeria the last month, and evidently, he'd fallen into the rhythm of life in Africa.

The guys in the Humvees behind him? Not so much.

One had slipped into a puddle deeper than the driver anticipated. Everyone had bailed out and climbed in the second vehicle. Now they were hanging off the sides holding their rifles. Maybe some locals would show up unexpectedly and take care of the problem for him. After all, Judah was the only one who looked like he belonged here.

Even if this place matched every memory in his life that he didn't want to remember.

The edge of town came into view. Judah hit the gas as the car bumped up onto asphalt. The road wasn't in much better condition than the dirt, but he skirted around potholes and headed for civilization. Knowing he might be successful and find a phone, the rush of adrenaline flooded him with strength and energy. He needed to focus, or he would lose his grasp on the situation at the last second. Then it would be over.

The first building he came to was boarded up and rundown. The chain-link fence around the outside guarded the structure. A couple of streets down, there was a petrol station and convenience store. Lights inside drew him like a beacon.

He pulled up out front and raced in because there was no one outside. The door slammed back on its hinges. The bell got stuck. "I need to use your phone."

His front smashed the counter as he collided with it. Several packets of snacks tumbled to the floor, but he didn't check to see what they were.

The man behind the counter lifted his sparse gray brows, shifting the skin on his wrinkled face.

"Please."

"Police won't help you out here."

Judah winced. "Do you have a gun?" It might be up to him to defend them from the men about to show up.

"Shotgun." But the man didn't move.

"How much do you want to keep this store, and how much do you want to walk away with nothing and retire?" Maybe the guy had insurance. But given what was about to happen, Judah was going to at least try and move it in the direction the guy wanted it to go in.

"You bring trouble to my store?"

Judah didn't know what to say.

The guy just sat there on his stool behind the counter. "I deal with trouble."

"And the phone?"

"One hundred British pounds."

So he had figured out the accent. "I don't suppose you have PayPal?"

The old man waved a gnarled finger. "Aisle two."

"I don't have time to charge it." He glanced at the windows and saw the Humvee pull in. "And neither do you."

"You want a phone, or not? Aisle two."

Judah ripped the phone from its packaging and pocketed it, along with the charger.

"Go. Out the back." The old man racked the shotgun. "I'll take out the trash."

Judah blinked. Too many action movies? "I'm sorry."

He did as instructed, running for the hallway to the exit at the end. He reached for the bar on the door.

And stopped.

A shotgun blast boomed down the hallway from the storefront. Glass shattered and the high sound of a man screaming filled the air. Followed by laughter, which he was pretty sure belonged to the old man. The guy really wanted to go out like this? Maybe he'd been sitting around for years just waiting for a situation where he could end it all in a blaze of glory.

When Judah had asked for help and a way out, this wasn't exactly what he'd meant.

But help was what the old man had done.

Judah whispered a prayer and pushed out the door. He ran through town, pumping his arms and legs without even thinking about it, dodging people. He raced through a market where he had to slow after colliding with an older woman. She made him think too much of the gnarled man.

Eyes wide, the woman gasped.

Judah kept going, not caring where he would end up. He just needed a place to sit and plug in the phone. And then he saw the white church at the end of the street. The cross on the roof, stretching up to the sky.

He stumbled and one hand grazed the ground.

He kept going. Through the little gate, along the path to the front door. His fingers slipped on the handle, leaving blood behind as he pushed his way in. The vestibule was empty. Judah spotted an outlet low on the wall, to the right. He hit the wall and slid down to sit. Breathing hard.

He pulled the phone out and managed to plug the thing in, though it took several tries. He had to wipe the blood off on his pant leg.

And they thought he could be an intelligence agent? Alone like this wasn't his favorite place, and it never would be. Having his brothers—his friends—behind him, watching his back? That was the best place to be as far as he was concerned.

Thinking of them caused tears to roll down his face.

Life had gone on while he was forced onto a different path. Could he go back? It wouldn't be to Soraya. Travers would never allow that, not when they'd intended to kill him today along with Yuri.

Isaac's father.

Judah knew what it felt like to suffer that loss.

He swiped the tickle from his face, brushing away the moisture but leaving a smear of blood given the state of his hands.

His breath hitched in his chest.

He stared at the phone. *Charge faster.* He needed to use it *now.*

White swished in front of his face. Judah blinked and looked up at the man of the cloth who stood there. "Greetings, friend." He looked between Judah and the outlet. "I'm thinking you needed more than just a charge, did you not?"

Whether that was true or not, Judah figured he would get

more than he bargained for choosing a church to get rescued in. "S'pose you're going to try and save my soul?"

The priest, or father, or whatever he was, crouched. Judah heard the pop of old knees. "Yes, Son. I think I am."

Judah had to admit, "That's probably a good idea." After all, he was a mess right now.

"Any trouble following you that I should know about?"

"I don't want to put anyone here in danger," Judah said. "I can leave."

"And rob me of the opportunity to save a wayward soul?" He seemed genuinely hurt by that, although it could simply be pretense. The part he played when he put those robes on. "Let's get you cleaned up and fed, and then we can talk about it."

"As long as I can make a phone call." The idea he'd be able to reach Zander was like a drug he was jonesing for. "I have friends who can come and pick me up."

At least, he hoped they would be willing to come all this way. Who knew how they felt about him now? Maybe it had been too long, and all they wanted was information from him. He'd be cut loose to make his own way back to Last Chance County to be with his sister.

That was the fear talking. Judah knew the Chevalier team. Even if he hadn't told them everything, there was no way they would give up on him. He hoped.

By the end of this, he might wind up getting saved in every way.

Or his fear would be proven right.

"Is that really necessary?" Soraya smoothed down the blanket that had been pulled up over her hospital gown.

The doctor said, "Yes."

Over by the window, Lana chuckled.

Soraya glared at both of them. "Fine." She thought Lana would leave the room, but she didn't.

"You think I've never had a difficult patient before?" The doctor shot her a look that made it seem like she actually had a personality, instead of just being cold and professional like so many medical people. "But you don't want to walk on those legs anytime soon. Are you going to argue with me that you don't need a good night of sleep?"

Soraya made a face. "Let me guess, you have kids?"

"If you think I sound like your mom," the doctor said, "I'm going to take that as a compliment."

Soraya trained a stare on Lana, who brushed hair back from her face. Her skin glinted. Clammy. She also looked a little pale. It might be from being at the explosion site, but Soraya wanted the medical professional to check anyway.

"How are you feeling?" The doctor pulled a tiny flashlight from her breast pocket and flicked it on. Lana stood still while the doctor shone the light in her eyes. "I'd like to take your temperature."

Lana shook her head. "I've been a little run down lately. Nauseous, maybe. But I don't think it's anything to worry about. We're not here for me."

Yet another reason Soraya had to be confident in the decision she'd made. That team of Judah's seemed friendly enough, but she didn't know them. Lana was the one who had helped her hide out when she needed to be safe. When Travers Industries was trying to kill her.

And when they captured her again? Lana was the one who had shown up in time to pull them all out of the rubble—Soraya and that team of six who'd been there for Judah, and maybe her too. But it wasn't like she knew them enough to trust them.

"Let me know if you change your mind."

Lana nodded. After the doctor headed out, she wandered over to the bed.

"She's right," Soraya said. "You don't look well."

Lana clasped her hand. "Probably just a bug I picked up somewhere."

"Thank you for coming to get me." Soraya brushed at the blanket again. "Who were those people who came to get their friend?"

"And you." Lana shook her head. "They would have taken you with them."

"Judah seemed nice." And now she had no idea where he was. "Maybe they are too. They did help pull me out." When Lana said nothing, Soraya continued, "Did I hear them say they found Jerry Travers in there? In a coma, I think."

"It looks that way." Lana blew out a breath and settled on the end of the bed, folding her arms and looking out the window.

Soraya would have rather the woman met her gaze. There was something about the fact she didn't face Soraya head-on that niggled inside her as a question she didn't know how to voice. "Who are they?"

Lana glanced over. "Tell me what happened."

Soraya didn't want to, but she reiterated everything with British intelligence—which seemed crazy just talking about it and not at all like her life. Then she told Lana everything with Raleigh and the "job" she'd been forced to do. The fact they had cameras in her parents' house.

Lana had handed her a phone as soon as they got in the car outside the facility. Soraya had spoken with both her parents, who assured her they were fine. Lana had jumped on the phone after and told Soraya's father she was sending someone to the house to remove the security system, so they no longer had to worry about being watched.

"How much of what you had to read can you remember?"

Soraya scrunched up her nose and rested her head on the pillow. "A lot of stuff about how I was so happy to be on board now, working with them to keep America safe." She shook her head even though it ached. The doctor had given her localized meds in her legs. She didn't want a cloudy head, so she'd declined narcotics. "How I value what Travers is doing so much that I jumped at the chance to work for them."

"So basically just a bunch of baloney PR stuff." Lana nodded.

"Yeah, I guess."

"So why threaten your family just to get that?"

"Because they needed it." Soraya stared at the window, thinking back through it all. The way Raleigh had paused at the doorway. Right before the alarm went off, she'd had a feeling there was something he wasn't telling her. Something he didn't want anyone else to know.

"What is it?" Lana asked.

"They blew the whole place, trying to kill all of us."

"That other team, Judah's friends, they told me Raleigh left with all his people right before the explosion. They expected a lot more resistance going in there, but Travers Industries just cut their losses and ran. Which means there was nothing to salvage in that facility. Just a whole lot of things that needed to be buried." Lana spoke with the kind of cold indifference that sounded as though she might have been talking about next week's weather.

Soraya winced. Lana had been amazing so far, but there was still an edge to the woman that seemed dark. Probably darker than Soraya wanted to admit seeing as she needed Lana's help and relied on her. "So they wanted us all dead, and all the information on the servers destroyed."

"I'm sure Chevalier got into that at the same time they were looking for you and Judah."

Soraya shuddered at the mention of his name. He could've been in there as well, for all she knew. "Where is he?" Maybe Lana knew, and she just didn't want to tell Soraya because it would upset her.

They'd hardly spent any time together, and yet there

seemed to have been this connection between her and Judah. Something she'd never had with anyone else. So how was she even supposed to know what it was?

She probably needed to call her mom again.

Lana squeezed Soraya's hand. "I don't know where he is, but I'm looking."

"Who are they, this Chevalier group?"

Soraya might have heard some things in the news about some of them, especially that one she realized now had been on the FBI's Ten Most Wanted list until recently. He was cleared. But they had been involved as a group with some serious dealings, given their connection to Stephen Gladstone. Maybe the rumors about them were true.

And now they were going up against Travers? She needed to get in front of her computer so she could find out who this Judah guy was.

Lana brushed hair back from her face. Her hand shook, her skin still pale and clammy. She really didn't look good. "They are my family."

"But you don't work with them?" Maybe she did on occasion, and just not right now.

Lana winced. "I tried to do the right thing, but they don't want to know me."

Soraya had thought they were nice people, helping out. Doing what they could. But how could that be true, now that she knew what they were really like? Soraya laid her other hand on Lana's this time. "I think I'm going to need your help to figure this out."

"After what Raleigh did to you," Lana said, "there's no way I'm going to let him get away with any of this."

"Thank you." Soraya smiled. "I don't think I can ever repay you for what you've done for me. I'm alive because of you."

"You're the one who stood up to them."

Soraya wasn't so sure about that. "Did I, though? They still got what they wanted and left us for dead."

"This isn't about anyone else. It's about you." Lana held her attention with that steady gaze of hers that made Soraya sure she could trust her. "Soraya, you've fought against Travers since you first learned what the truth is behind their PR scam. Now they tried to drag you into it and destroy your integrity. But we can't let them do that. We have to work together."

She didn't mention Chevalier. Maybe they were only interested in Judah, not taking down Travers. Both of which were the right thing to do.

Soraya had been alone long enough she knew it only allowed the fear to overcome her. She needed to focus. She didn't want to be alone anymore, so teaming up with someone she could trust was going to be the best option for her. Because after turning down Judah in that container, she wondered if teamwork might be the way to win at this.

Soraya nodded. "Together sounds good."

"I'll make the arrangements." Lana stood, swayed slightly, and straightened. Then she headed out like nothing had happened.

Soraya watched her leave. *Thank You, God, for her.*

Lana was the only one on her side.

16

———

Two days had passed since Judah made that call from the burner phone, leaving a voicemail on the company line. And nothing. No return call or rescue attempt. Neither had anyone shown up.

Judah pushed the extra T-shirts into the rucksack the minister had given him and zipped it closed. How long was he supposed to wait when it was so clear that no one was coming? He was kidding himself if he thought they would ever take him back.

He fought the hot burn of moisture in his eyes.

Maybe this was his life now.

"You're just gonna keep running?"

Judah spun around.

Zander stood in the doorway, leaning on the doorjamb with his arms folded and a bruise high on his cheekbone.

"What happened?" Judah could see from the look in his eyes that there was a reason he had been delayed. All the fear washed away at that moment, as if Judah had never been gone.

"Let's just get you home. We can talk on the way." Zander motioned with his chin to the hallway.

Judah grabbed the rucksack and looked around at the tiny bedroom. It was one of the rooms schoolchildren stayed in during the term. Right now they were on break, home with their families—except the ones who didn't have anywhere to go. The minister said those ones stayed here year-round.

He'd eaten breakfast with a couple of them yesterday. Tried to draw them into a conversation, something that had proven futile at best.

Not that he blamed them. In fact, they reminded him a lot of himself as a kid.

"You want to do something for these people?" Zander held that steady gaze on him.

Judah nodded. "Kids, mostly."

"Then we will."

As if it were that simple. Maybe in Zander's world, it was. Judah hadn't had the same experiences. But neither was worse than the other. They were simply the lives he and Zander had lived. Losing family members young. Serving in the military. Being part of Chevalier. Two existences, and yet Providence had seen fit to throw them together.

The minister met them at the front door, where Judah had stumbled in looking for a phone charger.

Judah held out his hand, and the minister shook it. "Any word on that shopkeeper?"

"He perished in the battle. However, he managed to take three men with him." The minister didn't seem especially cut up about that.

Judah didn't have time to get into it. "Thank you for following up. Did he have a family?"

"A daughter and granddaughter," the minister said. "They were killed a year ago by rebels."

Judah pushed out a breath.

"Thank you." Zander also shook his hand. "For everything."

The minister nodded, then glanced at Judah. "You remember what I said. And that my door is always open."

"Thank you." Judah wasn't sure how many times he would need to say it but figured that eventually, he wouldn't be able to get those words out.

Zander headed to the door and outside, followed by Judah. A car was parked at the curb.

Judah motioned. "That yours?"

"Yep."

It was on the tip of Judah's tongue to ask what had taken Zander so long to get there. After all, days had passed since he made that call.

While Zander drove, Judah pulled the phone out and looked at it. Not that anyone would have called him or sent a message except maybe Ted. But there was nothing, which made more sense if he were honest. No one even had this number.

"Did you tell Toni you found me?" Judah glanced over.

Zander looked at the phone in Judah's lap, his expression inscrutable, and Judah had never wanted to know what his boss was thinking more than he did right now. "I figured I'd let you tell her yourself when we get back."

"Because you're not going to give me her number?" The only one he had memorized was the Chevalier emergency line. The one he called that had brought Zander here. Who memorized phone numbers these days, anyway?

If Zander tried to take this phone away, they would have words. Even if it might be the right thing to do for operational security.

"You're on radio silence until we run down everything we both know about what's going on." Zander turned a corner for the main road heading toward the nearest airport.

Judah had studied a local map all morning, figuring he'd need to make his own way there.

"It's been weeks. You need to tell me everything that

happened since you and Badger were held captive. Last I heard from you, you were going to wait for me to come and get you."

"I thought it was you. When they…" Judah winced. "When British intelligence pulled up, saying I owe them, which wasn't exactly inaccurate. Except that the guy they think I cost them? He's alive."

"So what you've been doing isn't about Raleigh and Travers?"

There was something in his tone. A guardedness that said he was testing Judah. "Rather than hedging your bets about whether I'm going to tell the truth or not, maybe you could just ask me what happened. Because I've got a whole lot of information about all of this. Maybe even more than you."

"Is that right?"

He wanted to spill all of it right then, but something told Judah if he did that there was a chance Zander might not invite him to get on the plane. Maybe it was a fissure in him that let a tiny portion of insecurity leak out. However, given the way they had all reacted to Isaac's betrayal, Judah wasn't exactly anticipating a warm reaction.

Even he had harbored anger toward Isaac for walking away from the team. Judah figured he probably needed to apologize to the guy for that, considering it was unlikely Isaac would have done it if there was any choice.

"I didn't betray Chevalier. And I didn't walk away of my own accord." Not just that. "The first chance I got, I called you."

Zander navigated into the airport and pulled up alongside the plane. As he switched the car off, he turned to Judah. "No one thinks you betrayed us."

"You think Isaac did. *I* thought Isaac did."

"But you're not so sure now?" Zander asked.

"Let's just say, I've been through enough the past few weeks to know there's a reason why he walked away."

"Because he thought it was the only thing he could do." Zander reached for the door handle.

"You're not going to let me back with no questions asked, are you?"

"Would you respect me if I did?"

"No."

"Toni probably will." Zander paused. "But she's your sister. I'm your boss, and we're in the middle of trying to unravel a mystery that involves a former president. So I need to know who I can trust."

"I've been looking for a family a long time."

"I know." Zander nodded. "Chevalier is that for all of us. So we do what families do, and we talk it out. We figure out how to move on in a way that means we can trust each other." He clapped Judah on the shoulder. "But we can talk it all through on the plane."

"I didn't want to let you down." Judah felt like part of him had been cracked open, and that fissure was widening. He hadn't realized until now how much the guys of Chevalier meant to him. He'd never had a team like them around him. He didn't want to lose it.

He had plenty of intel to trade with Zander. But something in him said that wasn't what his friend was interested in, even if they were going to talk it all through. Judah intended to tell him all about Isaac's father, and the group of assassins associated with Travers Industries. And Soraya.

His heart squeezed in his chest just thinking of her.

Judah rubbed his palm over his left pectoral. Was she okay? Did they still have her? He tried to get the questions out but couldn't even speak.

Judah shoved the door open and stumbled toward the steps of the plane. Halfway up, Andre stepped into view at the top of the stairs. Then Badger appeared beside him. Andre had a bandage on the side of his forehead.

Judah wiped at the tickle on his cheek, and his fingers came away wet.

The two of them stepped back as he entered the plane with Zander right behind him.

Judah tried to speak, but the words clogged his throat.

Andre rolled his eyes. "Get over here, idiot."

He pulled Judah into a backslapping hug that made him wince. Then Badger's arms banded around both of them. Judah pushed out a long breath.

Zander squeezed the back of Judah's neck with his big palm.

Everything he wanted was right here. Especially knowing he would get back to Last Chance County and he'd see his sister and her fiancé. There was still something missing.

He looked at Zander through the tears in his eyes. "Where is she?"

"Soraya Adams?" Zander asked.

All Judah could do was nod and swipe away stupid tears. They were going to think he'd missed them.

Andre said, "Let's get going, and we can talk."

That didn't sound good.

"No, I can't come home. Not yet." Soraya sniffed. She leaned forward from her seat on the couch to the laptop on the coffee table. On the screen her mom and dad sat, arms intertwined, on the couch in their living room, where President Raleigh had been watching them.

Lana had ordered her people to remove the cameras. Now her people were stationed around the house, acting as bodyguards until the threat was over. It was something that still remained unfamiliar to Soraya even after everything she'd been through. Who lived this kind of life, where they had to guard their loved ones at all times?

"It's not safe for me to come home," she told her mom.

Nothing could induce her to do that while the threat was active. Raleigh had tried to kill them all, and the real Jerry Travers along with them. No one knew what he was currently up to. Whatever it was, Soraya figured none of them would like the aftermath.

That was why she wasn't going home until this was over. Until she had proven to the world what she knew to be real— that the former president cared only about power and not about the people he should've served. Or the ones who were trying to live honest lives.

There was no way Soraya would put her family in danger with someone like Raleigh after her. As soon as he found out they were all still alive, he would come after them again one way or another. There would be no escaping it.

She could see in her mom's eyes that moment her mom realized there would be no changing Soraya's mind. The conversation didn't last much longer, but it was enough for Soraya to know that her parents were safe now and being cared for so that she didn't need to worry.

Soraya only needed to worry about herself right now, according to Lana. The woman had been amazing so far, mustering all her people to help them figure out how to bring Raleigh down before he announced the rollout of this new phone system.

Soraya wished she had the evidence in hand to walk up to Capitol Hill in Washington, DC, and hand over proof that it was the worst idea the government had ever come up with. But so far, all she had was her word.

That word would be worth next to nothing after Raleigh broadcast all those recordings he'd had her make. There was already a social media campaign about how she was the newest employee of Travers Industries. Even though he thought he'd killed her, the man was still determined to use her for PR purposes. Maybe that had been the plan all along.

Raleigh had to be hiding something. Maybe an issue with the tech itself?

After all, if everything was working fine, he would've simply rolled it out on the original release date. Instead, he was working overtime to convince everyone it was all going fine. Overcompensating?

Soraya got up off the couch. The pain in her shins made her wince, but after a few days of rest, she was feeling much better than she had when they pulled her out of the rubble. Those people had saved her life. Good people, looking for their friend.

Not for the first time, she realized she didn't fit with them if she wanted to do this in a way that meant no one else got hurt. Lana could handle herself, and she had people. They seemed to be more like a family.

Something about Lana told her the woman could handle whatever came at them. But Soraya didn't know the same thing was true about those people. The ones Judah had called Chevalier. Maybe they didn't even know what they were getting into. Lana was the known, and they were the unknown here.

The last thing she wanted was to bring trouble to their doorsteps when they were only trying to find their friend.

Lana stood at the counter while the kettle boiled. After everything that'd happened it seemed strange to watch her do something so mundane. But this was real life, wasn't it? At least it was the life Soraya wished she had to go back to after all of this blew over.

"Did you find anything out about Judah?" Soraya had asked Lana to look into it. Judah had been at the facility, but no one knew where he was. She had no idea what had happened to him.

Lana glanced over, her face paler than it had been. Her eyes were a little glassy. She didn't look well at all. When Soraya had asked about it, she was shot down.

"Judah was in Africa," Lana finally said. "Now he's back with his friends."

"Oh." Soraya waited for more, but Lana turned back to watch the kettle. "That's good."

Lana retrieved the mug from the cupboard above the toaster. She brought it down with a shaky hand so hard it clattered on the counter.

"Are you okay?"

Lana started to nod. Or turn. As she moved, her eyes rolled back in her head, and she collapsed to the floor. Soraya rushed forward and got there a second before Lana's head would've hit the floor. She barely managed to catch the back of Lana's head and cradled it in the palm of her hand.

Her skin was clammy and flushed.

Soraya grabbed the cell phone on the counter beside the mug. She moved her thumb to tap the phone icon and saw the contact on the screen. *Hannah.* Who was this? Maybe she could call them for help.

She looked at Lana. 9-1-1 was probably best, but Soraya had always had the feeling Lana wanted nothing to do with legitimate law enforcement.

"Should I call this Hannah person?" She asked it aloud despite the fact Lana was unconscious.

Soraya bit her lip. "Okay, here goes."

But before she could tap the number, Lana grabbed her wrist and held fast.

Soraya looked down and saw her eyes were open. "Hey, you collapsed."

"Help me up."

"Maybe you should stay there, and I'll get someone to help?" Soraya had no idea what to do in a medical emergency. Sure, she watched a lot of hospital dramas, but when were those ever about the actual conditions—or realistic at all?

Lana shook her head. "Let me sit up."

Soraya did so but asked, "Is there something I should know?"

"I think it's poison." Lana blew out a long breath. "My head is swimming."

Soraya gasped. "You know that I would never have—"

"Not you. I know that." Lana closed her eyes for a second. "It happened a couple of weeks ago. I passed this guy on the street, and I felt a prick on my side. I think he injected me with something. I've been waiting for it to get worse ever since, but it must be slow acting. Really, really slow."

"Who would do this to you?"

Lana shook her head. "It doesn't matter. Raleigh obviously thinks I'm a threat if he's willing to pay someone to take me out. But he has no idea what he's up against."

"Please tell me you're not talking about me. Because I have no idea what to do next." Soraya had been trying to figure out a plan for the past couple of days. Ever since they showed up at this vacation rental. "And I have no idea how to stop him."

Honestly, if she admitted it to herself, Soraya was scared to move forward and combat Travers Industries. How could she possibly go up against the company with that amount of power? They would kill people she cared about.

They'd blown up the facility she was in, along with everyone else inside. Tried to murder them all and bury whatever evidence had been contained in the place. How she'd managed to survive was something Soraya was going to have to figure out. And she'd probably be wrestling with it for the rest of her life.

"I've been trying to figure out how to avoid it," Lana said, "but the truth is, we need help."

"From the rest of your people?"

Lana shook her head. "I don't want them involved in this."

"So how can we fight Travers?" Soraya shook her head.

"You need a doctor to check you out, and there's no way we can go up against Raleigh with just the two of us."

Lana stilled. "I'm glad you said that." She took the cell phone from Soraya and tapped the screen, swiping away the number for whoever Hannah was. Lana called a different number and put the phone to her ear.

"Who are you calling?"

Lana shifted the phone from her ear. "Whatever I say next, remember that we need help."

Soraya frowned.

"Yeah. It's Lana. Is Doctor Windermere available? Because I want to make a trade."

She shifted away from Lana. That didn't sound good at all.

The other woman grasped her wrist again, the way she had when Soraya thought she was unconscious. "Hang on."

Soraya started to shake her head.

"This is the only way to get this done." Lana paused. "Whether you agree or not."

17

____

"**S**he said *what?*"

Judah got up from his chair in the hospital waiting area. The whole team filled the place, along with Karina and Aria and friends from town.

They had told him the whole story on the way back from Africa. Before she left with Lana, the facility where they'd rescued Soraya had blown up. And while most of the team only suffered minor injuries, Eas had been dug out and transported back to Last Chance County. He was still unconscious, with swelling on his brain. They were waiting for the doctor's assessment.

Nora approached her husband.

Zander put an arm around her and said, "Lana called Ted. She needs to see Doctor Windermere, and she wants to give us Soraya Adams in exchange for a consult with him."

Even the second time, Judah still couldn't believe it.

Nora glanced up at her husband and frowned. "Is she sick?"

"I would imagine so." Zander squeezed her shoulder.

Across the other side of the group, Badger put his arm around Hannah. Lana was Nora and Hannah's mother and the mother of their teammate Isaac, who was currently in federal prison.

Judah didn't like the sound of it. "So she's trading Soraya like a commodity?" That wasn't any better than what Raleigh did with her. "This has to be some kind of bait and switch, like every other time she's asked for something."

Zander shrugged. "Every time she hands over information, it gives us a lead."

"Only because she knows more than we do. But can she share all of it? No, because that means we don't need her anymore."

"Either way, she'll be at the airport in a couple of hours." Zander's expression hardened. "That means we have time to make a plan. I don't want Lana around innocent people here at the hospital, or at the house, just in case she's targeted."

"We can put her in the bunker under the warehouse," Hannah suggested.

Zander shook his head. "I don't want her anywhere near our home." He glanced over where Aria stood huddled with her mom, all of them worried over Eas's prognosis.

"What about the cabin?" Andre said. "We can take shifts on detail. Keep an eye on the place, and make sure Windemere doesn't get hurt."

Judah took a half step back and sank into a chair. "Is it wrong that I don't want her anywhere near this town? Whether she's hurt or not, I don't know why I should care." Then he realized two of Lana's children were listening and winced. Probably he shouldn't have said that out loud, considering it likely sounded heartless.

The truth was, he wanted to see Soraya. Especially if Lana was willing to use her as a trading piece.

The last place she should be was with a woman like that when she was in danger. Chevalier could protect her. Lana didn't care about Soraya as much as he did. Judah might not know her well, but he cared about Soraya. Was Lana even capable of it?

The rest of the team had found relationships in the last few months. The fact that he was the last one still single was something Judah hadn't thought about much. The last thing he needed to do was latch on to the first eligible woman who came along. How could he know it was the real thing and not just him reaching for something he didn't have?

He needed to sort out his own feelings. But if Soraya needed to be kept safe, she should absolutely be with Chevalier. Not Lana.

"This is a game to her," Zander said. "Whether we want to play or not, Lana dragged us into this. There might not be anything we can do. But if she's calling us before anyone else, then it means she's got her back up against the wall." He shifted to his wife, and they faced each other. "Do you want to talk to her if she's ill?"

Nora nodded. She glanced at Hannah, but Andre spoke before Nora could say anything. "This has to be a trap. It has been practically every other time she came to us."

"The stakes are different this time," Hannah said. "We all want to take down Raleigh. She knows that, which means whatever she's giving us in exchange for medical treatment, it'll be useful."

Judah winced. They were talking about Soraya in the same vein as Lana was willing to use her.

He couldn't stay here and sit around when this was supposed to be about holding a vigil for Eas, and praying he would wake up soon. The doctor had told them his brain had swollen from the impact of debris falling on him. Considering they weren't too far from southern Utah, he'd been stable enough to be transported home from that disaster zone. But sitting around waiting was worse.

Judah pushed out of the seat and strode away from his friends. In a way, it seemed as though he hadn't been gone for weeks. And at the same time, it felt so foreign being here. He didn't know what to do with the feeling, even though the guys had told him everything was squared away.

Ted was currently holed up in his office, looking for anything he could find about Uzhas—the organization of assassins Isaac's father had run. Never mind that Ted was supposed to get married in a matter of days. When the wedding date was picked, no one thought the team would have to fight against a multinational corporation being overtaken by the former president.

There were so many things going on and so many people involved, Judah could hardly get it all straight in his head.

He jabbed at the button for the elevator. The closest one dinged. The doors slid open, and his sister strode out, along with her fiancé.

He'd been waiting for her to show up since he got back to town. But now that she was here, Judah couldn't even stomach having to talk about everything all over again. If Travers got anywhere near her, he didn't know what he was going to do.

"Jude—"

His back hit the wall, and he realized he'd retreated all the way across the elevator lobby. All he could see in his mind was that photo they'd shown him. The things they said they'd do to Toni and Jeff, if he didn't comply.

Judah's knees gave out, and they caught him—his sister on one side and his future brother-in-law on the other. Then his backside hit the tile floor, and the two of them sank down on either side of him.

His sister touched his cheek. "Talk to me."

He shook his head, swallowing back the lump in his throat.

"You know what happens when you bottle it up. You have to get it out, Jude."

Jeff squeezed his arm. As though he was content to sit

there for as long as it took. Much like Judah's sister would, but only because that was precisely how stubborn she was.

Beyond the two of them and this huddle, the rest of Chevalier and their significant others stood talking. Except for Karina and Aria, who were waiting to hear if Eas was going to be okay. And now things were getting worse again. Lana wanted to make a trade for Soraya. Who knew where Raleigh was and what he had up his sleeve?

The minister's words echoed in his head still. It seemed as though he'd done nothing but talk the whole time Judah stayed there.

He closed his eyes, but all he could see were those kids at that breakfast table. No family. No home.

Toni swiped her thumb over his cheek. "You need to talk."

She thought he was bottling it up? "I already told Zander everything," Judah said.

"The facts, right?" She squeezed the back of his neck. "Not the real stuff."

"I did a full debrief."

"That's what I'm talking about," she said.

Judah shook his head. "The first time I've seen you in weeks, and you're going to get all up in my face?"

"There's a reason we're all sitting on the floor, Jude." Toni wasn't going to let this go.

He wanted to push them away and stand, but that would only make things worse. The whole team would see him break down. Now that he was back, things were supposed to be fine. Normal.

"Tell me what you need."

He squeezed his eyes shut. Instead of those kids, this time, he saw Soraya's face. Her wide, fearful eyes mirrored everything inside of him as they fought together. Survived together.

He couldn't latch onto her. He wasn't going to find something real with the first woman who showed up in his life in a long time who brought with her the promise of everything he wanted. Life just didn't work like that.

"Jude—"

He opened his eyes. "I need Soraya."

Before anyone could say anything, Zander made a declaration. "I'll call Lana back. We're making the trade."

SORAYA DIDN'T BOTHER LOOKING out the airplane window. She was too wound up anyway and had been since she heard Lana on the phone telling whoever was on the other end that she would trade Soraya for medical care.

The only reason Lana hadn't been forced to tie Soraya up was that she had zero intention of being abducted again. If she was going anywhere, then it was because she chose to. Not because anyone forced her. If she was going to go with these people and not find the first opportunity to make a run for it, that would be her decision. She wouldn't be on this plane if Lana hadn't assured her these were the people from the facility. The ones who'd come to find her, along with their friend Judah.

Would he be with them now?

The plane touched down, jolting her in her seat. Lana had laid down hours ago. Since then, she had been in and out of consciousness in a way that worried Soraya. As soon as the airplane came to a stop, she unbuckled her seatbelt and crouched beside the other woman.

She touched Lana's shoulder. "We're here."

Her voice sounded scared, even to her own ears. The last thing she wanted to do was think about what her life had become. She'd done enough of that while she waited for her legs to feel better over the last couple of days.

Maybe it would never be better. Soraya certainly hoped

she could find a measure of happiness, no matter what happened.

But Lana didn't wake up.

Not even when the pilot opened the door and the stairs lowered.

The first man through the door held a pistol, his face familiar. This was the one who had pulled her from the rubble.

Soraya let out a breath she'd been holding. "Is that for me?"

She motioned to the gun, wondering if he intended to shoot her.

He looked around, then stowed it in a holster under his arm and glanced out the door. "It's clear." He turned back to her. "In case you forgot, I'm Zander."

Was she supposed to introduce herself? The less they knew about her the better, but that was probably futile.

The suited man who entered had graying hair and a distinguished look about him. He smiled in a way that was professional and nothing else. "I'm Doctor Windermere."

"I'm the collateral." Soraya hadn't meant for it to sound like that, but what else was she going to say? Wherever she was, she put the people around her in danger. Then she was traded like a set piece.

"And the patient?" Windermere spoke as though she hadn't said that.

Soraya motioned to the seat. "She hasn't regained consciousness in a couple of hours. She said it could be poison."

"Do you know what substance?" He crouched and put two fingers to Lana's neck.

Soraya shook her head. Should she have checked for Lana's pulse? "She didn't know what it was. She said it happened a couple of weeks ago."

Two more guys came in, the Hispanic one she'd seen

before and another guy with long hair carrying a backboard. They loaded Lana onto it and hauled her out. Yet more people came in, including Judah, then a black woman whose features resembled Judah's and a man with one arm.

She stared at him, soaking in his presence in a way she hadn't realized she would when she saw him. Part of her had wondered if he was even alive. Now he was here—one of these people. The kind who had accepted *her* in payment for medical services.

The guy named Zander took a step closer.

Soraya backed up.

"Z." Judah stayed him with a hand and motioned for them all to step back. Then he looked at her. "It's okay."

"I can't believe—" She stopped herself before any more came out. These people didn't need to hear her whining. Not when everything in her burned at them—and the world. It took Soraya a second to realize now that Lana was gone, being taken care of, she was actually angry at the woman.

While Lana was here, Soraya's off-the-charts empathy wouldn't let her get mad. She'd been worried if Lana would even survive.

Now that she was gone, all Soraya could think was that to save herself, Lana had given up Soraya.

"I know." Judah nodded. Then he motioned to the people behind him. "Believe me, we all know what it's like to be traded around by Lana."

And yet, they'd accepted her in payment. Even knowing that.

Judah continued, "We know that she exchanged you for medical care, but you're free to leave whenever you want."

The one-armed guy started to argue, but Judah shot him a look that shut the man up.

Soraya shuddered. "Travers will abduct me again. Or kill me."

Being with Lana had made her feel safe. But now there

was no one. Just a bunch of people she didn't know, and one she was very much attracted to. As much as she might want to rely on them, it was clear they had people in their lives they cared about. Vulnerable people.

She didn't want to put anyone else in danger.

"Stay with us," Judah said. "We'll keep you safe, and you can help us take Raleigh down."

"You don't know what he's like."

His brows rose.

She shook her head. "Okay, you know what he's like. You were there, too."

He frowned. "What did they do to you, Soraya?"

She shook her head and felt the burn of tears in her eyes. It was nothing worse than what they'd done to him. Why should it impact her so much more than he seemed to be affected by it?

He took a couple of steps closer to her. "You're safe with us."

"No, I'm not. I'm not safe anywhere." She shook her head. "If I'm here with you, everyone you care about is in danger. I can't let that happen."

The one-armed man said, "I like this girl."

Judah glanced over his shoulder. "Can you guys give us a sec?" He didn't even sound frustrated.

Zander flicked two fingers, and the one-armed guy called out, "Bro, tell her about your bacon sandwiches." Then they all left the airplane.

Judah turned back to Soraya. As he took another step, a muscle flicked in his jaw.

She wanted to ask what that comment had been about but didn't know if she could speak.

"We want the same thing," he said. "Even Lana does, although she'll do what we never would to get it."

Soraya swallowed. "And what is it we all want?"

"To stop Raleigh." He paused. "Everyone here knows the

risks. If we work together, the threat is spread across all of us so it's less for one person to carry."

"I'm supposed to put you all in danger and let you help me just so it's easier for me?" How could she do that when she had basically been passed to them as an asset? She'd thought going to Lana was the right thing.

"The fact you don't want to put us in danger is why we want to do it."

"Because you're so altruistic?" she asked.

"Raleigh and everyone who works for him has caused our family a lot of hurt and pain. One of my friends is in the hospital, and he might not wake up. None of us is willing to let Raleigh get away with this. He has to be stopped."

"That's what I was trying to do." Soraya sighed. "He destroyed my life and threatened my family."

"And yet, you managed to land in the perfect spot to take him down. Even despite everything that happened, or how you got here, you're right where you're supposed to be."

Soraya bit her lip. She didn't want this to be about the attraction between them. She didn't even know if he felt it. Maybe it was just her. Totally one-sided.

She felt a tear roll down her cheek.

He lifted a hand and swiped it away with his thumb. "I did that a lot today. But only because my sister ambushed me and everything rushed out in one go. All that we went through together, and everything that happened after." He winced. "I have this habit of pushing on and refusing to process. Eventually, it smacks me in the face."

"Even after she traded me to you guys, I still didn't want anything bad to happen to Lana. She saved my life. And now she did this? I don't know how I'm supposed to feel about her. But whatever it is, there's a lot of it."

"Where you are right now, you're safe to feel whatever you want to feel." His expression softened, and she watched his lips curl up. "The situation with Lana is complicated at best.

None of us are sure what to do with her. But there are plenty of people here for you to talk it over with. And together, we can make a plan."

"How am I supposed to take down Raleigh? I'm just a reporter, and he's taken everything from me."

Judah held out his hand. "Maybe a reporter is exactly what we need."

She stared at his palm.

"What do you say?" he asked. "Do you want to help us take him down?"

It was like he offered her the promise of being as strong as he was. Everything she didn't have, there in the palm of his hand.

Soraya laid her hand in his and held on. "Yes, I do."

18

———————

Hannah Yassick stared at the DNA test results on the computer screen long enough her eyes burned. She blinked, but the result didn't change no matter what she did.

Former president Raleigh was her father.

"Can you take a look at something for me?" She glanced up at Ted, the Chevalier Protection Specialists tech guy and all-around genius.

Hannah hit ALT-TAB, so the screen changed to her other open window, which happened to be her bank account. That was a sadder story than the latest turn her life had taken. She said, "What's that?"

Ted reached over and tapped the keyboard in front of her. An old Interpol file popped up on screen.

Her eyes widened. "Are you supposed to have access to this?"

Ted winced. "Just don't call the cops on me before I get married on Saturday. If anything happens, and I don't make it to that aisle, Jess will hunt me down and murder me herself."

"And then I'll be calling the cops on her." Hannah pointed out. She might not be a police detective anymore, but Ted's fiancé was. Jessica Ridgeman, who was about to become

Jessica Cartwright, worked for the Last Chance County Police Department.

"If you can find her." His eyebrows lifted above the fall of hair over his forehead.

"I'm sure plenty of people would be looking."

Warmth softened his features, despite the topic of conversation.

"What did you want me to look at?" Hannah needed a good distraction while the rest of the team headed to the airport to get the reporter Soraya Adams. They were also going to drive Windermere to the hospital so Lana could be treated in a private wing guarded by heavy security.

Raleigh didn't need to know that Lana was in Last Chance County.

No one needed a war on the home front.

Ted tapped a couple more keys. "This Interpol file is for Yuri Amrakov."

"Isaac's father?" It had to have been part of the giant packet of information they'd just received by file transfer.

Ted nodded. "There's a detailed rundown of all his holdings before he 'died.'" He made air quotes. "If you could go through it, cross-referencing the location where Judah was sent to find him, that would be a big help."

"Great." Hannah realized how that might've sounded and glanced up at Ted. "That wasn't sarcastic."

"I know." He returned to his desk, grabbed the chair, and wheeled it over. He sat by the corner of her desk. "Believe me when I say that I know how hard it is when you have a criminal for a family member. And when you know there's a chance you might see them, but you have no idea what you're going to say when you do."

Hannah winced. She'd heard the story of Ted, his brother Dean, and their father. "I know you do. And you're right, it is hard." She blew out a breath. "I want to talk to her. But we did that already, so what else is there to say? She handed me a gun and money. Like those were the answer to what I needed."

"Does anybody ever think their parent understands what they really need?" He made a face.

Hannah felt the bubble of laughter rise in her. "I think you might have a point there." She managed to smile.

Out in the hallway she heard the commotion of the rest of the team returning. Nora hadn't gone with them to the airport, but the others did. Now they were coming back with Soraya.

Hannah wanted to talk to the reporter again. They'd seen each other for a few moments before that facility exploded all around them. And now Hannah knew why Raleigh kept her there, so she could be his company spokesperson. But why do that and then try to kill her?

Zander strode in first. "You got everything Lana transferred over?"

Hannah nodded. It had happened as soon as the agreement was made.

"It's already proven useful," Ted said.

"Good." Zander motioned to the door. "Hannah?"

She got up and turned to Ted. "I'll be back in a minute to help. More coffee?"

He grinned. "You know it."

She took his empty mug and turned to Zander. "Any prognosis on when Eas might regain consciousness?"

"Windermere is going to check on him when he has Lana settled." He led the way to the living area of the house, where everyone was gathered, except Eas and his family.

Badger crossed the room and handed her bottled water. She made a face, because coffee had water in it, but drank some anyway.

"How is she?" Nora stood in the doorway.

Zander held out his hand.

She crossed to him and took it.

"Windermere doesn't know what she was poisoned with," he said, "but he can run some tests to try and find out."

The door opened again. Judah came in, leading the woman Hannah recognized from the facility. Someone who had spent more time with Hannah's mother than she had.

The emotion that rose in her was hot and nauseating. Hannah didn't like the sensation at all. It wasn't like her, or at least it wasn't usually like her. Given the one conversation she'd had with Hannah's mother, something about this woman meant Lana took Soraya under her wing.

Hannah stared at her, trying to see from the outward what that might be.

She didn't find anything.

Zander spoke again to Nora. "As soon as Windemere says you're good, you can go to the hospital and be with her."

They had to have talked about this, so Zander knew Nora wanted to see her mother. Her half-sister glanced at her. Nora had a particular look on her face, that older sister thing she seemed to do so naturally.

Hannah shook her head. If her mother wanted anything to do with her, it was up to Lana. She wasn't going to seek the woman out and get blown off all over again, given a handout and told to go on her way. Sure, Lana and her people had saved Hannah's life from a group of cartel crazies. But that didn't mean her mother wanted a relationship with her.

Badger tugged her under his shoulder. He knew how she felt. As much as she loved both him and these people who were her family now, there was still a hole in her even her adoptive parents hadn't managed to fill.

What is she like?

Hannah shook off the question. "I want to go online or on a news program. I'm going to tell everyone that Raleigh is my father."

While the room full of people absorbed that statement,

she considered it further. Yeah, so she'd spoken without thinking it through first.

Hannah had been in the news enough that some people would know who she was. She wasn't a complete unknown. Or someone everyone thought was crazy.

"Hannah."

She glanced up at Badger. "What?"

"You're just going to drop a bomb like that with no fore-thought?"

Geez, it was like he thought she was supposed to be a better person or something.

He grinned as though he knew her thoughts.

Hannah decided to move the conversation along instead of getting into that. "You think I haven't gone over it? I've been doing that ever since I found out." Then she spiraled into thoughts that her birth parents—Lana and Raleigh, the man they were up against—might have rubbed off on her. Or gifted her something, at least on the genetic level. "They want a fight? I'm going to use everything at my disposal to hit back at them."

She could see the concern in Badger's eyes. Concern for *her.* "But at what cost?"

"I don't care. They're not counting the cost of what they're doing." Hannah shrugged one shoulder as if no one were listening to their conversation. "So we hit back at Raleigh, and we get him scrambling to cover himself. If it's enough of a blow, then he's off his game. There's a chance we might be able to catch him on something."

She hoped that "something" would be in the packet of information Lana had sent to Ted that she had handed over along with Soraya in exchange for medical care. But wouldn't Lana have already used it if she had proof that could bring down Raleigh?

That meant Lana was desperate, unable to operate

because she needed medical care, and was looking for them to do the hard work for her.

"None of them will expect it." Hannah glanced around at the Chevalier team members.

"You don't think we should focus on the files she sent over?" Lucia said. "And what about talking to Soraya, getting as much as we can to use to bring down Raleigh?"

The reaction was visible. Judah sidestepped closer to Soraya, covering her.

Guess we know where you stand.

"That's what they think we'll be doing because that's what they've given us to do," Hannah said. "How can you guarantee this isn't just more manipulation? Lana has only ever used us for her own ends."

"Does she know Amrakov was alive a few days ago?" Judah asked them.

Hannah glanced over. "Do you know he's dead for sure now?"

"I saw him get shot."

"People saw him die the last time," Hannah paused. "And yet, he was still alive."

Judah opened his mouth, then closed it again.

Zander spoke up. "I already have someone verifying that. There's enough personnel in this room that we can tag-team everything. Judah, you and Soraya talk through everything you guys know. Andre and Lucia can take their statements. I want everything that happened from when Badger and Judah were taken until now."

There were several nods around the room.

Zander continued, "I'll work with Ted on the files. Hannah and Badger, figure out how we would release the information that Hannah is Raleigh's daughter. If we decide to go ahead with it, we need to know how to maximize the reveal to our advantage."

Any other time that would have sounded emotionless, as

would her suggesting it in the first place. But given it was her own suggestion, Hannah was all in to bring down Raleigh by whatever means necessary. She nodded. "Got it."

Badger frowned, but she was certain that he would see her point. At least if they talked it through. They didn't have to agree on everything, but if their relationship was going to work, he would need to understand where she was coming from. The same as she would do with him.

Nora said, "I think you're all forgetting about something."

Zander shook his head. "What's that?"

Nora set her hands on her hips. "The fact you all have appointments for tuxedo fittings at six o'clock." She glanced around the room. "And none of you is going to be late."

Judah shifted, turning to Soraya. "I don't suppose you're free on Saturday night, and you'd like to be my date for a wedding?"

Andre muttered something under his breath about bad ideas for first dates.

Hannah needed to pick up Aria and Karina's dresses in town. She'd promised she would, and it was more of a priority than taking care of Raleigh. As much as she wanted to be done with all of this danger so they could get to some peace and quiet. "The wedding is everyone's priority until Saturday. After that? Whatever we've got, we run with."

They were all hoping Eas at least woke up before then. Even if he couldn't attend the wedding, there could at least be good news.

Zander lifted his brows.

"Assuming…that's your order for the team. Which you run. Because you're the one in charge." Hannah winced.

"That's what I thought." Zander's serious face lasted for a second, then he grinned and looked at everyone. "What Hannah said goes."

Andre didn't seem to think that was especially funny, but everyone else did.

Judah said, "I'll put the kettle on, and we can all get to work."

As they dispersed, Nora came over. "When she's stable, do you want to go to the hospital with me and see Lana?"

Hannah had gone with her to meet their brother, Isaac. But this? She shook her head. "I think I just want to focus on Raleigh right now."

Before any of them could argue with her, Hannah strode from the room.

Like a coward.

19

Judah held still while the tailor eased in the sharp end of a pin in a spot where he didn't exactly want to get stuck.

The tailor sat back on his heels. "Okay, let's take a look at this."

While the tailor assessed his handiwork, Zander pushed aside the curtain of one of the dressing rooms and stepped out in his suit trousers and the white shirt he was wearing for the wedding. All of the guys in Chevalier were acting as ushers for Ted's wedding while Ted's brother Dean was his best man.

The two brothers sat beside each other on plastic chairs in the corner of the room, talking intently. Probably about everything that had come in from Lana. Ted even had a tablet in front of him, which meant he probably hadn't quit working even though they were currently getting fitted for tuxedos for the ceremony on Saturday.

"Everything good?" Zander asked.

Judah got the impression he wasn't asking about the tuxedo trousers. "Fine."

Ted and Dean got up from their chairs and came over. Badger and Andre emerged from their dressing rooms, and the tailor mumbled something about getting everyone an espresso.

Judah surveyed their collective expressions. "You guys are ganging up on me. You want me to lose it again, just so that you can feel like you're doing something to help me."

Dean shook his head. *Of course.* The guy was a counselor. He just happened to also be a qualified EMT and a former Navy SEAL. "That's not what's happening here. No one wants to see you having a hard time. We just don't want to see you bottling it up either."

Judah crossed his arms over his chest. "Maybe that's just how I deal with things. I take a long time to process, and I do it in my head."

"That's not dealing," Andre said. "Believe me, I should know."

Judah figured that was true, considering Andre had been married for years. Until Lucia showed up, none of them—except Zander and Badger, who had heard mention of it years ago—had even known about her. Or that Lucia and Andre had been estranged for most of their marriage.

"Maybe I should call Toni." Zander didn't reach for his phone, though.

"I don't need my sister here," Judah shot back.

"Because she'll see right through you?" Ted asked. "Trust me when I say I know something about older siblings. Ones you can't pull the wool over the eyes of. Things usually work out, but you have to be honest."

"It's not like I'm lying," Judah pointed out. "I told you guys everything that happened."

Only now all they had was a bunch of information and some possible leads. Things they needed to follow up on as soon as the wedding was over. They would bring down Raleigh. It was just that they would do what was right for their family first. That meant supporting Ted before they took care of business.

"You've been quiet since the hospital." Badger pinned him with a look.

"And you haven't?" Judah countered.

"None of us liked seeing Eas like that." Zander motioned with a hand. "Not knowing when he's going to wake up is the worst part. He's missing all of this. Life going on around him, and things moving on. He doesn't get to be part of taking down Raleigh. He might miss celebrating the next step in Ted's life."

Judah blinked away the burn of tears. "You know, this has never happened to me before. Except when Toni was in the hospital, after our uncle tried to kill her."

"What's never happened?" Ted asked.

Judah glanced around, then settled his gaze on the man getting married on Saturday. "Caring about people really sucks."

There were a couple of chuckles and a groan.

Judah blew out a breath. "I need a cup of tea."

Zander said, "Don't we all."

But Judah wondered if that was what it was. Given the fact Soraya was at the house, resting up and being interviewed by Hannah and Lucia he had to consider that her arrival had spurned all this. Or it was Ted's wedding. Knowing his friend was moving on, taking hold of the things that would make him happy. Or both. Meeting her. Finding himself at this point in his life.

Watching everyone around him settle.

It wasn't lost on Judah that everyone seemed to be pairing off with other people lately. Now he was the only one left, and he had to buy wedding gifts. Baby shower presents. Watch his sister plan her own ceremony.

Meanwhile, he'd been stuck for years, waiting for British SIS to track him down and call in their favor.

At least now he could honestly say he owed them nothing. That slate was wiped clean as far as he was concerned.

But this business with Raleigh was far from over. All he could do was pray that Travers Industries didn't make a move before Saturday or *on* Saturday. The last thing any of them needed was for something to disrupt the wedding.

The bell rang over the door, and Jeff walked in. His future brother-in-law clocked the whole scene, lifted his chin, and said, "Do they make these things with one arm or what?"

Judah said, "Either way, you might as well just buy one. No point renting it."

"You think I need a penguin suit?" Jeff came over to him.

"Because my sister is going to let you marry her in anything else? Or me?"

"I'm not marrying you. No matter if you ask nicely."

Judah rolled his eyes. "You know what I mean."

He gave Jeff a playful shove in the shoulder that had an arm attached. The other one had been blown off when an IED exploded, an event Zander had been present at. Along with Judah's sister, though none of them knew it at the time.

Judah said, "My sister isn't marrying some guy in jeans." When Jeff got in that accident, Judah had been halfway across the world with no idea his sister was working covert operations.

"Guess I am getting stuck with a needle as well, then." Jeff grinned.

Andre wandered over. "It's called 'tailoring,' bro."

Jeff said, "I thought that was for when married life made you soft around the middle."

Andre hooked an arm over Jeff's shoulders and pulled him into a loose headlock. Jeff punched him repeatedly in that not-so-soft middle.

Zander clapped his hands twice. "Now, now, children. It's story time, so take your seats."

The guy altering all of their tuxedos stared at them as though he wasn't sure what to make of a bunch of huge guys with their reputations standing around cracking jokes.

Judah let out a long breath and sat on the edge of the platform. The prick of the needle somewhere sensitive made him wince, but he didn't let anyone know. Except the tailor raised his brows. "We can get to that in a minute."

Zander motioned to him. "What is it?"

He wanted to say that he still didn't like that they were all here and Eas wasn't. Never mind that he had spent the last few hours in the hospital holding vigil with Karina. Aria had returned from her shift at work that the high schooler hadn't been able to get covered. They'd had their appointment for tuxedo fittings, and there was no change in Eas's situation, so they asked her to call if anything happened.

Instead, Judah said, "I want to be the one to tell Isaac about his father."

The guys all reacted in their own ways. It was clear none of them envied him the job of telling their former teammate that his father hadn't been dead. And yet, even though he'd been alive all this time, he was now dead. No matter what Hannah thought, Judah was sure Yuri Amrakov had been killed.

Unless MI-6 somehow faked his death.

The Brits would have no doubt co-opted him into working for them if that was true. But it was more likely to be Raleigh and Travers Industries. They were the ones who'd known where the head of Uzhas had been this entire time. They'd sent the British on a wild goose chase, feeding them false information, and meanwhile directed Judah to kill him. His friend's father. A man Isaac believed was dead. Instead of Judah carrying out the mission, the target was the one who was killed. But Judah had escaped before he could be killed as well.

Not just that, but the minute Chevalier showed up at the facility where he and Soraya had been held, Raleigh escaped and destroyed the whole place.

"I already got you on the visitor's roster," Zander said. "First thing Monday morning."

Judah had to bite the inside of his lip. His eyes were burning again.

Jeff bumped Judah's shoulder with his. "If everyone is busy, Toni and I will go with you."

"Thanks." Judah glanced from Jeff to Zander, who nodded. Good. Both of them agreed that Judah's family would be nowhere near this. "I appreciate it." He had to say it, even though he had no intention of taking Jeff up on his offer.

After all, the guy had a business to run.

And Judah was going to look out for the people he cared about, no matter what it took.

NORA SET the mug on the table in front of Soraya.

"Thank you." She knew who this woman was, given Soraya had covered the story of Stephen Gladstone. That article had recounted his entire life and career all the way to the revelation of his criminal activity and finally his death in prison.

Soraya figured this wasn't the right time to tell Nora she already knew everything about her. Well, everything about her father, at least. And Nora's part in his life.

What Nora had now was something entirely different. Even after finding out her non-profit was a front for her father's illegal business, Nora had managed to build a life. She was married to Zander, and the two of them seemed very happy. Plus, if Soraya wasn't mistaken, Nora was in the first trimester of pregnancy.

Which would also be awkward to bring up.

Hannah and Lucia sat on the other side of the table. Nora took the seat at the head.

Soraya shook her head. "Why do I get the impression maybe I should call my lawyer?" She glanced at Nora and smiled.

Nora returned it. "Not from me, right?"

"No, but the two of them?" Soraya left that comment hanging and pointed at Hannah and Lucia.

"I know what you mean," Nora said. "That's because Hannah, who is my half-sister, was a police detective. Lucia was a DEA agent."

"Ah. That's why you're supposed to take my statement since the guys are busy."

Hannah nodded. She didn't seem inclined to ask a question, though.

It was Lucia who said, "I know you're anticipating I'm going to ask about Raleigh and everything that happened with him. But we'll get to that."

Soraya was glad for it. Even just the mention of his name made her shiver.

"You're the first person we've met who has spent time recently with Lana," Lucia said. "There were a few days between when we saw you at the facility and when you arrived today. Can you tell us where you were?"

Soraya frowned. "A hospital. But I don't know where it was. Then she drove me to a rental house, and we stayed there for a few days. I could see she was getting worse, but she kept denying how bad it was."

Finally, Lana had admitted it was poison.

Nora stared at her fingers holding onto the handle of her mug. Soraya took a sip of her drink. Not the tea she wanted Judah to make her.

He'd been mentioning it so much she couldn't wait to try some. Then again, what if she didn't like it?

Maybe it would be a dealbreaker.

No, there were far too many things to think about right now other than a relationship between her and Judah.

Everyone here was preparing for the wedding on Saturday. After that, all of them would work hard to stop Raleigh—hopefully without further loss of life.

"What was she like?"

Nora's question came out of nowhere, surprising Soraya. She wasn't sure how to answer it and settled on, "Lonely, maybe. I felt like she was lying low. But every other time I saw her, she was surrounded by people in tactical gear carrying weapons. It was different seeing her in workout clothes and pajamas. Watching movies and eating popcorn."

They had both been recovering. It should have been relaxing, yet neither of them had really engaged—either with each other or with the attempt to entertain themselves.

Hannah sat back in her chair. "Watching movies?"

Soraya winced. "There weren't any books in the house." She shook her head because that was a crime as far as she was concerned. Especially considering that she hadn't been able to bring her e-reader with her. She usually read a book every day or two.

Lately it seemed like she couldn't concentrate on someone else's story no matter how hard she tried. It was such a strange feeling she'd even done an internet search on her symptoms, just in case there was something wrong with her.

Not being able to read just felt wrong.

Except for the possibility she might be addicted to reading—even if she could stop whenever she wanted to, thank you very much—there wasn't anything wrong with her. As far as vices went, reading was more cozy than dangerous. Especially this time of year when snow fell outside, and sipping a cup of peppermint hot chocolate sounded nice.

If there wasn't a psychotic former president trying to destroy them.

"I don't understand her at all." Hannah pushed back from the table and got up. She paced away a few steps, then came back. She set both fists on the table and leaned forward like a dog about to bite. "Just tell me she at least mentioned any of us."

Soraya winced. She couldn't imagine what it was like to have that kind of relationship with her mother. "I know when I met you guys at that facility that I didn't want to drag you into all this if you weren't already part of it."

"It's too late for that," Lucia said.

Soraya nodded. "I know now. But you seemed like nice people, so I wanted to keep you out of it if I could."

Lucia glanced at Hannah. "Maybe she's just a terrible judge of character."

"Speak for yourself." Hannah straightened. "I'm nice."

"*Nora* is nice," Lucia said. "You and I are cops."

Before she could continue, Nora said, "Thank you."

"So I'm not even on the scale?" Hannah lifted her hands, then let them fall back to her sides.

Lucia smirked. "Wherever you are on the scale, make some space for me too. Because I'm right there with you."

"The question is…," Hannah began.

Lucia finished. "Where is Soraya on the nice scale?"

"In time," Nora said. "I'm sure we'll learn for ourselves." She looked at them as though she were the teacher and Hannah and Lucia were the students.

Soraya was impressed. Again, she didn't need time to see what was clear about these people. "Is there a spot on the scale for 'I was trying to do the right thing, but I didn't think I'd get in this over my head'?"

Lucia and Hannah glanced at each other, then turned back to Soraya and said, "Yes," in tandem.

Nora smiled.

Soraya wanted to be friends with them, but this situation was strange. She felt like the whole world was some foreign land where she didn't speak the language. "I didn't think Lana would just trade me to you guys. She said she would help me take him down."

"Have you been looking into him long?" Hannah asked.

Soraya knew the former president was Hannah's father. But it was only because Judah had told her that she wasn't surprised by the information. "Long enough to know Travers should never release that phone system. It will give Raleigh and the company ultimate control over all the information contained in it. He'll be able to manipulate anything and everything he wants." She took a breath. "And long enough for him to realize I'm onto him and discredit me. They came after me and tried to kill me."

"And Lana helped you stay alive?" Lucia asked.

Soraya nodded. "She was probably using me from the beginning. Keeping me safe was a means to an end because I had something she didn't."

"I thought you gave her the chip before you went to Africa?" Lucia asked.

"True," Soraya said. "She's the one who had the chip in the first place. After she realized I was looking into Travers and getting too close to something, she had me take it to a contact I made. But he was with Travers. The only thing for me to do was lay low and get out of the country. That's how I met Judah."

All that trying to cover herself. Protect herself. It would be for nothing if the fallout hurt people.

"You're right." Hannah nodded. "She probably did use you. But Lana wouldn't have kept you around so long if she hadn't formed some kind of attachment. I'm not going to say she cared about you because we don't know if she's even capable of it. In her own way, though, she did the right thing. Which means she had a reason to make sure you lived."

"I don't know what to do with that."

Nora reached over and laid her hand on Soraya's. "It's the same thing Hannah and I have to do with the fact she left for a life that didn't include us. Make peace with it as much as we can."

Hannah glanced over at her. "How's that working for you?"

Nora looked down her nose at the younger woman, her half-sister. "I have no comment."

Both of them grinned. Lucia rolled her eyes, and Soraya exhaled her first full breath since she arrived here. Even though Lana had essentially betrayed her to these people in exchange for medical care, maybe they were right. Lana may very well have been taking care of her the best she could.

Soraya said, "She left me with people who are kind and entirely capable of protecting me."

Nora eyed her. "Are you asking if she did that with us, as well?"

Soraya shrugged. "I don't know much about it."

Hannah worked her mouth from side to side. "Maybe she did."

Lana had left Soraya in the hands of people with the capability, will, and integrity to get this done. She just hoped and prayed the cost wouldn't be too high.

20

———

Judah stirred the chunks of lamb and onions around the pan. Behind it, on the stove, potatoes boiled. Once those were done, he was going to mash them to make the top layer of the dish.

Zander wandered into the kitchen, sniffed, and then smiled. "Shepherd's pie?"

Judah nodded. "Should be enough for everyone, with plenty of leftovers for tomorrow's lunch."

"Good. We might need it before we head over to the church for the service."

Since the appointment with the tailor, most everyone had been researching Travers and Raleigh and everything they were up to. Trying to find a way to pin something on them. Otherwise, they were never going to convince anyone the rollout of this new phone system was anything other than a good thing.

Surely if Raleigh intended to control so much federal information, there had to be a pattern of behavior they could pull from to prove their suspicion. While it was possible that following the death of his wife, Raleigh had some kind of mental break, it was the least likely option. The rumors that surrounded his presidency suggested he tightly controlled information. Raleigh played the game of politics well, and many people had loved him.

Now he was just another businessman. One intent on his own agenda, with no boundaries over how he would get it done. And given everything that happened at that facility, it seemed as though Raleigh wanted everyone who knew the truth dead before the phone system was released.

"What's going on?" Zander asked.

Of course, he hadn't left. It figured he knew why Judah was making the dish his grandmother had taught him at twelve—the one he always made when he needed to think something through. He worked through the steps automatically, leaving his mind free to churn over what was happening around him.

Judah turned off the burner under the meat. He crossed his arms, leaned his hips back against the counter, and looked at his socks. The low-grade fear he'd been battling the last few days flared to life again.

"Jude," Zander prompted.

Judah nodded, then spat it out. "I know we have to be here for Ted's wedding, but this isn't a safe place. Raleigh knows we live here. If he even thinks we're alive, this is where he'll look for us first. For her."

"That's why our entire security system has been upgraded, and I have rotating teams walking the perimeter," Zander said. "We all know Soraya is the target. But it's a risk we're willing to absorb."

Judah glanced over at his boss. "After the wedding I think I'm going to make an appointment and talk to Dean. Figure out my head."

Toni hadn't been wrong about the fact he only pushed through and didn't bother to deal with everything that happened. But when too much occurred, it all came one after the other like dominoes falling on him.

There'd been no time to process. Not while he was scared, fighting for his life, and wanting to get back in the fold of his friends. Vulnerability wasn't a place he appreciated. Nor was going solo.

Judah needed people around him. He had to feel like he was part of something.

"You really like this girl." A small smile curled Zander's lips. Judah wondered if he was thinking about Nora back when they met. It was clear to everyone else on the team from the beginning that Nora had been unlike any other woman that *Zander* had met.

Judah started to shake his head but realized there wasn't much point denying it. "She isn't like anyone else."

"You're worried about her…or all of us?"

Maybe Judah was worried the team would realize how much Raleigh wanted Soraya and put her somewhere else. A place he couldn't watch her.

Judah didn't make shepherd's pie because he enjoyed the process. He could cook, but mostly it was boring and simply functional. No one wanted to eat toast or microwave stuff all the time. If he was going to eat, it would be something he enjoyed.

"Bro, get out of your head." Zander squeezed his shoulder. "Everything is tight. After the wedding tomorrow, we'll reassess and make a plan. There has to be a way to turn the tables on Raleigh."

"As long as it's not too late."

Soraya wandered in as far as the refrigerator and stopped. "Sorry. I didn't mean to interrupt."

"You're not." Judah shook his head. "I'm just making dinner."

Her expression shifted to something like wonder. As though he'd just told her he figured out how to perform surgery on a person without cutting them open.

She shifted her stance. "Travers Industries is about to start live-streaming their board meeting."

"You think the piece they had you record is going to be part of it?"

She nodded. "It felt like I was answering setup questions and giving a speech. Responding to things people said. I think they're going to edit it as though I'm there live."

"And you don't want to watch?" Zander said.

She shook her head.

Judah uncrossed his arms. "You can hang in here with me and help out. Assuming you can work a potato masher."

"I think I can handle it." She winked.

"I'll leave you guys to it." Zander passed her and then glanced back.

Whatever his expression was about, Judah just ignored it. Soraya wandered over. Judah stuck a fork in one of the potatoes. "Done. I'll get the colander."

"The what?"

Judah frowned. "The strainer?"

"Oh," she said. "I always just use the lid to drain the water over the sink."

"But then it inevitably slips, and you wind up with four potatoes down the drain." After he drained most of the water from the potatoes, Judah put the pan back on the stove.

"I didn't need those anyway." She grinned.

Judah fought against the tug that seemed intent on drawing him to her. As much as he didn't want to feel this pull, it was still there whether he liked it or not. "Why don't you tell me some of what Raleigh had to say about the phone system?"

She got a drink from the fridge. "The intro for the livestream has my picture on it, saying I'm the new head of public relations. The company spokesperson for new technology." She didn't twist the cap off the drink.

He moved to stand in front of her. "Tell me."

"It was all about how good the phone system is. How it's the best thing to keep America safe, and it's unhackable by the Chinese." She winced. "Like Raleigh didn't do a deal with them. He probably gave them a backdoor into it." She shook her head. "I could never prove that, so I don't know why I'm bringing it up now. We're supposed to be finding actual evidence. Not just more theories."

"It's okay to have hope. To believe that there is enough to dig up, and we'll be able to get this done." He knew how he would feel if he was being used the way she was.

Had Soraya been killed when the facility exploded, as Raleigh intended, the company would probably still do this and pretend she was alive. Maybe they didn't know she was. Travers would use her for marketing purposes regardless, to keep spouting the company line as an independent voice they had supposedly convinced around to their way of thinking.

They'd probably had Jerry Travers confined to that place, in his medical coma, for years. No one would ever know, now that the facility had been destroyed and the man they created to take his place was also dead.

"It seems strange to rely on people." She spoke softly. "I'm so used to working by myself."

"I like the team way better," he said. "Having people I can trust to watch my back, and we can work together."

In fact, he didn't like going alone at all. It tied into why his nature insisted he had a relationship even when one wasn't available. Romance sometimes took time, but his heart jumped for the first woman who came along every time. He just had to hold on while something solid built in its own time.

The way he always fell so hard and fast now just seemed cheap and flighty.

He didn't want to be that way with Soraya, as much as he was attracted to her and could see them having a relationship —because that would mean he got to kiss her.

She nodded, a small smile on her face. "I'm seeing that."

He shifted closer to her, and she didn't break the connection between them. He gave her ample opportunity to do it, just to be sure. "You want to be part of the team on this?" He paused, considering how she got here. "I know Lana handed you to us, and you can leave anytime you want—"

"Can I? I'm pretty sure Raleigh would have me killed or captured."

"There's always a risk. But you're safe here." He trusted Zander wouldn't do anything to put his pregnant wife at risk. Or any of the rest of them.

"And no one is distracted by this wedding happening tomorrow?"

"Speaking of which, do you want to be my plus one?" He'd already cleared it with Ted.

She smiled. "Nice deflection. And Hannah grabbed a dress for me when she was in town. I think they're all assuming I'll be there."

"It'll be the safest place. Unless you want to sit in the bunker."

She shook her head. "Not really."

Judah nodded. "Okay, then. Feel free to just come and hang out, I don't want to put any pressure on you to—"

Soraya closed the gap between them and pressed her lips to his.

Judah's reflex was to catch her up in his arms, but he forced himself to keep them by his sides. To let her guide this, whatever it was going to be. When she leaned back, he couldn't help but smile. "Don't apologize."

Her cheeks pinked.

"I've always jumped too fast into relationships. This, I'd like to take slow…if that's okay?"

She bit her lip. Nodded.

"I'd like to do this right." *For once.*

Because for whatever reason, this relationship seemed more important than any other.

I'D LIKE to do this right.

Judah's words replayed in her mind all the way to the hospital. Along with that look on his face and the feel of him.

Soraya had kissed him first. And while he hadn't outright rejected her, he hadn't pulled her to him or made any move to take things further. He'd left everything entirely in her control. And now that she had the chance to really overthink the whole thing, Soraya decided she liked that. Even if it also irritated her that he hadn't simply swept her away into his arms.

Now they were headed up in the elevator to the wing of the hospital where Dr. Windermere was treating Lana. Soraya shifted her weight, the ache in her shins making her want to find a chair. She was only here to provide support for Hannah and Nora. Both of them wanted to speak with their mother.

Everyone in Chevalier thought she should try and get Lana to open up. Given Lana had traded her to them in exchange for care, Soraya didn't want to hear what the woman had to say. It wasn't like they needed her to take Raleigh down.

Lana might think she was in the know, but no one could possibly understand everything. That would be impossible. Or it at least required an extensive network of people and resources.

The elevator doors opened.

Inside the hallway, two uniformed police officers guarded the darkened wing formerly part of the hospital. Nora greeted them both, but Soraya ignored the small talk in favor of trying to figure out what she was going to do next.

As they walked to the far end, she decided that whatever it might have been with her and Judah, it needed to be pushed out until after they took down Raleigh.

Why make this situation more complicated than it needed to be?

It wasn't as though she was good at relationships. She'd barely had one, just a handful of casual dates and nothing more to speak of. Now when she looked at Judah, it felt like electricity. For the first time, she understood what sparks were. Because that was exactly what she felt when she'd pressed her lips to his. Probably the reason why she'd done it in the first place.

Nora started to slow. Hannah did the same. Despite them being two very different women from different backgrounds, both were utterly consumed with nerves about facing their mother. Nora hadn't seen Lana since she was twelve. Hannah had only met her once, and the circumstances hadn't been exemplary. Now their mother was vulnerable, and it was clear neither one knew what to say to her. Especially if she might be dying.

Soraya figured it didn't matter when deep down every woman was that little girl who wanted to be loved by her mother. She said a prayer of thanks that her mom was just a mom—not the leader of a secret organization with questionable tactics and motives.

Nora came to a stop and turned to them in front of the door. "I don't know if I can——"

Soraya saw it was nothing but nerves. "I kissed Judah."

Nora gaped.

Hannah spun around with a similar expression on her face.

"I don't think he knew what to do with it." Soraya managed to chuckle. "I just laid one on him, and he let me. But he said he's interested, and he wants to take things slow."

Hannah snorted. "He'd be the first one of these boys to consider doing that. Not counting how Andre and Lucia ignored each other for years."

Nora turned to Hannah. "Is there something you need to tell everyone about you and Badger? Because I was thinking it's been a few weeks."

Hannah's eyebrows rose. "So we should be married, and then immediately pregnant, by now?"

Nora's cheeks flushed pink.

Before any of them could say more, Dr. Windermere stepped out of the room and closed the door behind him.

Nora and Hannah both leaned to look through the gap in the door, probably hoping to catch a glimpse of their mother.

Soraya said, "How is she?"

Windermere kept a placid expression on his face. Probably accustomed to doing so because of all his doctor training.

Delivering bad news couldn't be good, although it could be balanced with positive outcomes. She hoped he had more of the latter, but considering Eas was currently still unconscious, she wasn't sure that would be true right now.

"She's awake and is happy to talk to you." He glanced around.

Soraya wasn't sure who he was referring to specifically. Maybe he'd known they were all coming here and had asked Lana already.

Before either of the other two could change their minds, Soraya said, "Great. We'll head right in. What's her prognosis?"

"She's stable," Windermere said. "I'm treating her symptoms as best I can. But without knowing what she was poisoned with, I'm afraid I can't tell if there is an available remedy. And I may not discover the source before she's left unable to fight its onslaught."

Soraya nodded. "Thank you." She figured that meant if Hannah and Nora wanted to talk to her, then they should probably do it sooner rather than later. Otherwise, it would be too late.

Soraya pushed on the door and held it open for the other two. They came in much more slowly, guarded expressions on both their faces. Nora reached out and took Hannah's hand. Her pregnancy was barely noticeable. Had Soraya not already known that she was carrying a baby, she might not have guessed. But given everything else Lana was privy to, Soraya would be surprised if she didn't know that her daughter was pregnant.

The woman on the bed didn't look much like she had the last time Soraya had seen her. Dark circles ringed her eyes, casting shadows on her cheekbones. The blanket barely rose and fell with her breathing. Only the monitors beside the bed, and their steady beep, indicated she was alive.

Lana's eyes fluttered open.

Soraya stayed by the door while the other two moved to the bedside. The change in Lana was so stark Soraya had to search deep in those eyes for the woman she had been even just days ago. It was clear now how much she'd pretended to be fine.

What lay in the bed now was the honest truth.

Hannah spoke first. "Do you know who did this to you?"

Lana's gaze shifted to her younger daughter.

"If we can find them, we can find out what was used on you. The doctor will be able to reverse the damage."

Soraya wasn't sure that was possible, but hope was never a bad thing.

Lana's expression shifted. "It's the end. And I get to see the two of you."

"You're not going to fight this at all?" Nora's voice was thin. Soraya could only imagine seeing her mother for the first time in years and realizing quickly she had no intention of sticking around.

"My enemies will use everything at their disposal to destroy me." Lana took a breath as though it hurt to converse. "I will not let that happen to your child. They are not going to be a pawn, which means they cannot grow up in a world where my enemies use them to come after me."

"So you'll let them win?" A tear rolled down Nora's cheek, but she didn't bother to wipe it away.

"They won't."

Soraya frowned. That didn't sound good at all.

"Is this about the information you handed over with Soraya?" Hannah asked. "Is there something in there we should focus on?"

Lana glanced at her. After a minute, she said, "I can't imagine ending up anywhere else than right here. With the two of you."

Soraya's stomach dropped. "What did you do?"

21

"I t's been a long time coming."

Ted looked up from buttoning his shirt and saw his brother Dean in the doorway to his bedroom, wearing his own monkey suit.

Although, Ted had to admit Dean looked pretty good in his tuxedo. The guy was formerly a Navy SEAL and certified EMT. Now he ran a counseling center. Ted had always felt a little overshadowed by what his brother was capable of. But on his wedding day? Ted didn't need to worry about that. It might seem strange to think about it this way, but the bottom line was that today was about Ted. It wasn't about Dean.

Ted couldn't believe he was finally marrying Jess after all these months of waiting. Given everything he'd been through, it was time to realize this wasn't a competition, and he didn't need to prove himself. Most of the drama had occurred after Dean joined the Navy, and their father had free rein to coerce Ted into doing whatever he wanted. Which, for the most part, meant illegal hacking. But that was only where it started. Ted figured after all the counseling he'd gotten the last year or so —though, not from his brother but a coworker now on staff at the center—now was the time to embrace the future.

Their father was gone. Now it was about their lives.

Back in August, Ted had stood beside Dean as best man when his brother married Ellie—the one woman in the world who suited Dean perfectly. Ted was marrying Jess today, and Dean would stand beside him to return the favor.

The fact the Chevalier boys would stand with them as well wasn't lost on Ted. He was going to have the most heavily armed wedding party ever.

Dean came over, and the sight of him grew blurry. "What is it?" His brother grabbed the back of his neck and touched their foreheads together.

It didn't help. In fact, it made a couple of tears fall even though Ted tried to recall them.

"If I was marrying Jess I'd be scared, too."

Ted punched his brother in the stomach.

Dean only laughed, letting go and backing up a couple of steps like Ted had done nothing to him. But his brother's humor dissipated. Dean shot him a pointed look. "Tell me what you were thinking just now."

"Just that all of you will be standing there with me." Knowing Ted was upset, Dean would set the world on fire if that was what it took to fix it. Ted took a second and marveled over that. "I realized that my best man and my groomsmen are some of the most highly trained operators in the world."

"Good." Dean nodded. "Because this thing is going to go off without a hitch. I don't care if World War Three breaks out. Nothing is going to ruin today."

Ted felt the smile strain his lips and his brother blurred again.

"Nothing." Dean did the neck-squeeze thing again.

"Thanks." Ted swallowed.

Across the room on a chair mostly piled with clothes his tablet alarm went off.

Ted moved to it.

"You're not seriously working today, are you?" Dean folded his arms. "I figured you'd at least take a day off."

"Raleigh is up to something." Ted picked up the tablet. "I can feel it. Something is coming. It's like knowing you're going to get hit by a wave, but you haven't turned around yet to see how far away it is. Or how big it will be."

"Tomorrow you're leaving on your honeymoon. You think Jess is going to want you distracted checking your email every five minutes?"

"She's not going to be working any cases for the Last Chance PD." Ted glanced up. "You think she isn't going to be all over figuring out this Raleigh thing with me?"

"You're both going to work on your honeymoon?"

"We'll have the headspace to tackle it. And after he's been taken down, we'll take another week of vacation. Go somewhere."

Dean quirked an eyebrow.

"You know she loves a puzzle to solve," Ted added.

"So this is your wedding gift to her? Taking down the former president?"

Ted didn't want to find that funny. "You know what? It kind of is." He let out a breath. "But this is about keeping cops safe. Federal ones sure, but she's never going to let that go if she can help."

"I guess that's true enough." Dean had a guarded look on his face. One Ted knew well.

"You're worried about me."

Dean winced. "If you were stocking shelves at the grocery store for a living, I'd worry about you. Working on your computer is a little easier to stomach. Until gunmen come to the house to steal whatever you guys have that they want."

"Jess and I hid in the panic room for that."

"But the house has still been compromised." Dean paused. "Are you going to raise your children in that environment?"

"Whoa—"

"Please don't tell me you're getting married and you haven't talked about it."

"We have time. We're in agreement about that." Ted held the tablet to his chest. "Nora and Zander are going to raise their child here. Karina and Eas—" Ted choked on his friend's name. "Aria lives here."

Danger was at least somewhat mitigated by the panic room, and the bunker. Zander had made even more upgrades. Andre and Lucia wanted to build a townhouse of all things up on the hill behind the house. Things would change, but the way they made a family—all of them—wouldn't.

Dean held up his hands. "I didn't want to do this today. We should be talking about things that are happy, not looming threats. It's your wedding."

"It's another part of real life, which is not always happy," Ted said. "Sometimes there are sad parts." Hopefully more happy than sad, overall.

But whatever it was, he and Jessica had promised to face it all together. She loved him, and today she was going to pledge to stay by his side for the rest of their lives. As for him, he had family and loved what he did, but he'd never had anything that belonged solely to him. At least not that he could be proud of. Jess was the only woman he'd ever loved.

The tablet beeped again, breaking the flow of his thoughts. Ted looked at the screen and then felt his behind hit the chair.

"What is it?" Dean said.

Ted frowned at the screen. "The files that Lana put on the drive she gave us access to? They keep flagging with more and more unsolved Interpol cases."

"How do you have access to Interpol stuff?"

"Zander knows a guy." Ted shrugged one shoulder. "And the FBI works with them, so I was like, double covered in getting my foot in the door." A fissure of worry flared inside him. "I'm supposed to get on a video call with the new Director of Clandestine Service next week."

"Like an interview?"

He looked up at Dean. "They're deciding if they want to give Chevalier freelance work in the future. Part of the verification process includes checking me out."

"I know you're not proud of everything you did in the past, but anyone that can't see you're a good man is an idiot."

Ted grinned. Dean was his brother, so he was supposed to believe stuff like that, but it was still good to hear. "I'm hoping that marrying a police detective carries weight. Especially after I got fired from the department."

"Because you went on to bigger and better things."

Ted wasn't sure he'd ever get used to his brother's unwavering support. As much of a surprise as it was like an old, familiar comfort blanket.

"Tell me what's up with Interpol?" Dean leaned over to look at the tablet screen.

"Sure you want to get involved?" Ted didn't like the idea of his brother being targeted along with the rest of them any more than Dean did when he was hurt—or the victim in an incident. He'd tried for a long time to be strong enough to live up to his big brother's expectations. Sometimes it felt like an impossible standard, but the truth was that he loved that Dean set the bar high.

Ted wanted to achieve it. Because he knew even if he missed the mark, he'd still accomplish more than he would've otherwise.

"You're all over the place today," Dean said. "Maybe you should shelve this, or I'll go give it to Zander and he can take over. You can focus on…oh, I don't know. Maybe the fact you're getting *married* in a couple of hours."

"Let's see what we can get done in ninety minutes."

Dean eyed him. "Fine."

Ted scrolled through the notifications. "Every one of these

cases is a suspicious death. No one was ever prosecuted. Some were labeled murder and others weren't."

"So there's another assassin out there?"

"We know there's a whole group, though they recently lost their leader." Ted turned to his brother. "You know anyone in those circles you could reach out to?"

"You're thinking the loss of their leader leaves a power vacuum someone is going to fill?"

He hadn't been, but that was a good point. "Never mind."

"What?"

"There's exactly one person in all this who seems determined to scoop up power everywhere he can find it." Ted frowned. "I'd bet all the money I have saved up to buy a house on Raleigh being the new head of this assassin crew."

"You're buying a house?"

"Is that the point here?"

Dean shook his head. "You're moving out? Seriously?"

"We need our own space, and not just part of the house you're living in with Ellie."

"The house belonged to Jess's grandpa. She inherited it."

"You know she doesn't think of it that way. Jess is thinking about you guys raising a family there, and she loves what Ellie did with the yard. The two of you should make it your own." Ted let out a breath. "You know I love living with the boys. It's been different since you got married and moved out, and Stuart did the same. Things are changing. I'm not going to assume I'll still be living there in ten years. Or thirty. I'm making plans."

"There's a house for sale down the street from Ellie and me." Dean grinned. "Jess said it was 'cute.'"

"Call your Realtor. I want to know how much it is."

"Sure, I'll do it tomorr—"

Ted shook his head. "Right now. You know how the housing market is."

Dean chuckled all the way to the door. "I'll go find my phone. It's in my backpack."

Ted felt a sense of peace settle on him. Life was far too short not to move when something was so clear. That house might not be the one they would buy to start their lives, but he and Jess wanted a place of their own.

He just hoped it was big enough for a full-sized office *and* a panic room.

Ted scrolled through the results until his eyes burned. Dean hadn't come back yet, so he headed from his room to the living area of the big house. Despite the amount of people who lived here the place seemed empty. Even the dog was out.

He stared around, wondering where Dean had gone and thinking that he might move out. After living here for years, and practically growing up here, Ted didn't love the idea of leaving. But as he'd told Dean, things were changing.

Life was moving on.

"Dean?" He turned around and headed for the hall at the back of the house.

The back door was open.

A snowy breeze blew in from outside. Jess loved the snow, so it was fine with her to get married in winter. He just hoped more didn't dump—

Dean lay outside, facedown in the snow in his wedding clothes.

Ted ran out the door. "Dean!"

A wet red patch in his brother's hair had splashed on the snow. He'd gone down hard. He'd fought someone and been hurt.

"Dean!" Ted yelled, reaching for his brother's shoulder.

A sharp pain jabbed the side of his neck.

Ted tried to stand, but his legs had turned to noodles.

Everything went black.

22

Judah leaned between the front seat, where Zander drove, and the passenger seat, where Andre sat. All of them still needed to change into their wedding tuxedos. They'd been at the hospital all morning, checking on Eas to see if there were any signs he'd wake up soon.

"The app says the back door has been open. For how long?" Judah gripped the seats.

"Too long." Andre shifted in his seat.

It was wearing on all of them that Eas still hadn't regained consciousness. And as much as it affected them, it was clear it affected Karina so much more not knowing when the man she loved would wake up. No one wanted to say *if*, not even if none of them believed in the power of suggestion. Words had authority, but it wasn't as though they were going to jinx his recovery in any way by contemplating aloud the fact he might not pull through.

None of them wanted to even think about that, let alone speak it.

Zander yanked the wheel to the right, and they all braced. Judah planted a hand on the seat between him and Badger so he didn't careen over into the guy's shoulder. Before Zander even put the vehicle in park, three doors flew open and they ran to the front door as a group.

The girls were over at Dean's house with his wife, Ellie, who was Jess's sister, helping her get ready. Except for Soraya, who was at the hospital drifting between Karina and Dr. Windermere under off-duty police protection.

At the front door, all of them pulled out weapons. They entered the house using a key, then disabled the alarm, which had been set in "residence" mode for when someone was home. Still secure, but allowing for a modicum of freedom. It had been necessary in the past when the house was breached and people were home. But not as stringent in terms of security as there would be if no one was home.

Judah yelled, "Clear!" in the entryway.

They made their way through the living areas to the hall.

Andre yelled, "Clear!" Then he headed upstairs.

Badger went to the basement level, where there were a couple of rooms.

Judah found the back door open. "Zander!" Once his team leader caught up, he motioned to what he'd seen.

"Go!" Zander ordered.

Judah went to the doorway first, which he cleared just in case someone was lurking, then stepped into the daylight. "He's here!"

Dean lay on the snowy grass, out cold. Blood on the back of his head.

No one else was around.

Standing guard while Zander knelt beside their friend, Judah asked, "Is he breathing?"

"Pulse is faint, but it's there. His head doesn't look good. I'm calling…" Zander paused. "Darn."

"Yeah." Judah exhaled. "9-1-1?"

"I guess." Zander sighed.

Judah kept watch on the terrain around him while Zander shifted and pulled out his phone. He could track the guy's movements without even looking, just from the sound of clothing and the creak of his boots. There was a comfort to it. A familiarity he'd been without for weeks. No foundation, no support.

Judah took a breath and held it. He was back with them now and that was what mattered, not the time he'd spent under the thumb of British intelligence. Ted was supposed to be finding Casper Cunningham, but that was on the back burner with everything they'd gained from Lana about Raleigh and Travers.

It could be overwhelming if he thought about it all.

Andre and Badger piled out the back door.

Judah glanced over his shoulder. "Where's Ted?"

Badger shook his head. "Not inside. Out here?"

"Where would he be?" Judah swept his arm across the whole terrain behind the house. There weren't any footprints in the snow the team hadn't made themselves in the fresh powder this morning.

Andre got his phone out. "I'll track him."

Judah didn't like the sound of this. It made him want to call Soraya on the burner Ted had given her and make sure she was all right. Then check in with Windermere. Karina. Toni and Jeff—even if he'd been ignoring their calls. His sister meant well, but she hadn't needed to force that emotion out of him in the hospital, even if she thought it was necessary.

"Thank you." Zander hung up. "EMTs will be here in minutes, and they're going to call Conroy. Let him know what happened."

"What *did* happen?" Judah yelled the question louder than he wanted to.

Zander looked up from touching around the wound on Dean's head. "Judah, go look at the surveillance footage for the back door. If someone hit Dean, we'll see who they are. Find Ted," he ordered, as if he had one hundred percent confidence that Judah would be able to do it.

Something Judah needed to find in himself.

His grandmother had always told him that nothing in him was good, apart from what God put of Himself inside a person. Judah was fine with that. He needed as much of Him as possible. But he'd just never figured out how that worked in a person's life. He'd never managed to get past his own self, and what he understood of his abilities, to hit the point he had nothing more to give.

He could do nearly everything put in front of him. The only issue came when he sat back and thought about how he felt about it. What he couldn't handle was the pressure of fear that seemed to weigh on him like a ton of bricks. The guilt he felt, or the shame. That was too much to carry.

He didn't know how to handle it. Let alone process it and set it aside.

Instead of thinking more, he pushed all that from his mind and strode into the house. He jogged to Ted's office and used the computer off to the side that Ted had set up for them. Ted's computer was too confusing to use, although he said he put everything where he needed it—it was just that no one else could find anything on the thing.

Judah waited the interminable seconds for the thing to load. When it finally popped up, he logged into the program for their surveillance system and went back an hour—just in case. He scanned through the footage for the back door.

Eight minutes before, a dark-dressed figure had found Dean outside and hit him with a pipe. The figure disappeared from view.

Judah's stomach cramped, but he kept watching.

Minutes later, Ted came out the back door, reacting immediately to Dean being down. His brother crouched the way Zander had, but without someone to back him up. That led to the groom being stabbed in the neck with a needle. The guy hauled Ted away, behind the house.

Judah printed the image they had of the assailant. He'd worn his hood up, never looking at the camera.

A pro.

Judah clocked the direction he'd gone and ran from the office to the back door. The EMTs lifted Dean and whisked him away.

Badger said, "I'll go with them and call Ellie on the way."

"Get Jess as well," Judah said. They all turned to him. "The guy who did this? He took Ted."

Before they could respond, Judah tracked the guy around the house. Footsteps in the snow led across the open stretch behind the warehouse. He found two ruts in the snow where a vehicle had been parked.

Now it was gone.

He turned back, aware then that his pants were soaking wet from the snow. Andre was behind him. "He stuck Ted with a needle and took him away in whatever car was parked over here."

Andre turned to Zander. "Do we have surveillance out this far?"

Zander shook his head, a dark look on his face.

"This guy was a professional." Judah gritted his teeth. "He knew where to stand. Which way to turn so his face never hit the feeds. He took out the threat—Dean. Neutralized him so it was clear for him to take Ted and no one would stop him."

His stomach roiled so hard Judah had to turn to the side and spit out the acid that emerged in his throat. Thankfully he didn't heave. Instead, he inhaled a couple of icy breaths and got a lungful of brisk air.

"I can only think of one connection between our enemy and a professional hitman. Someone who could be hired to skillfully abduct the right person." Andre folded his arms.

"Why do they want Ted?" Judah asked. Maybe he didn't want to know. *Neither of them is dead.* He had to remember that.

"Good question," Zander said. "They didn't take anything

else, so either they don't know we have that information from Lana…or they don't care."

"Because all they wanted was Ted." Judah gritted his teeth.

And they'd taken him on his wedding day.

JUDAH PUSHED into the room ahead of Soraya. She wound her fingers around the inside of his elbow. When he glanced back, she said, "Let me."

There wasn't much she could do about it if his intention was to interrogate Lana into telling them what she might know about Ted's abduction.

The tension in the boys of Chevalier had been palpable. Each of them had gravitated to the woman they loved, seeking solace in a hug or the squeeze of a hand. Reminding them-selves of what they had while Karina stood with Aria, waiting for word on Eas.

Jess, who was supposed to marry Ted today, had been with her sister at Dean's bedside. The cop wanted firsthand infor-mation as soon as he woke up, not even wanting to look at the surveillance footage. At least according to what Badger had told the rest of them. Soraya didn't blame her. The last thing she would want to see was video of a loved one being stuck with a needle and abducted.

Soraya had to push away the empathy, or she would get sucked beneath its undertow. Instead of wallowing, they needed a plan.

She figured Jess—better known as Detective Ridgeman in Last Chance County—would agree with her on that.

"What happened?" Lana's voice lacked strength, but still managed to ring with authority.

Soraya stood beside Judah at the end of the bed. "Are you any better?"

"Not really. So what happened?"

When Judah said nothing, Soraya explained to Lana what he'd told her. The needle. Dean being injured. When she was done with her very brief report, she said, "Who would want to take Ted?"

"Who *wouldn't* want him? That's probably an easier question to answer."

Soraya frowned.

Lana continued, glancing at Judah, "Why do you think he hides in Last Chance County under your protection? It was that or work at an NSA facility, off book. He'd never be able to leave, and he wouldn't get a say on what he worked."

"Those are his only choices?" Soraya asked.

Lana nodded.

Beside Soraya, Judah shifted his stance as though trying to control his reaction. Exploding on Lana wasn't going to solve this problem. It might make them feel better for a moment, but if they wanted a way to move forward they'd need Lana's help.

Soraya had to put aside all of it. Lana had her reasons for what she said and did, and whether Soraya liked it or not didn't matter. What mattered was making sure Ted got home, and taking down Raleigh so he couldn't release that phone system.

Lana was dangerous—and in danger—just lying in a hospital bed under guard.

Soraya wasn't sure if the cops in the hall were there to protect Lana—or to protect others from her. Or maybe both. She wanted to mull over the fact that this woman's plan had been to be near her daughters. Had Lana been convinced this might be the end for her, and it could be her final opportunity to spend time with them?

They still had to get to the crux of why she and Judah were here.

"How do we get this done?" Soraya asked.

Lana shook her head, though she didn't seem confused. It was more of a challenge. "What are you asking for?"

Soraya figured Raleigh was the one who had taken Ted. And what did Raleigh need?

The phone system wasn't finished. In fact, she figured he was behind on it. People were waiting on him, and whoever was constructing the whole program hadn't finished. Maybe they even needed help—from the one guy who *could* finish it fast.

So they'd kidnapped Ted from his house. They could've killed his brother but didn't. Could've taken the files. Hadn't.

And why else, but for his skills?

Soraya gripped the rail at the foot of the bed. "How do we beat a guy with global reach and trained killers on his payroll?"

Lana leveled her with a steady gaze, even tucked in a hospital bed. "You drag the darkness into the light."

Soraya nodded.

Judah turned to her. "You know what that means?"

"Let's go." She took his hand and led him out, even if that meant Lana saw. It didn't matter at this point.

They headed for the hallway.

"Care to share?" Judah asked.

Even though the others were gathered in the hall, she turned to him. Frankly, if he was the only one here, that would be fine with her. All she needed was the one person she wanted to be around, even if doing this might take all of them.

She wanted to try that kissing thing again. Or the "going slow" that he'd suggested. A hug would be amazing right about now, but she didn't know how to ask for it.

The skin around his eyes shifted. "Are you—"

Before he could finish, and she could inevitably break down, Soraya slammed into him and slid her arms around his waist. She buried her face in the crook of his neck.

After a split second of surprise, he wrapped his arms around her.

Soraya let out an exhale. "I should stop ambushing you."

His chest rumbled as though he was laughing, but she didn't hear anything. "I'll let you know if there's a problem." He shifted and whispered in her ear, "I like hugs. They're basically amazing, but"—he pulled back—"you do need to answer my question as well."

"I know." Soraya whispered the words against his collar, her forehead pressed against his neck. She took another breath to steady herself and leaned back slightly. Not enough either of them had to let go because she agreed it was "basically amazing," as he'd put it. She loved the way he phrased things.

He lifted her chin. "What is it?"

"I need to be a reporter. Not a victim or even a friend. I need to do my job."

"That's what got you on Raleigh's radar in the first place." Judah frowned. "Unless you've forgotten."

"Believe me, I haven't."

The others gathered around them. Members of Judah's team and their significant others. It felt strange to be paired up with Judah like this. They'd never even gone out for coffee, and here they were in each other's arms, determined to take down the former president.

"We can't let him get away with any of this." The things he'd done were damning enough. Now Raleigh had ruined a young woman's wedding on top of it. "We need proof, which means we need to get evidence. Witness testimony." She ran out of ideas. "*Something.*"

"Isaac." Judah turned to Zander. "We're going to interview him. Officially."

Soraya felt the same as he did, caring little that there would be pushback. "We're past the time to play it safe.

Except with things we absolutely cannot afford to lose." She looked pointedly at Nora.

Zander got her meaning. "The two of you can head out as soon as the plane is ready. I'll make the call."

"What about me?"

Everyone turned to Hannah.

Her cheeks flushed. "I mean, Raleigh is my biological father." She shrugged. "If we can provide the conclusive DNA evidence, I can take that to the news media. Or Soraya can put it out on the internet. It'll be something no one can ignore."

Lucia nodded. "Even if they want further proof, it's at least enough to cast doubt on his integrity. Though, how it never came out during his presidential run is a huge question we'll have to answer."

Soraya said, "That's how tight he has everything. He handles it all personally, and he's not afraid to get dirty." His reputation came from people who had talked—White House employees and Secret Service agents that worked protecting him then but didn't now.

"What does he want with Ted?" Nora asked.

"The phone system isn't finished," Soraya replied. "I'm guessing Ted has the expertise to do it." None of them disagreed, so she figured that meant they all knew she was probably right.

Zander's phone buzzed. He pulled it from his front pocket and looked at the screen. "Eas woke up."

The relief among the group was palpable.

Soraya let out a breath and smiled. "That's great."

"Andre and Lucia, talk to Lana and find out what else she knows. Nora and I will sit with Karina, then I'll head back to the house to look through Ted's systems. Badger and Hannah, get Hannah's statement worked up, and we can figure out how we'll release it. Judah and Soraya, get to Virginia. I'll get you into the prison to visit Isaac, but I want as little time for

Raleigh to realize what we're doing as possible, so it'll be last minute."

They all nodded.

The elevator doors opened, and a blur of white whooshed out. Zander and Andre caught the blonde before she could slam into them. Mascara-laced tears trailed down her cheeks. "Where is he?"

Jess.

All that had happened to Soraya in that facility rushed back. Seeing Judah dragged out and taken to that room. Recording that video. The gunman standing over her. Raleigh's amusement.

She shuddered, and a whimper escaped her lips before she could stop it.

Judah pulled her away from the others. "Come on. Let's get to work."

23

E ven though he managed to sleep on the plane, Judah was still dragging when he walked into the private meeting room at the federal prison where Isaac was held. From what everyone had told him, it seemed this was precisely where his friend wanted to be.

Soraya entered behind him, and the two of them pulled out chairs at the table opposite Isaac. She sat forward while Judah leaned back, crossed one leg, and set his ankle on his knee.

Isaac motioned to Soraya but didn't take his gaze from Judah. "Who is this?"

It was the first time Judah had seen his former friend since Isaac betrayed Chevalier. He'd gone back to work for Lana—his mother—and shut that down when he took a stolen suitcase nuke and returned it to a military base, turning himself in. He'd been here in federal prison awaiting trial ever since.

Judah had heard about everyone else's visits with Isaac. Even Nora and Hannah, his half-sisters, had been here. But what Isaac had to say was something Judah wanted to hear for himself.

"She's probably your only hope." Judah shrugged one

shoulder. "If it's even possible for you to have hope. Most likely, you'll rot in here for the rest of your life."

"Nah." Isaac shook his head. "This isn't going to trial. One day you will hear that I was killed. Or I committed suicide. Who knows what story they'll tell. I'll be transferred to some prison that's not on any map or listed in any database. You'll never hear from me again, but I'll live a long and probably unpleasant life being 'questioned' about what I know."

"So why turn yourself in if you knew already that would be the inevitable outcome?" Judah asked. Soraya sat still and quiet beside him. Instead of jumping into the conversation and demanding answers, she was playing it cool without him even having to suggest it.

"You wouldn't believe me if I told you," Isaac said.

"Because I'd never think you had it in you to be altruistic. Or try to earn some kind of atonement?" Judah linked his fingers over his diaphragm.

Isaac was quiet for long enough that Soraya said, "Now we know why you're here, you should know there are several reasons why *we're* here."

"Because I care?" Isaac smirked.

"I get the impression you want the same thing we do," she continued. "And like Lana, you have a vastly different way of going about things."

Isaac gave a nod. "That's true enough."

Soraya just looked at him.

Judah watched Isaac's eyes narrow and figured he would just say it without Isaac having to ask. "Who would want to poison Lana?"

Isaac's attention whipped over to Soraya. "You're the reporter." He looked back at Judah. "Why? Is she dead?" Judah was aware there wasn't much love lost between Isaac and his mother. However, there was definite concern in his friend's gaze.

"Windermere is taking care of her," Judah said. "When we left, she was stable."

Isaac let out a breath. "She has a lot of enemies. Pinpointing one would be hard to narrow down unless you know what kind of poison it is. Sometimes that's like a calling card."

Judah figured that was likely true when a group of trained assassins was running around, working for Travers Industries now.

Soraya spoke. "Tell us the real reason you turned yourself in."

Isaac eyed her for a second. "There's a guy in here. He's a surgeon. Does plastic surgery. Like if you want to look like someone else."

"The way Raleigh did with Jerry Travers?" Judah asked.

Isaac nodded.

"So your plan is to get close to the doctor and convince him to testify about Raleigh taking over the company?" Soraya paused. "How Travers was in a coma, and he had another guy change his face to look like him?"

Judah studied his friend. Isaac didn't know that the double of Jerry Travers was dead. Or, who it had been. Judah would have to tell him that his father, Yuri Amrakov, was dead. Something Isaac had likely already believed for years.

Isaac glanced at Soraya. "Sure. Get him to testify. That's exactly what I was thinking."

"You don't need to be sarcastic." Judah let out a breath. "We're here trying to help you."

Isaac said, "Are you?"

Judah wasn't planning on telling him that Ted was missing. It had happened entirely too recently. There was no way Isaac could know about it. Not only that, but he cared about the kid. If there was nothing Isaac could do and no way for him to help, why leave him even more distressed than he needed to be?

Isaac shifted back to look at Soraya. "What else?"

"Who is this doctor?" she asked. "We're going to need to speak to him as well. If he has information on how to get close to Raleigh, then we need it."

"Chevalier must be desperate if you guys are here asking me for help."

"Everyone on the team is working something different," Judah said. "Lana is out of commission—"

"As if that means she's not up to something?" Isaac said.

"This one is all hands on deck." Judah sat forward in his chair. "That means you as well."

"So all is forgiven?"

"You think I don't understand being stuck between a rock and a hard place? I've been living there this entire time. And it is only a matter of time before British intelligence comes back because they realized Raleigh didn't kill me. Then I'll be stuck working for them again, whether I like it or not." Judah blew out a breath. "Except the favor they want from me? It's because I cost them a man of theirs. Only he isn't actually dead. I saw him alive and well." He motioned to Soraya. "He tried to kill both of us."

Isaac gasped. "Casper Cunningham?"

Judah didn't even bother wondering how on earth Isaac knew that name. He wasn't surprised about anything regarding his friend. The guy had been a CIA agent. Then he'd worked for Lana. He'd been lying all of his adult life. Covert operations were what he lived and breathed. Judah had never believed Isaac wasn't precisely where he wanted to be right now.

Isaac spoke quietly. "Just rip off the bandage."

"The man Raleigh got under the knife, the one who had enough plastic surgery he looks like Jerry Travers?"

"You found him?" Isaac asked. It seemed to be a genuine question, but his friend wasn't disclosing anything in his tone or expression.

Judah continued, "Raleigh sent me to kill the head of the assassins' guild. When I got there, it wasn't who I was expecting."

"But he's dead?"

Judah nodded. "It was Yuri Amrakov."

Isaac just stared at him.

"He wasn't dead, up until a few days ago." Judah winced. "Now, I'm sorry to say——"

"Don't bother being sorry for me that my father is dead. It would be a waste of time."

Judah didn't know what to say.

Soraya spoke up. "If I told you Raleigh was behind the scenes, taking over the entire company and that it included this group of trained killers, would you believe it?"

"In a heartbeat."

Judah followed up her question with one of his own. "What do you know about him that the rest of the country doesn't that would make you believe it so easily?"

"If you know where Lana is, and she's so stable, why don't you ask *her* that."

Soraya glanced over at Judah, who nodded and said, "We will. But tell me what you know about your father."

"Not much that will help you take down Raleigh." Isaac shrugged one shoulder. The chains that secured him to the floor between his feet jingled. "I tried to join that group of assassins just to find out who was leading them. Guess I know now why they dumped me in the middle of nowhere. I was surprised they didn't kill me, but that would draw too much attention."

They'd likely known who he was when Isaac first approached them. Judah figured Lana had told him to infiltrate the group, even knowing how dangerous it could be.

She hadn't even known the half of what he'd been walking into.

"And Yuri?" Judah wasn't about to say *your father*. That might not go down well.

"I guess they weren't as in love as she thinks." Isaac shrugged. "Because apparently he just wanted out."

"It seemed to me like Yuri was under Raleigh's thumb. Maybe he didn't have a choice being Travers or working for the company."

Isaac shook his head. "We always have a choice. Maybe it isn't one that anyone should have to live with, or it seems impossible. But sometimes even choosing death is better than the alternative."

Before Judah could ask what that meant, an alarm erupted from a speaker, high in the corner of the wall. "Code Red Lockdown. Repeat. We are in Code Red Lockdown."

Soraya pushed back her chair and stood. "What's happening?"

"Probably a riot in the cafeteria or the exercise yard." Isaac tipped his head to the side. "I'm sure it's nothing to worry about."

Judah leaned forward in his seat. "Where's the doctor currently?"

"Solitary confinement," Isaac said. "Two floors directly above us."

Judah figured this wasn't a coincidence at all.

SORAYA TRIED to assimilate all the information they had heard since they walked into this room. The man across the table was nothing like she had imagined. He seemed so different from all the research she'd done after Isaac turned himself in to military custody. And yet, in some ways also exactly as she thought he would be.

When he looked at her, or the guard stood in the corner, the stern expression on his face gave nothing away. But when he looked at Judah? The care and concern for his friend were there in his eyes.

"You guys stay here." The guard spoke for the first time. He pulled the door handle and let himself out into the hallway, grabbing his radio as he moved. The door clicked shut behind him.

He either naively assumed Isaac posed no threat because he was shackled…

Or he'd been paid off.

Isaac's head whipped around to them. "Out that door." He motioned with his chained hands. "Two doors down to the left is the stairs. You have two and a half minutes to get up to solitary, and the doors will open. Get the doctor and bring him to the boiler room behind the showers. He'll know where that is." Isaac took a breath. "You get him out, and he'll testify against Raleigh."

Soraya said, "Why would he do that?"

Isaac glanced at her. "Who do you think buried him in this place?"

Judah motioned to her, and she walked with him to the door.

"Nope. The two of you can't do this. Just one, since that's what my guy in the control room is looking for," Isaac said. "So the reporter stays here with me, and you can go take the good doctor to the exit."

"That's not gonna happen." Judah shook his head. "Soraya stays with me. Not you."

Isaac looked at an imaginary watch. "Tick-tock."

"It's fine. I'll stay." She didn't want them to lose out on this opportunity, even if she would feel better staying with Judah than Isaac. "Go get that guy out."

Judah pressed his lips together and made a frustrated sound deep in his throat. But he pulled the door open on the other side from where the guard had gone.

When it clicked shut, she turned to Isaac. But he was not what caught her attention.

The room was starting to fill with smoke.

"Did you know there was going to be a fire?"

Isaac frowned. "I had something to tell you…and you alone. Fire was not part of the plan."

The guard from the hallway rushed through the door. "Where's the other guy?"

"He went to see if the way out is clear," Soraya said.

The guard kicked Isaac's chair back from the table. Bending down, he used a key to unlink the chains from the floor. Part of her expected Isaac to attack the man as soon as he was free. But he simply sat in the chair, staring at the guard as he straightened.

"I'm not going back on our agreement," the guard said.

"Then you'll be given what you asked for." Isaac didn't move. "All you need to do is go back to your locker, check your cell phone, and see for yourself."

"I brought it with me." The guard glanced at his smart-watch. "And oops, I forgot to take this thing off." It vibrated. "Looks like the transfer is complete."

Isaac lifted his hands.

As the guard came near, Isaac moved faster than Soraya could even track. Then he wrapped the chain between his cuffed hands and feet around the guard's neck. The guard's eyes bulged, and he gasped for breath. His legs folded. He landed on his knees on the floor. Minutes later, he passed out completely and slumped on the floor. His hand opened, and what looked like an insulin pen rolled across the floor.

Soraya sucked in a breath that got stuck in her throat. She couldn't make a sound to scream.

"Let's clarify." Isaac straightened from the chair and bent to rifle through the man's pockets. "He was going to kill me… and probably you, too. After all, you're a witness."

"Why did he want to kill you? Did Raleigh send him?"

"Probably." Isaac found a key and unlocked the cuffs on his feet. Then his hands. "Does it matter?"

"It matters to me."

"That's why I didn't let him do it."

He was still talking when she whirled around to the door and pulled it open. She didn't get through. The door slammed shut in front of her face, missing her fingers by millimeters.

Isaac crowded at her back. "If you go anywhere in this place without me, that guard gets what he wanted. And you aren't going to enjoy the process whereby you wind up both broken *and* dead."

"You're not even going to bother to try and keep me alive?"

"One guy?" He waved at the guard. "Clearly, I can take care of you. But if there are fifteen of them? Neither of us wants to come up against that."

"This whole thing was a setup, wasn't it?" Soraya didn't know whether to scream or kick him. Surely there was another guard—one that wouldn't try to kill them—somewhere around here. But whoever it was would quickly realize Isaac and Judah were unaccounted for in the middle of a prison riot.

Isaac tipped his head to the side. "How is it even possible I could set up anything? I didn't know until two hours ago that you were coming here."

She stared into his dark blue eyes. A thousand experiences looked back. Deadly wisdom that wouldn't mean anything if he wasn't in the life he was living, where power was the only thing that mattered, and people were nothing but a commodity to be used and discarded.

Whatever he had felt for his friends was gone. Here, behind these bars.

He was only a prisoner now.

Not a brother or son. Or a friend.

"We need to go to Judah." She didn't like this man and

who he was without his friend. There was nowhere she wanted to be inside this prison except right by Judah's side. "I'll get out with him, and you can go back to your cell because you know it's the right thing to do."

He grinned, but there was no humor there.

"Well?"

"I will take you to Judah," he finally said.

"Good. And if anyone asks, I'm not putting in a good word for you." She needed to pretend she didn't care one bit about him. It wasn't what a reporter was supposed to be— impartial, even though it seemed as though no one in journalism was these days. The fact she only ever intended to report the truth was what got her into this mess in the first place.

He let out a rusty-sounding laugh. "Step outside and hug the wall. We'll have to move quickly."

She did as he ordered.

The hallway was empty, but the smoke smell lingered. A cloud poured from the vent at the top of the wall. They weren't going to be able to breathe free for long.

"All the way to the end," Isaac added.

He had her stand with her back to the wall while he opened the stairwell door. Thundering footsteps echoed up from floors below.

"It sounds clear. Go up." He practically shoved her to the concrete steps and hurried behind her, hanging onto her at times. Acting protective. As if he cared what happened to her when she wasn't convinced he did.

Maybe there was a speck of human decency inside him. Or he simply cared enough for his friend that he didn't want Judah to lose her. Even if they hadn't said or done anything that would indicate they were a couple, until Isaac asked them to separate, he'd evidently figured out that Soraya meant something to Judah.

"The doors in solitary should be opening soon."

"Doesn't that mean everyone in there will be let out?" She glanced back over her shoulder.

He stared at her for a second. "Yeah, that's generally what that means."

"This is a federal prison. There are people in here who should never have contact with another human. Not for the rest of their lives."

"That's a whole different wing. The doctor is up on the next level, and those people who are not fit for society? That's just every single person in here."

And they were walking right through that nightmare. *If you're going through hell…*

What was the saying? Oh yeah, they had to keep on going.

"Great," Isaac muttered.

She stopped at the next door he indicated. Isaac reached for the handle just as a different alarm blared above the first lockdown alarm still ringing.

She frowned. "I'm guessing that's not good."

"You'd be right about that." He ushered her in.

"Can your guy in the control room take care of it?"

Isaac frowned. "He's helping Judah. You want him distracted?"

Soraya shook her head.

"Come on, quickly. Before all the doors lock and we can't get anywhere until the fire department clears the whole building."

"Judah will be able to get out, right?" Soraya rushed into the hallway.

Isaac slammed into her back.

The two of them faced off with four men walking toward them. The one in front sneered. "Well, lookie what we have here."

24

The voices grew louder behind him. Some kind of commotion he didn't care about or have time for.

Judah ducked into the next cell in solitary confinement. So far he'd found two empty and one he hadn't stuck around in.

Things in this place were lethal, but he needed to focus on finding the doctor. Not trying to prevent every crime that would happen while the prison was under siege—or whatever was really going on. He didn't have time to fix this whole place, no matter what the others would think of his actions.

This next room wasn't a cell. It was storage.

Blood had pooled on the floor, where it was smudged and footprinted. Someone had been dragged in here and attacked. The second thing he realized was that he wasn't alone.

Judah spun around a split second before the man in a light-blue jumpsuit slammed into him. Covered in blood and gasping for breath, the man rushed at him. Judah figured the inmate wouldn't put up much of a fight. But underestimating anyone in a situation like this would be a bad idea. Especially a guy in federal prison.

The inmate, wielding a shank, swung a hand down.

Judah caught the man's wrist, halting the manufactured

weapon before it could make contact with him. He paused to give the doctor a second to realize that he wasn't a prisoner or a correctional officer. "I'm not here to hurt you."

The doctor's legs started to give out. Judah held onto him, turning the man so he could lie on the floor. All that was in here were shelves of cleaning supplies, a mop bucket, and two brooms. Across the doctor's chest were multiple stab wounds.

Judah didn't know where to apply pressure first. But it was clear this man wasn't going to last much longer if he went without medical care. "What happened?"

"Lungs…" The doctor gasped a breath that rattled in his chest. "Lungs filling." He gasped again. "Blood."

Judah didn't have much medical training, but he'd seen plenty of battlefield injuries. Even if the doctor had all the medical knowledge he needed, the fact it was something he was experiencing personally might throw him off enough to have any kind of reaction.

Shock. Hysteria.

"We need to get you out of here so you can get medical care." Judah shifted to pick the guy up. "There's a ride waiting for you."

Supposedly, that was what Isaac had planned. For them to get this guy out, but not Isaac himself? It was interesting he'd orchestrated it that way.

The doctor shook his head. "No time." He gasped. "Doesn't matter. Dead."

"You seriously think getting out doesn't matter? You were targeted, weren't you?" And Judah had left Soraya in Isaac's care to come here for this. He winced. He didn't even have a phone to record a dying declaration.

Judah didn't like at all the fact he had been forced to walk away from her. It only cemented in him the truth of how he felt about her. Isaac had better take care of her through this, or they would have serious words.

Lord.

He gritted his teeth and prayed the correctional officer outside the door down where they were would help out. But who knew how things would go in a situation like this? Certainly no one who'd shown up to work here in the prison today would've thought their day would go this direction.

The doctor said, "I was targeted after I got out of my cell." He swallowed. "There was a crowd in the hallway, and…shoved me in here."

So Judah had been right.

"No point trying to save me." He gasped. "I don't get to decide whether I live or die."

"Because Raleigh thinks you shouldn't live anymore? At least tell me what I need to know before it happens. Otherwise, what's the point?"

He had to appeal to this man's dignity. His sense of legacy. Doctors understood the power they had over people's lives. It would be no different for this one, considering how he had affected the world and everything that occurred in it.

In the hallway, someone slammed against the door.

Judah's head whipped around. The door handle rattled. He stared at it, praying the person didn't manage to get in. The last thing he needed right now was for whoever did this to come back and try again. "We really need to get you out of here."

The doctor shook his head.

"Then give me something, at least." Judah couldn't believe the guy was simply going to let his life end and not even attempt to pass on at least some information. "Tell me who did this to you."

"Does it matter? I'm guessing we both know Raleigh sent him."

Judah waited.

"Fine." The doctor frowned. He coughed, and blood appeared at the corner of his mouth. "I have a storage unit no one knows about. It's under a fake ID, and I'm certain

Raleigh never figured out it's there. You'll find everything you need to take him down if you go there." He rattled off the address.

"I'll remember." Judah had nothing to write it down with and no personal belongings on him.

"If you don't, I'm unlikely to care." The doctor's voice grew sluggish. He didn't have much time left.

"Anything else you want to say?"

The door thumped again as someone tried to break it down. Judah glanced over and saw smoke begin to seep under the door. It matched the smell in the air, laced with the tang of flames.

The doctor's chest jerked. He made a choking noise. "It's —" The life dissipated from his eyes, and his head relaxed to the left.

Judah lowered the man's eyelids.

He found the weapon the doctor had wielded, the one Judah assumed was used to kill him. It was slick in his fingers. He had to wipe the ridged, melted plastic, set in a way that left a point at the end. Once it was cleaned of the blood, he gripped it in his hand and stood to one side of the door.

Judah held his back to the wall, the weapon in front of him across his body. He used his left hand to release the handle on the door.

Two men wearing light blue jumpsuits rushed in and went immediately to the doctor, who lay on the ground. Dead.

Judah slipped out the door behind them.

A crowd had gathered at the end, blocking his view of the stairs.

Judah turned to go the other direction but then saw Isaac between two prisoners with their backs to him.

One moved, and Soraya cried out. "She comes with me." The man in front of them grabbed her arm and dragged her toward a room across the hall.

Judah ran toward the crowd. He tackled them all, shoving

one man into the next like a chain of cars rear-ending one another.

The man with Soraya didn't stop.

Judah kept shoving.

She saw him then. "Judah!"

The man didn't even look at him. Judah tossed the weapon he'd picked up from the floor to her. She missed it, stumbled, and fell to her knees. His heart sank, but then she grasped up the weapon. The man dragged her to her feet and slammed the door to one of the cells.

She was shut in there with him.

A fist came out of nowhere and smashed into the side of Judah's face. He reared back.

Isaac roared, and the man was tackled to the floor. The two of them thumped onto the old tiles. Isaac wailed on the guy, punching him over and over.

Judah shoved another man away. The third one came at him. Judah swept the guy's arm away with his left forearm, refusing to acknowledge the pain as bone hit bone. He used his right hand to punch the man's sternum.

Soraya screamed.

His breath came fast until all he could hear was the rushing in his ears.

He slammed into the door, but it didn't open. Judah reached for the handle, but there wasn't one. The cell had only an electronic lock. All of them had been armed so that no one went anywhere. They were stuck in this hallway.

Soraya was trapped in the cell with that inmate.

Judah pulled Isaac off the man. "Enough." He hauled his friend to his feet. "We need to get in there." Then he pointed at the room.

Isaac shook his head. "We can't get in there. I couldn't stop them."

"So much for your grand plan."

"I didn't know this would happen."

Judah glanced at him. "None of that matters if anything happens to her."

Soraya screamed again.

Judah pounded on the door. "Soraya!"

There was no lock. He couldn't shove it open. The thing was built to withstand force. He'd never be able to break it down.

"Soraya!" Tears gathered in his eyes. Judah slammed his fists against the door and yelled her name again.

"Out of the way!" A group of guys in SWAT gear raced into the hall.

Judah gasped.

"Who are—"

Judah spun around. Surely Isaac could…

He turned. "Isaac!"

But his friend was nowhere to be seen.

HIS HAND WAS up her shirt. There was no time to thank God that was only as far as he'd managed to get. When his body jerked against hers, she pulled her hand back.

Slick. Bloody.

She nearly dropped the shiv, but pushed all thought from her mind purposely.

Don't think. Just do it.

Again.

She shoved the shiv at him and stabbed it into his abdomen for a second time. Tears rolled down her cheeks.

The man who'd dragged her in here stumbled back. A criminal. A man who'd have taken more than she could afford to give if she didn't do this. He'd done enough. But he was still a human being. A life created like everyone who breathed—no matter what they chose to do with it.

Soraya didn't believe anyone was too far gone.

Or, she hadn't until now. Maybe she was the one who was past it, beyond redemption.

He clutched his abdomen, stumbled back, and went down on the floor. Blood soaked the jumpsuit. He looked up, teeth gritted, and bit off a foul string of words.

Soraya could only stare at him with the bloody shiv in view.

After a second, she realized she hadn't breathed and sucked in an inhale. Purely a reflex, it caught in the middle as she shuddered against the door.

Why.

That was all her mind could conjure. Nothing else, just that single word.

She'd come here to talk to Isaac, wanting to spend time with Judah. Trying to be part of the team to help take down Raleigh. And this happened? She hadn't asked for this or put herself in a position where it was possible.

And now she'd all but killed a man.

I didn't ask to be here. But you didn't have to do this.

Someone slammed into the door behind her.

Soraya got out of the way. Her feet tangled, and she leaned against the wall. She eyed the man she had stabbed. He laid back while his soaked chest rose and fell sharply. She didn't take her eyes from him as she slid down to the floor. With her back to the wall, her knees folded.

She tucked herself into the tightest ball possible and didn't even blink.

The door crashed open.

"Ma'am?" A rush of dark material moved in front of her. More than one.

Someone crouched. Not Judah. This was a uniformed local police officer, with SWAT on his vest.

"Ma'am?" He took hold of the shiv, then touched her elbow. "Let's get you out of here, okay?"

She said nothing, but managed to nod. She wanted to get

out of here more than anything. Where was Judah? Any second he was going to rush to her, and she would be in his arms.

But he wasn't in the room.

Or the hallway.

Several armed cops turned to her, identical expressions on their faces. Pity. They probably thought they were keeping it professional by not empathizing. She hated the looks on their faces and turned away from them.

"Let's go downstairs. Get you somewhere you can sit, and we'll have a medic come and look at you."

Soraya shook her head. "I'm unhurt."

He glanced at her, but she didn't look at the expression on his face. She didn't want to know what was there or how he felt about what happened to her.

All she wanted to do was find a quiet place to cry by herself.

Had she really thought she could do this? Now Soraya knew for sure this life was definitely not for her. Whatever qualified the men and women of Chevalier, she wasn't built—or trained—the same way. She wanted to know what had happened to Ted. She wanted the world to understand what Travers Industries was really up to.

Having her life in danger like this, where any moment could be her last, and she'd stare the end in the face when she least expected it? Soraya couldn't handle that.

She felt it. That moment when the emotion rose in her throat. When her lip began to quiver and tears rolled down her cheeks.

All she could do was lean against the wall in the stairwell.

"It's okay," the guy said.

She shook her head, breathless and unable to speak. It wasn't going to be okay. Not anymore, and maybe even not ever. She finally forced out the words, "Where is Judah?"

He stared at her for a second. "The guy you came in with?"

She managed to nod.

"He's helping his friend escape. They didn't tell you that?"

Soraya blinked.

"Sorry." He winced. "Guess they didn't let you in on that plan. So if you're thinking he's going to swoop in and carry you out, my recommendation is to not hold your breath for that. You'll wind up being disappointed."

They thought Judah had used her to help Isaac escape?

"You survived that back there on your own." He pointed up the stairs. "And it'll hit you later, what you just did. That's inevitable. But know this." He paused, an intent look fixed on her. "There aren't many people who could survive something like that. But you did."

"I killed that man."

"You'll carry that with you. Believe me, it'll be part of you for the rest of your life."

She took an honest look at him then. Red hair peeked out under the edge of a black helmet, light eyebrows, and thin lips. He had the hint of a scar under the stubble on his chin. Insignia on the vest and a uniform that consisted of dark green fatigues. Black boots. Belt and holster.

"One day, you'll wake up and realize you haven't thought about it in a while," he said. "Might take a few years. It might take the rest of your life, but you'll get there. You'll realize it isn't quite as close as it always had been."

He seemed so genuine, but she realized they were standing in a desolate hallway with the smell of smoke all around them.

"Should we get out of here?" She looked down the stairs and didn't hear anyone coming up. Once again, she was alone with a man she didn't know—though this time she wasn't trapped, and he was on the right side of the law instead of the wrong side.

He nodded. "That's a good idea."

"Which way?"

"Downstairs." He pointed a gloved finger. The space where a patch should've been attached to his sleeve was blank, just the fuzzy side of the Velcro. He'd probably had to rush here so fast he hadn't had time to grab it.

Soraya headed down. Slower than she'd have liked to walk, but it took her farther and farther from where she'd last seen Judah. That didn't seem good, even if this guy was right and she should stand on her own two feet. After all, she'd managed to get this far on her own.

Standing up for the truth.

Living on her own, on the run. Helping Mayeni find a safe place to be. Getting Zander and his team what they needed so Lana could get help.

Now this?

It might take some doing to find out where Ted was being held, but there was no way she would walk away and not do everything she could. After all, she knew what it felt like to be under Raleigh's thumb, captive and forced to do whatever he told her to do.

Ted had to be there to finish coding the software. So Travers Industries could push out the phone system. That *had* to have been why he was taken from his home. They hadn't killed anyone or stolen anything. It was a targeted attack because Ted was a means to an end, and they *needed* him. Unlike the rest of them, who had been nearly blown up in that facility.

Left for dead.

No longer needed.

She glanced over her shoulder. The look on the guy's face made her pull up short.

He said, "You okay?"

"Shaken up." Even the words sounded like she was nervous, which helped. That look on his face. It'd been...she didn't know how to describe it.

What was going on here?

"Is Judah this way?" She kept the question as benign as she could while her mind caught up, her thoughts running through everything and trying to figure out an answer.

"Sure. Just a little farther."

Soraya rounded the next stairwell. At the last second, before she passed the door, she reached for the handle.

A body slammed her into the door, and her jaw smashed the wood. Warm breath drifted over her cheek, and a man said, "Let's get a couple of things straight first."

With a British accent.

25

A ndre gripped his phone, standing in the hallway outside Lana's hospital room. "How is Eas doing?"

Zander was on the other end of the call. "Two makes two. Conroy is the police chief in town. Things are coming back as they should."

"That's good." Andre figured Eas had a strange set of questions to answer for his cognition test, but whatever worked. "Windermere is down there?"

Zander grunted. "He and the doc are glaring at each other. Maggie looks like she's about to make them an appointment for coworkers who can't get along."

"Like couple's therapy?"

Instead of answering Zander said, "I haven't heard from Judah yet."

"Doesn't mean something is wrong." Andre didn't expect them to call in until later. But with Ted gone, it felt like flying blind. "We have no idea where he was taken."

"Is that a statement or a question?"

"It's—"

"Unhelpful." Zander cut him off. "You think I wouldn't

rather be in the jet, across the other side of the country or wherever they took him? I want Ted back as much as you do. Jess is the *only* exception. We could go on. She…"

Andre clenched his teeth.

"Sorry."

"You don't need to apologize," Andre said. "I want to yell, too."

"Doesn't make it okay."

"I'd suggest going to the community center in town since they just put in the ball pit and one of those things where you get two huge foam jousting sticks. You stand on the rolling beam over the foam blocks, and we can wail on each other."

"But it doesn't seem right. Not now."

"No," Andre said. "It doesn't seem right." Not at all at a time like this.

Zander sighed.

"It's good Eas is awake. I bet Karina and Aria are glad."

"And the dog sitter. Will and Hollis have been watching Kuai for days."

Andre tried to think of a retort to convince Zander things were good. But how could they be? Ted was gone, and not only did they not know why except for a guess, but they also didn't know where to look for him.

Give him a door to kick down any day.

Not knowing was killing him.

Zander said, "Things like this happen. Nora could lose the baby. Windermere could have a stroke. That facility should've killed all of us, but instead we survived."

"So there's no rhyme or reason to any of it? It's just life?" Andre didn't know if he liked that answer at all.

"It's the life everyone lives in a fallen world. But we have hope."

"We do." Andre looked at his shoes.

"Even in the midst of the pain."

Andre said, "I'll pray for Nora."

"Thanks." Zander hung up.

Zander hadn't had much in his life that had gone right. Not until lately, when he'd met Nora. They'd set the world record—no one had checked, though—for marriage and then getting pregnant. Now they all had to face the fact he could lose Nora. Maybe that was what drove their relationship, neither of them wanting to wait when life was far too short to miss out on what you had right in front of you.

Said the man who waited twenty years to sort his marriage.

Since Lucia came back into his life, he'd had to come to terms with that whole thing the last couple of months. Seeing her face every day when he woke up helped.

Andre knew exactly what Jess was going through. She was a cop, so they'd had to have her coworkers lock her down to keep her from going after Ted. They'd had to promise to her that the second they knew where he was, they'd tell her so she could come with them and rescue him.

Jess Ridgeman might be an unknown they hadn't trained with, someone who should stay firmly on the honorable side of the law, but no one would say no to her. Not when they all knew they'd do the same thing. If Chevalier didn't tell Jess the second they knew where Ted was, she'd find out for herself and go anyway.

It was better to have her go with them there to act as backup.

Andre walked back to the room where Lana was resting in the hospital bed. His wife had probably gone in to interrogate the woman. Lucia would pull out all the tricks and tips she'd learned with the DEA and the sneaky stuff they'd taught her to get answers from Lana.

But he'd given her plenty of time.

Andre cracked the door and peered inside.

"We all wanna know." Lucia stood to his right, her arms

folded. She was getting frustrated, so he figured Lana hadn't said much that was useful. Yet.

Lana lay in the bed, looking frailer than he'd ever seen her before. Nothing like the woman who had pulled the rug out from under them more than once. Zander's mother-in-law, though neither he or Nora was about to invite her to family dinner—or allow her to be a grandmother to the baby they were expecting.

"How did you know where Karina was the whole time she was under the protection of the accountant's office?" Lucia asked. "At least tell me that."

"That isn't why I came here." Lana moaned.

Lucia shifted her stance and cocked her hip. "So your intention was to maintain operational security while you bribed us for medical care, and we won't be inclined to call the police and report your whereabouts?"

It really was too bad he appreciated her aggression. She was gorgeous when she was all fiery like that, in cop mode, but it wasn't going to get Lana to talk. As much as he wanted to watch this, conventional methods to get someone to open up likely didn't even apply here.

Lana sighed. "Tell that woman not to worry. I only got one file, so the whole business wasn't compromised."

"That woman?" Lucia said.

"Ellie. Melly." Lana frowned. "Millie. That's it. The one who married that FBI agent who likes to meddle. So you can tell Jeff not to worry, because none of the current clients are compromised."

"I'll forward the information on." Lucia nodded.

Andre had to catch the smile before it got out.

"Doesn't matter," Lana said. "I won't earn any favors, no matter what I give them."

"Who?"

Lana rolled her eyes. "Let's not kid ourselves. You guys have the local police and the FBI on speed dial. I'm surprised you don't know the president."

Andre was pretty sure Ted did, but it was far too close a connection with the Secret Service watching Raleigh. No one knew how far the former president's reach went. When they had the evidence, they had to go public everywhere at once. So there was no way for anyone to squash it.

"You're probably the one with the hardline to the president," Lucia said.

Lana only grinned. Considering her condition, it wasn't as deadly or impressive as it would've been just a few weeks ago.

Andre said, "Who did this to you?"

"Does it matter?" Lana said. "What's done is done. The future is the only thing that counts."

"It can't be secured." He leaned against the wall by the door. "No one can do that."

"I can try."

Lucia glanced at him, and they shared a look. As much as he might want to, trying to ensure the future was futile. They'd attempted it, and he and Lucia had spent twenty years as estranged spouses. All he wanted to do now was spend time with her.

Which meant as soon as everyone was secure and this was done, he and Lucia would be disappearing for two weeks. Preferably somewhere so warm he'd spend the whole time in shorts looking at her in a bikini. She must've caught the thought in his head because the corner of her lips curled up. He grinned back at her.

Lucia rolled her eyes on a head shake. "Ted is out there, and we have no way to find him, Lana."

Andre said, "Hannah found a flight that left the airport that's an hour away, a private plane. Fits the timeline. The flight plan filed said it was headed to Seattle. It never arrived."

No doubt there would be some NTSB investigation, but that was the least of Raleigh's worries. He had Ted.

"Is anyone looking for a crashed plane?" Lana asked. "Or one that landed where it wasn't supposed to?"

"Not the kind of thing that's easy to hide," Lucia replied.

Lana's eyes drifted closed.

Lucia mouthed, *Should we ask her about Soraya?*

He shrugged, not sure what she was hinting at.

"I have one more question," Lucia said.

Lana's brows rose, but her eyes didn't open. "Hmm?"

"Can we trust Soraya? Is she solid, or should we make concessions?"

The blanket over Lana's front rose and fell.

Andre shrugged. "Maybe she's asleep."

"I'm not." It took a few long seconds, then Lana said, "Soraya Adams is one of the best people I've ever met. She isn't built for this life, but she'll do the right thing." Her lips barely moved.

Andre frowned. Soraya had gone with Judah to speak with Isaac.

"I'm sure they're fine." His wife had a look on her face. She didn't want him to worry. They were supposed to be watching Lana and not leaving this post until the two cops on the detail were done with Jess and Ted's brother Dean and got back up here.

There was nothing they could do.

He felt the frown tug at his brows. "I should call and check they're good."

"Have Badger do it," Lucia suggested. "Hannah probably needs a break from figuring out their *plan*." Her words made Lana frown, but neither of them was going to tell her Hannah intended on making it public that Raleigh was her biological father.

This whole thing was a mess, but since Chevalier had arguably started it—or been there when it kicked off at least —they should see it through to the end.

Andre nodded. "I'll step out—"

The window beside Lucia exploded in a shower of glass. Her body spun from the force, and she fell to the ground. Lana jerked on the bed. Red blossomed on her chest.

Andre had his phone out before he realized he'd pulled it. He looked down at his own thumbs and watched from somewhere that felt far away as he dialed Zander. That didn't seem right. Was that right? Maybe he should…

"Andre!" Lucia yelled at him. Her mouth moved, but he couldn't hear what she said next.

He put the phone to his ear and said a single word, "Sniper."

Then there was only ringing in his ears.

Lucia crawled across the broken glass, blood smeared across her cheek. The ringing swelled, and he realized he could hear bits and pieces.

"…out…the way." She winced and lifted one hand. "In case…again."

He took her hand in his and looked at the damage to her palm, then turned her chin.

"We have to get Lana down from the bed." Lucia glanced over, assessing the situation.

"We do that," he said, "and we're in the line of fire."

"She has information. I just know it."

Andre wasn't sure he cared all that much, even if it was the right thing to do. Zander would be up here with backup in seconds, no doubt. But they could still act quickly.

"Wheel the bed out of the way of the window." He glanced around, then underneath it at the mechanics of the hospital contraption. "So she's clear."

Lucia started to crawl.

"No." He snagged her arm. "Stay out of the glass. I'll go."

"I love you." She laid a quick kiss on his lips and headed around the other side of the bed.

After they got the wheels unlocked, Andre braced his feet

on the bedside cabinet and said, "Pull." He grabbed the bed and pulled.

Lana's hand flopped over the side of the sheets, then her arm dangled down. Her fingers covered in blood.

Andre felt for a pulse.

"Is she…?"

26

Judah pounded down the hallway. *There's nothing you can do for Soraya.* The words were like a litany in his mind.

Two officers he'd met running away from that hallway with the locked door had assured him they were headed there to get it open and get her out. Soraya would be good. The officers would get her away from that guy.

He'd done all he could.

They wanted him to stand down and go with them. But there was no way he could leave Isaac loose. Judah was sure his friend would use this chance to try and escape. Especially now he knew that the doctor was dead. A way out had already been put into place.

Had Isaac planned on using it himself all this time?

A door on the right of the hallway opened and a man stumbled out, wearing only underwear and clutching his head. Judah reached for a gun he realized he wasn't carrying, because his fingers came up empty.

The man did the same thing, hands grasping at a holster he didn't have. More than anything else, that told Judah the guy was probably a prison guard.

"Someone hit you over the head and took your uniform?" Judah asked.

The guy blinked.

"Go find a colleague or a phone," Judah said. "Have someone look at your head."

There were enough uniformed SWAT guys around, and most of the prisoners had been put back in their cells or at least subdued.

Around the next corner was a sealed entry, beyond which there was an exit.

Both doors were open but likely wouldn't be for long. The prison staff would be getting all the locking mechanisms back up and running—and it would be harder to move around. That was why Isaac worked frantically at the exit bar, picking the security lock to get outside.

Judah stepped into the entryway with him, grabbed a fire extinguisher from the wall, and used it to prop the inside door open so he could get back in if he needed to. "Don't do this."

Isaac twisted something in the lock. "And spend the rest of my life here, or buried somewhere no one will ever find me? I don't think so." He pushed the door open.

Judah raced after him outside, where two uniformed cops waited beside a black and white car. Relief nearly had Judah sagging to the floor. They would arrest Isaac, and he'd be able to go back for Soraya.

She'll be okay.

She had to be. Judah couldn't face any other outcome when he was supposed to be protecting her. He was the one who'd brought her here.

He wanted to be sick just thinking about that inmate dragging her into a cell. Hearing her out would go a long way to helping him get over the guilt of knowing he'd been unable to help, but at the end of it she was the one who'd gone through something here. His feelings didn't factor in her healing. All he had to do was be supportive.

If he had a problem, he'd deal with it on his own.

He just hoped he'd be able to do that even with everything swirling around them. This might be the last thing they needed, but it had happened nonetheless.

One of the officers opened the back door. "Let's go. We don't have much time."

Judah came to a stop and frowned.

"Did you hear anything about the woman?" Isaac had one foot in the car.

"The emergency response team already got her out," the guy said. "She killed the guy who dragged her into the cell in solitary."

Judah couldn't process the information fast enough. This guy was legit, but he was helping Isaac as well? "What's going on?"

His former friend glanced back at him. "You won't stop me."

The look in Isaac's eyes said he fully understood Judah's determination, and yet he'd still asked about Soraya. No doubt not out of the goodness of his heart, but probably more likely because it would throw off Judah.

"I'm going to find you." Judah was determined it would happen sooner or later.

Isaac climbed into the car without a word.

One of the cops strode over and handed Judah a walkie talkie. "You come to a door you need open? Call in. They'll get you back through to the girl."

He climbed in. The driver shut the door, and the vehicle sped away seconds later.

Judah ran inside.

All the way back up to the floor where solitary was, radioing at almost every door to be let through by whoever they had in the control room working locks.

A guy in uniform halted him as soon as he emerged from the stairwell. "Not so fast."

Judah nodded. "I know. I'll give a statement about what happened with that doctor who is dead in there."

Given the shift in the man's expression, that wasn't the response he was expecting.

"But I also need to find my friend. She was in there?" Judah waved at the open door while his stomach roiled at the idea of what might have happened. "She really killed him?"

He'd tossed her the weapon, a kind of Hail Mary as the guys of Chevalier would've called it. But soon as the door locked, there was nothing else he could do. Maybe Judah was trying to convince himself he'd done everything he could. Or this was something he would live with for the rest of his life, a regret he would always carry.

"One of our officers took her downstairs." The man lifted his radio and asked for confirmation of her location. The reply came a few seconds later.

Judah just stared at him. "Did I hear that right? She isn't down there yet?" It hadn't taken that much time to get back and forth through the prison. Though Judah was in one wing, and it may have been a straight shot from here to the exit Isaac had taken, getting back to the front entrance might be a lot longer.

The man shrugged. "Maybe it's taking some time for them to make their way down there."

"I'm going to find her."

Judah didn't wait around for permission, just headed for the stairwell and made his way down. If it took looking over this whole place, then he was going to do that.

Maybe it was regret that drove him or the idea he should have been able to knock down an impenetrable door somehow. Given enough time, he might have figured out a way in. But at that moment, all he was thinking about was her scream. That she'd been trapped in that room, and there was nothing he could do to stop it but toss her a poor prison knife and hope for the best.

His breath came in gasps as he ran down. Worry caused a physical reaction, even while he forced his mind not to think about it.

He just needed to find her. That was all.

Isaac was gone. As Judah stumbled down the next flight of stairs, he realized he hadn't even mentioned it to the officer up there. His thoughts had been full of Soraya and not his renegade friend.

When this all shook out, they were going to say he'd helped Isaac escape. That Judah had given him a head start by not mentioning it to anyone. But who could he tell? Clearly some of them had been involved in the response, not just fakers dressed in uniform. So which officers could he trust? He didn't know who was good or who was allied with Lana in this situation.

Judah shoved his way through the entrance hall of the prison. He stumbled toward a couple of people and asked where she was but got met with looks of confusion. He didn't see her anywhere around, so he went outside.

The glaring sun blinded him until he raised a hand and covered his eyes.

"Bro, you need to stop." One of the officers got in front of him. "We need a statement from you, so quit running around everywhere like you have any kind of authority to do so."

Judah couldn't even form words. He shoved at the man and kept going.

Firetrucks, police cars, and even an ambulance had parked haphazardly between him and the spot where they'd left their vehicle.

"Soraya!" He yelled her name before he even caught up to the fact he'd seen her climbing into an ambulance.

The sight of it should have reassured him that she was being taken care of. But Judah just wanted to see for himself. To look in her eyes and know they were good. At that moment, nothing else mattered.

Not the officer who was probably about to tackle him to the ground.

Judah ran to the ambulance. He thought he might have knocked somebody over, or at least barely managed to keep from sideswiping them. He made it to the ambulance just as the doors were shutting.

The EMT was dressed in police uniform, much like the rest of the first responders on the scene.

Judah tried the back door, but it was locked. He raced to the front driver's door but got there just after the EMT closed it. Judah slammed a hand on the door and tried the handle. "Hey, wait a second!"

The guy stared back at him through the glass of the window.

Casper Cunningham.

The hitman smashed down the accelerator, and the ambulance lurched away. Judah jumped back, so it didn't run over his foot.

"Soraya!"

THE WHOLE AMBULANCE swayed when the driver hit the gas. The bed rolled to slam against the back doors. Soraya bit back the urge to cry out and looked down at the needle mark on the inside of her elbow.

She'd thought he was a cop.

Now she wondered if he didn't have some kind of medical training. He wasn't an EMT, though. That was for sure.

What was happening?

"Who are you?" She called out her question. Loud enough he would maybe hear her through the open window between the back compartment and the ambulance cab.

She heard a low chuckle and fisted her hands by her sides.

If she got up, maybe he would be able to see her if he looked in the rearview.

Was there a mirror like that? Did he even care?

She lifted her head, half expecting it to swim around as she lost consciousness. Wasn't that shot he'd given her meant to knock her out? She had no idea, and there wasn't time to figure out what was true if she was going to get out of this.

She rolled over and climbed off the bed onto the floor. Everything in her sank. It felt like being pinned. The pressure—even if it was only in her mind. The worst part of what'd happened to her today.

Once again she was somewhere she didn't want to be, held against her will.

Raleigh. That prisoner. This not-a-cop.

Soraya blew out a breath that expelled from her mouth in a shudder that brought tears to her eyes. They were all the same, and if it hadn't been for the fact she'd met so many good guys lately, she might be inclined to believe all men were like this.

Judah.

She'd heard him yell her name. Was he in pursuit? He'd tried to get into the cell in solitary as well. Those things weren't built to allow access without the credentials to unlock the door. He'd given her the tools to survive—even if she hated everything about what she'd done.

She needed to focus.

Soraya couldn't just lay here waiting for rescue. She was turning out to be tougher than she'd ever thought, even though the whole thing was horrible, and she never wanted to be in another situation like this one. Or the last two. Or all the ones before that.

Maybe she should move to a quaint town and become a librarian.

Soraya slid her body along the floor toward the back door

and got close enough she could pull down the handle. It was locked.

"What are you doing back there?" His voice had a British accent, and his tone sounded rusty. As though he didn't speak much. Or his vocal cords had been damaged.

She wasn't going to lift up and make herself visible. He needed to hear her voice over where she was supposed to be, so she crawled back up the bed. "Nothing. I'm not doing anything."

He grunted. Maybe he muttered something, but she couldn't hear the words.

Soraya's whole body hurt. She didn't think she had injuries, but she was exhausted, and everything ached enough that tears escaped the corners of her eyes and ran down to her hair.

"…taking your sweet time," he said. "There you are." The words he used next made her wince, but she didn't think he was talking about her.

Maybe Judah?

If that was true, it seemed like they might know each other. But how was that possible? Unless Raleigh told this guy about Judah. Was this one of those assassins? She didn't know what to make of that. It was too far beyond anything she'd ever experienced. Then again, so was nearly all of what was going on lately.

She expected lethargy to overtake her. For her to have to fight passing out. Instead, her thoughts remained clear. She wasn't being knocked out by whatever had been in that syringe.

"What did you give me?"

He didn't answer.

The ambulance continued to rumble down the road. No sirens that she could hear. Still, she got the sense he was driving faster than she would've done.

"I'm serious!" She was beyond frustrated, and he needed

to get that through his head. "What did you give me?" The question was a demand that she yelled, though the tears made her voice wobble a little.

He chuckled. "I'm sure you just caught something. Whatever it feels like, someone probably just sneezed on you."

"What was in that needle?"

His chuckle turned to outright laughter. "That's what she—" The ambulance swerved. "Oh, no, you don't."

Soraya couldn't catch herself in time. She squealed and rolled off the bed onto the floor again. The bed started to move. She grabbed the frame above the wheel, so the thing didn't slide sideways on top of her. Just in case.

She pushed out a breath between clenched teeth.

"Yeah, that's what it's like." His voice carried back to her.

The ambulance swayed. A cabinet opened, and a pile of packages flew out, spewing all over the bed and her.

Soraya ducked down in case anything heavy fell.

He straightened the vehicle out on the road, then turned a sharp corner. She felt the ambulance lift up on two wheels.

She screamed, and the sound morphed into her yelling, "What are you doing?" As she scrambled up, she saw a device on the shelf below the cabinets.

A radio?

Soraya clambered to it, ignoring the way the ambulance careening down streets made her sway. No way could she fall again. She had to get to whatever that was.

Switch on the side.

Lights came on. She fumbled with the handset. Should she be able to hear someone? She squeezed the buttons on both sides since it was like a radio receiver—or whatever this was called. "Hello? Hello, can anyone hear me?"

Static replied.

"Hello? I'm in an ambulance. I've been kidnap—"

Again, the rig careened to the side, this time swaying so hard it stayed up on two wheels. Soraya scrambled onto the bed so she didn't get trapped between it and the cabinets. That was the only thought she could manage as the engine screamed.

The driver swore loudly.

Soraya grabbed two cabinet handles, and the ambulance started to tip onto that side. She held her breath but didn't think squeezing her eyes shut would be a good idea.

At the last second, it fell back on all four wheels.

She lost her grip on the cabinets and tumbled over. Her head struck whatever was behind her, and she landed on her low back with her feet still on the bed.

Soraya screamed out all the pain and frustration, not caring that he would hear it.

Good.

She wanted him to participate in her suffering here since he was the cause. And not just that, but this really *hurt*.

She managed to pull her feet off the bed and get them in front of her on the floor between her and the window partition. All that separated her from the back and the front cab were a bunch of supplies that had fallen. Tools. Equipment.

A scalpel.

No, I can't.

There was no way she could stomach stabbing a man again. Not when she'd done precisely that in the solitary confinement cell.

Maybe this situation was worse.

She tried to move, and it certainly *felt* worse.

A sob worked its way up her throat. Soraya tried to breathe through the pain that wanted to stall her. She couldn't let it, especially when she *could* move. She just didn't want to feel what happened when she did.

Soraya gritted her teeth and got close enough to grab the scalpel.

She wrapped her fingers around the cold metal while the driver continued to careen around corners and nearly crashed the ambulance. Maybe he would hit a wall, and she wouldn't have to worry about what happened after because she wouldn't be around to hear about it.

"Oh no, you don't," he yelled.

She wanted to ask what was happening. Instead, she stayed quiet, hoping he forgot that she was back here.

She was really going to do this.

She had to get close enough she could pop up before he knew she was there. After that…she wasn't going to think about what she'd have to do.

Soraya would worry about the nightmares later.

Right now, she climbed onto the bed and toward the window. They turned a corner, but she managed to hold on and stay silent even though her back felt like one giant bruise.

With one hand, she grabbed the edge of the open partition. She swung at him, grasping the scalpel with the other, and looked in time to see his torso.

She ignored the face that whipped around to look at her, pushed out every thought, and slammed the blade into his shoulder.

He grabbed her arm.

She winced at the loud screech and realized it was her.

Screaming.

The ambulance turned and headed full speed into the side of a building.

Judah saw the ambulance barrel into the side of the house. He gripped the door handle, unable to look away. "Whoa."

The cop who was driving hit the brakes, coming up fast behind the ambo, and tapped the dash screen. He made a call that rang in the car's speakers.

"9-1-1. What's your emergency?"

"This is Sergeant Roberts." He gave his badge number. "We have a collision at the east side of the twelve-hundred block of O'Hare. I need fire and paramedics, plus backup."

"Copy that, Sergeant." The dispatcher asked a couple more clarifying questions and the sergeant answered.

Judah got out of the car. He had no weapon, but what did it matter? Between the sergeant and the car that had followed them as they sped away from the prison, there were enough cops around. He'd raised a ruckus over the fact it was Casper in the ambulance. They'd jumped in to help, something he was immensely thankful for. Though, it was likely because they thought all the fuss was about Isaac and his escape.

All he needed to do was get Soraya out of the back.

Judah ran his hands over his head, then squeezed the

back of his neck. The sergeant got out of the car. Once he knew she was okay, Judah could worry about Isaac being loose.

"Hey," Roberts said. "At least let me go first, yeah?" The guy drew his weapon.

Judah walked right behind him into the open hole on the side of the house.

"Police! If you're in here, call out!" Roberts stepped carefully around the ambulance.

Judah stopped at the back door and pulled the handle. It was wedged shut. The dented back corner put pressure on the door, so he couldn't get it open. He pulled on it anyway. "Come on."

It wouldn't budge—just like the cell door in solitary.

"Soraya! Can you hear me?"

"Over here."

Judah skirted the edge of the couch and looked at the back corner of the ambulance. It looked like they'd sideswiped something. He pounded on the side. "Soraya!" No sound came from inside, so he turned to the wreckage of whoever's home this was. "How long before fire gets here?" he asked Roberts. "We need to get that door open."

"Couple of minutes."

She might not have that long if she was bleeding out.

Judah prayed over that, just as he hoped and prayed no one was here in the living area when this ambulance crashed into the side of the house. "Hello? Is anyone hurt?" He crouched and looked under the ambulance but didn't see anything. Maybe the residents were all out, at work, or on vacation.

Please, Lord.

He turned to the sergeant. "You get the impression the residents were home?"

"Car isn't in the driveway, but it could be in the garage." They both stopped to listen, then Roberts pulled open the passenger door. He frowned and glanced at Judah. "Stay here. I need to check the other side."

Judah moved into the space he'd occupied. "There's blood."

He climbed in because no one was inside, praying Casper was injured but hadn't gone far—as fervently as he prayed Soraya was all right. The door on the other side was open. He looked in the hatch between the seats and got a view of the back.

"Soraya!"

Sirens whirled down the street, growing louder as they got closer. But it didn't make him feel any better.

Roberts shined his flashlight. "You see her?"

"Only her side. She isn't moving." Judah inhaled. "Soraya!"

Was she going to wake up? He was too big to climb back there.

"Fire department!" The call came from outside.

Judah stuck his head out the door. "Get the back open! There's someone in there hurt!" He didn't wait for the firefighter to acknowledge it, just turned back to Roberts. "Where's the driver?"

He shook his head. "Not here. I'm going to do a search."

"Backup?"

"Send them after me," Roberts said. "But the firefighters will walk through as well to check no one was home."

Judah nodded. He watched the direction Roberts went, then stared in the window. "Soraya, you've got to wake up." Tears gathered, stinging his eyes.

Was she dead?

The driver's seat was soaked in blood up high on the shoulder. Had Casper been injured in the crash? There wasn't any damage to the windshield, so a projectile hadn't come through the front window.

Heavy machinery whirred, and a hole emerged in the back door.

She still hadn't stirred.

He clambered out and noticed something shiny on the seat.

A scalpel covered in blood.

Judah's thoughts whirred like the Jaws of Life as he raced to the back, only to be stopped by the gloved hand of a uniformed firefighter.

The man frowned his caterpillar brows. "Stay back, sir."

"My friend is in there. She'll need immediate medical attention." He swallowed. *She's not dead. She can't be.*

"Then you let the EMTs get in there."

Judah nodded. "I'm good with that."

They were already waiting, duffels and gear over one shoulder. One held a backboard. The door was hauled open, groaning as it twisted on the hinges.

It was the hardest moment of his life to stand and watch as they called out to each other, and Soraya was loaded on the backboard. He helped carry it, and they probably only allowed it because he'd said nothing and hadn't moved.

Judah turned to the one who'd stopped him and stuck out his hand. "Thank you. No matter what happens. Thanks for getting her out."

There was a moment of pause, and the guy shook his hand.

Judah jogged to the ambulance and climbed in. He might've been kept out of the other bus, but no way would he get restricted from this. "Soraya."

The EMT glanced at him.

"I'll stay out of your way. Is she awake?"

The EMT was female and blonde. A tiny thing.

"I'm serious. I'll be no trouble."

"Just keep talking." She put a stethoscope in both ears and

listened to Soraya's chest. "With that accent, I'm sure you'll manage to convince me of whatever you want."

He wasn't sure that was a good thing but kept his mouth shut on the ride to the hospital. The heartrate monitor they hooked up to her beat steadily. He reached out and touched her ankle just to feel the warmth of her skin.

Had the cop found Casper? Would he come back to see Judah? One meant a whole lot of explaining. The other meant Judah needed to find a weapon.

Then there was Isaac.

Judah let out a long exhale and forced his mind to focus only on Soraya. He'd have to get Ted to—no, he couldn't. Ted was somewhere, probably being forced by Raleigh to work on the phone system. Judah squeezed his eyes shut. He'd have to get the number for Soraya's parents himself. Call, and tell them what had happened.

They would show up and demand real answers. Not the half-truths he'd tell them. Just enough truth to not make them targets.

"Rough day, huh?"

He looked at the EMT and her blue eyes. She'd probably seen some things she couldn't erase, but under it all, she still had hope. Probably down to the gold cross that hung around her neck. "It was a rough day."

"I can check your vitals. Just to make sure?"

He shook his head. "I'm good." Then he motioned to Soraya with his chin. "I just need her to be okay."

They pulled into the hospital, and Soraya was wheeled in. Orders he couldn't decipher were shouted back and forth.

Someone spoke to him.

Judah didn't understand their words. He could only stumble along until they took his elbow. "I need a phone." His behind hit a chair.

A guy in blue scrubs crouched in front of him, mouthing words.

Judah shook his head. "I just need to know if she's okay. And I need a phone."

The guy stared for a second, then pointed Judah to a phone on the counter at the reception desk.

He dialed Zander. The way he'd wanted to all those times when he was in Africa for weeks, working for the Brits.

Judah bent forward and tried to put his head between his knees. He heard Zander's voice, on the phone and then echoing in his other ear.

"Dude, stand up."

Judah straightened.

Badger, Hannah, his sister Toni, Jeff, and Zander walked toward him.

He stared while the phone made an angry tone in his ear.

His sister stopped right in front of him, one hand on her hip. "What did you get yourself into this time?"

"You're here." Judah wrapped her up in a bear hug until she squealed.

"Where else would I be?"

SORAYA CAME AWAKE to a tremendous sense of warmth. She was also tucked in—the way her mom used to do to her when she was little. Now she didn't do that, because she got so warm she had bad dreams. Night sweats. Terrors. This wasn't her. It was wrong.

Everything was wrong.

She gasped and opened her eyes.

A woman beside the bed laid down a magazine and smiled softly. Soraya saw elements of Judah's features in hers. The woman said, "Hi."

Soraya looked around and saw Judah on the other side of the bed. He was fast asleep in a chair with his body angled in a way that looked like it would be painful when he woke up. He was okay. She was the one in the hospital bed.

It all came back.

The solitary cell. The ambulance. The scalpel.

"I'm Toni."

Soraya looked back at the woman and swallowed. Her mouth tasted terrible. "Hi, Toni. I'm thirsty." She frowned, realizing what she'd said.

Toni grinned and brought over a cup with a straw. "Watch out. It's super cold like always." Her accent matched Judah's but with a softened quality to it. "I know your name is Soraya."

"Yeah."

"Want the bullet points update?"

"Sure." She didn't have the brainpower to ask for anything else, but she knew she didn't want to talk about bullets. Was that what this was about?

"Okay, the cops are outside." Toni settled back on the edge of the chair. "They'd like a statement from both of you when you're ready, but Judah wanted to wait until you woke up. Half of Chevalier and my husband-to-be are outside as well. They're planning because something is clearly kicking off. Isaac escaped, so he's out there, and Lana is back in Last Chance County in surgery. They're doing their best to get her stable, but it's touchy. She's been under the knife for hours. Apparently, the bullet nicked something."

"She was shot?"

Toni nodded. "Sorry. I can get you more information, but that's all I know about that."

"It's fine. I can go see her myself."

The moment the words came out of her mouth Soraya realized that was exactly what she'd do when she got out of here. Go back to Last Chance County and make sure Lana was all right.

She didn't want to walk into the line of fire, so she'd have to make sure it was safe since Lana got shot apparently. Soraya needed more details on that. But seeing her friend or a woman who *had* been her friend? That was important, even if it might be dangerous.

Soraya also needed to call her mom again.

Toni said, "Lana is surrounded by security, not just one person on the door. They gave up on the private wing and will move her to the middle of a public floor when she's out of surgery. Cops everywhere. She couldn't be safer."

Soraya nodded. "That's good."

It was a few seconds, then Toni broke the silence. "You okay?"

Soraya shook her head but didn't say anything. If she did, she was going to break down. That was the last thing she wanted to do in front of Judah's sister. The woman was tough, and she'd been through so much from what Judah had told her. They'd talked most of the way to the east coast before going to the prison. Now she knew Toni had survived because she was strong.

Soraya was nothing like her. All she'd managed was to be way too nosy, land herself on the radar of a powerful guy. And get kidnapped—several times.

She squeezed her eyes shut as the memories flooded back. The ones in the rear of the ambulance weren't as bad as the "up close with a dangerous man" memories she had. But being thrown around inside the ambulance when the crash happened hadn't felt good at all. Her entire body felt like one giant bruise, and the rest of it she didn't want to think about.

Now she was in the hospital. Surely that was a good outcome given the worst *hadn't* happened. She and Judah were alive. She didn't feel good, but it couldn't be serious if the doctors and nurses hadn't run in the moment she woke up.

But she still wasn't safe, was she?

"Has anyone heard from Ted?" Soraya bit her lip, part of her not even wanting to know the answer to her question.

Toni shook her head. "I'm sorry. We still don't know where he is."

"I'll bet Isaac could find out."

Toni frowned.

"I'm just saying." Chevalier had solid people, and they knew many folks with serious access. Why couldn't one of them help find their friend? They certainly didn't need her for that.

"See if you can come up with anything," Toni suggested. "It's always helpful to have someone in the mix with a different way of looking at things. It can be what makes the difference between a win and a loss. Like Judah throwing you that shiv."

Soraya didn't want to think about that.

"He told me. Sorry."

Soraya shook her head. "It all worked out, didn't it?"

Toni's eyes narrowed.

Soraya looked away, not wanting to get into something with a woman she'd only just met. It wasn't like Toni could help her get back to some kind of normal life with no danger nipping at her heels.

Toni began, "Soray—"

Judah groaned, shifted on the chair, and sat up, cutting off whatever his sister had been about to say. "Oh. Hey." He scrubbed his hands over his face. "Sis?"

Toni stood. "I'm gone. Gotta check in with the guys, anyway."

The door clicked shut.

"Hey." Judah leaned against the side of the bed.

Soraya looked up at him, but everything blurred. It didn't matter how hard she willed them away. The tears came.

"Hey." His voice softened. "It's okay. Everything is okay."

Soraya shook her head. It wasn't okay. Things were never going to be okay, not when she knew the taste of fear and just how quickly things could change.

"You're safe." His face was close.

She squeezed her eyes shut, and he held her for a few minutes while her tears leaked on his shoulder. Until she managed to say, "It's not okay." She lifted her chin and stared into those huge brown eyes. She still felt like she would never be safe again. "I don't think I can do this."

The muscles in his forehead flexed.

"I'm scared."

"I'll be with you. No matter what, I'm not going to leave again or let you face this alone."

She brushed off her cheeks, and he handed her a tissue, not saying anything while she cleaned up. "I'm sorry. I'm too scared. I can't live this life." She felt like she was confessing a sin. "I can't live your life."

"I'm not asking you to." He shook his head, confusion on his face.

"I need to find a safe place to go. Maybe police custody." Except there wasn't exactly a threat against her that they'd be able to verify. "Somewhere I can stay under the radar until this blows over."

"I thought you were going to help me—us, Chevalier— take down Raleigh?"

"I want to. He shouldn't be able to do what he does. I'm sorry about Ted. I'll help with that." She sniffed. "But I can't face down Raleigh. I can't see him. I can't—" Her voice cracked.

"You're not going to be doing this alone." He touched her cheek. "Not any of it."

But she was alone. And she'd been that way through so much of this, whether he intended otherwise or not. There was nothing he'd be able to do about it if something happened again. She would be trapped. Alone.

Terror buzzed in her, almost like it swam through her veins. A living thing.

"I can't." She shook her head. "I'm sorry. I want to help find Ted, but that's it."

She brushed away his hand from her face. The hardest thing she'd ever done. She wanted to take his hand and hold it, but that wouldn't help her stand on her own. The fear was too strong to rely on Judah, as much as she might want that. Maybe more than anything.

But she couldn't.

He had a job to do, and she shouldn't get in the way of that.

"I have to get on with my life. I have to get out of this world where I keep getting captured and hurt." She shook her head, determined to stay strong. "I can't do it."

He didn't need to have to protect her alongside doing his job. A guy like Judah had much more important things to do than babysit someone who was a liability.

Before he could say something that would change her mind or try to convince her, she said, "I think you should leave. Go do your job. It's important."

"Soraya—"

She shook her head, her stomach a mad flutter of nausea. She tried not to let him see. "Just go, Judah. I'm staying here, and you have a job to do."

He stared at her for a few moments. "You're not going to listen to anything I say, are you?"

She gripped the blanket. "Just find Ted."

"This isn't over."

The door clicked shut, and Soraya let the tears fall.

28

"That's what she said." Judah folded his arms. It was better than punching someone. "She's out."

Hannah frowned at him. Badger had left to visit the storage unit the doctor had told Judah about to see what was there.

Jeff leaned against the wall in the corner as though he intended to keep his place outside the inner circle of Chevalier. Since the guy had plenty going on in his life—not the least of which was marrying Toni—Judah didn't sweat it right now.

Andre and Lucia had stayed home, overseeing the hospital detail for Lana. They were also keeping Nora safe along with Eas, Karina, and Aria. Last Judah had heard, Nora was hanging out at the hospital with them to make things easier for them all. It was that, or stay in the bunker until someone got back to the house.

Judah didn't want to know how Zander dealt with being apart from the woman he loved—the one he'd married, who was now carrying his baby. But he figured he was about to get a taste of what it felt like.

"She's scared," he said. "She's been through a ton the last

few days. Maybe she'll work her way through it, but that could take time."

"We need her if this plan is going to work," Hannah reminded him.

He nodded. They'd have to tweak a lot if Soraya wasn't going to be part of it. Then again, in a way, it could play in their favor. "Sooner or later, Raleigh will run out of footage he coerced Soraya into making. He won't be able to use her anymore."

Raleigh would move on to the next part of his plan, or he would come after Soraya and try to abduct her again—which was the last thing she needed. Maybe it was better that she lay low. Even perhaps enrolling in Jeff and Toni's business, the one they worked side by side.

Judah strode to the man who would be his brother-in-law in a couple of months. "Can you get Soraya on the accountant's office client list?"

Jeff's eyebrows rose. Thanks to an IED a few years ago, the guy had one arm. There wasn't much that fazed him. Toni stood beside him, by the shoulder with no arm under it. As though she was inclined to protect his vulnerable side, which left Jeff's other arm free to use to defend that side. As though they were partners.

Something Soraya evidently didn't want to be with him.

Judah bit back what he wanted to say. "It's not like she can hide where Raleigh won't find her. Not with a bunch of trained assassins on his payroll. She's not safe anywhere in the world. She needs protection."

"Take Raleigh down," Jeff said. "Eliminate the threat."

"If it was that easy, we'd have done it already. I'm talking about contingencies. She might never be able to shake this."

Jeff said, "You care about her."

"Of course, I do!"

Toni looked like she was about to get all big-sister on him.

Instead, Jeff said, "So you want her to disappear where

you'll never see her again? Because this is stricter than witness protection, and there's no contact. Ever. She ceases to exist for you, and you both go on with your lives. Separately." He paused. "Is that something you're prepared to live with?"

"Will she be one hundred percent safe?" Judah glanced between them even though he already knew the answer.

"Is anyone?" Jeff asked rhetorically.

"You know what I mean."

"Raleigh will never find her." Jeff continued before Judah could argue with that. "I've been working on something. It's based on a rumor I heard a few years back about a town comprised entirely of people in witness protection. They're all too famous to show their faces anywhere, so they have to live completely separate from the world. An added layer of protection."

Judah didn't know how that would help clients of the Accountants Office, most of whom were former spies who'd been burned or ex-special forces. Anyone with the money to afford the service—though Jeff was apparently working on getting around that as well. People whose lives were under threat from organizations, or governments, who could find them anywhere.

So they had to disappear.

Completely.

Judah wandered to a chair and let his legs give out. He hung his head and gave his mind a few seconds to accept what his body was trying to tell him.

Zander sat beside him. "You okay?"

"Where's Ted?"

Zander pressed his lips into a thin line. Jeff and Toni sat, speaking low to each other in a way that made Judah want to rage at them for not doing more. But that wouldn't be fair. They were here to help, and they hadn't needed to come.

The fact was, they likely would do everything they could to help Soraya if she asked. Judah didn't care if he never saw her again. If it made Soraya safe? He would pay the whole bill himself.

Hannah sat opposite him and Zander. "I'm going on the five o'clock news here locally in a couple of hours. I'll tell everyone who will listen that Raleigh is my father. In a way no one will be able to contradict or discredit. He'll never escape the media storm this is going to create." She frowned. "I was also hoping Soraya would go with me."

"That would've backfired," Judah said. "Raleigh killed her credibility. And no one would believe she wasn't on that live meeting for real. She has no proof it was coercion."

"Witness statements still count for something." Hannah gave him what he thought of as her "cop" stare. Formerly a police detective, she was working on her Private Investigator license and with Chevalier. In the next few months, Judah had figured she'd settle on one side or the other. Considering Nora was her half-sister, she'd probably stick close to town so she could be there for her niece or nephew.

"If we're going to take down Raleigh, we need more than witness statements." Even though he wanted Ted back, so the kid could give his.

Sure, the guy was in his twenties, but considering he was basically their little brother, they all thought of him as a kid. Probably drove the kid crazy.

Judah rubbed an achy spot on his chest.

Zander squeezed his shoulder. "Badger is here."

Judah studied his face as he strode over. He shook his head slightly, and that long hair of his fell over his forehead. Badger swiped it back.

"Weren't you going to get a haircut for Ted's wedding?" Judah swallowed down the lump in his throat. It *would* happen. They were going to make sure of it.

Badger put his arm around Hannah. "She likes it like this."

"Wedding talk can wait," Zander said, his tone a little frustrated. "What happened at the storage unit?"

"Whole thing was cleaned out," Badger said. "There was nothing there, but I talked to the guy at the front desk and looked at his surveillance cameras. It was Isaac."

"He didn't bother to hide it?" Zander asked.

Badger shook his head.

Hannah twisted out from under his shoulder. "The guy just let you look at the footage?"

"I slipped him a couple of bills. We're square."

Zander said, "So Isaac cleaned it out?"

Badger nodded. "Whatever was there, he got to it first."

Judah scrubbed his hands over his face. Of course, Isaac got to it first. Nothing else about this had gone right, and now the guy was out of prison. "He's on the run from the feds as an escaped prisoner, and instead of hiding, he goes to the trouble of stopping by a storage unit that will help us, not him, and purposely gets his face on camera."

Hannah said, "The second that guy at the storage unit realizes it was him, he's going to call the cops to get a reward for the information."

"He could be trying to help," Zander said. "Isn't that what he's been doing this whole time?"

Badger shook his head. "I wish I knew what he was up to."

Judah was about to add his two-pence, but his phone chimed with a notification.

One by one, all of their phones went off—except his sister and Jeff.

Judah stared at the message. "Four-slash-seven." It was followed by a series of numbers he read off.

Zander said, "Latitude and longitude coordinates. Mine starts one-slash-seven."

"I'm six." Hannah looked up, a frown on her face. "Different coordinates than yours."

"Me too," Badger said. "And I'm five of seven."

Zander's phone buzzed again. "Andre and Lucia got the same thing. They're two and three."

"So who is seven?" Judah asked. "And what is this about?"

Zander's phone rang with an incoming call. "It's Jess."

Judah's thoughts snapped into place, and he stood. "If she's seven, then this is Ted. He sent us his location."

"Just me." Toni shut the door to Soraya's room behind her.

"Hi." Soraya didn't know what else to say. She'd basically yelled at Judah and told him to get out, then cried for a while on her own. The nurse had checked on her, and the doctor came by. She even used the phone and called her mom and dad, even though it was probably a security breach.

Now she had nearly zero energy and a full stomach of hospital food, which hadn't been so awful. Too bad she was emotional eating. She really hadn't needed both cookies, but guilt over food wasn't something she was willing to hold on to. Life was too short for that.

Her parents had gone to visit her aunt in California. It wouldn't keep them off Raleigh's radar if he wanted to get to them but might make them a tiny bit harder to find. It also gave them something to do rather than simply sitting around waiting for word about whether Soraya was alive or dead.

She let out a long sigh.

Toni eyed her. "I have news. If you want it."

Soraya nodded. "Better than sitting here feeling sorry for myself."

"There's no reason for that." Toni sat by the bed. "It's fine if that's how you feel, but no one is pitying you."

"I figured you'd be mad at me since I shut down Judah and told him I didn't want to help." Seeing the look on his face was the worst part, knowing she'd hurt his feelings.

"So you're going to do nothing?"

Soraya shook her head. Despite the fear, she couldn't in good conscience walk away. "Not if there's something I can do, especially if it might help Ted. But I don't want to be part of the team."

"You shouldn't be going on missions…or operations," Toni said. "You aren't trained, so there's no way to do it and not put you in harm's way. It's smart for you to steer clear of that. The team would have split focus, protecting you and doing their jobs."

That wasn't why she was still here, and determined to hide away, but it was a smart line of thinking. "I agree." She couldn't deny this was mostly about being too scared. "But why can't I shake the fear?"

"How about I fill you in on the latest?" Toni said. "Might get your mind off it."

"Sure." Soraya figured nothing would change, not yet.

"Seven sets of coordinates were sent to their phones. When they inputted each into a map, it gave them a circle."

"Places to look…for what?"

"Zander thought it was more of an attempt to point them in the right direction. Drawing lines from each point to the center gave them one place to look." Toni pulled out her phone. "A mansion in Richmond, Virginia."

"Do they think that's where Ted is?" Soraya asked. "Who owns the house?"

Toni grinned. "They think Ted sent the messages. His fiancée got one, too. She's on a plane already. The others already left, so they'll likely breach before she gets there to help. But your question was asked as well. By me, actually." Toni let out a sigh, which probably would've been laughter under different circumstances. "The house is legally owned by a shell corporation that doesn't exist."

"Private, or a business, or the government?" Soraya looked around. Like her laptop was going to be sitting around here, and she could just grab it. But she hadn't even taken it to Nigeria with her. She sighed. Nothing had felt right for weeks.

"Normally Ted would be researching that stuff. But since he's the victim here—"

"I don't like that word." She didn't even want to think about the fact she'd been one. So many times recently.

"The team could use your help."

"There it is." Soraya looked away.

"Isn't your instinct to research? To dig and find the truth?"

She nodded. "Until it put me on Raleigh's radar and I became public enemy number one."

"You can help by putting your skills to use…without putting your life on the line." Toni paused. "We have people in our lives who've trained for years to do that job. I gave it up. You've never done it. That means it's not the role we play in this scenario."

Soraya bit her lip. "My life is on the line either way."

"So we get you somewhere safe." Toni shifted. "Jeff and I run this business. It's like a private witness protection, for people who can't get government help to hide but who also can't show their faces in public without fearing for their lives. Sometimes *because* of the government."

"You run it?"

"Zander actually bought the company when the previous owner retired. He asked Jeff to run the business, and we've taken it on together."

"Helping people hide?"

Toni nodded. "New identities. A completely clean and anonymous life. There are many rules in some cases, and even a handful of people who had to have plastic surgery so facial recognition didn't know them anymore."

"That's what Raleigh did with Jerry Travers and the head of the assassin's guild."

"That doesn't mean there was a security breach. It just means the technology isn't as far-fetched as you might think."

Soraya wasn't sure she wanted to talk about that option yet. It sounded like a nuclear last chance for a life out of danger. Scary—and too good to be true. But considering everything scared her right now, maybe that wasn't surprising.

She decided to go back to talking about Ted and the team. "How long until we'll know if they're right that it's where Ted is being held?"

"A few hours." Toni sat back in the chair. "Plenty of time for me to tell you all about how the accountant's office could save your life."

"Why is it even called that?" That made no sense. It was probably very confusing, without getting the word out any way but by rumor. "How do you let people know about the service?"

"For years the accountant's office was only a rumor. I don't know who started it." Toni shrugged. "But I've met the woman who ran it before us. All the clients came by referral, or people started asking about the rumor and someone from the accountant's office would approach them. Anyone they could help, they did. No questions asked."

"What if someone doesn't know they need you until it's too late?"

"Hopefully they call Chevalier," Toni said. "But sometimes we can perform an extraction ourselves. It can be part of the service."

"Then why are you here, instead of being there to help get Ted out of that situation."

Toni frowned. "Jeff is with the team, and I'm here with you. That's what we decided."

Soraya started to object, but Toni held up a hand. "Besides, you could be a future client of the accountant's office, so we have a vested interest in keeping you safe."

"Probably out of my price range. And what will my parents do?"

"Some people take family with them."

"The program allows for that?" Soraya frowned.

"It's not a program as such," Toni said. "We provide a clean identity and what you'll need to get where you want to go. After that it's up to you. But if you need us, we have an emergency line."

"And Chevalier will show up?"

"Most likely." Toni smiled.

"It's a nice idea." Seeing Judah. Being free. But it seemed as though she would be using these good people just to obtain that dream. "Nicer than being scared…or getting abducted again."

Toni's expression darkened. "Did any of them…touch you?"

Soraya shook her head. "Not like that."

"Good." Toni looked like she just might have murdered someone if Soraya had said yes.

A light tap sounded on the door.

Soraya stiffened. Being here seemed like a cocoon of safety from the evil in the world. But Raleigh could find her anywhere, if he wanted to. He could hire an assassin to take her out. Isaac could show up again, for his own reasons. Who knew what would happen next?

Toni stepped outside for a second, then came back in. "Two FBI agents. I can confirm their credentials if you want to wait?"

Soraya bit her lip. She wanted to see their faces, but if they weren't who they claimed it would be too late by then. "What do they want?"

"Raleigh," Toni said. "Or so they say."

Soraya lifted her chin. "Do you have a gun?"

Toni grinned. "I like the way you think."

29

Jeff leaned forward in the cramped back seat. "We all know this could be a trap, right?"

Judah shot him a look. Along with Jeff and Badger, he was stuffed in the back seat of Zander's rental car. Hannah rode "shotgun" in the front. And why was it even called that?

"Does it matter?" Zander turned the corner so they all swayed to the left. "There it is."

Jeff took a deep breath as if he was going to speak again. Probably to tell them all that this might not even be where Ted was. Except for the fact the holding company that owned the property was mentioned in the cache of information Lana had handed over.

Judah nudged him. "Whatever you're gonna say, we all know already."

Jeff made a face.

"Maybe it's been a while since you've done this, so you're rusty. But the last thing you need is to psych yourself out before we even get there." Judah realized everyone was listening, and not just because they could hear him. "You wanna find Ted, right?"

Jeff gave a sharp nod. "It's usually not personal, okay? At least not since Toni…"

"I know." Judah figured changing the subject was a good idea. "How's Maggie?"

He figured asking Jeff about his mom would get his mind off what was going on.

"She's fine," Jeff said. "They released her after she got better from the salmonella thing, but she ended up sticking around the hospital with Windermere, so when Eas woke up, they were all there."

Hannah turned around. "You think they're gonna get married anytime soon, Maggie and the doc?"

No one said anything.

"What?"

"That's just…" Judah didn't know what to say.

"Wrong." Badger finished for him.

Hannah rolled her eyes. "You guys are—"

"We're here." Zander pulled over to the side of a residential street lined on both sides with gaping mansions.

Judah wasn't sure he'd ever want to live in a house like these. Too much upkeep. And all that square footage, knocking around so that it felt empty everywhere you went.

Hannah shoved open her door. "You all know Windermere and Maggie are dating. They're going to get married sooner or later, whether y'all like it or not."

Judah glanced at Badger. The two of them shook their heads.

"I agree with Badger." Jeff climbed out. "Not to mention I don't even want to think that stuff about my mom." He shuddered, but it seemed mostly fake.

Judah thought it was funny, though he agreed with the sentiment considering he experienced it himself thinking about Jeff marrying Toni. He wanted that with Soraya, if she was willing. For the first time in his life, he'd done the relationship thing right instead of jumping too far too fast.

Only she didn't want to be part of his life, did she?

She'd flat out said she couldn't handle it. Judah had no intention of pushing her into something she didn't want. So what was he supposed to do, other than get out of her way as she walked out the door?

Zander stepped in front of him. "You're on overwatch."

Judah started to object.

"No arguments." Zander turned, swirling his index finger in the air. "Let's go."

They spread out and came at the house from different entrances. Judah crossed the front yard and spotted a drain-pipe. He climbed to the second floor where there was a balcony above the front entrance.

"In position," Hannah said over comms. Probably satisfied about being the first one.

The others chimed in. Four compass points to breach the house.

Was Ted inside?

Judah didn't see anyone on the street out front. He climbed the peak of the roof and looked at the expansive back garden. "All clear from above."

He moved back to the front, passing the chimney. Voices drifted up from below. Judah peered down.

"You've got company, some spot where there's a fireplace." He figured the living room, but who knew where rich people put that stuff. Maybe it was a bedroom or the wall between two rooms.

"Copy that," Zander said. "Moving in now."

Did Soraya want to live in a place like this? Judah had never thought much about the future. His life had been a series of new starts. The latest one being when he took a job with Zander at Chevalier. He didn't expect it to be done anytime soon, but who knew what the future held? He'd never been one to settle down before.

For Soraya, it would be worth it. But she'd shut that down

pretty thoroughly. And even though he knew it was an emotional reaction down to all the fear she felt, he could understand it. He lived this life, and sometimes the fear made him nervous enough he hesitated or took a misstep.

Judah clocked the approaching car from down the street. He kept his eye on it while he crested the roof again. He couldn't look both ways at once, which was why he usually had someone up here with him. For Ted, it was a risk they were all going to take.

The car passed the house and kept going.

Soraya was safe. The team was going to make sure Ted got back to Jess, and they could get married.

"Nothing on the west side," Badger said.

"Nothing on the third floor." Hannah sounded breathy.

"I found the fireplace." Jeff's voice was soft.

"On my way," Badger said.

Judah could make out the shuffle of movement, but the comms system wasn't designed to pick up ambient noise. Just the voice of the operator.

A squeal cut across the open channel. Two suppressed shots popped off in quick succession. "Down!"

"Get down! Let me see your hands!"

Before Jeff and Zander could say more, Hannah cut across the feed. "Ted was here. He left a note on the bathroom mirror."

Judah's hands curled into fists by his side. He scanned the street in front, where a neighbor headed out. Something was brewing. He could practically feel the approach, like the slow roll of a storm. The tension in the air that preceded the first crack of lightning.

A van turned the corner at the end of the street. Behind the house, a street over, another similar vehicle did the same.

Judah announced, "We've got incoming."

"Get out of there, Jude." Zander's voice allowed no argument. "We're going to question these people. And whoever is coming, they'll either get in our way or they're going to help."

Judah figured he knew which it was. "I'm not leaving."

"The rest of you, go with him."

They started to argue.

Zander cut them off. "Go. Everyone."

Judah shimmied back down the drainpipe. Not quite as graceful as ascending it, and he ended up on his bottom in the peonies. But he brushed off the seat of his pants and ran for the car while the van did a slow drive by.

Maybe it was nothing.

The others walked out. He had the car running by then, and pulled up out front of the house. They all climbed in.

"Where are they?" Badger asked.

"So you can go to war on Zander's behalf?"

The van would do another circle in a second. Judah hit the gas and drove as fast as he could away from the house. He went south at the end, because the van had come from the north, and saw it pull out behind him from a parallel running street seconds later. Too far back for them to notice the Chevalier car. Hopefully.

"You think it's Raleigh…or the feds?" Hannah asked from the back seat.

"Right now," Judah said, "I figure those might be the same thing."

Jeff asked, "What did you find in the house that makes you think Ted was there?"

"How about a full computer setup and a notepad with his handwriting on it?" Hannah's voice quavered. "We're going to just let Zander get brought in by whoever is coming?"

Jeff said, "He probably figures if they work for Raleigh, he has a shot they'll take him to Ted. Or at least the same location. Either way the people in the living room will be answering his questions."

That was exactly what Judah figured Zander was doing—trying to get to Ted. "It's worth a try, at least. Worth the risk."

"He's going to get himself *killed*," Hannah said. "But he's the captain. So...what? He goes down with the ship."

"We're not happy about it, Han." Badger twisted around in the front seat. "But Zander's orders go."

"What's the plan? Because I didn't think this was a group who followed the letter of the law...or obeyed blindly."

Jeff chuckled.

"It's not funny," Hannah said. "Zander is in danger."

"He'll be okay," Badger told her. "He can also probably still hear you."

"He's right, Hannah." Zander's voice cut out a couple of times because of the distance, even though Judah had circled around and parked close enough they were still in range of each other. "But right now, I need you to call Nora."

"What's going on?" Badger asked.

"POLICE!"

"FBI! Freeze!"

The comms channel cracked and cut off.

"I'll call my sister."

Badger turned and shot Hannah a smile. But the expression he turned to Judah didn't hold the same warmth. "Cops?"

Judah shrugged.

"Hey—" Hannah's greeting cut off and she quieted.

Judah needed to drive them all back to the hospital. It hurt to leave the place where his boss might be in trouble. They could follow whoever took Zander out of there, or he could get back to Soraya. Strike back at Raleigh, with her help.

Since Zander had GPS on him, the answer was clear.

"And she didn't make it through the surgery?"

Soraya didn't like feeling at a disadvantage, but figured that was understandable under the watchful gaze of two federal agents and a police sergeant. They'd all introduced themselves. With no recording device and no notebook, she figured she wouldn't remember their names for long.

Toni shifted and pulled out her phone. "Sorry, Soraya. I have to take this."

Judah's sister left before Soraya could ask her who was calling. The door clicked shut and the cops just stared at her, assessing gazes all around. Until she had to fight a squirm. What did she have to hide?

"Can I help you gentlemen?" She glanced between them. "I thought you had questions."

"More like clarification. On a few things." The sergeant moved to one side of the bed and leaned against the wall. But there was nothing nonchalant about him. "I met your friend, Judah Havig. I chased the man driving the ambulance from the accident scene, but I lost him. He's in the wind."

It hadn't been an accident so much as her deliberate attempt to crash the ambulance after she'd stabbed that British guy in the neck.

"What can you tell me about him?"

"I don't know who he is, if that's what you're asking." Although, she'd guess it was the guy who'd shot up her apartment in Nigeria. But how was that tale going to make any sense? "I don't know his name, and I'm not sure if I can describe him except that he had a British accent."

The sergeant frowned. "That seems to be a theme here. What with your friend Judah, and his sister…" He motioned to the door.

That only served to distract her again with who might be on the other end of Toni's call—and whether the team had found Ted yet.

"Then there's our other issue." Special Agent Brennan had a blue tie and a dark mustache threaded with gray.

Soraya had only heard the man speak once, to give his name. "What's that?"

"Your recent appearance on the livestream board meeting of Travers Industries would indicate you're hard at work. On their payroll. Instead, you're running loose around a federal prison during a riot."

Did that mean she was in trouble legally? Maybe they thought she should have stayed in that tiny interview room, or they had issue with how she and Judah gained access to Isaac. Had the meeting itself been above board?

She had no idea.

For all Soraya knew, they had been sent by Raleigh to lock her down. Maybe not kill her. She didn't think this police sergeant was in cahoots. If they intended to take her with them, they'd probably have created some fictitious emergency for her to leave the hospital under their "protection." But they hadn't. And Toni's FBI contact had verified they were on the level.

Given everything she'd been through the last few days, Soraya wasn't going to jump to trust anyone right now.

Just thinking about what she landed in at that prison made her wince.

Brennan's mustache shifted as he studied her. "What is your relationship with Travers Industries and former president Raleigh?"

"There isn't a 'relationship.' And I don't like that word." She figured there'd be several truth bombs, but that was a good place to start. "I'd never met Raleigh until he kidnapped me and held me at a facility in Utah, which exploded, by the way." She told them about the recording, and the fact the real Jerry Travers had been there—in a coma.

The sergeant frowned. "What do you mean 'real'?"

"There was a guy who'd been given plastic surgery to look like Travers. The doctor who did the work was the man who died in solitary during the riot." Given all the blinking, they hadn't put that together. "Why are you all here?" She needed to know if they thought she was a suspect, or if they considered her a victim here. Or both. Who knew?

"We've received some disturbing reports about Jerry Travers, president Raleigh, and their company," the third man, an FBI agent, said. "But you say Travers is dead?"

She nodded. "Reports from where?"

"Let's say you weren't the first to vocalize the issues. And since then we've received a cache of information that includes Interpol files. There are several cases springing up as a result, and Raleigh is one of them."

That had to be what Lana had done. Not just handing over the files to Chevalier—but sending them to the feds as well.

"You can't let him release that phone system," Soraya said. "It gives Travers total control over the dissemination of information. They can do anything they want." She should have explained that better. They didn't seem convinced.

"Despite what you said on the live meeting?" the sergeant said.

"I wasn't there. It was prerecorded."

"Didn't look like it." Agent Brennan pinned her with a dark stare.

"So they did an excellent job of editing the footage they recorded when they held my parents at gunpoint and forced me to cooperate."

The agent's eyebrows rose. "Can your parents corroborate this?"

She shook her head. "They didn't know. But I watched them on Travers cameras in their house the whole time. They said they'd kill my parents unless I complied."

"An employee of the company…or Raleigh himself?"

"Raleigh."

The agent turned to his colleague. "If we can get the

computer that was used, we can likely verify from the hard drive."

"The whole facility exploded," Soraya added. "You're not going to find any evidence. That's been the issue this whole time. But if you have the cache, as you said, surely you can build a case?" They had to. With or without her testimony. All she wanted was to get this done. To be free of the threat of Raleigh—and the damage Travers's phone system would do to federal law enforcement and government agencies.

The fallout could be devastating.

And if she could be part of it? This was what Soraya wanted to do. Assuming these cops really were legit.

"We could use your help," the fed said. "And we can offer you protection, if that's an issue."

"It is." But accepting it from cops she didn't know? Soraya would rather hide in the bunker Chevalier had all mentioned. "I might have help with that, though. And no offense, but I know them. I don't know you guys."

Still, she wanted to do the right thing.

She continued, "You should come back when you've got an actual case." Because they were really only fishing for her to hand them something concrete. "Raleigh has gone unchecked for too long. He took my friend and me. Tried to kill us. Now he's taken another person I know, kidnapped him from his house on his wedding day."

"Was this reported to the police?" The sergeant shook his head. "I haven't heard anything about a victim."

"I'm sure it was, but the residence is nowhere near here." She frowned. "This isn't a local problem. Raleigh controls a group of trained killers that operate all over the world."

"Killers?" The fed frowned.

She nodded. "The man they gave plastic surgery to so that he looked like Jerry Travers was also the head of this 'guild of assassins' or whatever they called it. Now Raleigh controls them too. That's who the man in the ambulance was."

"A British assassin?" The fed's lips twitched. He glanced at his mustached colleague. "You believe he has assassins on his payroll?"

Both of them frowned.

The sergeant said, "You have to admit it sounds a little far-fetched."

"Why would I make it up? I have no reason to lie. This situation is too serious for that. Raleigh is trying to silence anyone who speaks up about the phone system."

"So why aren't you dead yet?" the fed asked.

"I've only narrowly escaped, believe me."

"I supposed the guy in the prison cell you killed was one of them?"

She frowned. "I don't think so." That wasn't why she'd been targeted. Was it?

Before she could think of something else to try and convince them she was telling the truth, one of the feds snorted. "We should go." He headed for the door.

The other fed frowned at her. "When you have something valuable to share, we'll talk again." He tossed his card on the end of the bed.

The sergeant stared at her.

She said, "What?"

"There's no point in lying to make Raleigh sound worse than he really is."

"You think that's what I was doing? I had to hide out in Nigeria for weeks because he tried to kill me."

The sergeant frowned.

"Whatever. If you're not going to believe me, why stick around."

He strode to the door. "We can't help you if you don't tell the truth."

Soraya said nothing.

What was the point? Her story sounded so far-fetched that it didn't seem like they were inclined to believe her even if it was the truth.

Alone in the room then, Soraya blew out a breath. The door handle turned slowly. Toni, coming back, probably. She needed good news. Hopefully—

A man stepped in wearing a beanie, glasses, and a heavy jacket. Behind the glasses his eyes were swollen and red-rimmed. As though he'd been crying.

"Isaac?"

30

"Take a left up ahead." Badger didn't lift his head. He just kept his attention on the phone, sat in the front seat.

Judah took the turn, wondering if the guy was just thinking what he should say to Hannah. It was a sticky situation as she hadn't had much of a relationship with her mother. They'd met only a couple of times and had barely managed to talk about personal things.

Still, Judah knew what it felt like to have that hole in your heart. He barely remembered his mother at this point, and none of it had been good. Toni—and soon Jeff—were his relatives at this point. But the space his grandmother had occupied in his life was a void now. One that hurt when he acknowledged its existence.

"Now a right," Badger said.

"Getting close?" Judah glanced over at Badger, who looked back at Hannah. "Bro?"

"Huh?" He looked at Judah, then the phone. "They stopped."

Judah slowed the car. "Hannah, how are you doing?"

"I'm focused on getting Zander and Ted back. What's

happening in Last Chance County can wait until we get there."

"Okay." Judah parked.

They approached on foot, through an industrial complex only half an hour from the house where Ted had been held.

As he peered around the corner, Judah said, "I'm guessing it's that warehouse with the armed guards all around, and snipers on the roof." He looked back at the three of them.

Jeff pulled out his phone. "I'll call for reinforcements. They're on standby already."

Judah frowned.

Badger turned to Jeff. "Who's on standby?"

"People I trust. They helped when we had to get Eas out of that mansion place in New York."

Judah shook his head. "Badger wasn't there. He was recovering from that chemical weapon." He'd been there at the time but didn't remember another team. Only a couple of women he hadn't recognized. "Friends of yours that work for the Accountant's Office?"

"Friends, yes. Vanguard is more of a freelance operation, though." Jeff paused. "Don't worry about who they are. They aren't going to volunteer that information. And running their photos or prints won't work either. You'll get no results, even if it's Ted doing the search."

Hannah frowned. "Great. More secretive people." She folded her arms. "You'd think we would have learned by now to steer clear."

"Sorry." Jeff winced.

Hannah moved over to Badger and leaned at the wall, her shoulder against his.

He kissed her forehead.

She said, "Later."

Judah wondered if she wasn't doing what he had after Nigeria. Bottling everything up so she didn't have to feel the weight of it. It was a good time to do that, considering the fact

Zander being brought there—which could be where Ted was being held—had to be the priority right now.

For all of them.

Judah still asked, "Are you sure? We can do this." He motioned to Jeff with a tip of his head. "Especially with backup coming."

"I want to help."

"Okay." Judah nodded, then turned back to the corner and looked around. He'd get spotted if his head was in view for too long, but he needed to assess the situation. "Maybe we create an emergency. A way to get Fire or PD inside there?"

The last thing he needed were for those men surrounding the place to be Secret Service but given Raleigh's involvement it was entirely possible.

He scanned the building.

"Any obvious vulnerabilities?" Badger asked.

"To guys with sniper rifles?" Judah answered. "No." His gaze snagged on a flashing light in an upstairs window. He frowned and watched it for a few seconds. "Does Ted know morse code?"

Badger shifted. "Why?"

"Just tell me. Yes…or no."

"I figure he does, but who knows?" Badger said. "Now answer *my* question."

Judah figured they'd end up arguing about who was in charge when Zander and Andre were both not here. Instead of clarifying, he said, "C-H…" He watched the flicker of the light. "E-V…A"

"Chevalier."

Judah nodded. "We need a way into that building. Ted is in there."

"They're both in there," Hannah said. "That means there's no time to lose."

"We can't rush in," Jeff pointed out. "That's only going to

result in failure. Wait for reinforcements, and we'll make a plan."

Hannah kept a stoic expression on her face. "How long?"

Judah figured her background in undercover work meant she could appear calm when inside she was anything but. Still, the truth of her feelings seeped through cracks in the façade she put up. "Twenty minutes, max. They'll be here. And we'll have a lot better chance."

Hannah nodded.

Judah's phone rang. It was his sister. "Yeah, Toni?"

"Long story, but Isaac is here."

His stomach flipped. "What?" They didn't need more problems right now.

"Two feds and a cop left. I was on a call with Andre, and I didn't see him go in but he's in there now. Talking to Soraya."

Everything in Judah wanted to run to her. She'd gone through too much. She didn't want to be part of this. "Talking?"

"He doesn't look like he's going to hurt her. They really are just talking. And they know I'm aware he's in there."

Judah frowned. "Make sure he doesn't hurt her. I don't like this."

The others gathered around him when he said that. Judah couldn't let go of his composure though. They didn't need to know how torn this made him.

"Me either," his sister said. "I'll keep her safe."

He wanted to ask her to promise him, but he trusted Toni. "Thanks."

He hung up and reiterated to the rest of them.

"That's not good," Badger announced.

Jeff frowned. "None of this is. But we know what we need to do."

"Split up," Judah said. "Get as close as you can without being seen, assess the situation, and report in. One of us might get near enough Zander connects back to the comms channel."

It was only a slim chance, but he was prepared to hope for the best.

After everyone picked a direction to come at the building from, they all dispersed. Judah said a prayer for the four of them, for Zander and Ted, and for Toni as she watched out for Soraya. He couldn't think about Soraya too much or he'd get sucked into the unfairness of it all that she didn't want to be part of his life.

He'd finally found a woman he could see himself wanting to settle down with, and she didn't like his life. Couldn't handle it.

Judah wanted to try and convince her she was stronger than she thought. But was that fair to her? Whatever she decided it had to be her choice. He prayed that at least she'd be past the gut reaction based on fear when she finally did.

Judah worked his way around a neighboring building and found a door. He broke in and went upstairs, looking for a spot where he could survey the protected building from a position of cover.

Three snipers walked the roof.

The comms channel crackled to life in his ear. "...anyone else?"

Judah frowned. "Say again." He studied the view out the window, keeping his body out of sight as best he could while he waited for the repeat.

"...working." The comms line crackled, but the little he'd heard sounded like Badger.

Judah pulled out his phone and sent a group text asking for updates. The cell signal in this building was rubbish, but it went through.

Instinct drew his awareness to the room behind him. Judah shifted his grasp on the phone, in case he had to use it as a weapon before he could get to the gun on his belt.

He looked over his shoulder, then turned around to face the man approaching slowly. Face paler than normal, a bandage on his neck with a red stain.

"She said she stabbed you." Judah wanted to fold his arms, but that would make the time it would take to draw his weapon longer. "I'm glad to see she scored a direct hit."

Casper Cunningham stayed several feet out of reach.

Judah's phone buzzed in his hand, but he didn't look at the screen. "What do you want, Casper?"

Ted was inside that building, and so was Zander now. They had a shot at getting their friends back—even if it was slim. This guy wanted to do this *now*?

"I figure I need you out of the way if I want a crack at snatching her again." Casper lifted a gun and pointed it at Judah's chest. "Put your weapon on the floor."

"What's going on?" Soraya was starting to hate being laid up in a hospital bed. She shifted and pushed the button to raise the bed.

The one to call security and get help was right there. She didn't push it.

If there was a problem, Toni would bust in and maybe shoot Isaac. But she didn't, because Soraya had waved her off. Something was up with Isaac and the reporter in her at least wanted to know what it was.

Isaac sniffed.

"If you're just here to kill me, get on with it." Soraya sighed. "I'm sick of being weak. I'll deal with the aftermath. Or not. Cause I'll be dead."

He winced. "That's what you think of me?"

"You're a federal fugitive," she said. "I'd love to know how you snuck unnoticed into a hospital. These places are supposed to be secure."

"You going to file a complaint?"

"Maybe. Let's just say the service has been sub par."

His lips twitched.

"What do you want?"

"I'm not here to kill you," he said. "I just didn't know where else to go."

"You left the prison with those dirty cops." No way would she give him any concessions, even if he did look like he was grieving. What was going on? He had to know something she didn't, or it wasn't related to anyone she knew. "I thought you had friends."

"Not good ones."

That was probably true. "You might've burned the bridge of getting anyone in Chevalier to trust you again."

"Unless I came here to see *you*."

"Why?" She needed an explanation. "And don't bother warning me my life is in danger. That's old news, and it was even before I went into that prison." She wanted to say *foolishly*, but it wasn't all the way true. She hadn't known any of that would happen.

"What did you tell those cops?"

"None of your business." As if she would tell him everything. Or anything at all. "What do you want, Isaac?" She was about to reach for that security button.

Surely Toni would realize this was wrong. All wrong.

"You need to take down Raleigh."

"I'm not trained like that." She shook her head. "I can't go up against him. Not if I want to survive."

"He'll kill you either way. He'll send assassins to kill all of us," Isaac said. "So why not do everything we can to take him down in the meantime."

"What did he do?"

Isaac swallowed. "Lana didn't survive the surgery. They'll say a bullet killed her, but she was weak from the poison."

Soraya gasped. "She's gone?"

"He won. Raleigh killed her." He looked at the window. Maybe wondering when another bullet was going to fly through the air. One that would hit him, or her.

"I'm so sorry for your loss."

He nodded. "You, too. I know you were friends."

"Did she send everything she gave Chevalier to the feds as well?"

"When she gave it, did she know she might not live?"

Soraya nodded. "Yes. I think she knew." Maybe not that she would get shot, but more likely that the poison didn't leave her much time to live.

"It wouldn't surprise me if she had a failsafe. One of her people could have sent the information to the feds as well." He slumped into the chair, and she realized she was seeing him in a rare state of rest. Or submission. He was losing his fight. And considering he was on the run, an escapee from federal prison, that might not be a good thing.

Still, he shouldn't get away with a crime if he'd committed one.

"What are you going to do now?" She kept her voice soft. The last thing she needed was for him to consider her a threat, or a target. She needed to know why he'd come to her, considering the risk inherent in having law enforcement looking for him in a wide-scale search.

"I don't think there's anywhere I can go." Isaac winced. "At least not where they'll willingly take me in. And why force someone to go to bat for me? I haven't earned it."

"So you come here because you've got no one?" Maybe he was *trying* to get caught because he had no other options. "I'd have figured you would flee the country. Hide out somewhere with no extradition."

"I don't even have the resources for that."

Soraya bit her lip. "Did you commit a crime?"

"They'll never stop chasing me. What does it matter what I've done?"

"Why not tell the truth?" It was her whole life to speak the truth, not because she needed people to hear her out. But because some people couldn't speak for themselves. Or they had no audience. No one who would listen.

Journalism, at its heart, was about getting people to hear.

If people even had ears to hear these days. Seemed like most folks had stopped listening a while back. Still, it wasn't as though she would give up who she was.

She studied him. "If you could tell everyone the truth, and you knew they'd hear you out, would you do it?"

He nodded.

"I'm going to get my phone." She pointed to it, not sure how he'd react to sudden movement.

"I'm not here to hurt you, Soraya. And I won't be mad that you think I might."

"Sorry."

"I gave up needing people to apologize a long time ago." His eyes flashed with sorrow.

Soraya fought the overwhelming need in her to empathize. She didn't want him to hurt more than he already did. This man had suffered. Was she going to wind up causing him even more pain? That was the last thing she needed on her conscience along with everything else.

She'd killed two people today. Assuming that British assassin guy was dead. If not, she'd tried anyway. They were both crimes no matter which way she looked at it.

She lifted her phone.

"If you want to turn me in, it's okay too. I didn't want to put you in an awkward position."

"It's probably too late for that," Soraya said. "But I doubt I'd notice at this point." She let her lips curl up.

He didn't return the smile, though his eyes did lighten a fraction.

She wanted to ease his burden more than just that, which seemed like such a small thing. And yet, it wasn't in her power to do it. Nor was it her place. This man had chosen to visit her, but at the end of the day she didn't mean much to him. They weren't connected except vicariously.

"What are you thinking?" he said.

Soraya logged into her favorite social media account. "Let's tell everyone the truth about Raleigh. About all of it."

He frowned.

"You want to tell the world why you don't deserve to be hunted? This is how we do it."

"You have no credibility and I'm a fugitive. Will people even listen?"

"If they do, we'll divide them over who believes us and who never will." She paused. "That's to be expected. But we don't need them to buy what we say, we just need to get them to doubt what Raleigh is up to and whatever he tells everyone."

"Okay." He nodded. "Let's do it."

"We'll have to be quick. The feds will come."

Toni was outside. Would she stop them? Could she help Isaac?

Soraya looked at the door.

Could the accountant's office give him a new life, one where he was free?

She looked back at Isaac. "Did you talk to Toni?"

"Let's just do this," he said. "You're right. We don't have much time."

Soraya started a livestream. "It's been a while, guys, but I haven't been gone. I've got a friend with me today, and he'd like to tell you some more of what you already know. That our freedoms are being eroded every day, and the government isn't doing anything to stop it."

In a lot of ways, they were the cause. Raleigh wasn't working with the government for this—as far as she knew. But at the core of it, she needed to trigger people into sharing the video and taking notice.

"This is Isaac Amrakov." She turned the phone toward Isaac, who sat beside her.

As he talked, sweat broke out on her forehead. Soraya took a couple of long breaths, trying to shake the feeling. Probably just nerves. After all, she was wrapped up in some serious stuff. A national, or even international, conspiracy. This wasn't small time, local crime anymore.

Would this even work?

"Now I'm an escaped fugitive," Isaac said, drawing her attention back to him. "And it's all because Raleigh wants to continue unchecked. He wants every means he can get his hands on to control not just this country, but the whole world. The police who are supposed to protect us. Every entity a person can go to for aid…or justice? He wants to control all of it."

The door flew open and slammed against the wall.

Toni motioned with her head.

Isaac turned to Soraya. "Tell them everything. It's time."

And then he was gone.

31

—————

Judah figured he was about to die. But who knew what was going to happen? As he stared at Casper Cunningham, all he could think about was Soraya. He never got the chance to tell her how he felt about her. But at least she was safe.

"What do you want?" Judah sighed. The guy might think he could get the upper hand. Which meant Judah couldn't let that happen.

"I know what they made you do." Casper's expression was unreadable.

The comms channel crackled, as if he needed to be reminded his teammates were out there. "We're here to get Zander and Ted out." Travers Industries, or whoever was in charge inside that guarded building probably knew already. "I can't do this with you right now."

"I'll help you," Casper said. "But you have to help me."

"And I'll just let you do that? Trust you?"

"I want out."

Judah still figured he would be shot at any second. "So go tell British intelligence you want out from under Raleigh."

Casper winced. It seemed genuine, but Judah was determined not to be fooled if he could help it. "I want out from all of it. I don't want this life anymore."

Judah could bargain with him. Ask for help in exchange for...what? Telling his sister about this guy? Surely the accountant's office could help Casper—if he really did want a new life. If he wasn't simply trying to escape the law, or the consequences of his actions. He could be planning to disappear to avoid the heat on him.

That wasn't something Judah wanted any part of.

His phone buzzed. "I can't talk about this right now." He looked at the screen.

Hannah and Jeff had encountered resistance. Badger was in position. Judah told them all he was ready. Only by drawing the attention of the snipers would he be able to provide enough of a distraction the others could slip inside.

He counted down the time he'd given them and formulated a plan. He scanned around him and found a piece of glass on the floor. Big enough this would work—and he prayed it would be enough.

If he had a long gun, this would be better. But considering these people could be Secret Service agents, he didn't want to shoot them before he knew for sure.

"You know as well as I do that Raleigh is the priority here," Judah said. "If Chevalier doesn't deal with him, he'll continue to go unchecked. It might be years before he's finally put out of business."

"You get what I've been doing for years, right?"

Judah didn't want to think too much about that. Not right now, when he had an operation to get on with.

"You want me to kill Raleigh?"

"You'd have done it before now, if it was possible. Right?"

Casper didn't answer that.

Judah looked out the window. If Casper was planning to kill him, he'd have done it already.

The sky was clear. If he could get enough refraction from

the sun across the glass, he could distract them into checking out this building—drawing them away from the building where Ted and Zander were.

Judah said, "I want Raleigh out of the picture, but we don't get justice—or answers—if he's dead."

"You think there's any way to do that with him still alive? He has everyone in his pocket."

Judah wasn't sure about that. "He doesn't have us." Chevalier would stand against Raleigh, even if it was the last thing they ever did. It was the right thing to do.

"I'm serious, man." Casper shifted behind him. "I'll help you—"

A boom split the air. The west end of the building erupted into a fireball that threw smoke out the roof vents and blew out all the windows.

Casper pressed a hand to the glass. "Whoa. Was that—"

Judah didn't bother waiting around for him to finish his question.

Please let that be Zander.

He raced to the stairs, and down. Out the door. He sprinted toward the sound of alarms.

A man hung partly over the edge of the roof. At first, Judah figured the guy was looking at the floors below, but he didn't move. Another man leaned over and dragged him back onto the roof.

If they were going to do this, now would be a good time.

Judah had his gun drawn as he ran for the closest door. All he could do was check to see if it was open.

Now his phone was going crazy, but there was no time. Something had jammed the comms channel, which was barely audible over the static. He wanted to pull the earpiece out and forget about it, but the audio could come back up at any point and he might miss something.

An armed man in black fatigues rounded the corner at the end of the building.

Judah lifted his gun and aimed before the man brought his rifle all the way around. He squeezed off two shots, and the man fell. The sound of gunfire was barely audible above the whirring sirens, alarms going off in the building.

Would emergency services get here in minutes?

He wouldn't object, assuming Chevalier didn't get arrested for that. He assumed Zander was the one who set off that explosion. Who else would have? Still, it wasn't like they were the bad guys.

The door was unlocked.

Judah stepped inside. When the door didn't click shut behind him, he hugged the wall.

Casper moved up next to him.

The door closed, casting the hallway in dim light except for the flashing orange from the ceiling. Judah figured Casper had come from inside. "What is this place?"

"Travers's off-site servers."

Judah almost felt bad for them. Ted was probably having a field day hooked up to their entire system. He almost hoped for Travers's sake that they had some safeguards in place, or they'd put Ted on an air-gapped computer.

Instead he said, "Good." After all, they already knew they were going to be destroyed. The smoke that laced the air was a prime example of that.

Judah pulled the first fire alarm he got to, which could set off every alarm in the building. Might be petty, but he wanted to create as much confusion and destruction as he could.

The hall branched off left and right at a T intersection.

"Left." Casper tilted his head.

"Toward the debris?"

Casper said nothing.

Judah turned the corner and spotted a man in black fatigues racing toward him, phone in one hand and a gun in the other.

Judah whistled.

The man lifted his gun and his face in tandem.

Judah put two bullets in his chest and then headed in that direction. Casper picked up the man's discarded gun.

Two men raced around the end. Judah lifted his gun on a reflex, finger to the trigger.

"Whoa." Zander lifted both hands.

Judah moved his finger and lowered the pistol. "Ted." He exhaled. The kid had a red knot on his forehead, and his white dress shirt was dirty. He looked rumpled but unhurt.

Zander's attention was on Casper. Even if he was hurt, the team leader would never let an unknown in on the fact he had a weakness.

Ted slammed into Judah, and they hugged for a second before Judah said, "Let's go." He handed Zander the weapon from his ankle, even though his boss made a face. "Deal with it. Let's go."

"And this guy?" Zander motioned to Casper.

Judah looked at each of them. "Is Raleigh here?"

Zander didn't take his attention from Casper, who said, "Raleigh is gearing up for his announcement."

"You're coming with us." Judah motioned for him to go ahead.

Before he turned, Casper sent him a look of such relief Judah had to believe it. He was grateful. He needed this new start.

Judah said, "This isn't over." Since he had to watch their backs as they exited, he unlocked the phone and handed it to Ted. "Group text."

Zander and Casper went first. Ted in the middle. Judah last, scanning hallways for more guards. Deep in the building he could hear the steady rapport of gunfire.

He should go help whoever it is.

"We're withdrawing," Ted said. "Yes?"

Zander's response came quicker than Judah's. "Everyone out."

"Watch for shots from the roof," Casper said. "There were a couple snipers up there."

Zander went outside first.

A man stepped out of a room behind them, moving fast.

The shot buzzed past Judah's ear and embedded in the wall beside him. Everyone crouched. Judah squeezed off a round while another gunshot blasted above his head.

Zander.

The man fell.

"Let's go," Zander ordered. "Everyone out."

Soraya tried not to think about how long she stared at the clock after Isaac disappeared with Toni. Sure, Judah's sister had asked if she would be all right alone for a few minutes. Why wouldn't she be? Soraya could barely think after everything.

She figured with that livestream, someone from Travers would be here soon to lock her down. Or the post would disappear, and her phone would wipe, or something like that.

Everything she'd tried to do, erased.

Instead, her phone had been blowing up since with notifications of comments and messages. The word was getting out. Some pushback, but mostly people who weren't surprised at all that a big tech company would be up to something like this.

She didn't like feeling trapped in this hospital bed. She'd rather be out of it, actively doing something rather than stuck in it but also actively doing something. She'd never been the type to sit around doing nothing when she could be productive. Working toward a goal.

Taking down Raleigh was definitely a goal. That livestream hadn't been about saving Isaac, so much as it had been about the ultimate end of getting people—and the government—to see the truth about the former president.

If it saved Isaac's life as well, and maybe meant he'd be free now, she figured everyone at Chevalier would be pleased. *Especially Judah.*

Okay, fine. She'd admit to herself at least that his opinion was the one she counted on. She didn't think she was the kind of person who could do what he did, but she still cared what he thought about her. And *especially* about the choices she made.

Her phone rang then.

Soraya frowned at the number. It took her a second to realize that was a California area code. Her aunt maybe? Considering her parents were there, Soraya answered. "Hello?"

"Hey, baby."

"Mom?" She didn't sound good at all. "What's going on? Is everything okay?"

"You don't need to worry about us." Her mom sounded like she was trying to be strong, but it was artificial. "You just need to do what you need to do—"

A low voice said, "Tell her."

Soraya frowned. She was about to speak when her dad said, "Honey?"

"Dad?" She pushed the hospital blankets back, as though jumping out of bed would solve anything. "What's going on?"

She'd barely got the question out when he said, "You're supposed to do what they say, but we love you and you're stronger than—"

A muffled thud sounded through the phone line.

"What's going on?" Even though in her heart of hearts, she knew. "Dad? Mom? What's happening?"

Toni was gone. Isaac was gone. The feds and that sergeant were all gone. None of Chevalier was here.

Maybe there was a security guard in the hallway, but she had no idea. Whoever it was had to have either looked the other way when Isaac left, or they hadn't noticed. Either way wasn't good.

"Do I have your attention?" the man asked.

"Who are you?" Soraya didn't know how to fight this. She had no help. Could she do another livestream? That was probably what brought this on in the first place. Doing it again might not help.

"I know you're in that hospital." His tone held no empathy, just a command. Did this man even have any feelings? "And right now, there's no one with you." How did he know that?

Soraya looked at her phone. Could she see his face somehow? He'd have to accept a video call in order to get a visual on the side of the call where her parents were.

She said, "Change the call to video. I want to see my parents." If she could stall long enough, would Toni come back in time to realize something was very wrong?

He huffed across the line. "You already heard from them. That's enough for proof of life."

"No. I want to see them."

Soraya heard a shuffle. Then her mom screamed. She gasped. "Stop! Okay, stop!"

The man came back on. "Get out of that bed. Go down the stairs, take the exit door on the first floor."

"And go where?"

"If you don't. There will be a finger on the ground and blood everywhere." Her mom whimpered and he continued, "Understood?"

She heard the threat under his voice, but just the words he spoke were enough. "Okay." She slid to the edge of the bed. "I don't have any shoes."

She realized then she'd said that aloud. How selfish did that sound? Her parents could be killed and she was worried about her feet hurting? She felt like a terrible person. A horrible daughter who got her parents killed.

Tears trickled from the corners of her eyes. Her mother would want her to pray, but no words would come. She couldn't even think. Soraya didn't have clothes, and the hospital gown was barely tied behind her.

She found the strings and did some fastening with the phone on speaker on the bed. "Don't hurt them." Her fingers fumbled with the last ties. She swiped away moisture from her cheek. "Please don't hurt them."

"Hurry up!"

Did he know where she was? Could he see her somehow? He knew she was alone. Maybe Raleigh had eyes inside the room. But if that was the case, then he'd know Isaac had been here. Toni and Isaac could be in danger right now. And there was no way for her to warn them.

Soraya's skin prickled with cold fear.

She tugged the blanket off the bed and tucked it around her shoulders, grasping the phone in its folds. "Where am I going?"

"Right. End of the hall. The stairs."

Bingo. He could see her.

Soraya looked both ways. There was no hospital staff that she could see, but that didn't mean she'd be spotted.

She walked as quickly as she could. A man in a side room, standing over a woman in the hospital bed, looked over. His expression didn't bode well for the woman's prognosis, and he didn't react as if he recognized her.

She pushed aside everything and prayed for both of them, which helped her keep her head above the water of her emotions.

As soon as the door to the stairs closed behind her, all that fell away. The clang of the steel door echoed down the empty stairwell. Like the hollow aftermath of death.

She couldn't let that happen. She didn't want to lose them.

Soraya needed to connect with her parents now. Again. She had to make sure everything was okay. "Hello?"

"He's waiting." The voice was far too loud beside her ear. Still on speaker.

She winced. "I'm going downstairs now. I need to know you aren't going to hurt my parents."

"I guess you'll just have to trust me."

Soraya took the stairs as quickly as she could, the concrete freezing under the soles of her feet. As she whispered down each step, her feet slipped and slid. She grasped the railing and whirled around every landing between floors, gasped for air and ignored the pounding in her head.

The last thing she wanted was to be in Raleigh's grasp again.

But how could she let her parents be hurt, or killed? This guy wasn't likely to stop at a finger. Things would be far worse when they were up against someone who would level an entire facility just to keep his activities quiet.

She reached the bottom and the EXIT door.

Behind her, the first-floor lobby teemed with an ocean of cops and other first responders. Small groups of officers threaded past each other through the halls.

Looking for Isaac?

Raleigh had picked the perfect time. *Please let him have escaped.* She didn't want Isaac to be in prison. Not when he didn't deserve it. She'd felt the fear in him, because it was something she was so accustomed to now. And the sensation made her want to hurl, the way she had all over Raleigh's computer keyboard.

All she could muster were dry heaves. That wasn't going to work.

Maybe he was only here to kill her.

Soraya pushed the door open and stepped outside. A rush of winter air blew in, ruffling everything. It cut through the blanket and hospital gown leaving her feeling like a popsicle. Her toes touched the snow and she hissed. A black town car was parked at the end of the street. The kind rich people use instead of taxis.

Was Raleigh inside?

"I see him." She held the phone in front of her and kept moving. That was better for her feet than standing still. She looked both ways, but not even a sharp cop on the lookout for Isaac was out here.

She was all alone.

The back door of the town car opened.

32

———

Judah saw the airplane the second they pulled into the airport and were let through security. Relief flowed through him, until he turned to the driver. Casper Cunningham. Who knew what ID the guy had used? Judah didn't plan on asking.

Jeff sat in the back. "She's still not answering."

Casper stopped the car behind the one they'd followed here, which held Badger and Hannah, Ted, and Zander.

As soon as they pulled up close to the hangar, Jess ran out. Judah climbed from their car and saw Andre and Lucia, who stayed by the plane, followed by Dr. Windermere, who strode after Jess's sprint toward Ted.

The kid climbed out of the car like a guy who'd been released from five years of captivity.

Jess slammed into him. Ted went back and both Badger and Zander steadied him so the two of them didn't fall. He was home. Even with everything else going on, there was a certain rightness to seeing Jess and Ted back together.

They needed an update on Dean and Eas.

Judah would've been right there except for Casper. He turned to him. "We have to know everything you do about

Raleigh and his operation. Otherwise, we have no hope of ending this."

Casper didn't look hopeful. He shook his head. "What's the point? You can't stop him."

"What does he have going on right now?"

"I might be on his payroll, but that doesn't put me in the inner circle," Casper said. "I got orders. You have to understand…it was nothing personal. I didn't think I had any other choice."

"What are you talking about?" Judah wanted to look around. Check the surrounding area for some incoming threat. But he couldn't do that and extrapolate from Casper's body language and the expression on his face. And he needed to know what this was.

"She probably isn't showing symptoms yet."

Judah said, "What are—"

Zander moved between them and shoved Casper back. "Talk. No complaints or excuses. We aren't making any deal. You tell us everything and *maybe* we don't put a bullet in *you* when this is done."

"I'm not proud of anything I've done," Casper said. "Not for a long time."

Judah figured that was probably true. He wasn't about to start sympathizing with the guy—even if Soraya probably would have seen that side of things. However, he could imagine what it was like to be forced into something.

No way out.

He'd lived enough to understand what that kind of powerlessness felt like. It was why he was part of Chevalier. To try and make a difference in the world. To fight for those who had no power to fight for themselves—because it had been taken from them.

Casper continued, "But I'll tell you what I know." He looked at Judah. "Not because I want something out of it."

"Good." Judah figured they could give him a whole lot.

Between Chevalier and the accountant's office they could get him free and in a brand-new life that was clear of all this threat—even if Raleigh were still in the world. But should it be because he'd earned it? Which of them had done enough good to warrant the guarantee of a happy life?

If it was even possible to expect nothing would ever go wrong. Which it wasn't.

Jeff wandered over. "Toni isn't answering. Have you heard from Soraya?"

Judah frowned. "Should I have?" He wasn't exactly expecting her to call. She knew he was busy with team business, and he'd heard the feds were there to talk to her. She was safe, right?

Andre and Lucia joined them while Badger and Hannah talked with Ted and Jess as Windermere took Ted's vitals.

Judah called her number, but she didn't answer. He pulled up the app Ted had designed that tracked their phones while they wouldn't be trackable using cell towers the traditional way law enforcement might try to do it. "She's not showing up. Maybe it's off."

Jeff put his phone to his ear and listened. After a few seconds he shook his head.

"You should go check on them." Zander motioned to Casper. "Take his car."

Judah nodded. "What are you going to do?"

Zander seemed okay even though he was kidnapped.

Judah said, "Was it you, or Ted, who blew half that building?"

Zander grinned.

Casper took a step back.

"Good." Judah figured he'd saved Ted, and that was what counted.

Zander stuck out his hand. Judah took it, and the shake morphed into a back-slapping hug. Zander motioned to the car. "Go make sure the women are okay."

Judah jogged to the car with Jeff. The guy could drive, but Judah figured he'd be the one to do it this time and not just because he was the one with two arms. "Good?"

Jeff buckled his seatbelt, then lifted his phone again. He put it to his ear.

Judah figured that meant he should just *go*. He peeled out of the airport as fast as he could without getting them in trouble and headed back to the hospital.

Jeff pushed out a breath and lowered his phone.

"Nothing?"

Jeff shook his head. "There's something I need to tell you. It's not Chevalier business, though."

Judah didn't like the sound of this. "What is it?"

"Isaac went to talk to Soraya." Before Judah could explode at him, Jeff continued, "Toni got him to our contacts. The ones who weren't at that facility helping."

Judah shook his head. "I didn't see anyone there. It was just us—and Casper."

"I know you didn't." Jeff paused. "If you had, it'd be because they wanted you to."

"I saw them in New York, during the Eas thing."

"Because it was necessary," Jeff said. "Don't ask questions about them."

"Need-to-know?" Judah exhaled a long breath. "You know why I'm not a spy? This is why. I don't need it in family business as well. Okay?"

"My family business and yours are going to stay two different things."

"Just tell me why Toni has Isaac. The guy is the subject of a search," Judah said. "Why isn't he long gone from here?"

They were a mile from the hospital now. Traffic was backed up, so he put the car in neutral and turned to Jeff. "Are you doing some kind of deal with him?"

"That was for Toni to figure out."

"Casper is going to ask for one as well." Judah didn't like it.

"Let's just worry about if everyone is safe before we debate the merits of my career, okay?" Jeff bent his head to his phone. "Toni was only going to be gone a few minutes, long enough to get Isaac out to the waiting car. That was half an hour ago."

Judah winced. "Traffic is nuts. I'm going to pull over. Let's walk, or we'll *be* half an hour."

He found a spot. Kind of. Casper's car would probably get towed.

They jogged down the sidewalk to the hospital. A federal incident response RV had been parked outside. "We need to get in without them seeing us."

"Or, we ask for an update on the hunt for Isaac." Jeff glanced at him. "Since we're concerned citizens."

He could call the sergeant. Roberts had given Judah his card. "Let's just find them. That's our priority. You might be helping Isaac, but he's on his own right now. Chevalier is up to our necks in this, and he hasn't exactly helped."

But was that really true?

It was easier to be mad at Isaac, but he'd given them leads over and over again. Judah didn't doubt he'd put himself in that prison—as much as a person could manipulate that stuff —purely to get close to that doctor.

Did they owe him whatever they could give? Chevalier would have to decide as a team.

Judah had just reached the conclusion that neither woman was here when his phone rang. "It's Zander." He slid his thumb across the screen. "What's going on?"

"Ted gave us something."

Judah put the call on speaker so Jeff could hear. What he wanted to do was run around the hospital, grab anyone he could find and demand to know where she was. His sister. Soraya. Either, or both of them.

Where were they?

Zander said, "Raleigh is going to announce the roll out of his new phone system tomorrow at a tech convention in New York City."

Judah winced. "It's ready to go live?"

"We're wheels up in thirty, so get the women and get back here."

He tried to get the words out, but nothing would come. Where were they?

Jeff said, "I'll stay and find them. You go."

"That's the last thing I want to do." Judah's stomach flipped over. It also rumbled, like now was the time to remind him he hadn't eaten. "But if what I think has happened, has happened, then I'll be going anyway."

"You think Raleigh has Soraya again?" Jeff's tone deepened.

Judah nodded. "I think he got her out of the hospital while Toni was helping Isaac."

"This isn't the accountant's office's fault," Jeff said. "He could have Toni as well."

"Figure it out." Judah bit the words off. What use was this guy being in his sister's life if she wasn't safe?

"What about Toni?" Zander asked.

Jeff said, "I'll find her." Given the look on his face, Judah figured his brother-in-law meant, *or else.* And if Raleigh had done anything to Toni? The consequences would be worse than what a group of assassins could ever do if Jeff got his hands on the guy.

Judah didn't blame him.

He glanced around, but she wasn't here. Neither of them was, and he needed to go right now. Jeff could confirm with security, or the staff, but the team was leaving.

He winced. "I'll be there. We need to take down Raleigh or this will never end."

Soraya held the hospital blanket tight around her and stared straight ahead out the front window. At least, what she could see of it. The windows gave her a view of the city rushing by on either side. But looking one way meant turning her back to Raleigh, and the other meant facing him. *Nope.* She didn't want to do either.

Not even after long minutes of him staring at her.

The time since they'd pulled onto the freeway, driving the same direction for more than an hour now without stopping.

She could feel his gaze on her shoulder and the side of her face, as though it burned. Not to warm her in a good way, that might feel comforting in light of the fact she was freezing cold. Instead it felt like a threatening, dangerous heat.

Not something she wanted to associate with a man who now had her under his control.

She could plead for her parents.

Soraya could ask him what he wanted with her.

Instead, she kept her mouth closed. Maintained her control. It was about the only thing she had control over right now.

If she thought too much, she would have to acknowledge that this was what she'd feared would happen again. Never mind that she'd fought two men and stabbed both recently. There weren't any weapons around her—she'd looked.

She felt as helpless as a child who didn't know what was happening and just wanted to feel safe again. Freezing and clammy, as if her body couldn't decide what temperature to be. The pounding in her head wasn't letting up. Were the meds the hospital had given her wearing off now?

The car raced up the freeway, heading north as far as she could tell by the signs.

Soraya felt the welling of emotion from deep inside her. In response, she bit down on the inside of her lip. The distracting pain helped for a moment before she felt the need to fragment. And after that, who knew what would happen?

This time there would be no rescue. Lana was dead.

She bit the inside of her lip again, but the tear escaped anyway. And now she tasted blood in her mouth. She wanted to sit back in the seat and close her eyes to combat the blinding headache that hammered against her skull. But how could she do that? Anything could happen with her eyes shut. Sitting like this she could almost see him out the corner of her eyes.

At least she would see it if he moved his hands toward her.

Soraya shuddered. This time not because she was so cold.

"Perhaps we should discuss why you felt the need to do that live video?"

Even his voice made her recoil. Soraya didn't move, though. She kept her body rigid on the seat. "I'm always going to tell the truth when I can."

"It was a foolish move."

"Yeah, well. I'm not going to quit doing what I can," she said. Maybe she should have said *what I'm best at.* But the words were out now. Why did she always think of a better thing to say afterward? She needed to mull that over later.

"…even listening to me?"

"Huh? Oh." Soraya glanced over enough to see his shoes. If she looked at his face, she would lose the tenuous hold she had on her composure. *You don't care.* "Sorry I didn't die when that facility exploded, by the way. That might've saved you some problems."

Just the thought of Chevalier and all the damage they could potentially do to Raleigh almost made her smile. Even if she wasn't the kind of person who could do that job, she respected their abilities.

Whether they found her in time—or at all.

If either happened she knew in a way she kept the thought close to her heart that Chevalier wouldn't let Raleigh get away with this. They would finish what they had started, save their friend, and make sure the phone system didn't roll out.

"Hmm. But then I wouldn't have the opportunity to achieve my ends."

"I'm the key to your whole plan, huh?" She wanted him to tell her it all, but that wasn't likely to happen. This wasn't an interview. The last thing she was in this situation was a reporter with any reputation or pull, where she could walk away whenever she wanted.

"Part of it, at least," he said.

"And you'd risk being out all that money if you lost the asset? All that work getting the video edited so everyone believed I was at that meeting when I was miles away looking into a group of assassins that happen to be on your payroll." Maybe one of them could kill her now.

She shifted again and looked at his shoes. This time she waved her hand. Let him think she barely cared—that she considered him little more than nothing.

A speck.

He said, "Money comes and goes. I'm after more than that, and with you there isn't much time."

"So you're after total world domination. As if you're not a giant cliché." She wanted to laugh, but the Lord knew there was nothing funny about this situation. Soraya figured He was the only one who knew what was happening right now. That was what her mom always told her about God. He was the one her mom always looked to when she had nothing else, and even when she had everything. All of it was down to Him.

"If that end were available to me? Certainly. But it's a fool's errand."

"You're not a fool," she said. "Blah-blah." She made the motion of a mouth moving with her fingers and thumb.

She wanted to think more about an all-powerful God who could scoop her out of this car and smite Raleigh anytime He wanted. Those were nice thoughts, even if she figured it was unlikely. Not something she'd ever reported as happening before. Just what she'd heard at Sunday school as a kid.

"You're right about one thing," he said. "I'm certainly not a fool."

She heard him shift on the seat and realized too late she didn't know what he was doing. *Lord, help me.* She had no savior in this. No one to find or rescue her.

She was entirely on her own.

Raleigh gripped a handful of the back of her hair. He spoke low, his mouth close to her ear so that his breath puffed against her skin.

She winced. The stinging pull on her scalp was enough to squeeze tears from her eyes.

He continued, "And I will not be made to look like one. Especially from some nothing reporter."

Every terrifying TV show about a narcissistic psychopathic killer rolled through her mind. As if she needed to be reminded. Yes, it was bad he thought of her as nothing. If he didn't value her life, he'd think nothing about doing whatever he wanted and *then* killing her.

"I will always tell the truth." It was an oath as well as a promise to him. "And do the right thing."

"I always get what I want." His breath whooshed in her ear canal.

She wasn't going to like anyone doing that to her for the rest of her life. However long or short that turned out to be.

He pulled her head back farther, until she could feel his shoulder and her back landed against the seat because she couldn't hold herself straight anymore.

"I will kill your parents."

She blew out a breath through gritted teeth. There was more, she was certain, but he said nothing else. "Don't hurt them."

"I will. That is certain." He sounded nothing like the man who had been president. "But the severity is up to you."

"What do you want from me?" She squeezed her eyes shut for a second, but that made it worse.

"We'll start simple, and maybe you won't screw this up." He ran his free hand over the bare skin of her knee. "I'd hate to have to punish you."

33

Music pumped from speakers stacked on top of each other on either side of the stage, and in a row above the front lip with the spotlights already rotating around the stage. A pack of dancers in sparkly shirts and tiny shorts kicked their legs in tandem to the music as the opening show of the tech convention got underway.

"Anyone else already have a headache?" Zander asked over comms.

Judah scanned the crowd but felt his lips curl up.

Badger responded, "That's cause you're old. You should be at home in front of the fire with slippers and a book."

"And my *wife*. Not three thousand strangers."

"I'd take the dog at this point," Hannah said. "Kuai is cute and all, but she barfed in my room the other day. That's not okay. Who do I tell? Do we have Human Resources?"

Someone chuckled. Maybe more than one person. All male, by the tone of it.

Two women brushed past Judah. Maybe they looked him over. He didn't much care. "I don't see her."

Lucia said, "She's here. You know Raleigh dragged her

back into this for a reason. He's got a plan, and this is the main event."

"The curtain will roll up? It's showtime?" Badger said.

Judah shook his head. "There's no curtain on this stage."

"You know what we mean," Lucia said. "She's here. We're going to find her."

Judah felt someone come up behind him. He glanced over his shoulder. "Gonna stab me in the back?" Because no one in the team could see who he was talking to, Judah added, "Casper?"

The guy wasn't on comms. Judah got the feeling no one cared where he went, though they'd care if he interfered. Casper wasn't someone they trusted, so even if he wanted to help, that wouldn't matter much when most of Chevalier was here.

Except for one teammate.

Judah indicated to Casper that he was talking through his earpiece. "How's Eas doing?"

Zander was the one who replied. "The doc said he's responding in leaps and bounds."

There was a pause, long enough for Judah to ask, "What?" while he scanned the crowd watching the show. Recording it on their phones instead of enjoying the experience. The dancers were on their second number—hopefully the last. Would Raleigh come out onstage as soon as the show started, or send out a warm-up act?

"Eas told me he's done with missions. He's in Last Chance County permanently now, and he'll work with us if needed but only in a support role."

Judah blew out a long breath.

Hannah said, "That's a big change for you guys."

"Girl, don't even ask us how we *feeeeeeel*," Andre said.

"Now's hardly the time for that."

"We'll talk about it later." Andre's tone indicated he wasn't interested in a discussion on the subject.

Judah figured Andre's intention was to duke it out later, the original guys on the team. Do something competitive and physical that would end up with a couple of visits to the doc and maybe stitches—if the win was hard fought enough. Unfortunately, with women on the team now, that meant someone with full operational clearance for Chevalier was left out of…team building.

"Yes," Lucia said. "We will talk about it later."

Badger chuckled.

"I'll be there," Hannah said. "Looking forward to it."

Andre groaned.

The music crescendoed to a finale, and the dancers flipped their hair, coming to a still pose. The crowd erupted. Judah wondered what this had to do with new technology. "Here goes."

A thin man in a suit jogged out onto the stage. He threaded through the dancers, calling out to the crowd with his hand-held microphone. "Ladies and gentlemen, is it great to be here or what?"

The audience cheered, a swell that sounded like a pride of wild animals. Loud enough Judah winced.

Casper moved closer to his side. "I don't see Raleigh anywhere."

"You know where he'd be?"

Casper shook his head.

"What did you mean when you said Soraya doesn't have much time?"

A muscle in Casper's jaw flexed.

"Tell me." Judah realized Casper hadn't had much time between taking Soraya from the prison and driving her in that ambulance to do much. But it might've been enough. "Did you poison her?" Judah figured he'd go to the logical end. "The way you poisoned Lana?"

The comms channel was quiet.

"She's dead. Did you know that?" Judah folded his arms.

"She was shot, and she didn't survive the surgery to remove the bullet." He realized Hannah could hear and winced. "People who care about Lana, who never got to know her well are going to have to say goodbye to her. They'll never get the chance to know her now. Because you took that chance away."

Casper said, "You want me to tell you what they do if you don't complete the mission?"

"You killed her."

"Lana…or your girlfriend?"

"Her name is Soraya." Judah grasped the collar of Casper's shirt. "And if *anything* happens to her in any of this, or what you did? I don't care. You'll pay for all of it."

Casper's expression shifted. He wanted to fight back, and yet he didn't.

Someone got between them. Just a hand, and Judah was pushed back. Andre on one side. Zander on the other.

Zander said, "Did you poison Soraya as well as Lana?"

The three of them surrounded Casper, staring down. It probably looked seriously intimidating and Judah was glad for that. He wasn't the tallest man in the world but made up for that in bulk. With his friends they certainly packed a punch— even without using their fists.

Unless they needed to use their fists.

Judah must have moved because Andre shoved him again. His phone buzzed in his pocket, but he ignored it.

Casper said, "She probably has a couple of weeks left."

Judah definitely moved then. One second he was headed to Casper with his fist raised, and the next he was lifted off the ground by Zander and turned around. When he got out of the hold and looked, Andre had Casper and they were ten feet away.

"Why did you stop me?"

"Because you'll solve this by beating on him?"

"Maybe not," Judah yelled in his boss's face. "But I'll feel better."

"No you won't. Not until you find her," Zander said. "Let's get looking."

Judah gritted his teeth.

The guy on stage had finished his intro crossed with a stand up comedy routine. The crowd not distracted by their altercation clapped, and the guy brought the girls back on.

"He's not bringing her onstage," Zander said.

Judah shook his head. "How do you know?"

"If he brings her here as his spokesperson after she made that live video with Isaac, no one will believe it. If she even sniffs like she's under duress he'll have no credibility. There's no way Raleigh will risk his plan for her to smile and shake hands."

"You're right. There's no way," Judah said. "But what is she here for?"

"Doesn't matter, because it won't work. We're going to find her before that," Zander said. "Yeah?"

Judah nodded.

"Let's go."

He pulled out his phone as they threaded through the crowd.

"Guys," Hannah's voice came over comms. "Found a program for stagehands. Raleigh is on in fifteen."

"Copy that," Zander said.

Judah checked his new text. "Jeff found Toni. He said it's all good."

Badger said, "Whatever that means."

"Exactly." But Judah didn't have time to figure it out, so he stowed his phone and they kept looking for Soraya. "Let's try and get backstage."

Zander nodded.

As they headed for a set of doors marked EMPLOYEES ONLY, Judah's heart started to beat faster. She only had weeks to live? Andre had better be getting the name of the poison from Casper. After what happened with Lana, his nerves were on a knife edge just thinking about Soraya going through the same thing. And not only that, but Nora and Hannah—and Isaac—had to be grieving the loss of their mother. Sure, it would happen in very individual ways and to different degrees, but they'd all had something taken from them that they would never be able to get back.

She has weeks.

Judah sniffed back the gathering emotion. Jeff had made sure Toni was good. Now Judah needed to make sure the same could be said of Soraya.

There was no way he would accept anything else.

He wanted a future with her however it came. And for that to happen, she had to *live*.

"Hey—" The word was barely heard across the comms channel before Hannah let out a noise that sounded like a mix of pain and surprise.

"Hannah!" Badger called out to her.

There was only a choked noise, and then nothing.

She was offline.

SORAYA STOOD up as soon as he entered. Raleigh was flanked by two Secret Service agents, until he crossed the threshold and they stayed out in the hall. He closed the door.

She only managed to hold it together because three of his staff members at Travers were in the room—a suited man, his tight-dress and stringy hair colleague and a stylist who'd done her hair and makeup. Soraya smoothed down the skirt suit jacket that didn't quite fit.

"We need to talk."

Raleigh kept his presidential expression. "I'm sure my staff can make sure everything is taken care of."

He'd locked her in a bare hotel room all night, and then shown up early this morning just as she was dozing off to a restless sleep and spent an hour dictating to her what was going to happen.

Thankfully the stylist was good with concealer, otherwise she would look terrible. But that might've played in her favor. Trying to convince the staffers she was here under duress had proven pointless. Maybe they were here under the same conditions. Who knew? They'd only stared blankly at her as she asked for help. Travers controlled everything, and they either were so accustomed to it they didn't step out of line anymore, or they knew they couldn't or life wouldn't be worth living.

They hadn't gotten far enough in the conversation for them to tell her what the consequences were. Or what happened to anyone else who tried. But she could imagine well enough.

"That's not what this is about," Soraya said. "I want a video call with my parents. I'm not doing this if I don't know you're going to keep your end of the deal."

The skin around his eyes shifted.

She straightened her shoulders and lifted her chin. "If you want my compliance, get them on first."

As far as she could tell, this was all his exit strategy. She just hadn't figured out what it entailed. He was going to put her on stage, she knew that much. But it couldn't be as a spokesperson. She wasn't going up there as a representative of Travers, that much was certain.

Her tired, over stressed, overly exhausted brain couldn't put the pieces together.

She had a part here, but without knowing the extent of what he wanted from her she could hardly figure out a plan to make it go wrong and get herself rescued.

Were Chevalier even here? She didn't want to hope, but part of her couldn't help it when it wasn't like she could do this on her own. She needed help. Preferably sooner, rather than later.

He stared at her as he ordered, "Everyone out."

They scurried to the door.

"You aren't worried I might try to kill you?" She knew he wasn't concerned about her. He didn't think she was a threat at all, not when he controlled everything. In his opinion she wouldn't dare try when there wasn't much she could try that constituted an issue he'd have to deal with.

As far as he was concerned, things were all going according to plan.

After everything she'd done, thinking Raleigh would be scrambling? The truth was more than a little disheartening.

She knew she was right when he sneered. "With the Secret Service outside?"

The presidential façade dropped, and she was left face to face with a predator. It was the last place she wanted to be, but what else was there to do? Soraya said, "I won't do anything you ask unless I speak with my parents again."

After all, how did she know he hadn't had them killed already? They could be lying dead somewhere. Casualties of a war she hadn't known she was getting into until it was too late to back out of the fight.

"You will do as I have instructed."

"Walk onto the stage?" She lifted her hands. "There has to be more to it than that."

"You will be given instructions as needed."

"I *need* to know what this is." She was ready to scream at him. "You can't just keep me here!"

He gave her a smug look. Not surprising, since in his mind he could do whatever he wanted.

"I talk to my parents, or you get nothing from me."

Poor choice of words. His eyes lit.

Soraya wanted to back up, away from him, but that would be a retreat. She wasn't going to back down.

Raleigh pulled out a phone, tapped the screen and put it to his ear. "Yeah, put them on. Video."

He turned the phone to her.

Soraya didn't care if he was handing it over or just showing it to her. She grabbed the device anyway and moved away from Raleigh because she couldn't stand to be near him anymore. "Mom? Dad?"

Their faces came into view. Her dad had a cut on his cheek, and a black eye. Her mom looked upset and disheveled, but unhurt. So far.

Soraya sank onto the seat where she'd had her makeup done. There was no mirror in here, so she had no idea what she looked like. "Hi."

"Honey, are you okay?" Her dad's voice shook and cracked. He swallowed. "Did they hurt you?"

"Don't worry about me." She didn't know what to say. How would they react if they knew she was going to roll over and do what she had to in order to save her parents, rather than standing up to the bully? They'd taught her to do exactly what she'd done. Tell the truth, fight even when the odds were stacked against her. But they probably never imagined she'd end up in a situation like this.

Soraya settled on saying, "Everything is going to be fine." Even though she had no idea if that was true.

Raleigh snatched the phone from her hand and hung up. "There. You saw them, and they're still alive. Now it's time to get this thing started."

She didn't get up.

Raleigh grabbed above her elbow and dragged her from the chair. Soraya gasped as pain flashed up her arm.

"Ow. You're hurting me."

"You'd be good to remember that. After today, no one will care where you disappear to." He shifted a fraction closer to her. Again the urge to retreat flared inside her. "How you live out the remainder of your life is very much up to me."

Soraya wanted to live up to who she was supposed to be, but

those old fears reared their heads. She didn't know how to deal with this. Couldn't fight him physically and mentally she wasn't recovered. Her whole body just wanted to fold so she could lay down. Sleep some. Would that even make her feel better?

"You're sweating already." His gaze drifted over her forehead. "We should do this quickly so we can move on."

She wanted to ask what that was about, but he'd already dragged her to the door and knocked on it with his fist.

A Secret Service agent entered. She didn't like him immediately, not the deep set eyes or the line of his jaw or the way he stared down at her.

Soraya pressed her lips together.

"Give her the shot. Let's get this done," Raleigh said. "It's almost time."

Before she could whirl around to Raleigh, the agent grabbed her arm with one hand. With the other, he jabbed an epi pen against the outside of her arm. Through her suit jacket. The needle end stabbed her.

Soraya cried out. "What are you doing?"

Raleigh opened the door. "Get her in place."

He was gone a second later.

Adrenaline raced through her, all the nerve endings in her body fired. It felt like touching a live socket and the sharp sting of all that electricity moving through her. But instead of a zap, it didn't dissipate.

She heard a low chuckle next to her ear. "He said I could get rid of your parents myself. I've seen your mom. It's going to be fun."

He slung an arm around her shoulder, and they were walking. The world around her blurred.

She heard a voice ask something. The body next to her replied, the words rumbling under her cheek.

Energy pulsed in her. A rush of power, as though the electric shock she'd received was giving her strength. She pushed against him because she could. She could do anything—whatever she wanted.

This felt great. She still couldn't see well, but that didn't matter. She was strong. Powerful. No one would be able to stop her.

She could do *anything*.

All her extremities agreed. Each finger on her hands waving in front of her face.

This is amazing!

"Ladies and gentlemen, President Raleigh!"

A crowd roared. The sound swelled in her ears, eclipsing everything else. Lights flashed in front of her face and blinded her except for that yellow glow.

A heavy body pressed her against a hard surface. "It won't be long now."

34

"There's a concentration of Secret Service agents in the west hall."

As soon as Badger said it, Judah shifted. His body wanted to turn and go in that direction. Anything to get to Soraya. Was she there? He needed to know what was happening with her, even while Chevalier worked to find Hannah and figure out what had happened to her.

Zander tapped the outside of his arm. "Come on."

Andre said, "I'm sure Casper has something to tell us about what Raleigh is up to here."

Judah surveyed the hall in front of them and realized why Zander had just picked up his pace. "We have something." He gave Badger their location.

Zander said, "We don't even know if it's her."

They closed in on the open door. Wedged the foot. Whoever it was, they were lying down. Probably unconscious. And the shoe was one Judah had seen before, even if he had never paid it much attention. "It's her."

Zander got Hannah's arm out of the way and pushed the door open. Before either of them could say anything, Badger asked, "How is she? I'm on my way to you."

No way were they going to be able to stop him. None of the team members would have even tried, because they all knew they would be doing the same thing if it was them.

Judah checked her head for injury. "Looks like she's been knocked out. But I don't feel a wound." She might have been strangled until she passed out. Or given something.

As soon as Badger reached them, Judah said, "I'm going to keep looking for Soraya."

Before either of them could object, he was already up and moving down the hallway. He checked each room and didn't find a single occupied until the end of the hall. As he opened the door, a woman let out a squeak. It was set up like a backstage makeup station, along with a dressing area.

"You're the stylist?"

She blinked, and he assessed her. Down on her luck. Not happy to be here. Scared of him, though she had little reason to feel that way.

Judah pulled out his phone and found a picture of Soraya, a screenshot from Isaac. The one he'd watched several times in the car on the way here.

He was so proud of her. Soraya was incredibly professional, knowledgeable, and a powerhouse as a reporter. Even if she thought only about what she was unable to do, he wanted to show her the magnitude of what she could accomplish. They might have different skills sets, but she was not someone who could be discounted.

"Have you seen this woman here?"

Her gaze flicked to the picture, and she gave a short nod.

"Where can I find her now?"

"Th-they…," she stuttered. "S-sending her onstage."

"Copy that," Lucia said. "I'll check backstage, both sides."

Judah was already at the door. "I'll be there to help."

He raced down the halls to a backstage area and pushed past the security guard, not even bothering to comprehend what the man said. Likely the guy would get on his radio immediately now, call in the breach, and have Judah removed. As if it were even possible for him to be dragged away from finding her.

As he ran, Andre's voice came on. "I'm going to need some backup."

Lucia said, "I'll keep looking for Soraya. Judah needs to get elsewhere than backstage. Everyone is looking for him."

"I don't care." He kept running, pushing between two people as he made his way down the hall. "Where is she?"

Commotion erupted behind him.

Lucia said, "I'll find her. Go help Andre."

"I'm on my way to him," Zander said. "Badger is taking Hannah to the medical station set up for attendees."

Good. That was good.

A suited man stepped out of a side room. His eyes locked on Judah with a purpose. Judah barreled into him, knocked the guy back, and heard the man's gun go flying. He kept going until two more men stepped in his path. He didn't recognize them until it was too late, and agents from British intelligence had shoved him into a room and knocked him on his behind.

He hissed out a breath, trying to gather his composure. The rest of them needed to know what had happened. But in the impact, his earpiece had gone flying. If he looked around for it, it would be entirely too obvious.

The door clicked shut. One man stepped forward, while the other remained by the door. Both held a gun in one hand.

"And what does MI-6 want?" Judah said it loud enough so that hopefully the rest of the team would hear. But not so loud it would be obvious he was trying to be heard.

It was the same man from the plane. And he stared down at Judah now. "Where is Casper Cunningham?"

"Ah, so you know he's alive." Judah didn't want to be on the floor, at a disadvantage. He shifted and got his feet under him so he could stand. When he was eye to eye with the agent, he said, "Is that really all you want?"

If they could get British intelligence to take out Raleigh, hopefully in revenge for betraying them in the exchange, it would certainly save Chevalier a lot of trouble.

"Raleigh is here," Judah said. "Are you really telling me you came here to find Casper, and not to also get revenge for Travers feeding you misinformation? If you know about him being alive, then you clearly know he's been working for Travers Industries all this time."

"Jerry Travers is dead."

"I know," Judah said. "That's why it's reasonable to conclude Raleigh is the one in control of it all." He wanted to tell the guy that if he was going to succeed at this, then the man really needed to be able to put the pieces together faster than he was.

The agent studied him with an assessing gaze. "I may have underestimated you."

"Most people do."

The door was kicked open. The agent guarding it fell to the ground as Zander rushed in, followed by Andre. And Casper Cunningham.

"Here." Andre shoved the assassin at the British intelligence agent.

The agent reacted on reflex, surprised enough he brought his hands up. Judah punched him in the low back. The man's knees collapsed. Judah pinned his hands behind his back, and Zander handed him something to secure them with. He'd already done the same with the guard before Judah even realized it.

Andre shoved Casper to a chair and drew his gun.

"I need to go find Soraya." Judah moved toward the door.

The British intelligence agent kicked out with his legs. Judah stumbled, whirled around, and returned the favor.

Both Zander and Andre shifted.

Judah realized they were listening to the comms channel. "What is it?" He glanced between them.

Zander said, "Raleigh is onstage."

"And Soraya?" He couldn't believe he still had no idea where she was. "Did Hannah wake up yet?" Maybe she knew something.

"Badger said Hannah told him it was Raleigh who hit her over the head." Zander's expression darkened.

Judah shook his head. "Now he's presenting, as if nothing ever happened?" He really needed the rest of the world to realize what Chevalier already knew—the truth of what Soraya and Isaac had put online.

He headed for the stage anyway, changing directions at the last minute when he saw a crowd of people who looked official. He didn't want to be delayed by anyone.

Judah worked his way through the audience from the edge and saw Raleigh with a microphone, talking about hope for the future. He turned, looking at the edges of the stage and then around the room. Avoiding the audience itself but taking in the periphery. Then back to the stage again. Where was she?

There.

She stood to one side of the stage, swaying. The man beside her wound an arm around her waist. The muscles in his forearm flexed. He was holding her far too tightly.

Judah headed for them. A man crossed in front of him, wearing a hat. Judah was so focused on Soraya he almost missed it.

He turned and grabbed for the man who had moved two steps beyond him, pulled the guy back, and spun him. Under the brim of the hat, former president Raleigh's eyes widened. If he was here, then who was on the stage?

Judah said, "What are you—"

The man shoved at him. Judah stumbled back two steps as the man ran away, far more spry than he'd have imagined. Pain speared through Judah's abdomen, and he gasped.

Behind him, a screech erupted. He turned to watch as Soraya raced onto the stage, weaving as though she were drunk.

The audience gasped. Someone screamed, and someone else yelled, "She's got a knife!"

Judah looked down. He moved his hand away from the front of his shirt.

Blood.

SORAYA BLINKED AGAINST THE LIGHTS, gripping in her hand whatever it was she held. As though it would steady her stumbling feet. Her head swam causing her to sway.

But she couldn't be waylaid. There was nothing that would stop her.

She was going to kill president Raleigh.

A couple more steps. Moving toward him, while he backed up. But not far enough she wouldn't do what she had to do. There would be no dissuading her. No matter the niggling note of disquiet at the back of her mind. She couldn't wait long enough to think on what that was.

Someone screamed. The high sound cut across the commotion.

It was going to be okay. Soraya was going to fix this.

She lunged at Raleigh with the knife. This was only going to end one way, with him dead and all of her problems over. Her parents would be safe. Soraya would be free to live her life. That had to be the end, and this was the only way to get it.

Fire birthed in her. Boiling up from deep inside. He had ruined everything, and her parents were dead because of him. There was no way she could let him live. Not when he had taken everything she had and destroyed everyone she loved.

Isaac?

She shook her head. No, that wasn't right. It was someone else, not him.

Raleigh backed up a couple more steps. He turned his head and yelled something she didn't hear.

She kept stalking toward him.

She would not be deterred.

Another face swam in her mind. One she wanted to stay with, and think on. After. She would do that after she was done with this.

Someone slammed into her. Soraya swung out with the knife, and her back hit the floor. The person grasped her wrist and held it down, but she would not loosen her grip on the weapon. The thing that was going to get her out of this.

"Where is the Secret Service?"

The question made no sense. But no one was asking her.

"No, don't let him leave."

Cameras flashed. Relentless lights that flickered across her perception. Soraya's eyes rolled back in her head, and she lost her grip on consciousness.

When she next became aware, Soraya was inside a room. She lay on the bed. Blinking, she glanced around. Some kind of medical suite. Was she at the hospital?

She groaned. Everything that had happened rushed back in a wave of nausea and the kind of distress that welled in her throat. Her nose filled, and her eyes began to sting. Tears leaked from the corners of her eyes.

What had she done? And all the flashing. Phone cameras and people watching. Everyone had seen her attempt to murder the former president. No one would believe her story now. And she thought Raleigh had destroyed her credibility earlier.

It would be so much worse going forward. It didn't matter

what she said, everyone would think she was completely unhinged.

But all she cared about, aside from her parents being okay, was one man.

Did Judah know? She thought he had been there but wasn't entirely sure when everything was a blur of anger and determination. Words going through her head that weren't her own. Things whispered in her ear until she could repeat them back. Until she was prepared to take a life over the things that had been done to her.

She tried to move. Both hands were secured by cuffs to either side of the bed. Chained to the rails.

Tears leaked from the corners of her eyes. What was happening?

She felt like she had the worst hangover ever.

The door opened. She must have made a noise to alert someone, because a uniformed police officer stuck his head in. Then he turned back to the hallway, and said, "She's awake."

***

"You HAVE to let me in there." Judah faced off with Sergeant Roberts.

The guy shook his head. "That's not happening. She tried to kill the former president and everyone saw. You think I can just wave the rules because you've decided they don't apply to you? That might fly in federal prison, but not with my case."

Judah bit back the response he wanted to give the man. This was a federal case, not an investigation that would belong to a local cop, even if he was a sergeant. The guy was likely looking to move up in the world, positioning himself in this in such a way he would be noticed.

"It's obvious to everyone that she was drugged." Lucia shifted forward, putting herself in front of Judah's shoulder. "She could be in there in medical distress."

"That's what trained professionals are for." As the sergeant motioned to the room, the cop opened the door again. A white-coated doctor stepped inside.

Before the door shut, the doctor glanced over.

"Casper," Judah whispered.

"What?" Roberts turned.

Judah wanted to shove everyone out of the way and see Soraya for himself. After she'd stumbled across the stage with that knife, nearly cutting Raleigh, he had to know if she was okay. "She didn't do this of her own volition." He moved to go after her.

Roberts held up a hand.

"She could be hurt."

Roberts lifted his brows. "And yet you're the one bleeding."

Lucia peered around to where Roberts motioned.

Judah shook his head. "I'm fine." As if he even cared about a cut.

"She's being taken care of," Roberts said. "And that woman stabbed two people that I know of. This attempt will be the third."

"And the fact I saw former president Raleigh in the audience seconds before it happened?" There wasn't enough time to explain all about the double of Travers the doctor had created out of Isaac's father. But it was still a fact of this case. "My colleagues are looking for him now. And when they find him? You're going to have to explain to everyone why you let him go free."

"Raleigh isn't the criminal here." Roberts' expression shifted in a way Judah was unsure he entirely believed that. "Unless you've got some kind of proof?"

"Your people are interviewing all of his staff, right?"

Roberts shrugged. "And what are they going to tell me?"

"How about the fact Soraya was held here against her will

after she posted that live video?" Lucia asked. "It's the reason Raleigh had her parents kidnapped."

They'd called Ted, who had gotten in contact with Jeff. Whoever these Vanguard people were that his future brother-in-law had on retainer, they'd been dispatched to locate Soraya's parents. Judah was hoping the word would come soon that they were okay.

It was time to clean up this entire mess.

But that meant finding Raleigh. Not the man who had been on the stage. Judah had concluded that it was a body double, as Travers had done with their founder. The man he had seen in the audience, the one who had run away from him, that had to be the real President Raleigh.

Zander and Andre had turned those two British agents over to the police to be questioned about why they were here, and gone after him.

Judah said, "Raleigh hated Soraya for exposing the truth behind his new phone system."

"You think no one else realized it might be problematic?" Roberts said.

Judah had no idea. "If there were issues, why was no one talking about them? Instead, a single reporter has her life destroyed by Raleigh all so he can keep pretending everything's fine. He used her over and over again, and now he drugged her and tried to get her to murder someone impersonating him."

"See?" Roberts said. "Even with all the files we got and all that Interpol stuff, that's the part I'm having trouble with. Body doubles?"

"Maybe it's just above your pay grade."

Lucia nudged Judah back. "I'm happy to walk you through all the evidence we have. So why don't you show me to your boss, and I'll do that."

"Just so long as Soraya doesn't go to prison," Judah said. "Because she's done absolutely nothing wrong."

Roberts narrowed his eyes.

Maybe he was one of those cops who thought everyone had done *something* wrong, and maybe the only innocent people in the world were little kids. The ones that didn't commit crimes, anyway.

Roberts nodded. "I'll take any evidence you have."

"Good," Lucia said. Judah agreed with her, given that the police were the ones that had to unpack this whole thing.

As the two of them walked away, Judah pulled out his phone and called Zander.

"O'Connell."

Judah said, "We need to get someone in to see Soraya. We're going to need to know what Casper gave Lana and Soraya." If they didn't know what poison she had been given, they weren't going to be able to give her an antidote.

"We handed over Casper along with those Brits. They're with the feds. We'll find out," Zander said.

"Casper went in to see Soraya." Judah squeezed the bridge of his nose—long enough to remember he'd broken it recently. *Ouch.* "What about Raleigh?" Things weren't settled unless the former president was in cuffs—or dead.

"Jeff's people are working on locating Soraya's parents. Ted is tracing all the calls between the cell towers locally and the West Coast, assuming they were still in California when Raleigh gave Soraya proof of life." Zander blew out a quick breath. He was moving fast.

"Did you find him?"

Zander only said, "Meet me in the west parking lot."

And then he hung up.

35

J udah raced between cars. The parking lot was open air on the west side of the convention center. Clouds hung low, threatening to dump the accumulated moisture on their heads. He ignored the malevolence above and headed for the row two aisles over where he could see several of his friends.

Zander stood still. Andre close by.

It wasn't until he drew close that he saw why they didn't move.

As he passed a van, he saw Badger grasping a man's shirt with both hands. Hannah stood close by. With no hat on, Judah realized it was the former president.

Hannah backed up a step. She lifted both hands and swiped at her cheeks. She was crying. Judah was unsurprised because this man was her father, and he had killed her mother. He realized then he would rather go to her and squeeze her shoulder in solidarity than take out any anger on the former president. Or, more likely it was because he knew Badger had that covered.

"Do we know it's actually him?" Judah glanced around.

Badger said, "It's him."

"And the Raleigh who is currently with Secret Service, inside this building?" Judah swung out with his hand not holding the gun and motioned at the giant concrete structure. He wanted to be back inside, but not because of the president. Because he wanted to be as close to Soraya as possible.

Andre said, "He's right. How do we know?"

"He was trying to escape." Hannah motioned to him, a hitch in her voice. "And the one that was supposed to be killed is playing his part in there while this one goes free. The fake one is the one who knocked me out, by the way."

Badger said, "It makes no sense that the fake Raleigh is the one trying to leave."

"What about a DNA test?" Zander asked. "That would prove who he is one way or another. And turning him over to the feds would also go a long way to lending credence to our story."

Judah said, "It's not like they're going to be able to argue with two Raleighs."

The sergeant he'd spoken with already thought he was crazy. Everyone in the world now thought the same about Soraya. Raleigh had done so much damage, Judah had no idea how they were going to get it all straight.

But what counted, was that they were all okay. The only casualty had been Lana. A life lost that they would grieve for sure. Especially her children. But the team itself and those they had brought into their lives were all alive and unharmed.

That was almost a miracle in itself.

If it stayed that way—and Soraya remained safe—Judah was going to think more on his granny's faith, and what that might mean for him.

Raleigh glanced between them. "You wouldn't turn me in. As if they'll believe any of you, when I can prove everything I've ever said is true. No one will ever convict me of anything."

"If you've managed to stay one step ahead of this so far." Zander stepped toward him. "I'll give you that much."

Andre said, "You had Stephen Gladstone killed in prison, didn't you?"

"What else would I do with a group of assassins?" Raleigh leveled a look of disgust at their teammate.

"It's over now." Judah was going to make sure of that, hopefully with Casper's help. He figured eventually he'd have to have a conversation with British intelligence. Explain one last time that he was off limits—if Zander hadn't already done that.

But that was a worry for tomorrow. Right now they had to figure out what to do with Raleigh.

Judah glanced at Andre. "Lucia is with the feds. Can she bring them out here to get him? Maybe they can bring the other Raleigh with them."

"Hey—"

Judah spun back around to see Badger jump back. Raleigh held a knife in his hand. Judah touched his stomach with his free hand reflexively, and it stung. He winced.

Badger said, "I don't think so. Not again."

Hannah pulled her gun out, lifted, and pointed at Raleigh. Judah wasn't sure she would be able to pull the trigger on a man she knew was her father—even if he also did terrible things.

Judah, Andre, and Zander all had their weapons out. Badger pulled his as well.

Hannah said, "I'd hate to have to shoot my own father, but I will if I have to."

Raleigh glanced at her, a look of disgust on his face. "Don't spare me any pity. I wouldn't do it to any spawn of Lana's."

Hannah stilled.

"Drop the knife, Raleigh." Zander lifted his chin in Badger's direction. "I thought you checked him for weapons?"

Badger winced. "He was clean."

"Obviously not."

Andre said, "Maybe you could put Badger on probation later, and we deal with this now."

Hannah shifted her stance, getting a better footing. "Drop the knife now. There's nothing you can do here that will end any way other than with you full of bullets, bleeding out on the ground. Is that how you want this to end?"

Andre had his phone out. "Yeah, babe. Bring everyone out here. Including the Raleigh that was attacked onstage."

The Raleigh they had in front of them still hadn't dropped the knife. His gaze flickered around each of them, as though he was formulating a plan. Exactly what did he think he was going to—

Raleigh let out a roar. He slashed at Hannah with the knife.

Five bullets hit his torso.

The former president jerked and then fell to the ground.

Zander sighed. "I guess he didn't want to face the consequences of his actions." He glanced at Hannah. "In more than one way."

Badger winced. "Okay. Just listen, all right? I patted him down. I don't know where he was hiding that knife, but I should have found it."

Two suited men raced across the parking lot toward them.

Andre said, "Incoming."

They all took a step back from the man on the ground. Each of them shifted their grip on their guns, holding them in a way that indicated they had no intention of using them and were fully prepared to lay them on the ground if instructed.

The men who approached were Secret Service agents. They drew out Sig Sauers, and the older said, "One of you had better explain what this is. Right now."

The thunder of footsteps from the other direction drew everyone's attention. Cops, along with Lucia, approached them. In the group were another handful of Secret Service agents, and a man who looked exactly like President Raleigh.

As much as Judah wanted to stick around for the explanation, he would rather be inside with Soraya. How long was this going to take before he could see her? He had to know what Casper had been doing in there.

Sergeant Roberts approached.

Judah said, "Do you want me to say I told you so, or are you going to figure that out for yourself?"

Zander shifted between them. "As you can see, the man on the ground—who may or may not be President Raleigh—has a weapon. As his intention was clearly to harm one of my teammates, lethal force was required."

Judah glanced at Hannah. Badger was over by her now, talking low to her. She nodded. Badger tugged her into his arms. Maybe she didn't know how she felt about her father's death, or maybe she considered him nothing to do with her. The real President Raleigh had been evil—a threat to every person in this country.

For all Judah knew, she was glad he was dead. She had even helped him get that way.

One of the Secret Service agents turned to Raleigh. "Sir?"

"I have absolutely no idea…" The fake Raleigh took a step back. "This is unbelievable."

Before he could turn and run, one of the agents grasped his elbow. "You're not going anywhere."

The fake president sputtered.

Judah realized he didn't know which was which, although he had an idea. "You might want to get a DNA test going."

Sergeant Roberts shook his head and glanced at Judah. "I should probably apologize for thinking you were crazy."

"Believe me, there have been a few times where I thought I was." Judah winced. "But you can do something for me."

"What's that?"

"After you're done interviewing Soraya Adams? Maybe you could let her go. She hasn't done anything."

Roberts said, "If that's our conclusion, then so be it. She'll be free to go."

Judah nodded. "Good."

Roberts shook his head.

Zander clapped Judah on the shoulder.

Judah said, "What?"

Hannah called over from her hug with Badger. He had turned her away from the mess that Raleigh had become so that she didn't have to look at it. "Let me guess," she said. "You need a cup of tea?"

Badger grinned. "Maybe it's Soraya who needs one."

Hannah smiled and leaned her head against Badger's shoulder. "I think you're right."

"So do I." As Lucia spoke, Andre tugged her under his shoulder.

Zander said, "I should go call my wife. See how she's doing, and get an update on Eas."

"Thanks, guys." Judah wasn't sure he could have done this without them. Never mind. He *definitely* couldn't have done it. Zander squeezed his shoulder. The others came over, and they ended up in a jumble of hugs together.

"We'll see you at home in a few days," Zander said. "With Soraya."

Judah wasn't sure exactly what was going to happen. He knew what he wanted, and even now the danger was over, life wouldn't be certain.

Did she want what he wanted?

Soraya walked out of the FBI office. The midday sun was so bright that she had to lift a hand and shade her eyes. Despite the fact it was absolutely freezing outside and she had no coat on, the sun still managed to shine valiantly.

Snow had collected on everything. Shoveled away by whoever the bureau hired for that, the sidewalk salted.

Ordinary, everyday things she could appreciate now. Because she was free.

And Raleigh wouldn't hurt anyone again.

The feds had asked her a million questions about Lana as well as the former president. Then there were the lengthy descriptions of everyone at Chevalier, and everything that had happened with them. As though the team were being vetted for some reason.

She couldn't make sense of any of it. And considering it wasn't the world she intended to live in, Soraya had answered the questions as best she could and not worried about anything else. Just telling the truth.

"Honey!"

She looked around, certain that was her mom's voice.

"Over here." Her mom waved, standing with her dad beside a huge white SUV.

They met halfway, laughing and hugging. Her mom kissed her cheek and probably left all her lipstick on Soraya's face. Her dad touched her cheeks after her, rubbing his thumbs as though either of them wanted to remove signs of her mother's affection.

Soraya laughed and gathered them both to her again.

She looked beyond them while they held her. Judah stood beside the SUV.

She was exhausted from what felt like days of talking to the police. Going over and over everything that had happened. She still felt the need to run to him and get a hug she knew would be *basically amazing.*

Judah smiled at her with a soft expression on his face. The last time they'd been together she'd yelled at him.

Her parents turned, taking both of her hands, one each, and led her toward him.

Her dad said, "We'll get in the back. You can sit up front, honey." He kissed her cheek.

Her mom squeezed her around the waist while Soraya blinked, trying to figure out what on earth was happening.

The door shut, and she was on the curb, alone with Judah. Relatively speaking at least, considering they were in public.

"Hey."

His smile widened. "Hello, Soraya."

"Everything good?"

He nodded. "You?"

"I think I might have a concussion. Because was it just me, or was that really weird?" She pointed at the car.

"Would it be weird if I asked you to have dinner with me…in Last Chance County?"

"Would it be weird if I said I might need to check with my parents first?"

He grinned. "It might have been your dad's idea."

She blinked.

"I took them by their house, and they packed suitcases each. The plane is waiting at the airport, and your parents have reservations at a vacation house in the mountains outside Last Chance County. It's about ten minutes from the Chevalier house."

"They're going on vacation?"

He nodded. "And they didn't want to be too far from you."

She felt her eyebrows rise. "So I don't have much choice?"

He shook his head. "You always have a choice. Thankfully, all the options here are good ones. No matter what you decide."

"But you have a preference?"

"I have a wedding to go to still, and I have a plus one that needs filling." He pushed off the SUV and closed the gap between them. "And it would be my very great honor if you would be my date when Ted and Jess finally manage to get married."

Her eyes filled. "Are they both okay?"

He nodded, but she still couldn't completely believe they'd all come through this. Raleigh hadn't won. They'd stopped him from managing to fake his own death so he could escape —something he'd planned for her to do. After Soraya had made that video with Isaac, and Raleigh had found the perfect person to try and frame as his murderer, everyone would believe she was unhinged enough to take his life. She believed he was evil, and had let everyone know it in no uncertain terms.

"And Toni…and Isaac?" she asked. Were they really okay as well? Maybe they hadn't made it out.

Another nod, though guarded. "Everyone is very much okay. Though, I don't think we'll be seeing Isaac much." He paused. "Can you tell me what happened with Casper? By the time I caught up to you again, they were taking you to the hospital under police protection. You were stable, and he's nowhere to be found."

She ran a hand through her hair, wishing she looked better than she probably did. If they were going to this wedding together, she'd have the chance to show Judah what she could look like when she wore a dress and heels, and did her hair and makeup.

Maybe after that, he would kiss her again.

Soraya realized she needed to answer his question. "Casper was dressed like a doctor. I was kind of freaked out, because I stabbed him before the ambulance crashed. I didn't know if he was there to hurt me. But he stayed on the other side of the room. And there was a cop in there, too."

Judah nodded. "That's the only reason I didn't shove my way in there, though I tried."

She laid a hand on his arm.

"He wanted out. That's what he told me."

She nodded. "He told me that he gave me the same poison he gave Lana, and the name of the antidote. He even cried."

Judah worked his mouth back and forth.

"He said I should tell the doctor when I got to the hospital. Otherwise, I wouldn't make it." She needed to ask, "Was he captured? Is he in jail?"

Judah shook his head. "No one knows where he is. But we'll find him."

"He did seem sorry."

"That doesn't excuse his actions." Judah blew out a breath. "You fought to keep your life. He took lives. And for what?" He glanced to the side, reached up with one hand, and squeezed the back of his neck. "I'm sorry. I should have been there."

"Taking down Raleigh was more important."

"You know what?" He shook his head. "In the moment, it wasn't." He held out his hand, palm up.

Soraya laid her hand in his.

"When it came down to it," he said, "all I could think about was you."

She stepped closer to him, so there was barely a space between them. "It was crazy, the way we met. But I'm glad it happened."

"It's going to be a good story we get to tell for years to come."

The back window of the car rolled down. Her mom called out, "Will you kiss already, so we can go? I'm not getting any younger."

Soraya's cheeks heated, and she groaned. This was the best day of her life, and the most thoroughly embarrassing. Judah was going to think her family was crazy. He would make excuses and—

He glanced over his shoulder. "Yes, ma'am." When he turned back to her, he said, "Your mom's orders."

Soraya lifted one brow.

Judah chuckled. "After this, I need a cup of tea."

His eyes widened, and she pressed her lips to his. With his arms wrapped around her, she slid hers up over his shoulders to touch the back of his neck. She kept it PG-rated since her parents were waiting. And hopefully looking the other way— or at their phones.

He smiled, his lips against hers.

It was about the sweetest thing ever.

When she lifted her head an inch, he said, "Thank you."

"For what?"

"Being strong, even when you didn't feel like it. For facing your fears, even if you didn't have much choice." He paused. "For helping Isaac tell the world the truth he needed to speak."

"And for being your date for the wedding?"

He winced. "Everyone has a date except me."

"Oh, so this is a pity thing?"

He laughed and hugged her to him. "Not on your life."

Soraya didn't know what the future held. She didn't feel like she'd lived her own life for months, and the chance to explore what could be—what might be, if she embraced it— held a promise that was different from anything she'd ever known. Like the potential and the wonder that came with the New Year, each December thirty-first bringing with it a fresh start. Another three hundred sixty-five days of possibility.

Of, what if?

For her, all of that was wrapped up in Judah. In the unspoken *what could be* that hung between them.

All Soraya knew was that she wanted to be around to find out.

To live the adventure with people she cared about.

And someone she loved.

EPILOGUE

Last Chance County

The sound of the string quartet warming up drifted through the open doors into the church lobby.

Aria smoothed down the front of her dress. "Showtime."

Her friend Jonah, the pastor's son, said, "What?" over the comms channel.

Yeah, so they'd co-opted the tech from the Chevalier house where Aria lived. But what else was she supposed to do? After the disaster of the last attempt to have this wedding, Ted and Jess needed things to go smoothly.

"Aria, you there?" That was Mateo, whose uncle was the police lieutenant. Both the guys were seniors, and she was a freshman, but they'd been nice to her at youth group. She also routinely kicked their butts on XBOX, and foosball, and cross-country—basically anything else competitive.

"Yes, I'm here."

"Bro, she's probably daydreaming about her wedding." Jonah snorted.

Mateo chuckled. "Is Sean even coming?"

Aria's face flamed. "Don't both of you have things to do?"

Zander and Nora strode past her, arm in arm.

Aria sighed. She heard her mom chuckle and glanced over.

Her dad stood beside her mom, who held Kuai's leash in her hand. "You're sure the dog is supposed to be part of this?" Karina asked, even though the dog was already dressed for the wedding.

Aria grabbed the leash. "You should both take your seats."

As if she hadn't been helping plan this wedding since she moved to town.

Aria had heard Jess and Ellie at the ice cream shop talking wedding details. After she'd given them a couple of suggestions she'd seen on Pinterest, they'd asked her to come on as co-wedding coordinator.

Aria wasn't going to let Jess down.

Her mom headed into the sanctuary. Eas hung back. Aria looked up at him, the comforting weight of the German shepherd against her leg. "Hey." It still felt weird calling him Dad.

He studied her. "Everything okay?"

Aria bit her lip.

Eas didn't move. Sometimes his focus had an unnatural stillness to it, but she thought it was cool. "What is it?" he said.

"Are you going to marry Mom?"

His expression softened in a way it only did with her mother. "When the time is right."

She wanted to stomp her foot, but she wasn't a kid anymore. She was almost fifteen.

He said, "Will you take my last name when I do?"

She nodded because she wanted that more than anything.

Eas leaned down and kissed her forehead. "I love you."

"Love you too, Dad."

He walked away. Over the comms channel Mateo said, "He scares me."

Jonah laughed. "Right?!"

"You guys are dorks." Aria rolled her eyes.

"That's why you get on with us," Mateo said. "Duh."

Andre and Lucia wandered past. He wore a dark suit, and she wore a floor-length blue dress. The two of them were breathtaking. In a different way than Zander and Nora, but no less impactful.

Over comms, Mateo said, "Dean and Ted are coming out of the pastor's conference room. They're taking their places."

Aria said, "Jonah, where's your dad?"

"Already at the front."

"Good."

Andre winked at her. Lucia squeezed her hand.

Aria heard a commotion behind her. Judah and Soraya walked in, followed by her parents. Toni and Jeff were part of the group, too. The couples fit together in a way that was so obvious it made her chest hurt. She wanted that with some-one…someday.

Maybe it would be Sean, maybe not.

Right now, she couldn't worry about it.

Aria held the door open. "People will be arriving soon." She glanced between Judah and Jeff. "Zander wants you both by the west door."

After ensuring Ted and Dean were at the church an hour ago, they'd gone back to fetch the women they loved.

Toni kissed her cheek.

Soraya squeezed her hand.

Mateo said, "I've got a rogue child in the west hallway."

Aria turned her attention to the comms channel. "Do you need help?"

"I've got it covered."

"Get that kid back to their parent," Aria said. "We're T-minus-twelve minutes until this thing starts."

Kuai barked.

Soraya's mom jumped back, startled. "Goodness."

The women giggled.

Jeff looked at Judah. "Does Zander know about this?"

Judah shrugged. "Maybe Ted needs an intern."

Aria nearly burst. "Tell my mom that. Please. You'll be able to convince her."

Judah slung an arm around her shoulders and hugged her. "Knock 'em dead, kid."

Badger swept through the front doors next, ahead of Hannah. He gave Aria a questioning look, and she nodded.

Hannah shook out her coat, dislodging the snow that had fallen on the walk over from their car. She glanced between them. "What's this?"

Aria smiled. "Your seats are on the left."

Badger nodded and led Hannah inside.

She waited. Three seconds after they entered the vestibule, Hannah squealed. "Mom! Dad!"

Aria grinned. People filed into the wedding, residents from town, and the entire police department and their families.

Two minutes before the time they'd been scheduled to arrive, the car pulled up with Jess and her sister Ellie inside.

Their mother hadn't responded to the invitation.

"She's early," Aria said. "Is everyone ready?"

Conroy Barnes, the police chief, strode from the sanctuary. "Now?"

Aria nodded. He was so good-looking she got tongue-tied. He also had the cutest baby *ever*, which was why she signed up for nursery on Sunday mornings—so she got to hold their son all the time.

Ellie came in first, followed by the bride.

Aria's eyes stung.

Jess grinned. "That's a good reaction. I like that." She smoothed down the front of her dress and took the flowers from her sister. "I'm hoping Ted chokes on his tongue."

Aria nodded. "He will."

Conroy chuckled. "Ready?"

Aria moved to the doors with Kuai and said, "Positions."

The music changed, and the pastor asked everyone to stand. Aria unclipped Kuai's leash and said, "Go ahead."

The dog walked down the aisle, a wreath of ribbons on her head. She trotted to the front, then laid down to the side by Aria's mom.

Ellie went next.

The police chief led Jess down the aisle, as her mentor and the closest thing to a parent she had. Aria watched from inside the back doors. Nothing was going to go wrong.

She leaned against the doors and watched the pastor begin the ceremony. So much had changed the last few months, she could hardly believe they'd gone from just her and her mom—and Kuai—to a family that burst at the seams.

So much love.

From halfway down the pews, Sean turned back to her. He gave her a thumbs-up.

Aria smiled.

When he looked back at the front, she wiped the happy tear from her cheek.

From behind the lobby doors, she heard the front open. Aria eased out into the lobby and nearly tripped over her shoes.

Four men in suits stood guard, wearing wired earpieces.

Aria said, "We might have a problem."

Mateo answered, "What is it?"

"Uh..." Aria couldn't even form the words to explain what was happening as the doors opened again and the president of the United States entered.

He smoothed down his tie, that flag pin on his lapel.

"Uh..."

"I'm late, aren't I?" To his credit, he seemed apologetic.

"The bride arrived early," Aria said. "She was in a hurry."

The president chuckled.

Footsteps raced down the hall on either side. Mateo stumbled to a stop on one side, Jonah on the other.

"Friends of yours?"

Aria nodded.

"Good friends, it looks like."

"Yes." She swallowed. "Um…sir."

The president said, "You can call me Albert."

"If you don't mind, Mr. President is fine." Aria winced. "We haven't had much luck with people in power recently."

"I'm aware of that." Thankfully he didn't seem mad. "If you wouldn't mind passing along this"—the president slid an envelope from inside his suit jacket and handed it over—"I'd be eternally grateful."

"Um, sure."

He nodded. "Thank you." Then glanced at Jonah and Mateo. "I believe you both might make fine Secret Service agents one day. Collins, you might want to give them a business card."

"Yes, sir. I think that's a good idea." The agent wandered to Mateo first, then Jonah.

The president said, "You, I think, might be better suited to being *behind* the Resolute desk, rather than guarding it."

Aria said, "We'll see."

The president chuckled. "I'll look forward to it. I can tell everyone I 'knew you then.'" He swept out, flanked by agents.

Mateo and Jonah walked over to stand beside her.

Aria looked down at the envelope in her hand.

Mateo broke the silence. "Whoa."

"You know that's right." Jonah stared at the business card in his hand. "My mom is gonna flip."

Aria snapped out of it. "Get back to your positions. This wedding isn't going to coordinate itself."

They both saluted and said, "Yes, ma'am."

Aria pulled open the back door just as Jess and Ted walked down the aisle. She held it for them, watching while they seemed not to know anyone else was around.

She would have that, too.

"Someday."

Thanks for reading *Last Line of Defense*, I really hope you enjoyed it! Please consider leaving a review, it helps others find their next read.

Continue on for a sneak peek of the next story in the Last Chance County universe, *Point of Impact*, which kicks off the "Last Chance Downrange" series and releases February 2022!

Also, find an excerpt from *Expired Refuge* - Book 1 in the *Last Chance County* series, and see how it all began…

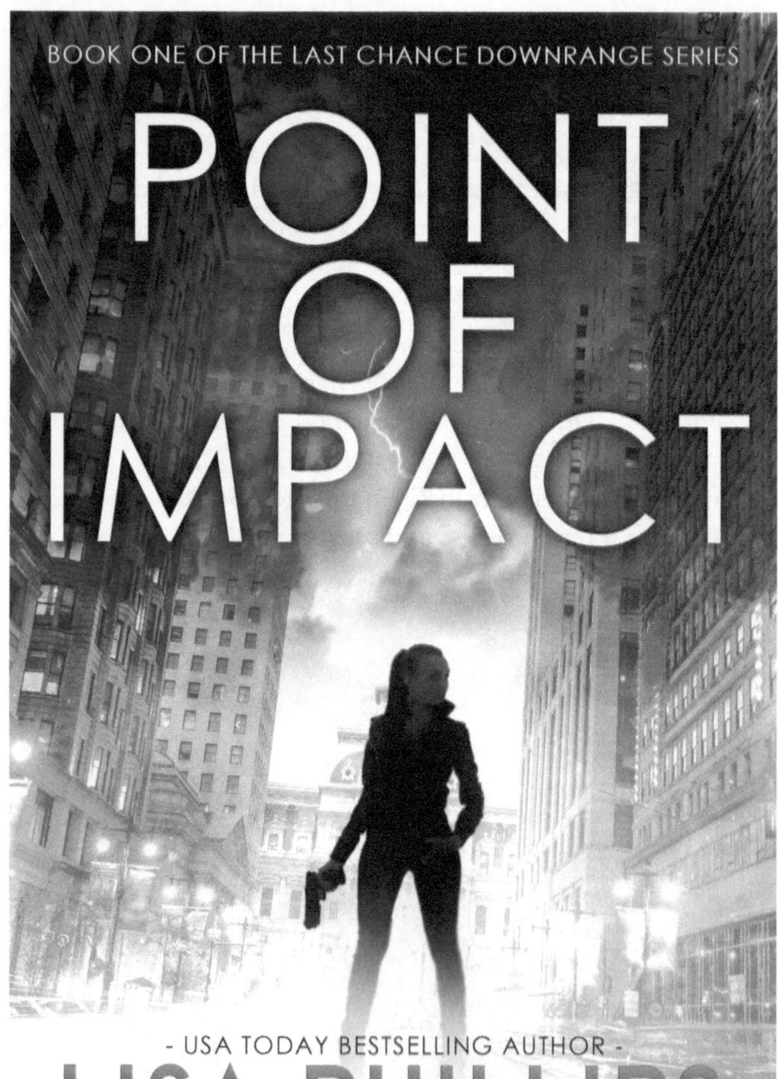
BOOK ONE OF THE LAST CHANCE DOWNRANGE SERIES
POINT OF IMPACT
- USA TODAY BESTSELLING AUTHOR -
LISA PHILLIPS
An old haunt.
A deadly killer at work.

Fifteen years after a serial killer tormented them, Addie and Jacob are living very different lives.

As an FBI Profiler, Addie is on the edge of burnout. When she returns home, she has to face down every nightmare she's ever had. Is the resurgence of a series of all too familiar deadly crimes the work of a former ally, or a mastermind who has been pulling her strings all along?

Recluse and artist Jacob likes his life. It's how he's managed to cope with who he became all those years ago. But he can't avoid the past any longer. Not when Addie walks back into town, and right back into his life.

The past returns in a wave of unexplained crimes. Addie and Jacob find themselves at the heart of it all, at the place where their lives were torn apart.

This stand-alone story is the start of the accountant's office series – a spinoff from Last Chance County.
A Christian romantic suspense novel.
Get Point of Impact now!
https://lastchancecounty.com/downrange-series

EXPIRED REFUGE

LAST CHANCE COUNTY BOOK ONE

eBook ISBN: 979-8-88552-025-6

Paperback ISBN: 979-8-88552-026-3

Publisher: Two Dogs Publishing, LLC Idaho, USA.

Cover design: Ryan Schwarz

Edited by: Jen Weiber

1

—————

According to intel, this was where it would go down. Police Lieutenant Conroy Barnes watched the feed on his laptop, which was sitting on a folding table in the janitor's closet of the high school. Low light meant it was hard to see what was happening. But he could make out enough.

The undercover was about to make the sale.

He could hear her every breath through the microphone. The second his officer made the exchange, cash for drugs, he was clear to move in.

Conroy watched as the dealer reached into a pocket. Even behind the door, he was ready to pull his weapon and step in. His officer was also armed and wearing a bulletproof vest. Not a foolproof plan, but she understood the risks, and they had been over all the contingencies.

The department was big enough they could have brought in several officers as backup, or even a couple of detectives. Each of them worked as part of a SWAT team when it was necessary. But tonight's operation had to be done discretely in order that word didn't get back to anyone that the police had snatched up this guy.

The drug dealer, who conducted business under the

moniker "Iceman," pulled a small baggie from his pocket. "You got the money?"

Conroy held his breath, watching the screen as he waited for the right words. He didn't like being the one on the other end of the video feed. He much preferred the front lines, but he also had a high profile in this town. His officer was new, which meant few people knew she was a cop.

So he'd put her in as an undercover.

And she was turning out to be seriously good at it. Though, with her history, he wasn't entirely shocked. She impressed him, but she was also his underling and barely twenty-four. He was creeping towards his thirties.

"Got it right here." Her voice was steady which shouldn't surprise him given everything he knew about Jessica Ridgeman. She might be green, but she was also proving to be a serious asset.

With just enough desperation in her voice, she said, "It'll be a good weekend."

That was the signal. Conroy shoved open the fire door and led with his weapon. Cold night air hit him like being slammed with a thousand ice picks.

"Police! Hands up!" He approached the suspect they had been surveilling who was still standing with Officer Ridgeman.

Iceman whipped around. Conroy saw him realize this had been a setup. He released the cash and pulled a knife.

"Drop it!" There was no way he would be so stupid as to hurt a cop just because he was about to be arrested. Then again, smart criminals didn't usually get caught this easily.

Dollar bills hit the ground. Iceman swiped the knife toward the customer, Jessica Ridgeman. She reacted with the reflexes of a police officer trained and, evidently, completely comfortable working undercover. Conroy had never seen someone under his command so cool in the face of a weapon. This newcomer to Last Chance County was going to fit in well.

She swiped at it with a flat palm, connecting with Iceman's wrist. The knife dropped.

"Hands up." Conroy held his gun aimed at the man. "You're under arrest."

The drug dealer grunted. Then he made the choice so many of them did when faced with poor odds.

He ran for it.

Iceman took off across the quad toward the field and the neighborhood behind the high school.

His officer took a half step back, shook out her hand, and said, "Ow."

"You okay, Jess?"

"I will be if you go arrest that guy, Lieutenant." She pulled her gun. "I'll get the car."

He took that as a green light and took off after the drug dealer. Iceman's real name was Simon Petrov and he seemed, by all accounts, a low-level guy. The man on the street dealing hand-to-hand with townspeople hooked on destruction. Not the boss.

Conroy wanted to sit Petrov down in his interview room and ask him to testify against the person who supplied him with the drugs. Whether that meant just straight testimony, or if it involved Petrov being put back on the street to get Conroy evidence on the one who got him the supply—a supply he then divided up and sold off for a cut. Conroy didn't mind either way if it got him the boss in cuffs.

Petrov made it all the way to the far end of the field. He went right through the break in the fence and took the walking path that ran along the back of the neighborhood.

Conroy pumped his arms and legs, his hiking boots pounding the salted path. Snow had been shoveled off the sidewalk for dog walkers and kids going to school, but he was going to send the landscaper a gift basket if he managed to get all the way to the end without slipping or sliding on the ice.

Petrov disappeared at the end of the path, turning into the

neighborhood. Mostly larger family homes at this end, he didn't figure anything good would come of Petrov breaking into one. The last thing Conroy needed was to spend the night working a hostage situation. Or a homicide scene. He'd worked exactly one murder in the last six months, and even a ratio that low didn't sit well with him.

One of his plans if he became the chief of police was to work on reducing violent crime. This town—affectionately known to all who lived here as Last Chance County—was supposed to be a safe haven, a place people could live their lives peacefully and quietly.

He'd grown up here, and during those years, as well as his years as a cop, Conroy had seen the best and worst of this place. He never wanted to be anywhere else. And except for the odd vacation in Hawaii during which he complained about the heat nearly constantly, driving his sister, her husband, and their kids crazy, Conroy was going to stay here until the day he died.

His earpiece crackled. Officer Ridgeman's voice came through loud and clear. "You copy me, Lieutenant?"

"Heading down Aspect now, about to cross Herrin Ridge."

The center of the neighborhood had a huge roundabout, grassed over in the middle with a kids play area where his niece and nephew loved to spend their time.

Petrov vaulted over a downed tree trunk and ran across the road to the center of the roundabout. Most of the snow here had melted, except for what was rolled into snowmen that now were nothing more than mounds of dirty, white stuff. Remnants of facial features and buttons—carrots and pieces of charcoal from someone's barbecue—lay on the frosty grass.

"He's on the north side of Aspect."

"Copy that," Ridgeman said. "I'm almost to Charmer."

That street ran along the top end of the neighborhood, a busy main road with strip malls on either side. A grocery store, a library, and the gym he worked out at. Plenty of potential spots for Petrov to come across another innocent bystander and make this situation more complicated than it already was.

"We need to cut him off at the light."

"I'm stuck behind a semi." And she sounded exceedingly irritated about that.

Conroy heard her use the sirens and knew she would have lights flashing. Ridgeman was a city girl, accustomed to employing defensive driving tactics just to change lanes. "Hurry it up, officer."

"Copy that."

She might have only been here two months, ever since her grandfather had gotten sick, but she was solid. Only on the job a few years, when he had been doing this for nearly twelve. Still, Ridgeman was going to be an asset to the team. It was that way with all the people in his department. He could tell who would fit, who would stick it out, and who wouldn't last.

Conroy picked up his pace, knowing the end of this foot chase was in sight.

It had to be.

The alternative was innocent citizens in danger.

Petrov had started to slow. Winded, maybe not sure where to run next considering he had a bullheaded police lieutenant right behind him.

Conroy called out, "Give it up, Petrov. There's nowhere to go."

But he didn't. Petrov glanced left, and then right. After that second of indecision, he raced toward the grocery store parking lot. What was he going to do, steal a car?

Conroy passed the chain-link fence that separated the neighborhood from the grocery store parking lot. A vehicle came out of nowhere. The driver slammed on his brakes, which locked and squealed as he started to slide on the icy asphalt toward Conroy.

He jumped out of the way and hit the ground, rolling as

his mind flashed back to that night. The screech of metal and the sound of the impact. Blood, everywhere.

"You okay, boss?"

He could hear the sirens now, and not over the comms.

"Lieutenant?"

"Yeah." He picked himself up off the ground and allowed the sound of approaching police sirens to relax him in the way it always did. Help was almost here, even if he was practically the boss now and she was only one of his officers.

He said, "I'm okay."

"I see Petrov. He's running past the front entrance."

"Let's cut him off."

Conroy ran toward the front doors of the grocery store and saw Petrov. A customer came out cart first, loaded with bags. She was a slender woman in skinny jeans and a huge, green coat. Her boots were edged with fluff that matched the collar of her jacket and her hood was up.

"Stop!" He yelled as loud as he could, both to Petrov and as a warning to the woman. "Police!"

She shifted immediately. There was a split second of decision-making before she rammed the shopping cart into Petrov's hip. He cried out and went down to the asphalt in a heap.

The woman didn't move. She just held onto the handle of her cart and watched.

Ridgeman pulled up in the car, lights flashing. She got out and held her weapon on Petrov while Conroy put the cuffs on.

"That was nice." He hauled Petrov to his feet and moved the guy toward Ridgeman. Conroy was breathing hard, harder than he would have liked. "Now I don't have to hit the gym on the way home. I already got my run in for the day."

Petrov said nothing.

"You good to take this one in, Officer?"

"Sure thing, Lieutenant." Ridgeman smirked, took hold of Petrov's arm and led him to the back of her black and white patrol car. She loaded him inside, glanced once back at Conroy with another smirk he didn't get, and then drove away.

Conroy turned to the woman. "Thanks for your help." Never mind that it had been dangerous. It also should never have been necessary for a civilian to get involved in the take-down of a suspect. He was still grateful, and it couldn't be denied that no one had been hurt.

"I'd say 'anytime' but that would be a lie." She squeezed the handle of her shopping cart and shoved it forward.

There was something about her that… "Hold up one second. I'm going to need you to sign some paperwork."

It was lame, and he didn't really need her to do it, but that was what had come out of his mouth. No taking it back now.

She turned and he saw her face in the yellow glow of the grocery store lights. A nasty gash ran down the side of her face in front of her right ear. "No, I really don't."

His jaw tightened. *Mia.*

It had been years since he had seen her last. And with all those images and sensations fresh in his mind, thanks to that car, the past rushed into the present and everything just kind of got blurred. Fear. Anger. Hurt. Why was she here?

He closed in on her.

Fury that she would put herself in danger like that almost overwhelmed him. "Then why get involved?"

"Reflex." Her eyebrows lifted. "One I will be seriously reconsidering in the future."

He stared at the injury on the side of her face. "How did you get hurt?"

"None of your business." Mia shoved at her shopping cart again. She headed for her father's truck parked in the center of the lot under a streetlight. "Good night. *Lieutenant.*"

Conroy should have gone over and offered to help with her bags. He also should probably have apologized for getting in her face.

He did neither of those things, instead opting to head back toward the high school to pick up their equipment.

As he turned, he spotted a car across the lot. A man sat inside.

Watching Mia.

2

———

Mia slammed the front door so hard the windows rattled. She winced, not just at the sound that screamed of potential for more home repairs on her father's tiny lake cabin, but also at the state of her shoulder, tweaked and still not healed.

She sighed to the quiet, empty home and then wandered across the threadbare rug to flop on the couch. Another wince.

She toed off her running shoes. Nothing wrong with her legs. She'd figured going for a morning jog wouldn't exactly hurt. Except that it did hurt. A lot.

She leaned her head back. Eyes closed.

The whole place smelled like her father and his old dog that had passed away. She breathed deep, her body covered in sweat despite the frigid temperatures outside.

Yeah, she wasn't doing so hot.

Infection? No. More like burnout plus injury, plus stress, plus emotional strain. The idea she might need to take *another* nap was the worst part of it. Every time she closed her eyes she saw Conroy and that look of confusion and surprise on his face.

Not that she minded the surprise. It was fine to throw a guy like that for a loop when the opportunity arose. She just didn't want to have anything to do with him.

Not now. Not ever.

Especially not now.

Her phone rang. Mia pushed aside that thought and answered it. "Tathers." The screen was cold against her good cheek.

"It's Hudson."

Tate Hudson. Calling back already? "That was fast."

"Best private investigator in Last Chance County."

"You should put that on your business card." Hesitation made her pause. "What did you find?" Mia didn't like her tone. Entirely too hurt, which happened constantly with regards to information about her sister.

"Train wreck, this kid. Wasn't hard, since I only had to follow the wake of destruction back to the source."

"And?" Her sister was only three years younger, so twenty-four. Hardly a kid, but for a man in his mid-forties, she figured anyone south of thirty was basically a child.

His turn to pause. "I almost want to give you this one for free, but I got a mortgage I'm paying extra on."

"Just tell me."

Mia half wondered if her sister was dead. A longtime junkie with a rap sheet, no one would have been surprised. But they would have grieved. All that light she'd had as a child, all that potential, gone now from the world.

Her father chose to bury his head in the sand. Case in point, the fact he was off hunting right now while she was here recuperating. No, she didn't need him to "take care of her," but she wouldn't have minded the company.

"I found her."

"Hudson—"

"Currently shacked up with a local dealer. A guy with a

whole lot of muscle and a stable of ladies of which your sister appears to be the queen bee."

Great. A "stable." She didn't even want to think about what that meant. "You saw her?"

"Talked to some acquaintances of mine…a few of his guys. Got the scoop. She's up there, living the high life."

"I'm sure." Just as Mia was sure it wouldn't look anything like the high life she might have chosen for her own life.

Mia squeezed the bridge of her nose. It was tempting to leave her to it, let Meena live her life however she wanted. But there were things left unsaid. "Thanks, Tate. I appreciate it."

"That's it? You're not planning on making the approach yourself, are you?"

She said, "You'd rather I pay you to do it?"

"I'd rather you didn't go in there without backup. You flash that badge of yours around, let them all know you're a federal agent, and you'll wind up full of more holes than you already have."

"I regret telling you about that." A long time ago now. And nothing to do with any of this.

Tate's sigh was loud enough she heard it over the phone. "I'm coming over."

"No, don't." He would end up seeing what a mess she was in. She'd have to take a shower to be presentable since she had just run four miles and now wasn't even sure she could get up to answer the door. Her legs were still shaking from the exertion of her run.

She shifted on the couch and planted her stocking feet on the coffee table. If he did come over, he could make her a sandwich. That would be fair.

"You even think about making a move, you tell me. Do *not* go in there without backup. This guy is a bad guy, Mia."

"It's sweet that you care."

He chuckled. "I just want my paycheck. After that, I'm not paid to worry."

She huffed a laugh out through her nostrils and smiled at the empty room. "I should go."

"Don't make me regret this."

"I won't do anything without calling you. I promise."

"Like you promised to pay me for mowing your lawn when your dad gave you the money and left for work?"

"I was twelve. I wanted to go to the movies." He'd been in his twenties, home from college for the summer. Doing odd jobs.

And he'd never once taken his shirt off when he mowed the lawn.

Tate groaned. "I went to the church and said a prayer of thanks when you swore that oath as an ATF agent. Finally landed on the right side of the law."

She had been kind of…precocious as a teen. Not as much as Meena, but more than her older sister Mara. Then Mara had been killed. After that, getting her way didn't seem to matter so much.

She said, "You mean like the prayer I uttered when the football captain went off to college? Or when he was sworn in as an FBI agent?" Not that she had prayed, considering church and all that wasn't really her thing. Not with the way she'd grown up. But that wasn't the point.

"Yeah, like that one." She could hear the smile in his voice.

"Life is funny that way." Too bad she was so busy working cases lately that she didn't have time to live it.

"Like a bad pun."

He'd wound up blowing out his knee, retiring, and becoming a local private investigator. She'd always figured there was more to the story, but since they were only friends—and not even good friends—it wasn't her place to pry about the real reason.

She decided to lighten this entire conversation. "Ain't that the truth?"

She figured she needed to either laugh about it or wind up crying. One dead sister and one as good as gone. Her career had stalled out while she stayed home and recuperated during the investigation of what had gone down. Everyone said she'd be cleared back to full duties, that the shooting had been justified.

Mia touched the scar in front of her right ear. Self defense.

Now she was here, wallowing in her dad's cabin. Trying to distract herself from the fact she was stuck here without a thing to do while someone else decided her fate. The alternative? She didn't even know where to begin, but she could start by figuring out what she would rather be doing with her life. Being a cop, even a federal one, was the only thing that had ever made sense to her.

"How about you do what you should be doing? That's resting, by the way." He paused long enough she wasn't sure he'd continue. Then he did. "I'll make the approach, see how Meena feels about meeting up with you and let you know what she says."

"What about this guy she's all shacked up with? He's going to be okay with that?"

Tate said, "I know what I'm doing."

"Sure you don't want backup?"

"I'll let you know. But I don't have the budget for a deputy, so don't get any ideas." He hung up.

Mia tossed the phone on the couch beside her.

Above the mantel was a framed picture. Herself, age nine. Standing between Meena, six, and Mara, eleven. Behind them was a Christmas tree. Last one they'd had that actually looked good, far as she could remember. The year before her mom took off. Before her dad realized he had to raise three girls on his own, with no idea how to do that.

Mara had died the summer before her senior year.

Mia descended into a tailspin after that, hitting junior year with a vengeance. It was a tailspin she'd managed to pull out of by reinventing herself in college. Thankfully she'd never run into any trouble with the law. That would've made becoming a federal agent problematic. Now she worked as an ATF agent out of the Seattle office, and it was widely known that if any of the agents ran into a teen through the course of an investigation, they should send Mia to talk to the kid. Mostly she figured the guys just didn't want to deal with drama.

Her sister Meena, on the other hand, had hit rock bottom right before ninth grade and never pulled herself out of it, despite Mia's attempts to convince her to turn her life around.

She knew where her sister was now. Shacked up with some local bad guy.

Mia just didn't know what to do about it. If her dad was here, or anywhere there was cell signal, then she would have talked with him about it. Which, according to him, defeated the purpose of "getting away from it all." He had a right to know where Meena was, and if he didn't know, then surely he at least cared about her enough to want to check in.

He parented like he did everything else. In "his own way." Which most of the time made no sense to anyone with no Y chromosome and part of the time seriously ticked her off. But she didn't want to spend her vacation—recuperation—time stewing over family stuff. She should have stayed home and gotten a hotel room until they were finally done dealing with the mold in her apartment building.

Mia shoved out of the couch.

Shower first.

Then food.

After that, she'd figure out what to do next.

Mia had wet hair and was assembling a sandwich when someone knocked on the door. A cop, if she wasn't mistaken. No one else rapped on a door like that.

And she only knew one cop in Last Chance County.

She pulled the door open and smiled sweetly. "Lieutenant, how nice to see you."

"Liar."

She shoved the door closed. Conroy Barnes put the toe of his boot between the door and the jam. Any other day she'd have fought it, but she didn't have the strength to go at it with him. Not with a messed up shoulder. "Move your foot!"

"I just wanna talk to you." He sounded tired.

She pushed the door against his foot and peered out through the tiny gap. He hadn't slept. She worked with enough alpha male cops to see he'd been up all night. Hopefully doing paperwork. She also hoped it had been mind-numbingly boring. "So talk."

He shook his head. "Inside."

"I'm not letting you in. We have nothing to say to each other." After what he'd done to her and to her family? "You have some nerve coming here, asking for time."

Not to mention whatever else he wanted.

"Mia."

"Don't do that." She knew all about him. "Don't put this on me. I don't care if your case got screwed up for whatever reason. It is *not* my fault."

His eyes narrowed. Piercing blue. She'd never really understood what that was supposed to look like. Until now. They were the color of that bright blue sky, so rare in Seattle. He even wore a suit. Dark blue tie with tiny gold dots.

He said, "You don't seem surprised I'm a cop."

She shrugged one shoulder and took inventory of her own state. At least she'd put on her good sweatpants when she got out of the shower. The sweater was thin and fitted, zipped up far enough it still gave him a view of her collar bones—which she'd always thought were her best asset.

What is wrong with you?

She'd gone crazy. Or this was some kind of torturous nightmare.

"Mia."

"What?" She snapped at him, mad at herself for finding him attractive. "Move your foot and then leave. I'm busy."

"Doing what? I heard you're ATF now. Is this time off? Because you should know your dad isn't back for another couple of weeks."

She was so surprised she let go of the door. He got his whole foot in, along with a leg. Now she wanted to slam the door on him for reals. Ouchie. "Why do you know my dad's hunting schedule?"

He shrugged, looking pretty pleased with himself that he knew something she didn't.

"Get out of my house."

"Not your house." The accusation was clear. She didn't belong here. "Your dad's house."

"The police chief is going to hear about this."

A shadow crossed his face.

She ignored it. "Get ready for a fight, because you're inviting a world of hurt down on yourself and your precious career. *Lieutenant.*"

"Don't bother the chief."

Sore subject. That was interesting. "Then leave."

If he didn't want her to call his boss, then he could end this right here. Before things got ugly.

He shook his head. "Not before we talk."

Talk? He was all grown up, pretending to be some good-guy police officer, and he wanted to talk to her?

"You and I." She wanted to scream and rage at him. "We have *nothing* to talk about."

"No?" He folded the arms of his jacket across an expansive chest. Had he been that big in high school? "Meena?"

She nearly choked. "Planning on killing another one of my sisters?"

He frowned, but not at her. Conroy Barnes tore through

her house to the back door and what amounted to her dad's yard beyond it. "Call 911. There's a prowler outside!"

Mia closed her eyes. She did get her phone, but she didn't call emergency services. Not when it was likely nothing but a deer outside.

Instead, she sent Tate a one word text.

Traitor.

3

———

Conroy stepped onto the frosty grass and winced. Wrong shoes. Coming to Mia's dad's cabin, he'd stupidly made the mistake of wearing his nice shoes. Something he wasn't about to think on, at least not overly much. It had nothing to do with her.

He held his gun loose in his hands and scanned the area. Beyond the grass and the half-height picket fence was the lane that led to the main road. The back of the house faced the lane where his silver, unmarked Jeep was parked. The front of the house faced the lake, with big, wide windows that Rich told him had been the selling point on the house. Mia's father had put all his money into buying the house at its exorbitant price, now fixing it up bit by bit as he had the cash to do so.

Conroy had even helped with the bathroom tile since he'd done his own only a few months before.

Shooting the breeze. Two single guys hanging out, chatting. Conroy's parents lived in Arizona now and came to visit in the summer. When they did that, Rich tended to be absent as they didn't exactly get along. But sure enough, when it came time to return home to their retirement house, Rich showed back up.

That the father of the girl who'd died was the one who felt he had to retreat never sat well with Conroy. But he and Rich had made their own kind of peace with it. Between the two of them, they'd figured out how to move on. Something his parents hadn't yet made the effort to do to get past the death of a young woman they had loved, who had been so closely tied to their son.

He kept walking, circling the house back to the front yard and the lake shore. Eight houses were tucked in this corner of the lake, nowhere near the dock located down the shore or the neighboring occupants. Summer parties. Speed boats. Other activities that went on at the party side. Rich kept to himself, and he liked the quiet here at this end of the lake.

Conroy spotted a dark figure, same jacket he'd seen just moments before. Just a flash of color and movement between two trees. It was gone so fast he wondered if he imagined it. Conroy stared at the spot but saw nothing else.

He walked to the front door and tried the handle. Locked. Had she shut him out, or shut herself in?

He rang the bell.

Mia opened it. Her wet hair hung straight over her shoulders. The depth of her eyes was so dark brown the color bled into her pupils. Same as her sister's, that olive-skinned, exotic beauty none of them even realized they had—that was, until Meena figured out how to use it to her advantage. Mia's sweater fit snug against her volleyball-player figure, over dark blue sweatpants with white letters down one leg.

"Yes?" She had her phone in her hand.

He sighed. "Did you call it in?"

"A prowler? It was probably a deer."

He didn't give her the chance to shove the door in his face this time. Conroy pushed it open and stepped between her and the door. He holstered his weapon and folded his arms across his chest. Suit. Tie. His nice shoes.

Conroy dismissed the idea he might have been trying to

make a good impression. It had nothing to do with last night, or the fact she seriously reminded him of her sister Mara. Not in a weird way, like he was trying to get back what he'd lost when Mara had died. More like he remembered the way life was then and that junior high kid he'd known, the one who had clearly had a crush on him.

Now Mia was all grown up, though she seemed not to have grown out of her gangly phase. She was still all arms and legs. Almost as tall as he, and that was in bare feet. He figured the guys she worked with teased her for being a "girl," and all treated her like their kid sister.

She looked at him, her expression like, "*well?*"

"It wasn't a deer."

"I'm not sure I care what it was."

Conroy said, "That guy you took down last night was a low-level drug dealer. We're working to get him to roll over on his supplier. I'm poking the bear, and I doubt I'll manage to pull this off without some form of retribution. So you need to keep your gun close…" He realized she didn't even have it out. "Where's your weapon?"

"In my backpack…I think." She shrugged one shoulder.

"Did you call your people at the ATF?"

"No." She blinked. "Why would I?"

Conroy said, "Get your gun. Keep it close, Mia. These people don't wanna go down, they want to keep making money and don't care who gets hurt in the process."

"Is that why you came here, to warn me about that guy you took down last night?"

"No." He'd received a very interesting call from Tate Hudson. "You wanna talk to Meena, that's fine. But be smart. Don't go walking in there without backup."

He didn't want to know what would happen. He would wait about ten minutes max before going in after her if she did try it. Mostly he figured she'd wind up going in there… and never coming back out. Sucked into a life she didn't want.

A life she shouldn't even know about, but probably already did, what with her experience as a federal agent.

"My relationship with my sister has nothing to do with you."

He winced. "I know this town, and I know the players involved in this. You don't want to get caught up with them."

She studied his face for a second, those dark eyes assessing him. "Is it this 'boss' you're trying to take down?"

"I have no evidence to back up my theory but, yes, that's what I think."

"It's *my* sister we're talking about."

"I know. I just want you to be careful."

"Why do you care? I'm a grown woman and a federal agent. Also, last time I checked, I was a free citizen of this country."

"Last Chance County is my jurisdiction. Unless you're working a case." Which he knew she wasn't since Tate confirmed she was home on leave. Recovering. He saw it in the way she moved. "You're hurt. This is not the time to stir something up. You need to be on your A-game for that."

Mia moved to the kitchen area, about ten feet from the entryway. A sandwich sat plated on the counter.

"You should eat. I should go." His stomach rumbled, probably because he'd only had coffee so far today.

"I don't need protection." She lifted her gaze. "But thanks for the warning."

He'd have said "friendly warning." She probably didn't think that was what this had been. Truth was, he cared about her. It had to do with his connection to her family, but also because of his job.

"Like I said, my jurisdiction." He looked at the back door, where he'd seen someone moving around outside. "If you hear or see anything, call it in."

There had been a man outside. Whether that had to do with Iceman's boss, he didn't know. Whether it was or not, it wasn't worth the risk of Mia being caught injured and off guard.

He pulled out a business card from his wallet and moved to her. "My cell is on the back. Please use it if you think you've seen someone. You have cop instincts, and I'm going to trust those. But I want you to call."

She didn't take the card.

Conroy tossed it on the counter. "You need a reference? Fine. Your father called me…about six years ago now. Someone slashed his truck tires. I helped him through that and caught the kids responsible. They'd been gearing up to more serious crimes. Namely, putting your father in the hospital."

"What. Why?"

Conroy said, "Dispute over stupid stuff—road rage escalated. Your dad pushed it and they didn't back down. Then they turned it back on him. So he called me."

"And you helped him. Caught the kids who were responsible."

That was what he'd said.

"And he let you."

Conroy said, "Yes."

She planted her palms on the counter. "Probably figured you needed to earn his trust back, so he gave you the chance when there was nothing big at stake." She swiped his card off the counter, turned to the cupboard under the sink and tossed it in the trash. "I don't need your brand of help."

"This could be serious. Someone was outside."

"Who?"

"I didn't get a good look at him. Dark jacket, hood up."

"Probably one of those kids you saved my dad from."

"It wasn't." They were all in county jail.

"I don't need your problems coming around here. I have enough going on."

She'd been hurt. That much was clear by the scar down

her face, an angry red scratch. Now it was light, he could see it wasn't as bad as he'd thought last night. But it was still bad. "Tell me what happened."

She jerked her head back. "It's none of your business. Just leave, Conroy."

Not "lieutenant?" Now he was Conroy, and she looked like she was about to cry. Which, considering the alternative, might be good. He'd rather that than her screaming at him. He could try and help her, and she might accept it instead of him having to leave.

Conroy needed to accept she was more than just a citizen to him. This was more than just him doing his job.

"If there's something going on with you, I might actually be able to help."

"I don't need anything from you."

"Mia—"

"Don't." She shook her head, eyes squeezed tight. "Even if there was someone outside, it was probably nothing. Just a nosy neighbor. Leave it alone, and leave me alone while you're at it." She opened her eyes and pinned him with a stare. "I'll be talking to Tate about being overbearing. There's nothing more I need from *either* of you."

Conroy pulled out another card and laid it where the first had been.

"I don't need to be kept safe. I can take care of myself."

"Good." She might need it. "Keep your eyes open and your gun close."

Conroy turned and headed for the front door.

"Whatever."

He pulled the door open and hauled it shut behind him. The slam rang out across the lake. A neighbor, unloading a leashed dog from the back of his truck next door, looked over. A puppy, by the look of it. But when it was done growing, the thing would be massive.

Conroy pretty much stomped back to the lane and his

Jeep. He didn't have the filter to not let frustration bleed into his walk. Why did she have to be so infuriating? Sure, it was clear she hadn't forgiven him, but he'd been there to do her a favor. He could've worked on making amends. If she'd have let him.

He beeped the locks on his car.

The world flashed orange and Conroy was hit by a wall of heat. The force of the blast threw him through the fence and onto the grass of Rich's back yard.

Conroy hit the ground and everything went black.

Find where you can continue reading *Expired Refuge*, learn about Last Chance County, and the other books based there at https://lastchancecounty.com

ALSO BY LISA PHILLIPS

The entire Chevalier Protection Specialists series:

Book 1: Last Taste of Freedom

Book 2: Last Hour till Sunrise

Book 3: Last One Still Standing

Book 4: Last Man to Survive

Book 5: Last Line of Defense

Find the whole series here:

www.lastchancecounty.com/chevalier-series

Find out about Lisa's other books at her website:

authorlisaphillips.com

Other series:

Last Chance County

Northwest Counter-Terrorism Taskforce

Double Down

WITSEC Town (Sanctuary)

Love Inspired Suspense titles

ABOUT THE AUTHOR

Find out more about Lisa Phillips, and other books she has written, by visiting her website: https://authorlisaphillips.com

Would you also share about the book on Social Media, leave a review on Lisa's page and share about your experience? Your review will help others find great clean fiction and decide what to read next!

Visit https://authorlisaphillips.com/subscribe where you can sign up for my NEWSLETTER and get free books!

www.ingramcontent.com/pod-product-compliance
Lightning Source LLC
Chambersburg PA
CBHW030914300726
48970CB00001B/152